Taking Off

Marian pulled her face away and gazed down at Duncan. His eyes were closed. She kissed the end of his nose. "I think I ought to tell you something," she said softly. "I'm engaged. I shouldn't be here."

"But you are here." Duncan smiled. "Actually, I'm glad you told me. It makes me feel a lot safer. Because really," he said, "I don't want you to think that all this means anything. It never really does, for me. It's all happening really to someone else."

But this was definitely happening to Marian. She was discovering what it meant to have sex without strings—and learning what it was to live without limits . . .

THE EDIBLE WOMAN

◆

"Genuine wit, insight, originality . . . so good!"
—*Publishers Weekly*

"A pleasure."

—*Kirkus Reviews*

Novels by
MARGARET ATWOOD

The Edible Woman
Life Before Man
Surfacing

Published by
WARNER BOOKS

MARGARET ATWOOD

THE EDIBLE WOMAN

WARNER BOOKS

A Warner Communications Company

WARNER BOOKS EDITION

Copyright © 1969 by Margaret Atwood
All rights reserved.

This Warner Books Edition is published by arrangement with
Little, Brown and Company in association with the Atlantic Monthly Press.

Warner Books, Inc.
666 Fifth Avenue
New York, N.Y. 10103

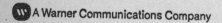 A Warner Communications Company

Printed in the United States of America

First Warner Books Printing: June, 1983

Reissued: April, 1989

10 9 8 7 6 5 4

For J.

"The surface on which you work (preferably marble), the tools, the ingredients and your fingers should be chilled throughout the operation. . . ." (Recipe for Puff Pastry in I. S. Rombauer and M. R. Becker, *The Joy of Cooking*.)

Part One

1

☐ I know I was all right on Friday when I got up; if anything I was feeling more stolid than usual. When I went out to the kitchen to get breakfast Ainsley was there, moping: she said she had been to a bad party the night before. She swore there had been nothing but dentistry students, which depressed her so much she had consoled herself by getting drunk.

"You have no idea how soggy it is," she said, "having to go through twenty conversations about the insides of peoples' mouths. The most reaction I got out of them was when I described an abscess I once had. They positively drooled. And most men look at something besides your *teeth*, for god's sake."

She had a hangover, which put me in a cheerful mood—it made me feel so healthy—and I poured her a glass of tomato juice and briskly fixed her an alka-seltzer, listening and making sympathetic noises while she complained.

"As if I didn't get enough of that at work," she said. Ainsley has a job as a tester of defective electric toothbrushes for an electric toothbrush company: a temporary job. What she is waiting for is an opening in one of those little art galleries, even though they don't pay well: she wants to meet the artists. Last year, she told me, it was actors, but then she actually met some. "It's an absolute fixation. I expect they all carry those bent mirrors around in their coat pockets and peer into their own mouths every time they go to the john to make sure they're still cavity-free." She ran one hand reflectively through her hair, which is long and red, or rather auburn. "Could you imagine kissing one? He'd say 'Open wide' beforehand. They're so bloody one-track."

"It must have been awful," I said, refilling her glass. "Couldn't you have changed the topic?"

Ainsley raised her almost non-existent eyebrows, which hadn't been coloured in yet that morning. "Of course not," she said. "I pretended to be terribly interested. And naturally I didn't let on what my job was: those professional men get so huffy if you know anything about their subject. You know, like Peter."

Ainsley tends to make jabs at Peter, especially when she isn't feeling well. I was magnanimous and didn't respond. "You'd better eat something before you go to work," I said, "it's better when you've got something on your stomach."

"Oh god," said Ainsley, "I can't face it. Another day of machines and mouths. I haven't had an interesting one since last month, when that lady sent back her toothbrush because the bristles were falling off. We found out she'd been using Ajax."

I got so caught up in being efficient for Ainsley's benefit while complimenting myself on my moral superiority to her that I didn't realize how late it was until she reminded me. At the electric toothbrush company they don't care what time you breeze in, but my company thinks of itself as punctual. I had to skip the eggs and wash down a glass of milk and a bowl of cold cereal which I knew would leave me hungry long before lunchtime. I chewed through a piece of bread while Ainsley watched me in nauseated silence and grabbed up my purse, leaving Ainsley to close the apartment door behind me.

We live on the top floor of a large house in one of the older and more genteel districts, in what I suppose used to be the servants' quarters. This means there are two flights of stairs between us and the front door, the higher flight narrow and slippery, the lower one wide and carpeted but with stair-rods that come loose. In the high heels expected by the office I have to go down sideways, clutching the bannister. That morning I made it safely past the line of pioneer brass warming-pans strung on the wall of our stairway, avoided catching myself on the many-pronged spinning-wheel on the second-floor landing, and sidestepped quickly down past the ragged regimental flag behind glass and the row of oval-framed ancestors that guard the first stairway. I was relieved to see there was no one in the downstairs hall. On level ground I strode towards the door, swerving to avoid the rubber-plant on one side and the hall table with the écru doily and the round brass tray on the other. Behind the velvet curtain to the right I could hear the child performing her morning penance at the piano. I thought I was safe.

But before I reached the door it swung silently inward upon its hinges, and I knew I was trapped. It was the lady down below. She was wearing a pair of spotless gardening gloves and carrying a trowel. I wondered who she'd been burying in the garden.

"Good morning, Miss MacAlpin," she said.

"Good morning." I nodded and smiled. I can never remember her name, and neither can Ainsley; I suppose we have what they call a mental block about it. I looked past her towards the street, but she didn't move out of the doorway.

"I was out last night," she said. "At a meeting." She has an indirect way of going about things. I shifted from one foot to the other and smiled again, hoping she would realize I was in a hurry. "The child tells me there was another fire."

"Well, it wasn't exactly a fire," I said. The child had taken this mention of her name as an excuse to stop practising, and was standing now in the velvet doorway of the parlour, staring at me. She is a hulking creature of fifteen or so who is being sent to an exclusive private girls' school, and she has to wear a green tunic with knee-socks to match. I'm sure she's really quite normal, but there's something cretinous about the hair-ribbon perched up on top of her gigantic body.

The lady down below took off one of her gloves and patted her chignon. "Ah," she said sweetly. "The child says there was a lot of smoke."

"Everything was under control," I said, not smiling this time. "It was just the pork chops."

"Oh, I see," she said. "Well, I do wish you would tell Miss Tewce to try not to make quite so much smoke in future. I'm afraid it upsets the child." She holds Ainsley alone responsible for the smoke, and seems to think she sends it out of her nostrils like a dragon. But she never stops Ainsley in the hall to talk about it: only me. I suspect she's decided Ainsley isn't respectable, whereas I am. It's probably the way we dress: Ainsley says I choose clothes as though they're a camouflage or a protective colouration, though I can't see anything wrong with that. She herself goes in for neon pink.

Of course I missed the bus: as I crossed the lawn I could see it disappearing across the bridge in a cloud of air pollution. While I was standing under the tree—our street has many trees, all of them enormous—waiting for the next bus, Ainsley came out of the house and joined me. She's a quick-change artist; I could never put myself together in such a short time. She was looking a lot healthier—possibly the effects of makeup, though you can never tell with Ainsley—and she had her red hair piled up on top of her head, as she always does when she goes to work. The rest of the time she wears it down in straggles. She had on her orange and pink sleeveless dress, which I judged was too tight across the hips. The day was going to be hot and humid; already I could feel a private atmosphere condensing around me like a plastic bag. Maybe I should have worn a sleeveless dress too.

"She got me in the hall," I said. "About the smoke."

"The old bitch," said Ainsley. "Why can't she mind her own business?" Ainsley doesn't come from a small town as I do, so she's not as used to people being snoopy; on the other hand she's not as afraid of it either. She has no idea about the consequences.

"She's not that old," I said, glancing over at the curtained windows of the house; though I knew she couldn't hear us. "Besides, it wasn't her who noticed the smoke, it was the child. She was at a meeting."

"Probably the w.c.t.u.," Ainsley said. "Or the i.o.d.e. I'll bet she wasn't at a meeting at all; she was hiding behind that damn velvet curtain, wanting us to think she was at a meeting so we'd *really* do something. What she wants is an orgy."

"Now Ainsley," I said, "you're being paranoid." Ainsley is convinced that the lady down below comes upstairs when we aren't there and looks round our apartment and is silently horrified, and even suspects her of ruminating

12

over our mail, though not of going so far as to open it. It's a fact that she sometimes answers the front door for our visitors before they ring the bell. She must think she's within her rights to take precautions: when we first considered renting the apartment she made it clear to us, by discreet allusions to previous tenants, that whatever happened the child's innocence must not be corrupted, and that two young ladies were surely more to be depended upon than two young men.

"I'm doing my best," she had said, sighing and shaking her head. She had intimated that her husband, whose portrait in oils hung above the piano, had not left as much money as he should have. "Of course you realize your apartment has no private entrance?" She had been stressing the drawbacks rather than the advantages, almost as though she didn't want us to rent. I said we did realize it; Ainsley said nothing. We had agreed I would do the talking and Ainsley would sit and look innocent, something she can do very well when she wants to—she has a pink-and-white blunt baby's face, a bump for a nose, and large blue eyes she can make as round as ping-pong balls. On this occasion I had even got her to wear gloves.

The lady down below shook her head again. "If it weren't for the child," she said, "I would sell the house. But I want the child to grow up in a good district."

I said I understood, and she said that of course the district wasn't as good as it used to be: some of the larger houses were too expensive to keep up and the owners had been forced to sell them to immigrants (the corners of her mouth turned gently down) who had divided them up into rooming houses. "But that hasn't reached our street yet," she said. "And I tell the child exactly which streets she can walk on and which she can't." I said I thought that was wise. She had seemed much easier to deal with before we had signed the lease. And the rent was so low, and the house was so close to the bus stop. For this city it was a real find.

"Besides," I added to Ainsley, "they have a right to be worried about the smoke. What if the house was on fire? And she's never mentioned the other things."

13

"What other things? We've never *done* any other things."

"Well . . ." I said. I suspected the lady down below had taken note of all the bottle-shaped objects we had carried upstairs, though I tried my best to disguise them as groceries. It was true she had never specifically forbidden us to do anything—that would be too crude a violation of her law of nuance—but this only makes me feel I am actually forbidden to do everything.

"On still nights," said Ainsley as the bus drew up, "I can hear her burrowing through the woodwork."

We didn't talk on the bus; I don't like talking on buses, I would rather look at the advertisements. Besides, Ainsley and I don't have much in common except the lady down below. I've only known her since just before we moved in: she was a friend of a friend, looking for a room-mate at the same time I was, which is the way these things are usually done. Maybe I should have tried a computer; though on the whole it's worked out fairly well. We get along by a symbiotic adjustment of habits and with a minimum of that pale-mauve hostility you often find among women. Our apartment is never exactly clean, but we keep it from gathering more than a fine plum-bloom of dust by an unspoken agreement: if I do the breakfast dishes, Ainsley does the supper ones; if I sweep the living-room floor, Ainsley wipes the kitchen table. It's a see-saw arrangement and we both know that if one beat is missed the whole thing will collapse. Of course we each have our own bedroom and what goes on in there is strictly the owner's concern. For instance Ainsley's floor is covered by a treacherous muskeg of used clothes with ashtrays scattered here and there on it like stepping-stones, but though I consider it a fire-hazard I never speak to her about it. By such mutual refrainings—I assume they are mutual since there must be things I do that she doesn't like—we manage to preserve a reasonably frictionless equilibrium.

We reached the subway station, where I bought a package of peanuts. I was beginning to feel hungry already. I offered some to Ainsley, but she refused, so I ate them all on the way downtown.

We got off at the second-last stop south and walked a block together; our office buildings are in the same district.

"By the way," said Ainsley as I was turning off at my street, "have you got three dollars? We're out of scotch." I rummaged in my purse and handed over, not without a sense of injustice: we split the cost but rarely the contents. At the age of ten I wrote a temperance essay for a United Church Sunday-school competition, illustrating it with pictures of car-crashes, diagrams of diseased livers, and charts showing the effects of alcohol upon the circulatory system; I expect that's why I can never take a second drink without a mental image of a warning sign printed in coloured crayons and connected with the taste of tepid communion grape-juice. This puts me at a disadvantage with Peter; he likes me to try and keep up with him.

As I hurried towards my office building, I found myself envying Ainsley her job. Though mine was better-paying and more interesting, hers was more temporary: she had an idea of what she wanted to do next. She could work in a shiny new air-conditioned office-building, whereas mine was dingy brick with small windows. Also, her job was unusual. When she meets people at parties they are always surprised when she tells them she's a tester of defective electric toothbrushes, and she always says, "What else do you do with a B.A. these days?" Whereas my kind of job is only to be expected. I was thinking too that really I was better equipped to handle her job than she is. From what I see around the apartment, I'm sure I have much more mechanical ability than Ainsley.

By the time I finally reached the office I was three-quarters of an hour late. None commented but all took note.

2

☐ The humidity was worse inside. I waded among the ladies' desks to my own corner and had scarcely settled in behind the typewriter before the backs of my legs were stuck to the black leatherette of the chair. The air-conditioning system, I saw, had failed again, though since it is merely a fan which revolves in the centre of the ceiling, stirring the air around like a spoon in soup, it makes little difference whether it is going or not. But it was evidently bad for the ladies' morale to see the blades dangling up there unmoving: it created the impression that nothing was being done, spurring their inertia on to even greater stasis. They squatted at their desks, toad-like and sluggish, blinking and opening and closing their mouths. Friday is always a bad day at the office.

I had begun to peck languidly at my damp typewriter when Mrs. Withers, the dietician, marched in through the back door, drew up, and scanned the room. She wore her usual Betty Grable hairdo and open-toed pumps, and her shoulders had an aura of shoulder pads even in a sleeveless dress. "Ah, Marian," she said, "you're just in time. I need another pre-test taster for the canned rice pudding study, and none of the ladies seem very hungry this morning."

She wheeled and headed briskly for the kitchen. There is something unwiltable about dieticians. I unstuck myself from my chair, feeling like a volunteer singled out from the ranks; but I reminded myself that my stomach could use the extra breakfast.

In the tiny immaculate kitchen she explained her problem while spooning equal portions of canned rice pudding into three glass bowls. "You work on questionnaires, Marian, maybe you can help us. We can't decide whether to have them taste all three flavours at the same meal, or each flavour separately at subsequent meals. Or perhaps we could have them taste in pairs—say, Vanilla and

Orange at one meal, and Vanilla and Caramel at another. Of course we want to get as unbiased a sampling as possible, and so much depends on what else has been served—the colours of the vegetables for instance, and the tablecloth."

I sampled the Vanilla.

"How would you rate the colour on that?" she asked anxiously, pencil poised. "Natural, Somewhat Artificial, or Definitely Unnatural?"

"Have you thought about putting raisins in it?" I said, turning to the Caramel. I didn't wish to offend her.

"Raisins are too risky," she said. "Many don't like them."

I set down the Caramel and tried the Orange. "Are you going to have them serve it hot?" I asked. "Or maybe with cream?"

"Well, it's intended primarily for the time-saver market," she said. "They naturally would want to serve it cold. They can add cream if they like, later, I mean we've nothing really against it though it's not nutritionally necessary, it's fortified with vitamins already, but right now we want a *pure* taste-test."

"I think subsequent meals would be best," I said.

"If we could only do it in the middle of the afternoon. But we need a family reaction. . . ." She tapped her pencil thoughtfully on the edge of the stainless steel sink.

"Yes, well," I said, "I'd better be getting back." Deciding for them what they wanted to know wasn't part of my job.

Sometimes I wonder just which things are part of my job, especially when I find myself calling up garage mechanics to ask them about their pistons and gaskets or handing out pretzels to suspicious old ladies on street corners. I know what Seymour Surveys hired me as—I'm supposed to spend my time revising the questionnaires, turning the convoluted and overly-subtle prose of the psychologists who write them into simple questions which can be understood by the people who ask them as well as the people who answer them. A question like "In what percentile would you place the visual impact value?" is not useful. When I got the job after graduation I con-

17

sidered myself lucky—it was better than many—but after four months its limits are still vaguely defined.

At times I'm certain I'm being groomed for something higher up, but as I have only hazy notions of the organizational structure of Seymour Surveys I can't imagine what. The company is layered like an ice-cream sandwich, with three floors: the upper crust, the lower crust, and our department, the gooey layer in the middle. On the floor above are the executives and the psychologists—referred to as the men upstairs, since they are all men—who arrange things with the clients; I've caught glimpses of their offices, which have carpets and expensive furniture and silk-screen reprints of Group of Seven paintings on the walls. Below us are the machines—mimeo machines, I.B.M. machines for counting and sorting and tabulating the information; I've been down there too, into that factory-like clatter where the operatives seem frayed and overworked and have ink on their fingers. Our department is the link between the two: we are supposed to take care of the human element, the interviewers themselves. As market research is a sort of cottage industry like a hand-knit sock company, these are all housewives working in their spare time and paid by the piece. They don't make much, but they like to get out of the house. Those who answer the questions don't get paid at all; I often wonder why they do it. Perhaps it's the come-on blurb in which they're told they can help to improve the products they use right in their own homes, something like a scientist. Or maybe they like to have someone to talk to. But I suppose most people are flattered by having their opinions asked.

Because our department deals primarily with housewives, everyone in it, except the unfortunate office-boy, is female. We are spread out in a large institutional-green room with an opaque glassed cubicle at one end for Mrs. Bogue, the head of the department, and a number of wooden tables at the other end for the motherly-looking women who sit deciphering the interviewers' handwriting and making crosses and checkmarks on the completed questionnaires with coloured crayons, looking with their scissors and glue and stacks of paper like a superannuated

18

kindergarten class. The rest of us in the department sit at miscellaneous desks in the space between. We have a comfortable chintz-curtained lunchroom for those who bring paper-bags, and a tea and coffee machine, though some of the ladies have their own teapots; we also have a pink washroom with a sign over the mirrors asking us not to leave our hairs or tea leaves in the sink.

What, then, could I expect to turn into at Seymour Surveys? I couldn't become one of the men upstairs; I couldn't become a machine person or one of the questionnaire-marking ladies, as that would be a step down. I might conceivably turn into Mrs. Bogue or her assistant, but as far as I could see that would take a long time, and I wasn't sure I would like it anyway.

I was just finishing the scouring-pad questionnaire, a rush job, when Mrs. Grot of Accounting came through the door. Her business was with Mrs. Bogue, but on her way out she stopped at my desk. She's a short tight woman with hair the colour of a metal refrigerator-tray.

"Well, Miss MacAlpin," she grated, "you've been with us four months now, and that means you're eligible for the Pension Plan."

"Pension Plan?" I had been told about the Pension Plan when I joined the company but I had forgotten about it. "Isn't it too soon for me to join the Pension Plan? I mean—don't you think I'm too young?"

"Well, it's just as well to start early, isn't it," Mrs. Grot said. Her eyes behind their rimless spectacles were glittering: she would relish the chance of making yet another deduction from my pay-cheque.

"I don't think I'd like to join the Pension Plan," I said. "Thank you anyway."

"Yes, well, but it's obligatory, you see," she said in a matter-of-fact voice.

"Obligatory? You mean even if I don't want it?"

"Yes, you see if nobody paid into it, nobody would be able to get anything out of it, would they? Now I've brought the necessary documents; all you have to do is sign here."

I signed, but after Mrs. Grot had left I was suddenly quite depressed; it bothered me more than it should have.

It wasn't only the feeling of being subject to rules I had no interest in and no part in making: you get adjusted to that at school. It was a kind of superstitious panic about the fact that I had actually signed my name, had put my signature to a magic document which seemed to bind me to a future so far ahead I couldn't think about it. Somewhere in front of me a self was waiting, pre-formed, a self who had worked during innumerable years for Seymour Surveys and was now receiving her reward. A pension. I foresaw a bleak room with a plug-in electric heater. Perhaps I would have a hearing aid, like one of my great-aunts who had never married. I would talk to myself; children would throw snowballs at me. I told myself not to be silly, the world would probably blow up between now and then; I reminded myself I could walk out of there the next day and get a different job if I wanted to, but that didn't help. I thought of my signature going into a file and the file going into a cabinet and the cabinet being shut away in a vault somewhere and locked.

I welcomed the coffee break at ten-thirty. I knew I ought to have skipped it and stayed to expiate my morning's lateness, but I needed the distraction.

I go for coffee with the only three people in the department who are almost my own age. Sometimes Ainsley walks over from her office to join us, when she is tired of the other toothbrush-testers. Not that she's especially fond of the three from my office, whom she calls collectively the office virgins. They aren't really very much alike, except that they are all artificial blondes—Emmy, the typist, whisk-tinted and straggly; Lucy, who has a kind of public-relations job, platinum and elegantly coiffured, and Millie, Mrs. Bogue's Australian assistant, brassy from the sun and cropped—and, as they have confessed at various times over coffee-grounds and the gnawed crusts of toasted Danishes, all virgins—Millie from a solid girl-guide practicality ("I think in the long run it's better to wait until you're married, don't you? Less bother."), Lucy from social quailing ("What would people *say*?"), which seems to be rooted in a conviction that all bedrooms are wired for sound, with society gathered at the other end tuning its earphones; and Emmy, who is the office hypochondriac, from the belief that it would make her sick, which it probably would. They are all interested in travelling: Millie has lived in England, Lucy has been twice to New York, and Emmy wants to go to Florida. After they have travelled enough they would like to get married and settle down.

"Did you hear the laxative survey in Quebec has been cancelled?" Millie said when we were seated at our usual table at the wretched, but closest, restaurant across the street. "Great big job it was going to be, too—a product test in their own home and thirty-two pages of questions." Millie always get the news first.

"Well I must say that's a good thing," Emmy sniffed. "I don't see how they could ask anybody thirty-two pages about *that*." She went back to peeling the nailpolish off her thumbnail. Emmy always looks as though she is coming unravelled. Stray threads trail from her hems, her lipstick sloughs off in dry scales, she sheds wispy blonde hairs and flakes of scalp on her shoulders and back; everywhere she goes she leaves a trail of assorted shreds.

I saw Ainsley come in and waved to her. She squeezed into the booth, saying "Hi" all round, then pinned up a strand of hair that had come down. The office virgins responded, but without marked enthusiasm.

"They've done it before," Millie said. She's been at the company longer than any of us. "And it works. They figure anybody you could take past page three would be a sort of laxative addict, if you see what I mean, and they'd go right on through."

"Done what before?" said Ainsley.

"What do you want to bet she doesn't wipe the table?" Lucy said, loudly enough so the waitress would overhear. She carries on a running battle with the waitress, who wears Woolworth earrings and a sullen scowl and is blatantly not an office virgin.

"The laxative study in Quebec," I said privately to Ainsley.

The waitress arrived, wiped the table savagely, and took our orders. Lucy made an issue of the toasted Danish—she definitely wanted one without raisins this time. "Last time she brought me one *with* raisins," she in-

21

formed us, and I told her I just couldn't stand them. I've never been able to stand raisins. Ugh."

"Why only Quebec?" Ainsley said, breathing smoke out through her nostrils. "Is there some psychological reason?" Ainsley majored in psychology at college.

"Gosh, I don't know," said Millie, "I guess people are just more constipated there. Don't they eat a lot of potatoes?"

"Would potatoes make you *that* constipated?" asked Emmy, leaning forward across the table. She pushed several straws of hair back from her forehead and a cloud of tiny motes detached themselves from her head and settled gently down through the air.

"It can't be only the potatoes," Ainsley pronounced. "It must be their collective guilt-complex. Or maybe the strain of the language-problem; they must be horribly repressed."

The others looked at her with hostility: I could tell they thought she was showing off. "It's awfully hot out today," said Millie, "the office is like a furnace."

"Anything happening at your office?" I asked Ainsley, to break the tension.

Ainsley ground out her cigarette. "Oh yes, we've had quite a bit of excitement," she said. "Some woman tried to bump off her husband by short-circuiting his electric toothbrush, and one of our boys has to be at the trial as a witness; testify that the thing couldn't possibly short-circuit under normal circumstances. He wants me to go along as a sort of special assistant, but he's such a bore. I can tell he'd be rotten in bed."

I suspected Ainsley of making this story up, but her eyes were at their bluest and roundest. The office virgins squirmed. Ainsley has an offhand way of alluding to the various men in her life that makes them uncomfortable.

Luckily our orders arrived. "That bitch brought me one *with* raisins again," Lucy wailed, and began picking them out with her long perfectly-shaped iridescent fingernails and piling them at the side of her plate.

As we were walking back to the office I complained to Millie about the Pension Plan. "I didn't realize it was obligatory," I said. "I don't see why I should have to pay into their Pension Plan and have all those old crones like Mrs. Grot retire and feed off my salary."

"Oh yes, it bothered me too at first," Millie said without interest. "You'll get over it. Gosh, I hope they've fixed the air-conditioning."

3

□ I had returned from lunch and was licking and stamping envelopes for the coast-to-coast instant pudding-sauce study, behind schedule because someone in mimeo had run one of the question sheets backwards, when Mrs. Bogue came out of her cubicle.

"Marian," she said with a sigh of resignation, "I'm afraid Mrs. Dodge in Kamloops will have to be removed. She's pregnant." Mrs. Bogue frowned slightly: she regards pregnancy as an act of disloyalty to the company.

"That's too bad," I said. The huge wall-map of the country sprinkled with red thumbtacks like measles, is directly above my desk, which means that the subtraction and addition of interviewers seems to have become part of my job. I climbed up on the desk, located Kamloops, and took out the thumbtack with the paper flag marked DODGE.

"While you're up there," Mrs. Bogue said, "could you just take off Mrs. Ellis in Blind River? I hope it's only temporary, she's always done good work, but she writes that some lady chased her out of the house with a meat cleaver and she fell on the steps and broke her leg. Oh, and add this new one—a Mrs. Gauthier in Charlottetown. I certainly hope she's better than the last one there; Charlottetown is always so difficult."

When I had climbed down she smiled at me pleasantly, which put me on guard. Mrs. Bogue has a friendly, almost cosy manner that equips her perfectly for dealing with the interviewers, and she is at her most genial when she wants something. "Marian," she said, "we have a little problem. We're running a beer study next week—you know which

23

one, it's the telephone-thing one—and they've decided up-stairs that we need to do a pre-test this weekend. They're worried about the questionnaire. Now, we could get Mrs. Pilcher, she's a dependable interviewer, but it *is* the long weekend and we don't like to ask her. You're going to be in town, aren't you?"

"Does it have to be this weekend?" I asked, somewhat pointlessly.

"Well, we absolutely have to have the results Tuesday. You only need to get seven or eight men."

My lateness that morning had given her leverage. "Fine," I said, "I'll do them tomorrow."

"You'll get overtime, of course," Mrs. Bogue said as she walked away, leaving me wondering whether that had been a snide remark. Her voice is always so bland it's hard to tell.

I finished licking the envelopes, then got the beer questionnaires from Millie and went through the questions, looking for trouble-spots. The initial selection questions were standard enough. After that, the questions were designed to test listener response to a radio jingle, part of the advertising campaign for a new brand of beer one of the large companies was about to launch on the market. At a certain point the interviewer had to ask the respondent to pick up the telephone and dial a given number, whereupon the jingle would play itself to him over the phone. Then there were a number of questions asking the man how he liked the commercial, whether he thought it might influence his buying habits, and so on.

I dialled the phone number. Since the survey wasn't actually being conducted till the next week, someone might have forgotten to hook up the record, and I didn't want to make an idiot of myself.

After a preliminary ringing, buzzing and clicking a deep bass voice, accompanied by what sounded like an electric guitar, sang:

Moose, Moose,
From the land of pine and spruce,
Tingly, heady, rough-and-ready. . .

24

Then a speaking voice, almost as deep as the singer's, intoned persuasively to background music,

> *Any real man, on a real man's holiday—hunting, fishing, or just plain old-fashioned relaxing—needs a beer with a healthy, hearty taste, a deep-down manly flavour. The first long cool swallow will tell you that Moose Beer is just what you've always wanted for true beer enjoyment. Put the tang of the wilderness in* YOUR *life today with a big satisfying glass of sturdy Moose Beer.*

The singer resumed:

> *Tingly, heady,*
> *Rough-and-ready,*
> *Moose, Moose, Moose, Moose,* BEER!!!

and after a climax of sound the record clicked off. It was in satisfactory working order.

I remembered the sketches I'd seen of the visual presentation, scheduled to appear in magazines and on posters: the label was to have a pair of antlers with a gun and a fishing-rod crossed beneath them. The singing commercial was a reinforcement of this theme; I didn't think it was very original but I admired the subtlety of "just plain old-fashioned relaxing." That was so the average beer-drinker, the slope-shouldered pot-bellied kind, would be able to feel a mystical identity with the plaid-jacketed sportsman shown in the pictures with his foot on a deer or scooping a trout into his net.

I had got to the last page when the telephone rang. It was Peter. I could tell from the sound of his voice that something was wrong.

"Listen, Marian, I can't make it for dinner tonight."

"Oh?" I said, wanting further explanation. I was disappointed, I had been looking forward to dinner with Peter to cheer me up. Also I was hungry again. I had been eating in bits and pieces all day and I had been counting on something nourishing and substantial. This meant an-

25

other of the T.V. dinners Ainsley and I kept for emergencies. "Has something happened?"

"I know you'll understand. Trigger"—his voice choked—"Trigger's getting married."

"Oh," I said. I thought of saying "That's too bad," but it didn't seem adequate. There was no use in sympathizing as though for a minor mishap when it was really a national disaster. "Would you like me to come with you?" I asked, offering support.

"God no," he said, "that would be even worse. I'll see you tomorrow. Okay?"

When he had hung up I reflected upon the consequences. The most obvious one was that Peter would need careful handling the next evening. Trigger was one of Peter's oldest friends; in fact, he had been the last of Peter's group of oldest friends still left unmarried. It had been like an epidemic. Just before I'd met him two had succumbed, and in the four months since that another two had gone under without much warning. He and Trigger had found themselves more and more alone on their bachelor drinking sessions during the summer, and when the others did take an evening off from their wives to go along, I gathered from Peter's gloomy accounts that the flavour of the evening was a synthetic substitute for the irresponsible gaiety of the past. He and Trigger had clutched each other like drowning men, each trying to make the other the reassuring reflection of himself that he needed. Now Trigger had sunk and the mirror would be empty. There were the other law students of course, but most of them were married too. Besides, they belonged to Peter's post-university silver age rather than to his earlier golden one.

I felt sorry for him, but I knew I would have to be wary. If the other two marriages had been any indication, he'd start seeing me after two or three drinks as a version of the designing siren who had carried off Trigger. I didn't dare ask how she had done it: he might think I was getting ideas. The best plan would be to distract him.

While I was meditating Lucy came over to my desk. "Do you think you can write a letter to this lady for me?" she asked. "I'm getting a splitting headache and I really can't think of a thing to say." She pressed one elegant hand to her forehead; with the other she handed me a note written in pencil on a piece of cardboard. I read it:

Dear Sir, The cereal was fine but I found this in with the raisins. Yours Truly, (Mrs.) Ramona Baldwin.

A squashed housefly was scotch-taped to the bottom of the letter.

"It was that raisin-cereal study," Lucy said faintly. She was playing on my sympathies.

"Oh, all right," I said; "have you got her address?"

I made several trial drafts:

Dear Mrs. Baldwin; We are extremely sorry about the object in your cereal but these little mistakes will happen. Dear Mrs. Baldwin; We are so sorry to have inconvenienced you; we assure you however that the entire contents of the package was absolutely sterile. Dear Mrs. Baldwin; We are grateful to you for calling this matter to our attention as we always like to know about any errors we may have made.

The main thing, I knew, was to avoid calling the housefly by its actual name.

The phone rang again; this time it was an unexpected voice.

"Clara!" I exclaimed, conscious of having neglected her. "How *are* you?"

"Shitty, thanks," Clara said. "But I wonder if you can come to dinner. I'd really like to see an outside face."

"I'd love to," I said, my enthusiasm half-genuine: it would be better than a T.V. dinner. "About what time?"

"Oh, you know," Clara said. "Whenever you come. We aren't what you'd call punctual around here." She sounded bitter.

Now I was committed I was thinking rapidly of what this would involve: I was being invited as an entertainer and confidante, someone who would listen to a recital of Clara's problems, and I didn't feel like it. "Do you think I could bring Ainsley too?" I said. "That is, if she isn't into anything." I told myself it would be good for Ainsley to have a wholesome dinner—she had only had a coffee at the coffee-break—but secretly I wanted her along to take off a bit of the pressure. She and Clara could talk about child psychology.

"Sure, why not?" Clara said. "The more the merrier, that's our motto."

I called Ainsley at work, carefully asking her whether she was doing anything for dinner and listening to her accounts of the two invitations she had received and turned down—one from the toothbrush murder trial witness, the other from the dentistry student of the night before. To the latter she had been quite rude: she was never going out with him again. She claimed he had told her there would be artists at the party.

"So you aren't doing anything then," I said, establishing the fact.

"Well, no," said Ainsley, "unless something comes along."

"Then why don't you come with me to Clara's for dinner?" I was expecting a protest, but she accepted calmly. I arranged to meet her at the subway station.

I left the desk at five and headed for the cool pink Ladies' Room. I wanted a few minutes of isolation to prepare myself for coping before I set out for Clara's. But Emmy, Lucy and Millie were all there, combing their yellow hair and retouching their makeup. Their six eyes glittered in the mirrors.

"Going out tonight, Marian?" Lucy asked, too casually. She shared my telephone line and naturally knew about Peter.

"Yes," I said, without volunteering information. Their wistful curiosity made me nervous.

4

□ I walked down towards the subway station along the late-afternoon sidewalk through a thick golden haze of heat and dust. It was almost like moving underwater. From a distance I saw Ainsley shimmering beside a telephone pole, and when I had reached her she turned and we joined the lines of office workers who were funnelling down the stairs into the cool underground caverns below. By quick manoeuvring we got seats, though on the opposite sides of the car, and I sat reading the advertisements as well as I could through the screen of lurching bodies. When we got off again and went out through the pastel corridors the air felt less humid.

Clara's house was a few blocks further north. We walked in silence; I thought about mentioning the Pension Plan, but decided not to. Ainsley wouldn't understand why I found it disturbing: she'd see no reason why I couldn't leave my job and get another one, and why this wouldn't be a final solution. Then I thought about Peter and what had happened to him; Ainsley, however, would only be amused if I told her. Finally I asked her if she was feeling better.

"Don't be so concerned, Marian," she said, "you make me feel like an invalid."

I was hurt and didn't answer.

We were going uphill at a slight angle. The city slopes upwards from the lake in a series of gentle undulations, though at any given point it seems flat. This accounted for the cooler air. It was quieter here too; I thought Clara was lucky, especially in her condition, to be living so far away from the heat and noise of downtown. Though she herself thought of it as a kind of exile: they had started out in an apartment near the university, but the need for space had forced them further north, although they had not yet reached the real suburbia of modern bungalows and station-wagons. The street itself was old but not as attractive as our street: the houses were duplexes, long and narrow, with wooden porches and thin back gardens.

"Christ it's hot," Ainsley said as we turned up the walk that led to Clara's house. The grass on the doormat-sized lawn had not been cut for some time. On the steps lay a nearly-decapitated doll and inside the baby-carriage was a large teddy-bear with the stuffing coming out. I knocked, and after several minutes Joe appeared behind the screen door, harried and uncombed, doing up the buttons on his shirt.

"Hi Joe," I said "here we are. How's Clara feeling?"

"Hi, come on through," he said, stepping aside to let us past. "Clara's out back."

We walked the length of the house, which was arranged in the way such houses usually are—living-room in front, then dining-room with doors what can be slid shut, then kitchen—stepping over some of the scattered obstacles and around the others. We negotiated the stairs of the back porch, which were overgrown with empty bottles of all kinds, beer bottles, milk bottles, wine and scotch bottles, and baby bottles, and found Clara in the garden sitting in a round wicker basket-chair with metal legs. She had her feet up on another chair and was holding her latest baby somewhere in the vicinity of what had once been her lap. Clara's body is so thin that her pregnancies are always bulgingly obvious, and now in her seventh month she looked like a boa-constrictor that has swallowed a watermelon. Her head, with its aureole of pale hair, was made to seem smaller and even more fragile by the contrast.

"Oh hi," she said wearily as we came down the back steps. "Hello Ainsley, nice to see you again. Christ it's hot."

We agreed, and sat down on the grass near her, since there were no chairs. Ainsley and I took off our shoes; Clara was already barefoot. We found it difficult to talk: everyone's attention was necessarily focussed on the baby, which was whimpering, and for some time it was the only person who said anything.

When she telephoned Clara had seemed to be calling me to some sort of rescue, but I felt now that there was nothing much I could do, and nothing she had even expected me to do. I was to be only a witness, or perhaps a kind of blotter, my mere physical presence absorbing a little of the boredom.

The baby had ceased to whine and was now gurgling. Ainsley was plucking bits of grass.

"Marian," Clara said at last, "could you take Elaine for

a while? She doesn't like going on the ground and my arms are just about falling off."

"I'll take her," said Ainsley unexpectedly.

Clara pried the baby away from her body and transferred it to Ainsley, saying "Come on, you little leech. I sometimes think she's all covered with suckers, like an octopus." She lay back in her chair and closed her eyes, looking like a strange vegetable growth, a bulbous tuber that had sent out four thin white roots and a tiny pale-yellow flower. A cicada was singing in a tree nearby, its monotonous vibration like a hot needle of sunlight between the ears.

Ainsley held the baby awkwardly, gazing with curiosity into its face. I thought how closely the two faces resembled each other. The baby stared back up with eyes as round and blue as Ainsley's own; the pink mouth was drooling slightly.

Clara raised her head and opened her eyes. "Is there anything I can get you?" she asked, remembering she was the hostess.

"Oh no, we're fine," I said hastily, alarmed by the image of her struggling up out of the chair. "Is there anything I can get you?" I would have felt better doing something positive.

"Joe will come out soon," she said as if explaining. "Well, talk to me. What's new?"

"Nothing much," I said. I sat trying to think of things that would entertain her, but anything I could mention, the office or places I had been or the furnishings of the apartment, would only remind Clara of her own inertia, her lack of room and time, her days made claustrophobic with small necessary details.

"Are you still going out with that nice boy? The good-looking one. What's-his-name. I remember he came by once to get you."

"You mean Peter?"

"Yes she is," said Ainsley, with a hint of disapproval. "He's monopolized her." She was sitting cross-legged, and now she put the baby down in her lap so she could light a cigarette.

"That sounds hopeful," Clara said gloomily. "By the

way, guess who's back in town? Len Slank. He called up the other day."

"Oh really? When did he get in?" I was annoyed that he hadn't called me too.

"About a week ago, he said. He said he'd tried to phone you but couldn't get hold of your number."

"He might have tried Information," I said drily. "But I'd love to see him. How did he seem? How long is he staying?"

"Who is he?" Ainsley asked.

"Oh, no-one you'd be interested in," I said quickly. I couldn't think of two people who would be worse for each other. "He's just an old friend of ours from college."

"He went to England and got into television," said Clara. "I'm not just sure what he does. A nice type though, but he's horrible with women, sort of a seducer of young girls. He says anything over seventeen is too old."

"Oh, one of those," Ainsley said. "They're such a bore." She stubbed out her cigarette in the grass.

"You know, I got the feeling that's why he's back," Clara said with something like vivacity. "Some kind of a mess with a girl; like the one that made him go over in the first place."

"Ah," I said, not surprised.

Ainsley gave a little cry and deposited the baby on the lawn. "It's wet on my dress," she said accusingly.

"Well, they do, you know," said Clara. The baby began to howl, and I picked her up gingerly and handed her over to Clara. I was prepared to be helpful, but only up to a point.

Clara joggled the baby. "Well, you goddamned fire-hy-drant," she said soothingly. "You spouted on mummy's friend, didn't you? It'll wash out, Ainsley. But we didn't want to put rubber pants on you in all this heat, did we, you stinking little geyser? Never believe what they tell you about maternal instinct," she added grimly to us. "I don't see how anyone can love their children till they start to be human beings."

Joe appeared on the back porch, a dishtowel tucked apron-like into the belt of his trousers. "Anybody for a beer before dinner?"

Ainsley and I said Yes eagerly, and Clara said, "A little vermouth for me, darling. I can't drink anything else these days, it upsets my bloody stomach. Joe, can you just take Elaine in and change her?"

Joe came down the steps and picked up the baby. "By the way," he said, "you haven't seen Arthur around anywhere, have you?"

"Oh god, now where has the little bugger got to now?" Clara asked as Joe disappeared into the house; it seemed a rhetorical question. "I think he's found out how to open the back gate. The little bastard. Arthur! Come here, darling," she called languidly.

Down at the end of the narrow garden the line of washing that hung almost brushing the ground was parted by two small grubby hands, and Clara's firstborn emerged. Like the baby he was naked except for a pair of diapers. He hesitated, peering at us dubiously.

"Come here love, and let mummy see what you've been up to," Clara said. "Take your hands off the clean sheets," she added without conviction.

Arthur picked his way over the grass towards us, lifting his bare feet high with every step. The grass must have been ticklish. His diaper was loose, suspended as though by will-power alone below the bulge of his stomach with its protruding navel. His face was puckered in a serious frown.

Joe returned carrying a tray. "I stuck her in the laundry basket," he said. "She's playing with the clothes pins."

Arthur had reached us and stood beside his mother's chair, still frowning, and Clara said to him, "Why have you got that funny look, you little demon?" She reached down behind him and felt his diaper. "I should have known," she sighed, "he was so quiet. Husband, your son has shat again. I don't know where, it isn't in his diaper."

Joe handed round the drinks, then knelt and said to Arthur firmly but kindly, "Show Daddy where you put it." Arthur gazed up at him, not sure whether to whimper or smile. Finally he stalked portentously to the side of the garden, where he squatted down near a clump of dusty red chrysanthemums and stared with concentration at a patch of ground.

"That's a good boy," Joe said, and went back into the house.

"He's a real nature-child, he just loves to shit in the garden," Clara said to us. "He thinks he's a fertility-god. If we didn't clean it up this place would be one big manure field. I don't know what he's going to do when it snows." She closed her eyes. "We've been trying to toilet-train him, though according to some of the books it's too early, and we got him one of those plastic potties. He hasn't the least idea what it's for; he goes around wearing it on his head. I guess he thinks it's a crash-helmet."

We watched, sipping our beer, as Joe crossed the garden and returned with a folded piece of newspaper. "After this one I'm going on the pill," said Clara.

When Joe had finally finished cooking the dinner we went into the house and ate it, seated around the heavy table in the dining-room. The baby had been fed and exiled to the carriage on the front porch, but Arthur sat in a high-chair, where he evaded with spastic contortions of his body the spoonfuls of food Clara poked in the direction of his mouth. Dinner was wizened meat balls and noodles from a noodle mix, with lettuce. For dessert we had something I recognized.

"This is that new canned rice pudding; it saves a lot of time," Clara said defensively. "It's not too bad with cream, and Arthur loves it."

"Yes," I said. "Pretty soon they'll be having Orange and Caramel too."

"Oh?" Clara deftly intercepted a long drool of pudding and returned it to Arthur's mouth.

Ainsley got out a cigarette and held it for Joe to light. "Tell me," she said to him, "do you know this friend of theirs—Leonard Slank? They're being so mysterious about him."

Joe had been up and down all during the meal, taking off the plates and tending things in the kitchen. He looked dizzy. "Oh yes, I remember him," he said, "though he's really a friend of Clara's." He finished his pudding

34

quickly and asked Clara whether she needed any help, but she didn't hear him. Arthur had just thrown his bowl on the floor.

"But what do *you* think of him?" Ainsley asked, as though appealing to his superior intelligence.

Joe stared at the wall, thinking. He didn't like giving negative judgments, I knew, but I also knew he wasn't fond of Len. "He's not ethical," he said at last. Joe is an Instructor in Philosophy.

"Oh, that's not quite fair," I said. Len had never been unethical towards me.

Joe frowned at me. He doesn't know Ainsley very well, and tends anyway to think of all unmarried girls as easily victimized and needing protection. He had several times volunteered fatherly advice to me, and now he emphasized his point. "He's not someone to get ... mixed up with," he said sternly. Ainsley gave a short laugh and blew out smoke, unperturbed.

"That reminds me," I said, "you'd better give me his phone number."

After dinner we went to sit in the littered living-room while Joe cleared the table. I offered to help, but Joe said that was all right, he would rather I talked to Clara. Clara had settled herself on the chesterfield in a nest of crumpled newspapers with her eyes closed; again I could think of little to say. I sat staring up at the centre of the ceiling where there was an elaborately-scrolled plaster decoration, once perhaps the setting for a chandelier, remembering Clara at highschool: a tall fragile girl who was always getting exempted from Physical Education. She'd sit on the sidelines watching the rest of us in our blue-bloomered gymsuits as though anything so sweaty and ungainly was foreign enough to her to be a mildly-amusing entertainment. In that classroom full of oily potato-chip-fattened adolescents she was everyone's ideal of translucent perfume-advertisement femininity. At university she had been a little healthier, but had grown her blonde hair long, which made her look more medieval than ever: I had thought of her in connection with the ladies sitting in rose-gardens on tapestries. Of course her mind wasn't like that, but I've always been influenced by appearances.

35

She married Joe Bates in May at the end of our second year, and at first I thought it was an ideal match. Joe was then a graduate student, almost seven years older than she was, a tall shaggy man with a slight stoop and a protective attitude towards Clara. Their worship of each other before the wedding was sometimes ridiculously idealistic; one kept expecting Joe to spread his overcoat on mud puddles or drop to his knees to kiss Clara's rubber boots. The babies had been unplanned: Clara greeted her first pregnancy with astonishment that such a thing could happen to her, and her second with dismay; now, during her third, she had subsided into a grim but inert fatalism. Her metaphors for her children included barnacles encrusting a ship and limpets clinging to a rock.

I looked at her, feeling a wave of embarrassed pity sweep over me; what could I do? Perhaps I could offer to come over some day and clean up the house. Clara simply had no practicality, whe wasn't able to control the more mundane aspects of life, like money or getting to lectures on time. When we lived in residence together she used to become hopelessly entangled in her room at intervals, unable to find matching shoes or enough clean clothes to wear, and I would have to dig her out of the junk pile she had allowed to accumulate around her. Her messiness wasn't actively creative like Ainsley's, who could devastate a room in five minutes if she was feeling chaotic; it was passive. She simply stood helpless while the tide of dirt rose round her, unable to stop it or evade it. The babies were like that too; her own body seemed somehow beyond her, going its own way without reference to any directions of hers. I studied the pattern of bright flowers on the maternity smock she was wearing; the stylized petals and tendrils moved with her breathing, as though they were coming alive.

We left early, after Arthur had been carried off to bed screaming after what Joe called "an accident" behind the living-room door.

"It was no accident," Clara remarked, opening her eyes. "He just loves peeing behind doors. I wonder what it is. He's going to be secretive when he grows up, an undercover agent or a diplomat or something. The furtive little bastard."

Joe saw us to the door, a pile of dirty laundry in his arms. "You must come and see us again soon," he said, "Clara has so few people she can really talk to."

5

□ We walked down towards the subway in the semi-dusk, through the sound of crickets and muffled television sets (in some of the houses we could see them flickering blue through the open windows) and a smell of warm tar. My skin felt stifled, as though I was enclosed in a layer of moist dough. I was afraid Ainsley hadn't enjoyed herself: her silence was negative.

"Dinner wasn't bad," I said, wanting to be loyal to Clara, who was after all an older friend than Ainsley; "Joe's turning into quite a good cook."

"How can she stand it?" Ainsley said with more vehemence than usual. "She just lies there and that man does all the work! She lets herself be treated like a *thing*!"

"Well, she is seven months pregnant," I said. "And she's never been well."

"*She's* not well!" Ainsley said indignantly. "She's flourishing; it's him that's not well. He's aged even since I've known him and that's less than four months. She's draining all his energy."

"What do you suggest?" I said. I was annoyed with Ainsley: she couldn't see Clara's position.

"Well, she should *do* something; if only a token gesture. She never finished her degree, did she? Wouldn't this be a perfect time for her to work on it? Lots of pregnant women finish their degrees."

I remembered poor Clara's resolutions after the first baby: she had thought of it as only a temporary absence. After the second she had wailed, "I don't know what we're doing wrong! I always try to be so careful". She had always been against the pill—she thought it might change

37

her personality—but gradually she had become less adamant. She had read a French novel (in translation) and a book about archaeological expeditions in Peru and had talked about night school. Lately she had taken to making bitter remarks about being "just a housewife". "But Ainsley," I said, "you're always saying that a degree is no real indication of anything."

"Of course the degree in itself isn't," Ainsley said, "it's what it stands for. She should get organized."

When we were back at the apartment I thought of Len, and decided it wasn't too late to call him. He was in, and after we'd exchanged greetings I told him I would love to see him.

"Great," he said, "when and where? Make it some place cool. I didn't remember it was so bloody hot in the summers over here."

"Then you shouldn't have come back," I said, hinting that I knew why he had and giving him an opening.

"It was safer," he said with a touch of smugness. "Give them an inch and they'll take a mile." He had acquired a slight English accent. "By the way, Clara tells me you've got a new roommate."

"She isn't your type," I said. Ainsley had gone into the living-room and was sitting on the chesterfield with her back to me.

"Oh, you mean too old, like you, eh?" My being too old was one of his jokes.

I laughed. "Let's say tomorrow night," I said. It had suddenly struck me that Len would be a perfect distraction for Peter. "About eight-thirty at the Park Plaza. I'll bring a friend along to meet you."

"Aha," said Len, "this fellow Clara told me about. Not serious, are you?"

"Oh no, not at all," I said to reassure him.

When I had hung up Ainsley said, "Was that Len Slank you were talking to?"

I said yes.

"What does he look like?" she asked casually.

I couldn't refuse to tell her. "Oh, sort of ordinary. I don't think you'd find him attractive. He has blond curly hair and horn-rimmed glasses. Why?"

"I just wondered." She got up and went into the kitchen. "Want a drink?" she called.

"No thanks," I said, "but you could bring me a glass of water." I moved into the living-room and went to the window seat where there was a breeze.

She came back in with a scotch on the rocks for herself and handed me my glass of water. Then she sat down on the floor. "Marian," she said, "I have something I need to tell you."

Her voice was so serious that I was immediately worried. "What's wrong?"

"I'm going to have a baby," she said quietly.

I took a quick drink of water. I couldn't imagine Ainsley making a miscalculation like that. "I don't believe you."

She laughed. "Oh, I don't mean I'm already pregnant. I mean I'm going to get pregnant."

I was relieved, but puzzled. "You mean you're going to get married?" I asked, thinking of Trigger's misfortune. I tried to guess which of them Ainsley could be interested in, without success; ever since I'd known her she had been decidedly anti-marriage.

"I knew you'd say that," she said with amused contempt. "No, I'm not going to get married. That's what's wrong with most children, they have too many parents. You can't say the sort of household Clara and Joe are running is an ideal situation for a child. Think of how confused their mother-image and their father-image will be; they're riddled with complexes already. And it's mostly because of the father."

"But Joe is marvellous!" I cried. "He does just about everything for her! Where would Clara be without him?"

"Precisely," said Ainsley. "She would have to cope by herself. And she would cope, and their total upbringing would be much more consistent. The thing that ruins families these days is the husbands. Have you noticed she isn't even breast-feeding the baby?"

"But it's got teeth," I protested. "Most people wean them when they get teeth."

"Nonsense," Ainsley said darkly, "I bet Joe put her up to it. In South America they breast-feed them much longer than that. North American men hate watching the basic mother-child unit functioning naturally, it makes them feel not needed. This way Joe can give it the bottle just as easily. Any woman left to her own devices would automatically breast-feed as long as possible: I'm certainly going to."

It seemed to me that the discussion had got off the track: we were talking theory about a practical matter. I tried a personal attack: "Ainsley, you don't know anything at all about babies. You don't even like them much. I've heard you say they're too dirty and noisy."

"Not liking other people's babies," said Ainsley, "isn't the same as not liking your own."

I couldn't deny this. I was baffled: I didn't even know how to justify my own opposition to her plan. The worst of it was that she would probably do it. She can go about getting what she wants with a great deal of efficiency, though in my opinion some of the things she wants—and this was a case in point—are unreasonable. I decided to take a down-to-earth approach.

"All right," I said. "Granted. But why do you want a baby, Ainsley? What are you going to *do* with it?"

She gave me a disgusted look. "Every woman should have at least one baby." She sounded like a voice on the radio saying that every woman should have at least one electric hair-dryer. "It's even more important than sex. It fulfills your deepest femininity." Ainsley is fond of paper-back books by anthropologists about primitive cultures: there are several of them bogged down among the clothes on her floor. At her college they make you take courses in it.

"But why now?" I said, searching my mind for objections. "What about the job at the art gallery? And meeting the artists?" I held them out to her like a carrot to a donkey.

Ainsley widened her eyes at me. "What has having a baby got to do with getting a job at an art gallery? You're always thinking in terms of either/or. The thing is *wholeness*. As for why now, well, I've been considering this for some time. Don't you feel you need a sense of purpose? And wouldn't you rather have your children

40

while you're young? While you can enjoy them. Besides, they've proved they're likely to be healthier if you have them between twenty and thirty."

"And you're going to keep it," I said. I looked around the living-room, calculating already how much time, energy and money it would take to pack and move the furniture. I had contributed most of the solider items: the heavy round coffee table donated from a relative's attic back home, the walnut drop-leaf we used for company, also a donation, the stuffed easy-chair and the chesterfield I had picked up at the Salvation Army and re-covered. The outsize poster of Theda Bara and the bright paper flowers were Ainsley's; so were the ash trays and the inflatable plastic cushions with geometric designs. Peter said our living-room lacked unity. I had never thought of it as a permanent arrangement, but now it was threatened it took on a desirable stability for me. The tables planted their legs more firmly on the floor; it was inconceivable that the round coffee table could ever be manipulated down those narrow stairs, that the poster of Theda Bara could be rolled up, revealing the crack in the plaster, that the plastic cushions could allow themselves to be deflated and stowed away in a trunk. I wondered whether the lady down below would consider Ainsley's pregnancy a breach of contract and take legal action.

Ainsley was getting sulky. "Of course I'm going to keep it. What's the good of going through all that trouble if you don't keep it?"

"So what it boils down to," I said, finishing my water, "is that you've decided to have an illegitimate child in cold blood and bring it up yourself."

"Oh, it's such a bore to *explain*. Why use that horrible bourgeois word? Birth is legitimate, isn't it? You're a prude, Marian, and that's what's wrong with this whole society."

"Okay, I'm a prude," I said, secretly hurt: I thought I was being more understanding than most. "But since the society is the way it is, aren't you being selfish? Won't the child suffer? How are you going to support it and deal with other people's prejudices and so on?"

"How is the society ever going to change," said Ainsley

41

with the dignity of a crusader, "if some individuals in it don't lead the way? I will simply tell the truth. I know I'll have trouble here and there, but some people will be quite tolerant about it, I'm sure, even here. I mean, it won't be as though I've gotten pregnant by accident or anything."

We sat in silence for several minutes. The main point seemed to have been established. "All right," I said finally, "I see you've thought of everything. But what about a father for it? I know it's a small technical detail, but you will need one of those, you know, if only for a short time. You can't just send out a bud."

"Well," she said, taking me seriously, "actually I have been thinking about it. He'll have to have a decent heredity and be fairly good-looking; and it will help if I can get someone co-operative who will understand and not make a fuss about marrying me."

She reminded me more than I liked of a farmer discussing cattle-breeding. "Anyone in mind? What about that dentistry student?"

"Good god no," she said, "he has a receding chin."

"Or the electric toothbrush murder-witness man?"

She puckered her brow. "I don't think he's very bright. I'd prefer an artist of course, but that's too risky genetically; by this time they must all have chromosome breaks from L.S.D. I suppose I could unearth Freddy from last year, he wouldn't mind in the least, though he's too fat and he has an awfully stubbly five o'clock shadow. I wouldn't want a fat child."

"Nor one with heavy stubble either," I said, trying to be helpful.

Ainsley looked at me with annoyance. "You're being sarcastic," she said. "But if only people would give more thought to the characteristics they pass on to their children maybe they wouldn't rush blindly into things. We know the human race is degenerating and it's all because people pass on their weak genes without thinking about it, and medical science means they aren't naturally selected out the way they used to be."

I was beginning to feel fuzzy in the brain. I knew Ainsley was wrong, but she sounded so rational. I thought I'd
42

better go to bed before she had convinced me against my better judgment.

In the room, I sat on the bed with my back against the wall, thinking. At first I tried to concentrate on ways to stop her, but then I became resigned. Her mind was made up, and though I could hope this was just a whim she would get over, was it any of my business? I would simply have to adjust to the situation. Perhaps when we had to move I should get another roommate; but would it be right to leave Ainsley on her own? I didn't want to behave irresponsibly.

I got into bed, feeling unsettled.

6

☐ The alarm clock startled me out of a dream in which I had looked down and seen my feet beginning to dissolve, like melting jelly, and had put on a pair of rubber boots just in time only to find that the ends of my fingers were turning transparent. I had started towards the mirror to see what was happening to my face, but at that point I woke up. I don't usually remember my dreams.

Ainsley was still asleep, so I boiled my egg and drank my tomato juice and coffee alone. Then I dressed in an outfit suitable for interviewing, an official-looking skirt, a blouse with sleeves, and a pair of low-heeled walking shoes. I intended to get an early start, but I couldn't be too early or the men, who would want to sleep in on the holiday, wouldn't be up yet. I got out my map of the city and studied it, mentally crossing off the areas I knew had been selected for the actual survey. I had some toast and a second cup of coffee, and traced out several possible routes for myself.

What I needed was seven or eight men with a certain minimum average beer consumption per week, who would be willing to answer the questions. Locating them might be more difficult than usual, because of the long weekend. I knew from experience that men were usually more unwilling than women to play the questionnaire game. The streets near the apartment were out: word might get back to the lady down below that I had been asking the neighbours how much beer they drank. Also, I suspected that it was a scotch area rather than a beer one; with a sprinkling of teetotalling widows. The rooming-house district further west was out, too: I had tried it once for a potato-chip taste-test and found the landladies very hostile. They seemed to think I was a government agent in disguise, trying to raise their tax by discovering they had more lodgers than they claimed. I considered the fraternity houses near the university, but remembered the study demanded answerers over the age-limit.

I took the bus, got off at the subway station, paused to note down my fare as "Transportation" on my expenses time-sheet, and crossed the street. Then I went down a slope into the flat treeless park spread out opposite the station. There was a baseball diamond in one corner, but nobody was playing on it. The rest of the park was plain grass, which had turned yellow; it crackled underfoot. This day was going to be like the one before, windless and oppressive. The sky was cloudless but not clear: the air hung heavily, like invisible steam, so that the colours and outlines of objects in the distance were blurred.

At the far side of the park was a sloping asphalt ramp, which I climbed. It led to a residential street lined with small, rather shabby houses set close together, the two-storey shoe-box kind with wooden trim round the windows and eaves. Some of the houses had freshly-painted trimmings, which merely accentuated the weatherbeaten surfaces of the shingled fronts. The district was the sort that had been going downhill for some decades but had been pushed uphill again in the past few years. Several refugees from the suburbs had bought these city houses and completely refinished them, painting them a sophisticated white and adding flagstone walks and evergreens in cement planters and coachlamps by the doors. The redone houses looked flippant beside the others, as though they had chosen to turn their backs with an irresponsible light-heartedness upon the problems of time and shabbiness and puritan weather. I resolved to avoid the transformed houses when I began to interview. I wouldn't find the right sort of people there: they would be the martini set.

There is something intimidating about a row of closed doors if you know you have to go up and knock on them and ask what amounts to a favour. I straightened my dress and my shoulders and assumed what I hoped was an official but friendly expression, and walked as far as the next block practising it before I had worked up resolution enough to begin. At the end of the block I could see what looked like a fairly new apartment-building. I made it my goal: it would be cool inside, and might supply me with any missing interviews.

I rang the first doorbell. Someone scrutinized me briefly through the white semi-transparent curtains of the front window; then the door was opened by a sharp-featured woman in a print apron with a bib. Her face had not a vestige of makeup on it, not even lipstick, and she was wearing those black shoes with laces and thick heels that make me think of the word "orthopaedic" and that I associate with the bargain-basements of department stores.

"Good morning, I represent Seymour Surveys," I said, smiling falsely. "We're doing a little survey and I wonder if your husband would be kind enough to answer a few questions for me?"

"You selling anything?" she asked, glancing at my papers and pencil.

"Oh, no! We have nothing to do with selling. We're a market research company, we merely ask questions. It helps improve the products," I added lamely. I didn't think I was going to find what I was looking for.

"What's it about? she asked, the corners of her mouth tightening with suspicion.

"Well, actually it's about beer," I said in a tinsel-bright voice, trying to make the word sound as skim-milk like as possible.

Her face changed expression. She was going to refuse, I thought. But she hesitated, then stepped aside and said in a voice that reminded me of cold oatmeal porridge, "Como in."

I stood in the spotless tiled hallway, inhaling the smell

45

of furniture-polish and bleach, while she disappeared through a door farther on, closing it behind her. There was a murmured conversation; then the door opened again and a tall man with grey hair and a severe frown came through it, followed by the woman. The man wore a black coat even though the day was so warm.

"Now young lady," he said to me, "I'm not going to chastize you personally because I can see you are a nice girl and only the innocent means to this abominable end. But you will be so kind as to give these tracts to your employers. Who can tell but that their hearts may yet be softened? The propagation of drink and of drunkenness to excess is an iniquity, a sin against the Lord."

I took the pamphlets he handed me, but felt enough loyalty to Seymour Surveys to say, "Our company doesn't have anything to do with *selling* the beer, you know."

"It is the same thing," he said sternly, "it is all the same thing, 'Those who are not with me are against me, saith the Lord.' Do not try to whiten the sepulchres of those traffickers in human misery and degradation." He was about to turn away, but said to me as an afterthought, "You might read those yourself, young lady. Of course you never pollute your lips with alcohol, but no soul is utterly pure and proof against temptation. Perhaps the seed will not fall by the wayside, nor yet on stony ground."

I said a faint "Thank you," and the man extended the edges of his mouth in a smile. His wife, who had been watching the small sermon with frugal satisfaction, stepped forward and opened the door for me, and I went out, resisting the reflex urge to shake both of them by the hand as though I was coming out of church.

It was a bad beginning. I looked at the tracts as I walked to the next house. "TEMPERANCE," commanded one. The other was titled, more stirringly, "DRINK AND THE DEVIL". He must be a minister, I thought, though certainly not Anglican, and probably not even United. One of those obscure sects.

No-one was at home in the next house, and at the one after that the door was opened by a chocolate-smeared urchin who informed me that her daddy was still in bed.

At the next one though I soon knew that I had come at last to a good place for head-hunting. The main door was standing open, and the man I could see coming towards me several moments after I had rung was of medium height but very thickly built, almost fat. When he opened the screen door I could see that he had only his socks on his feet, no shoes; he was wearing an undershirt and a pair of bermuda shorts. His face was brick-red.

I explained my errand and showed him the card with the average-beer-consumption-per-week scale on it. Each average is numbered, and the scale runs from 0 to 10. The company does it that way because some men are shy about naming their consumption in so many words. This man picked No. 9, the second from the top. Hardly anybody chooses No. 10; everyone likes to think there's a chance that somebody else drinks more than he does.

When we had got that far the man said, "Come on into the living room and sit down. You must be tired walking around in all the heat. My wife's just gone to do the shopping," he added irrelevantly.

I sat down in one of the easy-chairs and he turned down the sound on the T.V. set. I saw a bottle of one of Moose Beer's competitors standing on the floor by his chair, half-empty. He sat down opposite me, smiling and moping his forehead with his handkerchief, and answered the preliminary questions with the air of an expert delivering a professional verdict. After he had listened to the telephone commercial he scratched the hair on his chest thoughtfully and gave the sort of enthusiastic response for which a whole seminary of admen had no doubt been offering daily prayers. When we finished and I had written down the name and address, which the company needs so it won't re-interview the same people, got up, and began to thank him, I saw him lurching out of his chair towards me with a beery leer. "Now what's a nice little girl like you doing walking around asking men all about their beer?" he said moistly. "You ought to be at home with some big strong man to take care of you."

I pressed the two Temperance pamphlets into his damp outstretched hand and fled.

I shuffled through four more complete interviews without much incident, discovering in the process that the questionnaire needed the addition of a "Does not have phone . . . End interview" box and a "Does not listen to radio" one, and that men who approved of the chest-thumping sentiments of the commerical tended to object to the word "Tingly" as being "Too light," or, as one of them put it, "Too fruity". The fifth interview was with a spindly balding man who was so afraid of expressing any opinions at all that getting words out of him was like pulling teeth with a monkey-wrench. Every time I asked him a new question he flushed, bobbed his adam's-apple, and contorted his face in a wince of agony. He was speechless for several minutes after he had listened to the commercial and I had asked him, "How did you like the commercial? Very Much; Only Moderately; or Not Very Much?" At last he managed to whisper, feebly, "Yes."

I had now only two more interviews to get. I decided to skip the next few houses and go to the square apartment-building. I got in by the usual method, pressing all the buttons at once until some deluded soul released the inner door.

The coolness was a relief. I went up a short flight of stairs whose carpeting was just beginning to wear thin, and knocked at the first door, which was numbered Six. I found this curious because from its position it should have been numbered *One*.

Nothing happened when I knocked. I knocked again more loudly, waited, and was about to go on to the next apartment when the door swung inward noiselessly and I found myself being looked at by a young boy whom I judged to be about fifteen.

He rubbed one of his eyes with a finger, as if he had just got up. He was cadaverously thin; he had no shirt on, and the ribs stuck out like those of an emaciated figure in a medieval woodcut. The skin stretched over them was nearly colourless, not white but closer to the sallow tone of old linen. His feet were bare; he was wearing only a pair of khaki pants. The eyes, partly hidden by a rumpled mass of straight black hair that came down over the forehead, were obstinately melancholy, as though he was assuming the expression on purpose.

We stared at each other. He was evidently not going to say anything, and I could not quite begin. The questionnaires I was carrying had suddenly become unrelated to anything at all, and at the same time obscurely threatening. Finally I managed to say, feeling very synthetic as I did so, "Hello there, is your father in?"

He continued to stare at me without a tremor of expression. "No. He's dead," he said.

"Oh." I stood, swaying a little; the contrast with the heat outside had made me dizzy. Time seemed to have shifted into slow-motion; there seemed to be nothing to say; but I couldn't leave or move. He continued to stand in the doorway.

Then after what seemed hours it occurred to me that he might not actually be as young as he looked. There were dark circles under his eyes, and some fine thin lines at the outer corners. "Are you really only fifteen?" I asked, as though he had told me he was.

"I'm twenty-six," he said dolefully.

I gave a visible start, and as if the answer had stepped on some hidden accelerator in me I babbled out a high-speed version of the blurb about being from Seymour Surveys and not selling anything and improving products and wanting to ask a few simple questions about how much beer he drank in an average week, thinking while I did so that he didn't look as though he ever drank anything but water, with the crust of bread they tossed him as he lay chained in the dungeon. He seemed gloomily interested, much as one would be interested (it at all) in a dead dog, so I extended the average-weekly-consumption card towards him and asked him to pick his number. He looked at it a minute, turned it over and looked at the back, which was blank, closed his eyes, and said "Number six."

That was seven to ten bottles per week, high enough to qualify him for the questionnaire, and I told him so. "Come in then," he said. I felt a slight sensation of alarm as I stepped over the threshold and the door closed woodenly behind me.

We were in a living room of medium size, perfectly square, with a kitchenette opening off it on one side and

49

the hallway to the bedrooms on the other. The slats of the venetian blind on the one small window were closed, making the room dim as twilight. The walls, as far as I could tell in the semi-darkness, were a flat white; there were no pictures on them. The floor was covered by a very good Persian carpet with an ornate design of maroon and green and purple scrolls and flowers, even better, I thought, than the one in the lady down below's parlour which had been left her by her paternal grandfather. One wall had a bookcase running its whole length, the kind people make themselves out of boards and bricks. The only other pieces of furniture were three huge, ancient and overstuffed easy chairs, one red plush, one a worn greenish-blue brocade, and one a faded purple, each with a floor-lamp beside it. All exposed surfaces of the room were littered with loose papers, notebooks, books opened face-down and other books bristling with pencils and torn slips of paper stuck in them as markers.

"Do you live here alone?" I asked.

He fixed me with his lugubrious eyes. "It depends what you mean," he intoned, "by 'alone'."

"Oh, I see," I said politely. I walked across the room, trying to preserve my air of cheerful briskness while picking my way unsteadily over and around the objects on the floor. I was heading towards the purple chair, which was the only one that didn't have a rat's-nest of papers on it.

"You can't sit there," he said behind me in a tone of slight admonishment, "that's Trevor's chair. He wouldn't like you sitting in his chair."

"Oh. Is the red one all right then?"

"Well," he said, "that's Fish's, and he wouldn't mind if you sat in it; at least I don't think he would. But he's got his papers in it and you might mess them up." I didn't see how by merely sitting on them I could possibly disorganize them any more, but I didn't say so. I was wondering whether Trevor and Fish were two imaginary playmates that this boy had made up, and also whether he had lied about his age. In this light his face could have been of a ten-year-old. He stood gazing at me solemnly, shoulders hunched, arms folded across his torso, holding his own elbows.

"And I suppose yours is the green one then."

"Yes," he said, "but I haven't sat in it myself for a couple of weeks. I've got everything all arranged in it."

I wanted to go over and see exactly what he had got all arranged in it, but I reminded myself that I was there on business. "Where are we going to sit then?"

"The floor," he said, "or the kitchen, or my bedroom."

"Oh, not the bedroom," I said hurriedly. I made my way back across the expanse of paper and peered around the corner into the kitchenette. A peculiar odour greeted me—there seemed to be garbage bags in every corner, and the rest of the space was taken up by a large pots and kettles, some clean, others not. "I don't think there's room in the kitchen," I said. I stooped and began to skim the papers off the surface of the carpet, much as one would skim scum from a pond.

"I don't think you'd better do that," he said. "Some of them aren't mine. You might get them mixed up. We'd better go into the bedroom." He slouched across to the hall and through an open doorway. Of necessity I followed him.

The room was a white-walled oblong box, dark as the living room: the venetian blind was down here too. It was bare of furniture except for an ironing-board with an iron on it, a chess set with a few scattered pieces in a corner of the room, a typewriter sitting on the floor, a cardboard carton which seemed to have dirty laundry in it and which he kicked into the closet as I came in, and a narrow bed. He pulled a grey army-blanket over the tangle of sheets on the bed and crawled onto it, where he settled himself crosslegged, backed into the corner formed by the two walls. He switched on the reading-lamp over the bed, took a cigarette from a pack which he replaced in his back pocket, lit it, and sat holding the cigarette before him, his hands cupped, like a starved buddha burning incense to itself.

"All right," he said.

I sat down on the edge of the bed—there were no chairs—and began to go through the questionnaire with him. After I had asked each question he would lean his head back against the wall, close his eyes, and give the

51

answer; then he would open his eyes again and watch me with barely-perceptible signs of concentration while I asked the next.

When we got to the telephone commercial he went to the phone in the kitchen to dial the number. He stayed out there for what seemed to me a long time. I went to check, and found him listening with the receiver pressed to his ear and his mouth twisted in something that was almost a smile.

"You're only supposed to listen once," I said reproachfully.

He put down the receiver with reluctance. "Can I phone it after you go and listen some more?" he asked in the diffident but wheedling voice of a small child begging an extra cookie.

"Yes," I said, "but not next week, okay?" I didn't want him blocking the line for the interviewers.

We went back to the bedroom and resumed our respective postures. "Now I'm going to repeat some of the phrases from the commercial to you, and for each one I would like you to tell me what it makes you think of," I said. This was the free-association part of the questionnaire, meant to test immediate responses to certain key phrases. "First, what about 'Deep-down manly flavour?' "

He threw his head back and closed his eyes. "Sweat," he said, considering. "Canvas gym shoes. Underground locker-rooms and jock-straps."

An interviewer is always supposed to write down the exact words of the answer, so I did. I thought about slipping this interview into the stack of real ones, to vary the monotony for one of the women with the crayons—Mrs. Weemers, perhaps, or Mrs. Gundridge. She'd read it out loud to the others, and they would remark that it took all kinds; the topic would be good for at least three coffee-breaks.

"Now what about 'Long cool swallow?' "

"Not much. Oh, wait a moment. It's a bird, white, falling from a great height. Shot through the heart, in winter; the feathers coming off, drifting down. . . . This is just like those word-game tests the shrink gives you," he
52

said with his eyes open. "I always liked doing them. They're better than the ones with pictures."

I said, "I expect they use the same principle. What about 'Healthy hearty taste?' "

He meditated for several minutes. "It's heartburn," he said. "Or no, that can't be right." His forehead wrinkled. "Now I see. It's one of those cannibal stories." For the first time he seemed upset. "I know the pattern, there's one of them in the *Decameron* and a couple in Grimm's; the husband kills the wife's lover, or vice versa, and cuts out the heart and makes it into a stew or a pie and serves it up in a silver dish, and the other one eats it. Though that doesn't account for the Healthy very well, does it? Shakespeare," he said in a less agitated voice, "Shakespeare has something like that too. There's a scene in *Titus Andronicus,* though it's debatable whether Shakespeare really wrote it, or . . ."

"Thank you." I wrote busily. By this time I was convinced that he was a compulsive neurotic of some sort and that I'd better remain calm and not display any fear. I wasn't frightened exactly—he didn't look like the violent type—but these questions definitely made him tense. He might be tottering on an emotional brink, one of the phrases might be enough to push him over. Those people are like that I thought, remembering certain case histories Ainsley has told me; little things like words can really bother them.

"Now, 'Tingly, heady, rough-and-ready?' "

He contemplated that one at length. "Doesn't do a thing for me," he said, "it doesn't fit together. The first bit gives me an image of someone with a head made out of glass being hit with a stick: like musical glasses. But rough-and-ready doesn't do anything. I suppose," he said sadly, "that one's not much use to you."

"You're doing fine," I said, thinking of what would happen to the I.B.M. machine if they ever tried to run this thing through it. "Now the last one: 'Tang of the wilderness.' "

"Oh," he said, his voice approaching enthusiasm, "that one's easy; it struck me at once when I heard it. It's one of those technicolour movies about dogs or horses. 'Tang

53

of the Wilderness' is obviously a dog, part wolf, part husky, who saves his master three times, once from fire, once from flood and once from wicked humans, more likely to be white hunters than Indians these days, and finally gets blasted by a cruel trapper with a .22 and wept over. Buried, probably in the snow. Panoramic shot of trees and lake. Sunset. Fade-out."

"Fine," I said, scribbling madly to get it all down. There was silence while we both listened to the scratching of my pencil. "Now, I hate to ask you, but you're supposed to say how well you think each of these five phrases applies to a beer—Very Well, Medium Well, or Not Very Well At All?"

"I couldn't tell you," he said, losing interest completely. "I never drink the stuff. Only scotch. None of them are any good for scotch."

"But," I protested, astonished, "you picked Number Six on the card. The one that said seven to ten bottles per week."

"You wanted me to pick a number," he said with patience, "and six is my lucky number. I even got them to change the numbers on the apartments; this is really Number One, you know. Besides, I was boréd; I felt like talking to someone."

"That means I won't be able to count your interview," I said severely. I had forgotten for the moment that it wasn't real.

"Oh, you enjoyed it," he said, smiling his half-smile again. "You know all the other answers you've been getting are totally dull. You have to admit I've livened up your day considerably."

I had a twinge of irritation. I have been feeling compassion for him as a sufferer on the verge of mental collapse, and now he had revealed the whole thing as a self-conscious performance. I could either get up and leave at once, showing my displeasure, or admit that he was right. I frowned at him, trying to decide what to do; but just then I heard the front door opening and the sound of voices.

He jerked forward and listened tensely, then leaned back against the wall. "It's only Fish and Trevor. They're my room-mates," he said, "the other two bores. Trevor's the mother bore: he's going to be shocked when he finds me with my shirt off and a capital-G girl in the room.

There was a brown-paper crunkle of grocery-bags being set down in the kitchen, and a deep voice said, "Christ, it's hot out there!"

"I think I'd better go now," I said. If the others were all like this one I didn't think I would be able to cope. I gathered my questionnaires together and stood up, at the same time as the voice said "Hey Duncan, want a beer?" and a furry bearded head appeared in the doorway.

I gasped. "So you do drink beer after all!"

"Yes, I'm afraid so. Sorry. I didn't want to finish, that's all. The rest of it sounded like a drag, and I'd said all I wanted to say about it anyway. Fish," he said to the beard, "this is Goldilocks." I smiled rigidly. I am not a blonde.

Another head now appeared above the first: a white-skinned face with receding lightish hair, skyblue eyes, and an admirably-chiselled nose. His jaw dropped when he saw me.

It was time to leave. "Thank you," I said coolly but graciously to the one on the bed. "You've been most helpful."

He actually grinned as I marched to the doorway and as the heads retreated in alarm to let me pass he called, "Hey, why do you have a crummy job like this? I thought only fat sloppy housewives did that sort of thing."

"Oh," I said with as much dignity as I could muster, and not intending to justify myself by explaining the high—well, higher—status of my real job, "we all have to eat. Besides, what else can you do with a B.A. these days?"

When I was outside I looked at the questionnaire. The notes I had made of his answers were almost indecipherable in the glare of the sunlight; all I could see on the page was a blur of grey scribbling.

7

☐ Technically I was still one and a half interviews short, but I had enough for the necessary report and the questionnaire changes. Besides, I wanted to have a bath and change before going to Peter's and the interviewing had taken longer than I expected.

I got back to the apartment and threw the questionnaires on the bed. Then I looked around for Ainsley, but she was out. I gathered together my washcloth, soap, toothbrush and toothpaste, put on my dressing gown, and went downstairs. Our apartment has no bathroom of its own, which helps to account for the low rent. Perhaps the house was built before they had them, or perhaps it was felt that servants didn't need bathrooms; at any rate, we have to use the second floor bathroom, which makes life difficult at times. Ainsley is always leaving rings, which the lady down below regards as a violation of her shrine. She leaves deodorants and cleansers and brushes and sponges in conspicuous places, which has no effect on Ainsley but makes me feel uneasy. Sometimes I go downstairs after Ainsley has taken a bath and clean out the tub.

I had wanted to soak for a while, but I had barely scrubbed away the afternoon's film of dust and bus fumes when the lady down below began making rustling and throat-clearing noises outside the door. This is her way of suggesting that she wants to get in: she never knocks and asks. I clambered upstairs again, dressed, had a cup of tea, and set out for Peter's. The ancestors watched me with their fading daguerreotyped eyes as I went down the stairs, their mouths bleak above their stiff collars.

Usually we went out for dinner, but when we didn't the pattern was that I would walk over to Peter's and get something to cook at a store on the way—one of those small grubby stores you sometimes find in the older residential districts. Of course he could have picked me up at the house in his Volkswagen, but he is made irritable by errands; also I don't like to give the lady down below too much food for speculation. I didn't know whether we were going out for dinner or not—Peter had said nothing about it—so I dropped in at the store just to be on the safe side. He would probably have a hangover from the celebration of the night before and wouldn't feel like a full-scale dinner.

Peter's apartment-building is just far enough away to make getting there by transportation-system more bother than it's worth. It's south of our district and east of the university, in a run-down area, nearly a slum, that is scheduled to be transformed over the next few years by high-rise apartments. Several have been completed but Peter's is still under construction. Peter is the only person who lives there; he does so temporarily, at only a third of the price they'll charge when the building is finished. He was able to make this deal through a connection he acquired during a piece of contract manipulating. Peter's in his articling year as a lawyer and doesn't have extravagant amounts of money yet—for instance he couldn't have afforded the apartment at its list price—but his is a small firm and he's rising in it like a balloon.

All summer whenever I went to the apartment I had to thread my way through piles of concrete blocks near the entrance to the lobby, around shapes covered with dusty tarpaulins on the floor inside, and sometimes over troughs for plaster and ladders and stacks of pipes on the stairway going up; the elevators aren't in working order yet. Occasionally I would be stopped by workmen who didn't know about Peter and who would insist that I couldn't go in because nobody lived there. We would then have arguments about the existence or non-existence of Mr. Wollander, and once I'd had to take some of them up to the seventh floor with me and produce Peter in the flesh. I knew there wouldn't be any men working as late as five on Saturday though; and they probably had the whole long weekend off anyway. Generally they seem to go about things in a leisurely manner, which suits Peter. There's been a strike or a layoff too which had held things up. Peter hopes it will go on: the longer they take, the longer his rent will be low.

Structurally the building was complete, except for the finishing touches. They had all the windows in and had scrawled them with white soap hieroglyphics to keep people from walking through them. The glass doors had been installed several weeks before, and Peter had got an extra set of keys made for me: a necessity rather than just a convenience, since the buzzer-system for letting people in had not yet been connected. Inside, the shiny surfaces—tiled floors, painted walls, mirrors, light-fixtures—which would later give the building its expensive gloss, its beetle-hard internal shell had not yet begun to secret themselves. The rough grey underskin of subflooring and unplastered wall-surface was still showing, and raw wires dangled like loose nerves from most of the sockets. I went up the stairs carefully, avoiding the dirty bannister, thinking how much I had come to associate weekends with this new-building smell of sawn boards and cement-dust. On the floors I passed, the doorways of the future apartments gaped emptily, their doors as yet unhung. It was a long climb up; as I reached Peter's floor I was breathing hard. I would be glad when the elevators were running.

Peter's apartment, of course, has been largely finished; he'd never live in a place without proper floors and electricity, no matter how low the rent. His connection uses it as a model of what the rest of the apartments will be like, and shows it to the occasional prospective tenant, always phoning Peter before he arrives. It doesn't inconvenience Peter much: he's out a lot and doesn't mind people looking through his place.

I opened the door, went in, and took the groceries to the refrigerator in the kitchenette. I could tell by the sound of running water that Peter was taking a shower: he often is. I strolled into the living room and looked out of the window. The apartment isn't far enough up for a good view of the lake or the city—you can only see a mosaic of dingy little streets and narrow backyards, and you aren't low enough to see clearly what the people are doing in them. Peter hasn't put much in the living room yet. He's got a Danish-modern sofa and a chair to match and a hi-fi set, but nothing else. He says he'd rather wait and get good things than clutter the place up with cheap things he doesn't like. I suppose he is right, but still it will help when he gets more: his two pieces of furniture are made to look very spindly and isolated by the large empty space that surrounds them.

I get restless when I'm waiting for anyone, I tend to pace. I wandered into the bedroom and looked out the window there, though it's much the same view. Peter has the bedroom nearly done, he's told me, though for some tastes it might be slightly sparse. He has a good-sized sheepskin on the floor and a plain, solid bed, also good sized, second-hand but in perfect condition, which is always neatly made. Then an austere square desk, dark wood, and one of those leather-cushioned office swivel-chairs that he picked up second-hand too; he says it's very comfortable for working. The desk has a reading lamp on it, a blotter, an assortment of pens and pencils, and Peter's graduation portrait in a stand-up frame. On the wall above there's a small bookcase—his law books on the bottom shelf, his hoard of paperback detective novels on the top shelf, and miscellaneous books and magazines in between. To one side of the bookcase is a pegboard with hooks that holds Peter's collection of weapons: two rifles, a pistol, and several wicked-looking knives. I've been told all the names, but I can never remember them. I've never seen Peter use any of them, though of course in the city he wouldn't have many opportunities. Apparently he used to go hunting a lot with his oldest friends. Peter's cameras hang there too, their glass eyes covered by leather cases. There's a full-length mirror on the outside of the cupboard door, and inside the cupboard are all of Peter's clothes.

Peter must have heard me prowling. He called from inside the bathroom, "Marian? That you?"

"I'm here," I called back. "Hi."

"Hi. Fix yourself a drink. And one for me too—gin and tonic, okay? I'll be out in a minute."

I knew where everything was. Peter has a cupboard shelf well-stocked with liquor, and he never forgets to refill the ice-cube trays. I went to the kitchen, and carefully assembled the drinks, remembering not to leave out the twist of lemon-peel Peter likes. It takes me longer than average to make drinks: I have to measure.

I heard the shower stop and the sound of feet, and when I turned around Peter was standing in the kitchen doorway, dripping wet, wearing a tasteful navy-blue towel.

"Hi," I said. "Your drink's on the counter."

He stepped forward silently, took my glass from my hand, swallowed a third of its contents and set it on the table behind me. Then he put both of his arms round me.

"You're getting me all wet," I said softly. I put my hand, cold from holding the icy glass, on the small of his back, but he didn't flinch. His flesh was warm and resilient after the shower.

He kissed my ear. "Come into the bathroom," he said.

I gazed up at Peter's shower-curtain, a silver plastic ground covered with curve-necked swans in pink swimming in groups of three among albino lily-pads; it wasn't Peter's taste at all, he'd bought it in a hurry because the water kept running over the floor when he showered, he hadn't had time to look properly and this one had been the least garish. I was wondering why he had insisted that we get into the bathtub. I hadn't thought it was a good idea, I much prefer the bed and I knew the tub would be too small and uncomfortably hard and ridgey, but I hadn't objected: I felt I should be sympathetic because of Trigger. However I had taken the bath mat in with me, which softened the ridges.

I had expected Peter to be depressed, but though he wasn't his usual self he certainly wasn't depressed. I couldn't quite figure out the bathtub. I thought back to the other two unfortunate marriages. After the first, it had been the sheepskin on his bedroom floor, and after the second a scratchy blanket in a field we'd driven four hours to get to, and where I was made uneasy by thoughts of farmers and cows. I suppose this was part of the same pattern, whatever the pattern was. Perhaps an attempt to assert youthfulness and spontaneity, a revolt against the stale doom of stockings in the sink and bacon fat congealed in pans evoked for him by his friends' marriages. Peter's abstraction on these occasions gave me the feeling that he liked doing them because he had read about them somewhere, but I could never locate the quotations. The field was, I guessed, a hunting story from one of the outdoorsy male magazines; I remembered he had worn a plaid jacket. The sheepskin I placed in one of the men's glossies, the kind with lust in pent-houses. But the bathtub? Possibly one of the murder mysteries he read as what he called "escape literature"; but wouldn't that rather be someone drowned in the bathtub? A woman. That would give them a perfect bit to illustrate on the cover: a completely naked woman with a thin covering of water and maybe a bar of soap or a rubber duck or a blood-stain to get her past the censors, floating with her hair spread out on the water, the cold purity of the bathtub surrounding her body, chaste as ice only because dead, her open eyes staring up into those of the reader. The bathtub as a coffin. I had a fleeting vision: what if we both fell asleep and the tap got turned on accidentally, lukewarm so we wouldn't notice, and the water slowly rose and killed us? That would be a surprise for the connection when he came to show his next batch of apartment-renters around: water all over the floor and two naked corpses clasped in a last embrace. "Suicide," they'd all say. "Died for love." And on summer nights our ghosts would be seen gliding along the halls of the Brentview Apartments, Bachelor, Two-Bedroom and Luxury, clad only in bath towels. . . .

I shifted my head, tired of the swans, and looked instead at the curving silver nozzle of the shower. I could smell Peter's hair, a clean soap smell. He smelled of soap all the time, not only when he had recently taken a shower. It was a smell I associated with dentists' chairs and medicine, but on him I found it attractive. He never wore sickly-sweet shaving lotion or the other male substitutes for perfume.

I could see his arm where it lay across me, the hairs arranged in rows. The arm was like the bathroom: clean and white and new, the skin unusually smooth for a man's. I couldn't see his face, which was resting against

61

my shoulder, but I tried to visualize it. He was, as Clara had said, "good-looking"; that was probably what had first attracted me to him. People noticed him, not because he had forceful or peculiar features, but because he was ordinariness raised to perfection, like the youngish well-groomed faces of cigarette ads. But sometimes I wanted a reassuring wart or mole, or patch of roughness, something the touch could fix on instead of gliding over.

We had met at a garden party following my graduation; he was a friend of a friend, and we had eaten ice-cream in the shade together. He had been quite formal and had asked me what I planned to do. I had talked about a career, making it sound much less vague than it was in my own mind, and he told me later that it was my aura of independence and common sense he had liked: he saw me as the kind of girl who wouldn't try to take over his life. He had recently had an unpleasant experience with what he called "the other kind". That was the assumption we had been working on, and it had suited me. We had been taking each other at our face values, which meant we had got on very well. Of course I had to adjust to his moods, but that's true of any man, and his were too obvious to cause much difficulty. Over the summer he had become a pleasant habit, and as we had been seeing each other only on weekends the veneer hadn't had a chance to wear off.

However the first time I had gone to his apartment had almost been the last. He had plied me with hi-fi music and brandy, thinking he was crafty and suave, and I had allowed myself to be manipulated into the bedroom. We had set our brandy snifters down on the desk, when Peter, being acrobatic, had knocked one of the glasses to the floor where it smashed.

"Oh leave the damn thing," I said, perhaps undiplomatically; but Peter had turned on the light, gone for the broom and dustpan, and swept up all the bits of glass, picking the larger ones up carefully and accurately like a pigeon pecking crumbs. The mood had been shattered. We had said goodnight soon afterwards, rather snappishly, and I hadn't heard from him after that for over a week. Of course things were much better now.

Peter stretched and yawned beside me, grinding my

arm against the porcelain. I winced and withdrew it gently from beneath him.

"How was it for you?" he asked casually, his mouth against my shoulder. He always asked me that.

"Marvellous," I murmured; why couldn't he tell? One of these days I should say "Rotten," just to see what he would do; but I knew in advance he wouldn't believe me. I reached up and stroked his damp hair, scratching the back of his neck; he liked that, in moderation.

Maybe he had intended the bathtub as an expression of his personality. I tried thinking of ways to make that fit. Asceticism? A modern version of hair shirts or sitting on spikes? Mortification of the flesh? But surely nothing about Peter suggested that; he liked his comforts, and besides it wasn't his flesh that was being mortified: he had been on top. Or maybe it had been a reckless young-man gesture, like jumping into the swimming pool with your clothes on, or putting things on your head at parties. But this image didn't suit Peter either. I was glad there were no more of his group of old friends left to be married: next time he might have tried cramming us into a clothes closet, or an exotic posture in the kitchen sink.

Or maybe—and the thought was chilling—he had intended it as an expression of *my* personality. A new corridor of possibilities extended itself before me: did he really think of me as a lavatory fixture. What kind of a girl did he think I was?

He was twining his fingers in the hair at the nape of my neck. "I bet you'd look great in a kimono," he whispered. He bit my shoulder, and I recognized this as a signal for irresponsible gaiety: Peter doesn't usually bite.

I bit his shoulder in return, then, making sure the shower lever was still up, I reached out my right foot—I have agile feet—and turned on the COLD tap.

8

☐ By eight-thirty we were on our way to meet Len. Peter's mood, whatever it had been, had changed to one which I hadn't yet interpreted, so I didn't attempt conversation as we drove along. Peter kept his eyes on the road, turning corners too quickly and muttering under his breath at the other drivers. He hadn't fastened his seat belt.

He had not been pleased at first when I told him about the arrangements I'd made with Len, even when I said, "I'm sure you'll like him."

"Who is he?" he had asked suspiciously. If it wasn't Peter I would have suspected jealousy. Peter isn't the jealous type.

"He's an old friend," I said, "from college. He's just got back from England; I think he's a T.V. producer or something." I knew Len wasn't that high on the scale, but Peter is impressed by people's jobs. Since I had intended Len as a distraction for Peter I wanted the evening to be pleasant.

"Oh," said Peter, "one of those arts-crafts types. Probably queer."

We were sitting at the kitchen table, eating frozen peas and smoked meat, the kind you boil for three minutes in the plastic packages. Peter had decided against going out for dinner.

"Oh no," I said, eager to defend Len, "quite the opposite."

Peter pushed his plate away. "Why can't you ever *cook* anything?" he said petulantly.

I was hurt: I considered this unfair. I like to cook, but I had been deliberately refraining at Peter's for fear he would feel threatened. Besides, he had always liked smoked meat before, and it was perfectly nourishing. I was about to make a sharp comment, but repressed it. Peter after all was suffering. Instead I asked, "How was the wedding?"

Peter groaned, leaned back in his chair, lit a cigarette, and gazed inscrutably at the far wall. Then he got up and poured himself another gin-and-tonic. He tried pacing up and down in the kitchen, but it was too narrow, so he sat down again.

"God," he said, "poor Trigger. He looked terrible. How could he let himself be taken in like that?" He continued in a disjointed monologue in which Trigger was made to sound like the last of the Mohicans, noble and free, the last of the dinosaurs, destroyed by fate and lesser species, and the last of the dodos, too dumb to get away. Then he attacked the bride, accusing her of being predatory and malicious and of sucking poor Trigger into the domestic void (making me picture her as a vacuum-cleaner), and finally ground to a halt with several funereal predictions about his own solitary future. By solitary he meant without other single men.

I swallowed the last of my frozen peas. I had heard this speech twice before, or something like it, and I knew there was nothing I could say. If I agreed with him, it would only intensify his depression, and if I disagreed he would suspect me of siding with the bride. The first time I had been cheerful and maxim-like, and had attempted consolation. "Well, it's done now," I had said, "and maybe it'll turn out to be a good thing in the end. After all, it isn't as though she's robbing the cradle. Isn't he twenty-six?"

"*I'm* twenty-six," Peter had said moodily.

So this time I said nothing, remarking to myself that it was a good thing Peter had got this speech over with early in the evening. I got up and dished him out some ice-cream, which he took as a sympathetic gesture, putting his arm round my waist and giving me a gloomy hug.

"God, Marian," he said, "I don't know what I'd do if you didn't understand. Most women wouldn't, but you're so sensible."

I leaned against him, stroking his hair while he ate his ice-cream.

We left the car in one of the usual places, on a side-street behind the Park Plaza. As we started to walk along I put my hand through Peter's arm and he smiled down at me abstractedly. I smiled back at him—I was glad he was out of the teeth-gritting mood he had been in while driving—and he brought his other hand over and placed it on top of mine. I was going to bring my other hand up and place it on top of his, but I thought if I did then mine would be on top and he'd have to take his arm out from underneath so he'd have another hand to put on top of the heap, like those games at recess. I squeezed his arm affectionately instead.

We reached the Park Plaza and Peter opened the plate glass door for me as he always does. Peter is scrupulous about things like that; he opens car doors too. Sometimes I expect him to click his heels.

While we waited for the elevator I watched our double image in the floor-to-ceiling mirror by the elevator doors. Peter was wearing one of his more subdued costumes, a brownish-green summer suit whose cut emphasized the functional spareness of his body. All his accessories matched.

"I wonder if Len's up there yet," I said to him, keeping an eye on myself and talking to him in the mirror. I was thinking I was just about the right height for him.

The elevator came and Peter said "Roof, please," to the white-gloved elevator girl, and we moved smoothly upwards. The Park Plaza is a hotel really, but they have a bar at the top, one of Peter's favourite places for a quiet drink, which was why I had suggested it to Len. Being up that high gives you a sense of the vertical which is rare in the city. The room itself is well-lit, not dark as a drain like many others, and it's clean. No one ever seems to get offensively drunk there, and you can hear yourself talk: there's no band or singer. The chairs are comfortable, the décor is reminiscent of the eighteenth century, and the bartenders all know Peter. Ainsley told me once that she had been there when someone threatened to commit suicide by jumping to the wall of the patio outside, but it may have been one of her stories.

We walked in; there weren't many people, so I immediately spotted Len, sitting at one of the black-topped tables. We went over and I introduced Peter to him; they shook hands, Peter abruptly, Len affably. The waiter appeared promptly at our table and Peter ordered two more gin-and-tonics.

"Marian, it's good to see you!" Len said, leaning across the corner of the table to kiss my cheek; a habit, I reflected, he must have picked up in England, as he never used to do it. He had put on a little weight.

"And how was England?" I asked him. I wanted him to talk and entertain Peter, who was looking grumpy.

"All right, I guess; crowded, though. Every time you turn around you bump into somebody from here. It's getting so you might as well not go there at all, the place is so cluttered up with bloody tourists. I was sorry, though," he said, turning to Peter, "that I had to leave; I had a good job going for me and some other good things too. But you've got to watch these women when they start pursuing you. They're always after you to *marry* them. You've got to hit and run. Get them before they get you and then get out." He smiled, showing his brilliantly-polished white teeth.

Peter brightened perceptibly. "Marian tells me you're in television," he said.

"Yes," Len said, examining the squarish nails of his disproportionately large hands; "I haven't got anything at the moment but I ought to be able to pick up something here. They need people with my experience. News reports. I'd like to see a good commentary programme in this country, I mean a really good one, though god knows how much red tape you have to go through to get anything done around here."

Peter relaxed; anyone interested in news reports, he was probably thinking, couldn't be queer.

I felt a hand touch my shoulder, and looked around. A young girl I'd never seen before was standing there. I opened my mouth to ask her what she wanted, when Peter said, "Oh. It's Ainsley. You didn't tell me she was coming along." I looked again: it *was* Ainsley.

"Gosh, Marian," she said in a breathless semi-whisper, "you didn't tell me this was a *bar*. I sure hope they don't ask me for my birth certificate."

Len and Peter had risen. I introduced Ainsley to Len, much against my better judgement, and she sat down in the fourth chair. Peter's face had a puzzled expression. He had met Ainsley before and hadn't liked her, suspecting her of holding what he called "wishy-washy radical" views because she had favoured him with a theoretical speech about liberating the Id. Politically Peter is conservative. She had offended him too by calling one of his opinions "conventional", and he had retaliated by calling one of hers "uncivilized". Right now, I guessed, he could tell she was up to something but was unwilling to rock her boat until he knew what it was. He required evidence.

The waiter appeared and Len asked Ainsley what she would have. She hesitated, then said timidly, "Oh, could I have just a—just a glass of gingerale?"

Len beamed at her. "I knew you had a new roommate, Marian," he said, "but you didn't tell me she was so young!"

"I'm sort of keeping an eye on her," I said sourly, "for the folks back home." I was furious with Ainsley. She had put me in a very awkward position. I could either give the game away by revealing she had been to college and was in fact several months older than me, or I could keep silent and participate in what amounted to a fraud. I knew perfectly well why she had come: Len was a potential candidate, and she had chosen to inspect him this way because she had sensed she'd have difficulty forcing me to introduce them otherwise.

The waiter returned with her gingerale. I was amazed that he hadn't asked for her birth-certificate, but upon reflection I decided that any experienced waiter would assume thet no girl who seemed so young would dare to walk into a bar dressed like that and order gingerale unless she was in reality safely over-age. It's the adolescents who overdress that they suspect, and Ainsley was not overdressed. She had dug out from somewhere a cotton creation I'd never seen before, a pink and light-blue gingham check on white with a ruffle around the neck. Her hair was tied behind her head with a pink bow and on one of her wrists she had a tinkly silver charm-bracelet. Her makeup was understated, her eyes carefully but not noticeably shadowed to make them twice as large and round and blue, and she had sacrificed her long fingernails, biting them nearly to the quick so that they had a jagged schoolgirlish quality. I could see she was determined.

Len was talking to her, asking her questions, trying to draw her out. She sipped at her gingerale, giving short, shy answers. She was evidently afraid of saying too much, aware of Peter as a threat. When Len asked her what she did, however, she could give a truthful answer. "I work at an electric toothbrush company," she said, and blushed a warm and genuine-looking pink. I almost choked.

"Excuse me," I said, "I'm just going out on the patio for a breath of air." Actually I wanted to decide what I should do—surely it was unethical of me to let Len be deceived—and Ainsley must have sensed this, for she gave me a quick warning look as I got up.

Outside, I leaned my arms against the top of the wall, which came almost to my collarbone, and gazed out over the city. A moving line of lights ran straight in front of me till it hit and broke against and flowed around a blob of darkness, the park; and another line went at right-angles, disappearing on both sides into the distance. What could I do? Was it any of my business? I knew that if I interfered I would be breaking an unspoken code, and that Ainsley was sure to get back at me some way through Peter. She was clever at such things.

Far off on the eastern horizon I saw a flicker of lightning. We were going to have a storm. "Good," I said out loud, "it'll clear the air." If I wasn't going to take deliberate steps, I'd have to be sure of my self-control so I wouldn't say something by accident. I paced the terrace a couple of times till I felt I was ready to go back in, noting with a faint surprise that I was wobbling slightly.

The waiter must have been around again: there was a fresh gin-and-tonic in my place. Peter was deep in a conversation with Len and scarcely acknowledged my return. Ainsley sat silent, her eyes lowered, jiggling her ice cube around in her gingerale glass. I studied her latest version of herself, thinking that it was like one of the large plump dolls in the stores at Christmas-time, with washable rubber-smooth skin and glassy eyes and gleaming artificial hair. Pink and white.

I attuned myself to Peter's voice; it sounded as though it was coming from a distance. He was telling Len a story, which seemed to be about hunting. I knew Peter used to go hunting, especially with his group of old friends, but he had never told me much about it. He had said once that they never killed anything but crows, groundhogs and other small vermin.

"So I let her off and Wham. One shot, right through the heart. The rest of them got away. I picked it up and Trigger said, 'You know how to gut them, you just slit her down the belly and give her a good hard shake and all the guts'll fall out.' So I whipped out my knife, good knife, German steel, and slit the belly and took her by the hind legs and gave her one hell of a crack, like a whip you see, and the next thing you know there was blood and guts all over the place. All over me, what a mess, rabbit guts dangling from the trees, god the trees were red for yards. . . ."

He paused to laugh. Len bared his teeth. The quality of Peter's voice had changed; it was a voice I didn't recognize. The sign saying TEMPERANCE flashed in my mind: I couldn't let my perceptions about Peter be distorted by the effects of alcohol, I warned myself.

"God it was funny. Lucky thing Trigger and me had the old cameras along, we got some good shots of the whole mess. I've been meaning to ask you, in your business you must know quite a bit about cameras . . ." and they were off on a discussion of Japanese lenses.

Peter's voice seemed to be getting louder and faster—the stream of words was impossible to follow, and my mind withdrew, concentrating instead on the picture of the scene in the forest. I saw it as though it was a slide projected on a screen in a dark room, the colours luminous, green, brown, blue for the sky, red. Peter stood with his back to me in a plaid shirt, his rifle slung on his shoulder. A group of friends, those friends whom I had never met, were gathered around him, their faces clearly visible in the sunlight that fell in shafts down through the anonymous trees, splashed with blood, the mouths wrenched with laughter. I couldn't see the rabbit.

I leaned forward, my arms on the black table-top. I wanted Peter to turn and talk to me, I wanted to hear his normal voice, but he wouldn't; I studied the reflections of the other three as they lay and moved beneath the polished black surface as in a pool of water; they were all chin and no eyes, except for Ainsley's eyes, their gaze resting gently on her glass. After a while I noticed with mild curiosity that a large drop of something wet had materialized on the table near my hand. I poked it with my finger and smudged it around a little before I realized with horror that it was a tear. I must be crying then! Something inside me started to dash about in dithering mazes of panic, as though I had swallowed a tadpole. I was going to break down and make a scene, and I couldn't.

I slid out of my chair, trying to be as inconspicuous as possible, walked across the room avoiding the other tables with great care, and went out to the Ladies' Powder Room. Checking first to make sure no one else was in there—I couldn't have witnesses—I locked myself into one of the plushy-pink cubicles and wept for several minutes. I couldn't understand what was happening, why I was doing this; I had never done anything like it before and it seemed to me absurd. "Get a grip on yourself," I whispered. "Don't make a fool of yourself." The roll of toilet paper crouched in there with me, helpless and white and furry, waiting passively for the end. I tore some of it off and blew my nose.

Some shoes appeared. I watched them carefully from under the door of my cell. They were, I decided, Ainsley's shoes.

"Marian!" she called. "Are you all right?"

"Yes," I said. I wiped my eyes and came out.

"Well," I said, trying to sound controlled, "getting your sights set?"

"We'll see," she said coolly. "I have to find out more about him first. Of course you won't say anything."

"I suppose not," I said, "though it doesn't seem ethical.

It's like bird-liming, or spearing fish by lantern or something."

"I'm not going to *do* anything to him," she protested. "It won't hurt." She took off her pink bow and combed her hair. "But what's wrong? I saw you start to cry at the table."

"Nothing," I said. "You know I can't drink very much. It's probably the humidity." By now I was perfectly under control.

We walked back to our chairs. Peter was talking at full speed to Len about the different methods of taking self-portraits: with reflecting images in mirrors, self-timers that let you press the shutter-release and then run to position and pose, and long cable-release with triggers and air-type releases with bulbs. Len was contributing some information about the correct focussing of the image, but several minutes after I had sat down he gave me a quick peculiar look, as though he was disappointed with me. Then he switched back to the conversation.

What had he meant? I glanced from one to the other. Peter smiled at me in the middle of one of his sentences, fondly but from a distance, and then I thought I knew. He was treating me as a stage-prop; silent but solid, a two-dimensional outline. He wasn't ignoring me, as perhaps I had felt (did that account for the ridiculous flight?)—he was depending on me! And Len had looked at me that way because he thought I was being self-effacing on purpose, and that if so the relationship was more serious than I had said it was. Len never wished matrimony on anyone, especially anyone he liked. But he didn't know the situation; he had misinterpreted.

Suddenly the panic swept back over me. I gripped the edge of the table. The square elegant room with its looped curtains and muted carpet and crystal chandeliers was concealing things; the murmuring air was filled with a soft menace. "Hang on," I told myself. "Don't move." I eyed the doors and windows, calculating distances. I had to get out.

The lights flicked off and on and one of the waiters called "Time, gentlemen." There was a pushing back of chairs.

We descended in the elevator. Len said as we stepped off, "The evening's young, why don't you all come over to my place for another drink? You can take a look at my teleconverter," and Peter said "Great. Love to."

We went out through the glass doors. I took Peter's arm and we walked on ahead. Ainsley had cut Len out from the herd and was allowing him to keep her safely behind.

On the street the air was cooler; there was a slight breeze. I let go of Peter's arm and began to run.

9

□ I was running along the sidewalk. After the first minute I was surprised to find my feet moving, wondering how they had begun, but I didn't stop.

The rest of them were so astonished they didn't do anything at all for a moment. Then Peter yelled, "Marian! Where the hell do you think you're going?"

I could hear the fury in his voice: this was the unforgivable sin, because it was public. I didn't answer, but I looked back over my shoulder as I ran. Both Peter and Len had started to run after me. Then they both stopped and I heard Peter call, "I'll go get the car and head her off, you try to keep her out of the main drag," and he turned around and sprinted off in the other direction. This disturbed me—I must have been expecting Peter to chase me, but instead it was Len who was galloping heavily along behind me. I turned my head to the front just in time to avoid collision with an old man who was shambling out of a restaurant, then glanced back again. Ainsley had hesitated, not knowing which of them to follow, but now she was bouncing off in the direction Peter had taken. I saw her wobble in a flounce of pink and white around the corner.

I was out of breath already, but I had a good head start on them. I could afford to slow down. Each lamp post as I passed it became a distance-marker on my

73

course: it seemed an achievement, an accomplishment of some kind to put them one by one behind me. Since it was bar-closing time there were quite a few people on the street. I grinned at them and waved at some as I went by, almost laughing at the surprise on their faces. I was filled with the exhilaration of speed; it was like a game of tag. "Hey! Marian! Stop!" Len called behind me at intervals.

Then Peter's car turned the corner in front of me on to the main street. He must have driven around the block. That's all right, I thought, he's got to go across to the other lane, he won't be able to reach me.

The car was on the far side of the road, coming towards me; but there was a gap in the line of traffic, and it spurted forward and swivelled into a reckless U-turn. It was parallel to me now, slowing down. I could see Ainsley's round expressionless face peering at me through the back window like a moon.

All at once it was no longer a game. The blunt tank-shape was threatening. It was threatening that Peter had not given chase on foot but had enclosed himself in the armour of the car; though of course that was the logical thing to do. In a minute the car would stop, the door would swing open . . . where was there to go?

By this time I had passed the stores and restaurants and had come to a stretch of large old houses set well back from the street, most of which, I knew, were no longer lived in but had been coverted into dentists' offices and dress-making establishments. There was an open wrought-iron gateway. I plunged through it and ran up the gravel drive.

It must have been some sort of private club. The front door of the house had an awning over it, and the windows were lit up. As I hesitated, hearing Len's footsteps pounding nearer along the sidewalk, the front door started to open.

I couldn't be caught there; I knew it was private property. I leapt the small hedge by the side of the driveway and skittered diagonally across the lawn into the shadows. I visualized Len pelting up the driveway and colliding with the outraged forces of society, which I pictured as a group of middle-aged ladies in evening dress, and was momentarily conscience-stricken. He was my friend. But he had taken sides against me and would have to pay the price.

In the darkness at the side of the house I paused to consider. Behind me was Len; on one side was the house, and on the other two sides I could see something that was more solid than the darkness, blocking my way. It was the brick wall attached to the iron gate at the front; it seemed to go all the way around the house. I would have to climb it.

I pushed my way through a mass of prickly shrubberies. The wall was only shoulder high; I took off my shoes and threw them over, then scrambled up, using branches and the uneven bricking of the wall as toe-holds. Something ripped. The blood was throbbing in my ears.

I closed my eyes, knelt for a moment on the top of the wall, swaying dizzily, and dropped backwards.

I felt myself caught, set down and shaken. It was Peter, who must have stalked me and waited there on the side-street, knowing I would come over the wall. "What the hell got into you?" he said, his voice stern. His face in the light of the streetlamps was partly angry, partly alarmed. "Are you all right?"

I leaned against him and put my hand up to touch his neck. The relief of being stopped and held, of hearing Peter's normal voice again and knowing he was real, was so great I started to laugh helplessly.

"I'm fine," I said, "of course I'm all right. I don't know what got into me."

"Put on your shoes then," Peter said, holding them out to me. He was annoyed but he wasn't going to make a fuss.

Len heaved himself over the wall and landed on the earth with a thunk. He was breathing heavily. "Got her? Good. Let's get out of here before those people get the police after us."

The car was right there. Peter opened the front door for me and I slid in; Len got into the back seat with Ainsley. All he said to me was, "Didn't think you were the hysterical type." Ainsley said nothing. We pulled away from the curb and rounded the corner, Len giving directions. I would rather have gone home, but I didn't want to cause Peter any more trouble that night. I sat up straight and folded my hands in my lap.

We parked beside Len's apartment building, which as far as I could tell at night was of the collapsing brown-brick ramshackle variety, with fire-escapes down the outside. There was no elevator, just creaky stairs with dark wooden railings. We ascended in decorous couples.

The apartment itself was tiny, only one main room with a bathroom opening to one side and a kitchen to the other. It was somewhat disarranged, with suitcases on the floor and books and clothes strewn about: Len evidently hadn't finished moving into it yet. The bed was immediately to the left of the door, doubling as a chesterfield, and I kicked off my shoes and subsided onto it. My muscles had caught up with me and were beginning to ache with fatigue.

Len poured the three of us generous shots of cognac, rummaged in the kitchen and managed to find some coke for Ainsley, and put on a record. Then he and Peter began to fiddle with a couple of cameras, screwing various lenses onto them and peering through them and exchanging information about exposure times. I felt deflated. I was filled with penitence, but there was no outlet for it. If I could be alone with Peter it would be different, I thought; he could forgive me.

Ainsley was no help. I saw she was going to keep up her little-girls-should-be-seen-and-not-heard act, as the safest course to follow. She had settled into a round wicker basket-chair, like the one in Clara's back yard except that this one had a quilted corduroy cover in egg-yolk yellow. I'd experienced those covers before. They're kept on by elastic, and they have a habit of slipping off the edges of the chair if you wiggle around too much and closing up around you. Ainsley sat quite still though, holding her coca cola glass in her lap and contemplating her own reflection on the brown surface inside it. She registered neither pleasure nor boredom; her inert patience was that of a pitcher-plant in a swamp with its hollow bulbous leaves half-filled with water, waiting for some insect to be attracted, drowned, and digested.

76

I was leaning back against the wall, sipping at my co-gnac, the noise of voices and music slapping against me like waves. I suppose the pressure of my body had pushed the bed out a little; at any rate, without thinking much about anything I turned my head away from the room and looked down. I began to find something very attractive about the dark cool space between the bed and the wall.

It would be quiet down there, I thought; and less humid. I set my glass down on the telephone-table beside the bed and glanced quickly around the room. They were all engrossed: no one would notice.

A minute later I was wedged sideways between the bed and the wall, out of sight but not at all comfortable. This will never do, I thought; I'll have to go right underneath. It will be like a tent. It didn't occur to me to scramble back up. I eased the bed out from the wall as noiselessly as I could, using my whole body as a lever, lifted the fringed border of the bedspread, and slid myself in like a letter through a slot. It was a tight fit: the slats were unusually low for a bed, and I was forced to lie absolutely flat against the floor. I inched the bed back flush with the wall.

It was quite cramped. Also there were large rolls and clusters of dust strewn thickly over the floor like chunks of mouldy bread (I thought indignantly, What a pig Len is! Doesn't he sweep under his bed, then re-considered: he hadn't been living there long and some of the dust may have been left over from whoever lived there before). But the semi-darkness, tinted orange by the filter of the bed-spread that curtained me on all four sides, and the coolness and the solitude were pleasant. The raucous music and staccato laughter and the droning voices reached me muffled by the mattress. In spite of the narrowness and dust I was glad I didn't have to sit up there in the reverberating hot glare of the room. Though I was only two or three feet lower than the rest of them, I was thinking of the room as "up there". I myself was under-ground, I had dug myself a private burrow. I felt smug.

One male voice, Peter's I think, said loudly, "Hey, where's Marian"? and the other one answered, "Oh, probably in the can." I smiled to myself. It was satisfying to be the only one who knew where I really was.

The position, however, was becoming more and more of a strain. The muscles in my neck were hurting; I wanted to stretch; I was going to sneeze. I began to wish they would hurry up and realize I had disappeared, so they could search for me. I could no longer recall what good reasons had led me to cram myself under Len's bed in the first place. It was ridiculous: I would be all covered with fluff when I came out.

But having taken the step I refused to turn back. There would be no dignity at all in crawling out from under the bedspread, trailing dust, like a weevil coming out of a flour-barrel. It would be admitting I had done the wrong thing. There I was, and there I would stay until forcibly removed.

My resentment at Peter for letting me remain crushed under the bed while he moved up there in the open, in the free air, jabbering away about exposure times, started me thinking about the past four months. All summer we had been moving in a certain direction, thinking we were static. Ainsley had warned me that Peter was monopolizing me; she saw no reason why I shouldn't, as she termed it, "branch out". This was all very well for her but I couldn't get over the subjective feeling that more than one at a time was unethical. However it had left me in a sort of vacuum. Peter and I had avoided talking about the future because we knew it didn't matter: we weren't really involved. Now, though, something in me had decided we were involved: surely that was the explanation for the powder-room collapse and the flight. I was evading reality. Now, this very moment, I would have to face it. I would have to decide what I wanted to do.

Someone sat down heavily on the bed, mashing me against the floor. I gave a dusty squawk.

"What-the-hell!" whoever it was exclaimed, and stood up. "Someone's under the bed."

I could hear them conferring in low tones, and then Peter called, much louder than necessary, "Marian, are you under the bed?"

"Yes," I answered in a neutral voice. I had decided to be non-committal about the whole thing.

"Well, you'd better come out now," he said carefully. "I think it's time for us to go home."

They were treating me like a sulking child who has locked itself in a cupboard and has to be coaxed. I was amused, and indignant. I considered saying, "I don't want to," but decided that it might be the last straw for Peter, and Len was quite capable of saying, "Aw, let her stay under there all night, Christ *I* don't mind. That's the way to handle them. Whatever's eating her, that'll cool her off." So instead I said, "I can't I'm stuck!"

I tried to move: I *was* stuck.

Up above, they had another policy-meeting. "We're going to lift up the bed," Peter called, "and then you come out, got that?" I heard them giving orders to each other. It was going to be a major feat of engineering skill. There was a scuffling of shoes as they took their positions and got purchase. Then Peter said "Hike!" and the bed rose into the air, and I scuttled out backwards like a crayfish when its rock has been upset.

Peter stood me up. Every inch of my dress was furred and tufted with dust. They both started to brush me off, laughing.

"What the hell were you doing under there?" Peter asked. I could tell by the way they were picking off the larger pieces of dust, slowly and making an effort to concentrate, that they'd put away a lot of brandy while I was below ground.

"It was quieter," I said sullenly.

"You should have told me you were stuck!" he said with magnanimous gallantry. "Then I would have got you out. You look a sight." He was superior and amused.

"Oh," I said, "I didn't want to interrupt you." I had realized by this time what my prevailing emotion was: it was rage.

The hot needle of anger in my voice must have penetrated the cuticle of Peter's euphoria. He stepped back a pace; his eyes seemed to measure me coldly. He took me by the upper arm as though he was arresting me for jay-walking, and turned to Len. "I really think we'd better be pushing along now," he said. "It's been awfully pleasant. I hope we can get together again sometime soon. I'd really like to see what you think of my tripod." Across the room Ainsley disengaged herself from the corduroy chair-cover and stood up.

I wrenched my arm away from Peter's hand. I said frigidly, "I'm not going back with you. I'll walk home," and bolted out the door.

"Do whatever the hell you like," Peter said; but he began to stride after me, abandoning Ainsley to her fate. As I pelted down the narrow stairs I could hear Len saying, "Why don't we have another drink, Ainsley? I'll see that you get home safely; better let the two love-birds settle their own affairs," and Ainsley protesting with alarm, "Oh, I don't think I should. . . ."

Once I was outside I felt considerably better. I had broken out; from what, or into what, I didn't know. Though I wasn't at all certain why I had been acting this way, I had at least acted. Some kind of decision had been made, something had been finished. After that violence, that overt and suddenly to me embarrassing display, there could be no reconciliation; though now that I was moving away I felt no irritation at all towards Peter. It crossed my mind, absurdly, that it had been such a peaceful relationship: until that day we had never fought. There had been nothing to fight about.

I looked behind me: Peter was nowhere in sight. I walked along the deserted streets, past the rows of old apartment buildings, towards the nearest main street where I could get a bus. At this hour though (what hour was it?) I'd have to wait a long time. The thought made me uneasy: the wind was now stronger and colder and the lightning seemed to be moving closer by the minute. In the distance the thunder was beginning. I was wearing only a flimsy summer dress. I wondered whether I had enough money to take a taxi, stopped to count it, and found I hadn't.

I had been walking north for about ten minutes, past the closed icily-lighted stores, when I saw Peter's car draw up to the curb about a hundred yards ahead of me. He got out and stood on the empty sidewalk, waiting. I walked on steadily, neither slackening my pace nor changing direction. Surely there was no longer any reason to run. I was no longer involved.

When I was level with him he stepped in front of me. "Would you kindly permit me," he said with iron-clad politeness, "to drive you home? I wouldn't want to see you get drenched to the skin." As he spoke, a few heavy preliminary drops were already coming down.

I hesitated. Why was he doing this? It might be only the same formal motive that prompted him to open car doors—almost an automatic reflex—in which case I could accept the favour just as formally, with no danger; but what would it really involve if I got into the car? I studied him; he had clearly had too much to drink, though clearly also he was in near-perfect control of himself. His eyes were a little glazed, it was true, but he was holding his body stiffly upright.

"Well," I said doubtfully, "really I'd rather walk. Though thank you just the same."

"Oh come along Marian, don't be childish," he said brusquely, and took my arm.

I allowed myself to be led to the car and inserted into the front seat. I was, I think, reluctant; but I did not particularly want to get wet.

He got in and slammed his own door and started the motor. "Now perhaps you'll tell me what all that nonsense was about," he said angrily.

We turned a corner and the rain hit, blown against the windshield by sharp gusts of wind. At any moment we were going to have, as one of my great-aunts used to say, a trash-mover and a gully-washer.

"I didn't request to be driven home," I said, hedging. I was convinced that it hadn't been nonsense, but also acutely aware that it would look very much like nonsense to any outside observer. I didn't want to discuss it; in that direction there could only be a dead end. I sat up straight in the front seat, staring through a window out of which I could see little or nothing.

"Why the hell you had to ruin a perfectly good evening I'll never know," he said, ignoring my remark. There was a crack of thunder.

"I don't seem to have ruined it much for you," I said. "You were enjoying *your*self enough."

"Oh so that's it. We weren't entertaining you enough. Our conversation bored you, we weren't paying enough attention to you. Well, next time we'll know enough to save you the trouble of coming with us."

This seemed to me quite unfair. After all, Len was my friend. "Len's *my* friend, you know," I said. My voice was beginning to quaver. "I don't see why I shouldn't want to talk with him a little myself when he's just got back from England." I knew even as I said it that Len was quite beside the point.

"Ainsley behaved herself properly, why couldn't you? The trouble with *you* is," he said savagely, "you're just rejecting your femininity."

His approval of Ainsley was a vicious goad. "Oh, SCREW my femininity," I shouted. "Femininity has nothing to do with it. You were just being plain ordinary *rude!*" Unintentional bad manners was something Peter couldn't stand to be accused of, and I knew it. It put him in the class of the people in the deodorant ads.

He glanced quickly over at me, his eyes narrowed as though he was taking aim. Then he gritted his teeth together and stepped murderously hard on the accelerator. By that time the rain was coming down in torrents: the road ahead, when it could be seen at all, looked like a solid sheet of water. When I made my thrust we'd been going down a hill, and at the suddenly-increased speed the car skidded, turned two-and-a-quarter times round, slithered backwards down over someone's inclined lawn, and came to a bone-jolting stop. I heard something snap.

"You maniac!" I wailed, when I had ricochetted off the glove-compartment and realized I wasn't dead. "You'll get us all killed!" I must have been thinking of myself as plural.

Peter rolled down the window and stuck his head out. Then he began to laugh. "I've trimmed their hedge a bit for them," he said. He stepped on the gas. The wheels spun for an instant, churning up the mud of the lawn and leaving (as I later saw) two deep gouges, and with a grinding of gears we moved up over the edge of the lawn and back onto the road.

I was trembling now from a combination of fright, cold, and fury. "First you drag me into your car," I chittered, "and brow-beat me because of your own feelings of guilt, and then you try to *kill* me!"

Peter was still laughing. His head was soaking wet, even from the brief exposure to the rain, and the hair was plastered down on his head, the water trickling from it over his face. "They're going to see an alternation in their landscape gardening when they get up in the morning," he chuckled. He seemed to find wilfully ruining other people's property immensely funny.

"You seem to find wilfully ruining other people's property immensely funny," I said, with sarcasm.

"Oh, don't be such a killjoy," he replied pleasantly. His satisfaction with what he considered a forceful display of muscle was obvious. It irritated me that he should appropriate as his own the credit due to the back wheels of his car.

"Peter, why can't you be *serious*? You're just an overgrown adolescent."

This he chose to disregard.

The car stopped jerkily. "Here we are," he said.

I took hold of the doorhandle, intending, I think, to make a final unanswerable remark and dash for the house; but he put his hand on my arm. "Better wait until it lets up a bit."

He turned the ignition key and the heartbeats of the windshield-wipers stopped. We sat silently, listening to the storm. It must have been right overhead; the lightning was dazzling and continuous, and each probing jagged fork was followed almost at once by a rending crash, like the trees of a whole forest splitting and falling. In the intervals of darkness we heard the rain pounding against the car; water was coming through in a fine spray around the edges of the closed windows.

"It's a good thing I didn't let you walk home," Peter said in the tone of a man who has made a firm and proper decision. I could only agree.

During a long flickering moment of light I turned and

saw him watching me, his face strangely shadowed, his eyes gleaming like an animal's in the beam from a car headlight. His stare was intent, faintly ominous. Then he leaned towards me and said, "You've got some fluff. Hold still." His hands fumbled against my head: he was awkwardly but with gentleness untangling a piece of dust that was caught in my hair.

I suddenly felt limp as a damp kleenex. I leaned my forehead against his and closed my eyes. His skin was cold and wet and his breath smelled of cognac.

"Open your eyes," he said. I did: we still had our foreheads pressed together, and I found myself at the next bright instant gazing into a multitude of eyes.

"You've got eight eyes," I said softly. We both laughed and he pulled me against him and kissed me. I put my arms around his back.

We rested quietly like that for some time in the centre of the storm. I was conscious only that I was very tired and that my body would not stop shivering. "I don't know what I was doing tonight," I murmured. He stroked my hair, forgiving, understanding, a little patronizing.

"Marian." I could feel his neck swallow. I couldn't tell now whether it was his body or my own that was shuddering; he tightened his arms around me. "How do you think we'd get on as . . . how do you think we'd be, married?"

I drew back from him.

A tremendous electric blue flash, very near, illuminated the inside of the car. As we stared at each other in that brief light I could see myself, small and oval, mirrored in his eyes.

10

□ When I woke up on Sunday morning—it was closer to Sunday afternoon—my mind was at first as empty as though someone had scooped out the inside of my skull like a cantaloupe and left me only the rind to think with.

I looked around the room, scarcely recognizing it as a place I had ever been before. My clothes were scattered over the floor and draped and crumpled on the chairback like fragments left over from the explosion of some life-sized female scarecrow, and the inside of my mouth felt like a piece of cotton wool stuffing. I got up and wavered out to the kitchen.

Clear sunshine and fresh air were shimmering in through the open kitchen window. Ainsley was up before me. She was leaning forward, concentrating on something that was spread out in front of her, her legs drawn up and tucked under her on the chair, her hair cascading over her shoulders. From the back she looked like a mermaid perched on a rock: a mermaid in a grubby green terry-cloth robe. Around her on a table-top pebbled with crumbs lay the remnants of her breakfast—a limp starfish of a banana peel, some bits of shell, and brown crusts of toast beached here and there, random as driftwood.

I went to the refrigerator and got out the tomato juice. "Hi," I said to Ainsley's back. I was wondering whether I could face an egg.

She turned around. "Well," she said.

"Did you get home okay?" I asked. "That was quite a storm." I poured myself a large glassful of tomato juice and drank it bloodthirstily.

"Of course," she said. "I made him call a taxi. I got home just before the storm broke and had a cigarette and a double scotch and went straight to bed; god, I was absolutely exhausted. Just sitting still like that takes a lot out of you, and then after you'd gone I didn't know how I was going to get away. It was like escaping from a giant squid, but I did it, mostly by acting dumb and scared. That's very necessary at this stage, you know."

I looked into the saucepan that was sitting, still hot, on one of the burners. "You through with the egg water?" I switched the stove on.

"Well, what about you? I was quite worried, I thought maybe you were really drunk or something; if you don't mind my saying so you were behaving like a real idiot."

"We got engaged," I said, a little reluctantly. I knew she would disapprove. I manoeuvred the egg into the saucepan; it cracked immediately. It was straight out of the refrigerator and too cold.

Ainsley lifted her barely-nubile eyebrows; she didn't seem surprised. "Well, if I were you I'd get married in the States, it'll be so much easier to get a divorce when you need one. I mean, you don't really know him, do you? But at least," she continued more cheerfully, "Peter will soon be making enough money so you can live separately when you have a baby, even if you don't get a divorce. But I hope you aren't getting married right away. I don't think you know what you're doing."

"Subconsciously," I said, "I probably wanted to marry Peter all along." That silenced her. It was like invoking a deity.

I inspected my egg, which was sending out a white semi-congealed feeler like an exploring oyster. It's probably done, I thought, and fished it out. I turned on the coffee and cleared a space for myself on the oilcloth. Now I could see what Ainsley was busy with. She had taken the calendar down from the kitchen wall—it had a picture of a little girl in an old-fashioned dress sitting on a swing with a basket of cherries and a white puppy—I get one every year from a third cousin who runs a service station back home—and making cryptic marks on it with a pencil.

"What're you doing?" I asked. I whacked my egg against the side of my dish and got my thumb stuck in it. It wasn't done after all. I poured it into the dish and stirred it up.

"I'm figuring out my strategy," she said in a matter-of-fact voice.

"Really Ainsley, I don't see how you can be so cold-blooded about it," I said, eyeing the black numbers in their ordered rows.

"But I need a father for my child!" Her tone implied I was trying to snatch bread from the mouths of all the world's widows and orphans, incarnate for the moment in her.

"Okay, granted, but why Len? I mean it could get complicated with him, after all he *is* my friend and he's

86

had a bad time lately; I wouldn't want to see him upset. Aren't there lots of others around?"

"Not right now; or at least nobody who's such a good specimen," she said reasonably, "and I'd sort of like the baby in the spring. I'd like a spring baby; or early summer. That means he can have his birthday parties outside in the back yard instead of in the house, it'll be less noisy. . . ."

"Have you investigated his ancestors?" I asked acidly, spooning up the last strand of egg.

"Oh yes," said Ainsley with enthusiasm, "we had a short conversation just before he made his pass. I found out his father went to college. At least there don't seem to be any morons on his side of the family, and he doesn't have any allergics either. I wanted to find out whether he was Rh Negative but that would have been a little pointed, don't you think? And he *is* in television, that means he must have something artistic in him somewhere. I couldn't find out much about the grandparents, but you can't be too selective about heredity or you'd have to wait around forever. Genetics are deceptive anyway," she went on; "some real geniuses have children that aren't bright at all."

She put a decisive-looking checkmark on the calendar and frowned at it. She bore a chilling resemblance to a general plotting a major campaign.

"Ainsley, what you really need is a blueprint of your bedroom," I said, "or no, a contour map. Or an aerial photograph. Then you could draw little arrows and dotted lines on it, and an X at the point of conjunction."

"Please don't be frivolous," she said. Now she was counting under her breath.

"When's it going to be? Tomorrow?"

"Wait a sec," she said, and counted some more. "No. It can't be for a while. At least a month anyway. You see, I've got to make sure that the first time will do it; or the second."

"The first time?"

"Yes," she said, "I've got it all worked out. It's going to be a problem though, you see it all depends on his psychology. I can tell he's the sort that'll get scared off if I act too eager. I've got to give him lots of rope. Because as soon as he gets anywhere, I can just hear it, he'll go into the old song-and-dance about maybe we'd better not see each other any more, wouldn't want this to get too serious, neither of us should get tied down and so on. And he'll evaporate. I won't be able to call him up when it's really essential, he'd accuse me of trying to monopolize his time or of making *demands* on him or something. But as long as he hasn't got me," she said, "I can have him whenever I need him."

We ruminated together for some moments.

"The place is going to be a problem too," she said. "It's all got to seem accidental. A moment of passion. My resistance overcome, swept off my feet and so forth." She smiled briefly. "Anything pre-arranged, meeting him at the motel for instance, wouldn't do at all. So it's either got to be his place, or here."

"Here?"

"If necessary," she said firmly, sliding off her chair. I was silent: the thought of Leonard Slank being undone beneath the same roof that also sheltered the lady down below and her framed family-tree was disturbing to me; it would almost be a sacrilege.

Ainsley went into her bedroom, humming busily to herself, taking the calendar with her. I sat thinking about Len. I was again having stirrings of conscience about allowing him to be led flower-garlanded to his doom without even so much as a word of warning. Of course he had asked for it, in a way, I supposed, and Ainsley seemed determined not to make any further claims on whoever she singled out for this somewhat dubious, because anonymous, honour. If Leonard had been merely the standardized ladies'-man I wouldn't have worried. But surely he was, I reflected as I sipped my coffee, a more complex and delicately-adjusted creature. He was a self-consciously-lecherous skirt-chaser, granted; but it wasn't true as Joe had said, that he had no ethical sense. In his own warped way he was a kind of inverted moralist. He liked to talk as though everyone was out for nothing but sex and money, but when anyone provided a demonstration of his theories in real life, he reacted with scalding critical invective. His blend of cynicism and idealism had a lot to do with his preference for "corrupting", as he called it, greenish girls, as opposed to the more vine-ripened variety. The supposedly pure, the unobtainable, was attractive to the idealist in him; but as soon as it had been obtained, the cynic viewed it as spoiled and threw it away. "She turned out to be just the same as all the rest of them," he would remark sourly. Women whom he thought of as truly out of his reach, such as the wives of his friends, he treated with devotion. He trusted them to an unrealistic degree simply because he would never be compelled by his own cynicism to put them to the test: they were not only unassailable but too old for him anyway. Clara, for instance, he idolized. At times he showed a peculiar tenderness, almost a sloppy sentimentality, towards the people he liked, who were few in number; but in spite of this he was constantly accused by women of being a misogynist and by men of being a misanthropist, and perhaps he was both.

However, I could think of no specific way in which Ainsley's making use of him as she had planned could damage him irreparably, or even much at all, so I consigned him to whatever tough-minded, horn-rimmed guardian angels he might possess, finished the granular dregs of my coffee, and went to dress. After that I phoned Clara to tell her the news; Ainsley's reaction had not been very satisfying.

Clara sounded pleased, but her response was ambiguous. "Oh, good," she said, "Joe will be delighted. He's been saying lately that it's about time you settled down." I was slightly irritated: after all, I wasn't thirty-five and desperate. She was talking as though I was simply taking a prudent step. But I reflected that people on the outside of a relationship couldn't be expected to understand it. The rest of the conversation was about her digestive upsets.

As I was washing the breakfast dishes I heard footsteps coming up our stairs. That was another variation of the door-opening gambit employed by the lady down below: she would let people in quietly without announcing them, usually at times of disintegration like Sunday afternoons, doubtless hoping that we'd be caught in some awkward state, with our hair up in curlers or down in wisps, or lolling about in our bathrobes.

"Hi!" a voice said, halfway up. It was Peter's. He had already assumed impromptu visiting privileges.

"Oh *hi,*" I answered, making my voice casual but welcoming. "I was just doing the dishes," I added inanely as his head emerged from the stairwell. I left the rest of the dishes in the sink and dried my hands on my apron.

He came into the kitchen. "Boy," he said, "judging from the hangover I had when I woke up, I must've been pie-eyed last night. I guess I really tied one on. This morning my mouth tasted like the inside of a tennis-shoe." His tone was half-proud, half-apologetic.

We scanned each other warily. If there was going to be a retraction from either side, this was the moment for it; the whole thing could be blamed on organic chemistry. But neither of us backed down. Finally Peter grinned at me, a pleased though nervous grin.

I said, solicitously, "Oh that's too bad. You *were* drinking quite a lot. Like a cup of coffee?"

"Love one," he said, and came over and pecked me on the cheek, then collapsed on one of the kitchen chairs. "By the way, sorry I didn't phone first—I just felt like seeing you."

"That's okay," I said. He did look hung-over. He was carelessly dressed, but it's impossible for Peter to dress with genuine carelessness. This was an arranged carelessness; he was meticulously unshaven, and his socks matched the colour of the paint-stains on his sports-shirt. I turned on the coffee.

"Well!" he said, just as Ainsley had but with a very different emphasis. He sounded as though he'd just bought a shiny new car. I gave him a tender chrome-plated smile; that is, I meant the smile to express tenderness, but my mouth felt stiff and bright and somehow expensive.

I poured two cups of coffee, got out the milk and sat down in the other kitchen chair. He put one of his hands over mine.

"You know," he said, "I didn't think I was intending—

90

what happened last night—at all." I nodded: I hadn't thought I was, either.

"I guess I've been running away from it."

I had been, too.

"But I guess you were right about Trigger. And maybe I was intending it, without knowing it. A man's got to settle down sometime, and I am twenty-six."

I was seeing him in a new light: he was changing form in the kitchen, turning from a reckless young bachelor into a rescuer from chaos, a provider of stability. Somewhere in the vaults of Seymour Surveys an invisible hand was wiping away my signature.

"And now things are settled I feel I'm going to be much happier. A fellow can't keep running around indefinitely. It'll be a lot better in the long run for my practice too, the clients like to know you've got a wife; people get suspicious of a single man after a certain age, they start thinking you're a queer or something." He paused, then continued, "And there's one thing about you, Marian, I know I can always depend on you. Most women are pretty scatterbrained but you're such a sensible girl. You may not have known this but I've always thought that's the first thing to look for when it comes to choosing a wife."

I didn't feel very sensible. I lowered my eyes modestly and fixed them upon a toast crumb that had eluded me when I wiped the table. I wasn't sure what to say— "You're very sensible too" didn't seem appropriate.

"I'm very happy too," I said. "Let's take our coffee into the living room."

He followed me in; we set our cups on the round coffee table and sat down on the chesterfield.

"I like this room," he said, glancing over it. "It's so homey." He put his arm around my shoulders, and we sat in what I hoped was a blissful silence. We were awkward with each other. We no longer had the assumptions, the tracks and paths of our former relationship to guide us. Until we'd established the new assumptions we wouldn't know quite what to do or say.

Peter chuckled to himself.

"What's funny?" I asked.

"Oh, not much. When I went out to get the car I found

three shrubs caught underneath it; so I just took a drive past that lawn. We made a neat little hole in their hedge." He was still pleased with himself about that.

"You big silly idiot," I said fondly. I could feel the stirrings of the proprietary instinct. So this object, then, belonged to *me*. I leaned my head against his shoulder.

"When do you want to get married?" he asked, almost gruffly.

My first impulse was to answer, with the evasive flippancy I'd always used before when he'd asked me serious questions about myself, "What about Groundhog Day?" But instead I heard a soft flannelly voice I barely recognized, saying, "I'd rather have you decide that. I'd rather leave the big decisions up to you." I was astounded at myself. I'd never said anything remotely like that to him before. The funny thing was I really meant it.

11

☐ Peter left early. He said he needed to get some more sleep and he advised me to do the same. However I wasn't at all tired. I was filled with a nervous energy which refused to dissipate itself in the restless forages I made through the apartment. This afternoon held that special quality of mournful emptiness I've connected with late Sunday afternoons ever since childhood: the feeling of having nothing to do.

I finished the dishes, sorted the knives and forks and spoons into their compartments in the kitchen drawer, though I knew they wouldn't stay put for long, scanned the magazines in the living room for the seventh time, my attention snagging briefly but with new significance on such titles as "ADOPTION: YES OR NO?," "YOU'RE IN LOVE—IS IT REAL? A TWENTY-QUESTION QUIZ," and "HONEYMOON TENSIONS," and fiddled with the controls of the toaster, which had been burning things. When the telephone rang I jumped for it eagerly: it was a wrong number. I suppose I could have talked with Ainsley, who was still in her bedroom; but somehow I didn't think it would be much help. I wanted to do something that could be finished, accomplished, though I didn't know what. Finally I resolved to spend the evening at the laundromat.

We do not, of course, use the lady down below's laundry facilities. If she has any. She never allows anything as plebeian as washing to desecrate the well-kept expanse of her back lawn. Maybe it's that she and the child just never get their clothes dirty; perhaps they have an invisible plastic coating. Neither of us has been in her cellar or even heard her acknowledge the existence of one. It's possible that washing is, in her hierarchy of the proprieties, one of those things that everyone knows about but nobody who is at all respectable discusses.

So when the mounds of unwearable clothes become intolerable and the drawersful of wearable ones are all but empty, we go to the laundromat. Or, usually, I go alone: I can't hold out as long as Ainsley can. Sunday evening is a better time to go than any of the rest of the weekend. There are fewer elderly gentlemen tying up and de-aphidizing their rose-bushes, and fewer elderly ladies, flowery-hatted and white-gloved, driving or being driven up to the houses of other elderly ladies for tea. The nearest laundromat is a subway-stop away, and Saturdays are bad because of the shoppers on the bus, again elderly ladies hatted and gloved, though not as immaculately; and Saturday evenings bring out the young movie-goers. I prefer Sunday evenings; they are emptier. I don't like being stared at, and my laundry bag is too obviously a laundry bag.

That evening I looked forward to the trip. I was anxious to get out of the apartment. I warmed up and ate a frozen dinner, then changed to my laundromat clothes— denims, sweatshirt, and a pair of plaid running-shoes I'd picked up once on impulse and never wore anywhere else—and checked my purse for quarters. I was stuffing the pertinent garments into my laundry bag when Ainsley wandered in. She'd been closeted in her bedroom most of the day, engaging in heaven-knows-what black magic practices: brewing up an aphrodisiac, no doubt, or making wax dolls of Leonard and transfixing them with

93

hatpins at the appropriate points. Now some intuition had alerted her.

"Hi, going to the laundromat?" she said with careful nonchalance.

"No," I said, "I've chopped Peter up into little bits. I'm camouflaging him as laundry and taking him down to bury him in the ravine."

She must have thought this remark in bad taste. She did not smile. "Look, would you mind very much throwing in a few of my things while you're there? Just essentials."

"Fine," I said, resigned. "Bring them along." This is standard procedure. It's one of the reasons Ainsley never has to go to the laundromat.

She disappeared, and came back in a few minutes with both arms around a huge heap of multicolored lingerie.

"Ainsley. Just essentials."

"They're all essentials," she said sulkily; but when I insisted I couldn't get it all into the bag she divided the pile in half.

"Thanks a lot, that's a real lifesaver," she said. "See you later."

I trailed the sack behind me down the stairs, picked it up, slung it over my shoulder and staggered out the door, intercepting a frigid look in passing from the lady down below as she glided out from behind one of the velvet curtains that hung at the entrance to the parlour. She meant, I knew, to convey her disapproval of this flagrant exhibition of soilage. We are all, I silently quoted at her, utterly unclean.

Once I had settled myself on the bus I propped the laundry bag beside me on the seat, hoping it looked from a distance enough like a small child to fend off the righteous indignation of those who might object to working on the Lord's Day. I was remembering a previous incident, a black-silk-swathed old lady with a mauve hat who had clutched at me one Sunday as I was getting off the bus. She was disturbed not only because I was breaking the fourth commandment, but also because of the impious way I had dressed in order to do it: Jesus, she implied, would never forgive my plaid running-shoes. Then I concentrated on one of the posters above the windows, a colourful one of a young woman with three pairs of legs skipping about in her girdle. I must admit to being, against my will, slightly scandalized by these advertisements. They are so public. I wondered for the first few blocks what sort of person would have enough response to that advertisement to go and buy the object in question, and whether there had ever been a survey done on it. The female form, I thought, is supposed to appeal to men, not to women, and men don't usually buy girdles. Though perhaps the lithe young woman was a self-image; perhaps the purchasers thought they were getting their own youth and slenderness back in the package. For the next few blocks I thought about the dictum I'd read somewhere that no well-dressed woman is ever without her girdle. I considered the possibilities suggested by the word "ever". Then for the rest of the journey I thought about middle-aged spread: when would I get it?—maybe I already had it. You have to be careful about things like that, I reflected; they have a way of creeping up on you before you know it.

The laundromat was just along the street from the entrance to the subway station. When I was actually standing in front of one of the large machines I discovered I had forgotten the soap.

"Oh fiddlesticks!" I said out loud.

The person stuffing clothes into the machines next to mine turned towards me.

He looked at me without expression. "You can have some of mine," he said, handing me the box.

"Thank you. I wish they'd put in a vending machine, you'd think they'd have the sense to." Then I recognized him: it was the young man from the beer interview. I stood there holding the box. How had he known I'd forgotten my soap? I hadn't said it out loud.

He was scrutinizing me more closely. "Oh," he said, "now I know who you are. I didn't place you at first. Without that official shell you look sort of—exposed." He bent over his machine again.

Exposed. Was that good or bad? I checked quickly to make sure no seams were split or zippers undone; then I began to cram the clothes hastily into the machines, putting darks in one and lights in the other. I didn't want him to be finished before I was so that he would be able to watch me, but he was done in time to observe several of Ainsley's lacy frivolities being flung through the door.

"Those yours?" he asked with interest.

"No," I said, flushing.

"Didn't think so. They didn't look like you."

Had that been a compliment or an insult? Judging by his uninflected voice it had been merely a comment; and as a comment it was accurate enough, I thought wryly.

I shut the two thick glass doors and put the quarters in the slots, paused till the familiar sloshing sound informed me that all was well, then went over to the line of chairs provided by the management and sat down in one of them. I'd have to wait it out, I realized; there was nothing else to do in that area on Sundays. I could have gone to a movie, but I didn't have enough money with me. I'd even forgotten to bring a paperback to read. What could I have been thinking of when I left the apartment? I don't usually forget things.

He sat down next to me. "The only thing about laundromats," he said, "is that you're always finding other people's pubic hairs in the washers. Not that I mind particularly. I'm not picky about germs or anything. It's just rather gross. Have some chocolate?"

I glanced around to see if anyone had heard, but we were alone in the laundromat. "No thanks," I said.

"I don't like it much either but I'm trying to quit smoking." He peeled the chocolate bar and slowly devoured it. We both stared at the long line of gleaming white machines, and especially at those three glass windows, like portholes or aquaria, where our clothes were going round and around, different shapes and colours appearing, mingling, disappearing, appearing again out of a fog of suds. He finished his chocolate bar, licked his fingers, smoothed and folded the silver wrapper neatly and put it in one of his pockets, and took out a cigarette.

"I sort of like watching them," he said; "I watch laundromat washers the way other people watch television, it's soothing because you always know what to expect and you don't have to think about it. Except I can vary my programmes a little; if I get tired of watching the same stuff I can always put in a pair of green socks or something colourful like that." He was talking in a monotone, sitting hunched forward, his elbows on his knees, his head drawn down into the neck of his dark sweater like a turtle's into its shell.

"I come here quite a lot; sometimes I just have to get out of that apartment. It's all right as long as I have something to iron; I like flattening things out, getting rid of the wrinkles, it gives me something to do with my hands, but when I run out of things to iron, well, I have to come here. To get some more."

He wasn't even looking at me. He might have been talking to himself. I leaned forward too, so I could see his face. In the blue-tinged fluorescent lighting of the laundromat, a light that seems to allow no tones and no shadows, his skin was even more unearthly. "I have to get out, it's that apartment. In the summer it's like a hot, dark oven, and when it's that hot you don't even want to turn on the iron. There isn't enough space anyway but the heat makes it shrink, the others get too close. I can feel them even in my own room with the door closed; I can tell what they're doing. Fish barricades himself into that chair and hardly moves, even when he's writing, and then he tears it all up and says it's no good and sits there for days staring at the pieces of paper on the floor; once he got down on his hands and knees and tried to put them together again with scotch-tape, and failed of course, and threw a real scene and accused both of us of trying to use his ideas to publish first and stealing some of the pieces. And Trevor, when he isn't away at summer school or heating the apartment up cooking twelve-course dinners, I'd just as soon eat canned salmon, practises his fifteenth-century Italian calligraphy, scrollwork and flourishes, and goes on and on about the quattrocento. He has an amazing memory for detail. I guess it's interesting but somehow it isn't the answer, at least not for me, and I don't think it really is for him either. The thing is, they repeat themselves and repeat themselves but they never get anywhere, they never seem to finish anything. Of

97

course I'm no better, I'm just the same, I'm stuck on that wretched term paper. Once I went to the zoo and there was a cage with a frenzied armadillo in it going around in figure-eights, just around and around in the same path. I can still remember the funny metallic sound its feet made on the bottom of the cage. They say all caged animals get that way when they're caged, it's a form of psychosis, and even if you set the animals free after they go like that they'll just run around in the same pattern. You read and read the material and after you've read the twentieth article you can't make any sense out of it anymore, and then you start thinking about the number of books that are published in any given year, in any given month, in any given week, and that's just too much. Words," he said, looking in my direction finally but with his eyes strangely unfocussed, as though he was really looking at a point several inches beneath my skin, "are beginning to lose their meanings."

The machines were switching into one of their rinsing cycles, whirling the clothes around faster and faster; then there was more running water, and more churning and sloshing. He lit another cigarette.

"I gather you're all students, then," I said.

"Of course," he said mournfully, "couldn't you tell? We're all graduate students. In English. All of us. I thought everyone in the whole city was; we're so totally inbred that we never see anyone else. It was quite strange when you walked in the other day and turned out not to be."

"I always thought that would be sort of exciting." I didn't really, I was trying to be responsive, but I was conscious as soon as I'd closed my mouth of the schoolgirl gushiness of the remark.

"Exciting." He snickered briefly. "I used to think that. It looks exciting when you're an eager brilliant undergraduate. They all say, Go on to graduate studies, and they give you a bit of money; and so you do, and you think, Now I'm going to find out the real truth. But you don't find out, exactly, and things get pickier and pickier and more and more stale, and it all collapses in a welter of commas and shredded footnotes, and after a while it's like

98

anything else: you've got stuck in it and you can't get out, and you wonder how you got there in the first place. If this were the States I could excuse myself by saying I'm avoiding the draft, but, as it is, there's no good reason. And besides that, everything's being done, it's been done already, fished out, and you yourself wallowing around in the dregs at the bottom of the barrel, one of those ninth-year graduate students, poor bastards, scrabbling through manuscripts for new material or slaving away on the definitive edition of Ruskin's dinner-invitations and theatre-stubs or trying to squeeze the last pimple of significance out of some fraudulent literary nonentity they dug up somewhere. Poor old Fischer is writing his thesis now, he wanted to do it on Womb Symbols in D.H. Lawrence but they all told him that had been done. So now he's got some impossible theory that gets more and more incoherent as he goes along." He stopped.

"Oh, what is it?" I said, to joggle him out of silence.

"I don't really know. He won't even talk about it anymore except when he's loaded, and then no one can understand him. That's why he keeps tearing it up—he reads it over and he can't understand any of it himself."

"And what are you doing yours on?" I couldn't quite imagine.

"I haven't got to that point yet. I don't know when I ever will or what will happen then. I try not to think about it. Right now I'm supposed to be writing an overdue term paper from the year before last. I write a sentence a day. On good days, that is." The machines clicked into their spin-dry cycle. He stared at them, morosely.

"Well, what's your term-paper on then?" I was intrigued; as much, I decided, by the changing contours of his face as by what he was saying. At any rate I didn't want him to stop talking.

"You don't really want to know," he said. "Pre-Raphaelite pornography. I'm trying to do something with Beardsley, too."

"Oh." We both considered in silence the possible hopelessness of this task. "Maybe," I suggested somewhat hesitantly, "you're in the wrong business. Maybe you might be happier doing something else."

He snickered again, then coughed. "I should stop smoking," he said. "What else *can* I do? Once you've gone this far you aren't fit for anything else. Something happens to your mind. You're overqualified, overspecialized, and everybody knows it. Nobody in any other game would be crazy enough to hire me. I wouldn't even make a good ditch-digger, I'd start tearing apart the sewer-system, trying to pick-axe and unearth all those chthonic symbols—pipes, valves, cloacal conduits. . . . No, no. I'll have to be a slave in the paper-mines for all time."

I had no answer. I looked at him and tried to picture him working at a place like Seymour Surveys; even upstairs with the intelligence men; but without success. He definitely wouldn't fit.

"Are you from out of town?" I asked finally. The subject of graduate school seemed to have been exhausted.

"Of course, we all are; nobody really comes from here, do they? That's why we've got that apartment, god knows we can't afford it but there aren't any graduate residences. Unless you count that new pseudo-British joint with the coat of arms and the monastery wall. But they'd never let *me* in and it would be just as bad as living with Trevor anyway. Trevor's from Montreal, the family is sort of Westmount and well-off; but they had to go into trade after the war. They own a coconut-cookie factory but we aren't supposed to refer to it around the apartment; it's awkward though, these mounds of coconut cookies keep appearing and you have to eat them while pretending you don't know where they come from. I don't like coconut. Fish was from Vancouver, he keeps missing the sea. He goes down to the lakeshore and wades through the pollution and tries to turn himself on with seagulls and floating grapefruit peels, but it doesn't work. Both of them used to have accents but now you can't tell anything from listening to them; after you've been in that braingrinder for a while you don't sound as though you're from anywhere."

"Where are you from?"

"You've never heard of it," he said curtly.

The machines clicked off. We both got wire laundry-carts and transferred our clothes to the dryers. Then we sat down in the chairs again. Now there wasn't anything to watch; just the humming and thumping of the dryers to listen to. He lit another cigarette.

A seedy old man shuffled through the door, saw us, and shuffled out again. He was probably looking for a place to sleep.

"The thing is," he said at last, "it's the inertia. You never feel you're getting anywhere; you get bogged down in things, water-logged. Last week I set fire to the apartment, partly on purpose. I think I wanted to see what they would do. Maybe I wanted to see what *I* would do. Mostly though I just got interested in seeing a few flames and some smoke, for a change. But they just put it out, and then they ran around in frenzied figure-eights like a couple of armadilloes, talking about how I was 'sick' and why did I do it, and maybe my inner tensions were getting too much for me and I'd better go see a shrink. That wouldn't do any good. I know about all that and none of it does any good. Those types can't *convince* me anymore, I know too much about it, I've been through that already, I'm immune. Setting fire to the apartment didn't change anything, except now I can't flex my nostrils without having Trevor squeal and leap a yard and Fischer look me up in his leftover freshman Psych. textbook. They think I'm mad," He dropped his cigarette stub on the floor and ground it underfoot. "I think they're mad," he added.

"Maybe," I said cautiously, "you should move out."

He smiled his crooked smile.

"Where could I go? I couldn't afford it. I'm stuck. Besides, they sort of take care of me, you know." He hunched his shoulders further up around his neck.

I looked at the side of his thin face, the high stark ridge of his cheekbone, the dark hollow of his eye, marvelling: all this talking, this rather liquid confessing, was something I didn't think I could ever bring myself to do. It seemed foolhardy to me, like an uncooked egg deciding to come out of its shell: there would be a risk of spreading out too far, turning into a formless puddle. But sitting there with the plug of a fresh cigarette stoppering his mouth he didn't appear to be sensing any danger of that kind.

Thinking about it later, I'm surprised at my own detachment. My restlessness of the afternoon had vanished; I felt calm, serene as a stone moon, in control of the whole white space of the laundromat. I could have reached out effortlessly and put my arms around that huddled awkward body and consoled it, rocked it gently. Still, there was something most unchildlike about him, something that suggested rather an unnaturally old man, old far beyond consolation. I thought too, remembering his duplicity about the beer-interview, that he was no doubt capable of making it all up. It may have been real enough; but then again, it may have been calculated to evoke just such a mothering reaction, so that he could smile cleverly at the gesture and retreat further into the sanctuary of his sweater, refusing to be reached or touched.

He must have been equipped with a kind of science-fiction extra sense, a third eye or an antenna. Although his face was turned away so that he couldn't see mine, he said in a soft dry voice, "I can tell you're admiring my febrility. I know it's appealing, I practise at it; every woman loves an invalid. I bring out the Florence Nightingale in them. But be careful." He was looking at me now, cunningly, sideways. "You might do something destructive: hunger is more basic than love. Florence Nightingale was a cannibal, you know."

My calmness was shattered. I felt mice-feet of apprehension scurrying over my skin. What exactly was I being accused of? Was I exposed?

I could think of nothing to say.

The dryers whirred to a standstill. I got up. "Thanks for the soap," I said with formal politeness.

He got up too. He seemed again quite indifferent to my presence. "That's all right," he said.

We stood side by side without speaking, pulling the clothes out of the dryers and wadding them into our laundry bags. We shouldered our laundry and walked to the door together, I a little ahead. I paused for an instant at the entrance, but he made no move to open the door for me so I opened it myself.

When we were outside the laundromat we turned, both at once so that we almost collided. We stood facing each

other irresolutely for a minute; we both started to say
something, and both stopped. Then, as though someone
had pulled a switch, we dropped our laundry bags to the
sidewalk and took a step forward. I found myself kissing
him, or being kissed by him, I still don't know which. His
mouth tasted like cigarettes. Apart from that taste, and an
impression of thinness and dryness, as though the body I
had my arms around and the face touching mine were really made of tissue paper or parchment stretched on a
frame of wire coathangers, I can remember no sensation
at all.

We both stopped kissing at the same time, and stepped
back. We looked at each other for another minute. Then
we picked up our laundry bags, slung them over our
shoulders, turned around, and marched away in opposite
directions. The whole incident had been ridiculously like
the jerky attractions and repulsions of those plastic dogs
with magnets on the bottoms I remembered getting as
prizes at birthday parties.

I can't recall anything about the trip back to the apartment, except that on the bus I stared for a long time at an
advertisement with a picture of a nurse in a white cap and
dress. She had a wholesome, competent face and she was
holding a bottle and smiling. The caption said: GIVE THE
GIFT OF LIFE.

12

□ So here I am.

I'm sitting on my bed in my room with the door shut
and the window open. It's Labour Day, a fine cool sunny
day like yesterday. I found it strange not to have to go to
the office this morning. The highways outside the city will
be coagulating with traffic even this early, people already
beginning to come back from their weekends at summer
cottages, trying to beat the rush. At five o'clock everything will have slowed down to an ooze out there and the
air will be filled with the shimmer of sun on miles of

metal and the whining of idling motors and bored children. But here, as usual it's quiet.

Ainsley is in the kitchen. I've hardly seen her today. I can hear her walking about on the other side of the door, humming intermittently. I feel hesitant about opening the door. Our positions have shifted in some way I haven't yet assessed, and I know I would find it difficult to talk with her.

Friday seems a long time ago, so much has happened since then, but now I've gone over it all in my mind I see that my actions were really more sensible than I thought at the time. It was my subconscious getting ahead of my conscious self, and the subconscious has its own logic. The way I went about doing things may have been a little inconsistent with my true personality, but are the results that inconsistent? The decision was a little sudden, but now I've had time to think about it I realize it is actually a very good step to take. Of course I'd always assumed through highschool and college that I was going to marry someone eventually and have children, everyone does. Either two or four, three is a bad number and I don't approve of only children, they get spoiled too easily. I've never been silly about marriage the way Ainsley is. She's against it on principle, and life isn't run by principles but by adjustments. As Peter says, you can't continue to run around indefinitely; people who aren't married get funny in middle age, embittered or addled or something, I've seen enough of them around the office to realize that. But although I'm sure it was in the back of my mind I hadn't consciously expected it to happen so soon or quite the way it did. Of course I was more involved with Peter all along than I wanted to admit.

And there's no reason why our marriage should turn out like Clara's. Those two aren't practical enough, they have no sense at all of how to manage, how to run a well-organized marriage. So much of it is a matter of elementary mechanical detail, such as furniture and meals and keeping things in order. But Peter and I should be able to set up a very reasonable arrangement. Though of course we still have a lot of the details to work out. Peter is an ideal choice when you come to think of it. He's attractive and he's bound to be successful, and also he's neat, which is a major point when you're going to be living with someone.

I can imagine the expressions on their faces at the office when they hear. But I can't tell them yet, I'll have to keep my job there for a while longer. Till Peter is finished articling we'll need the money. We'll probably have to live in an apartment at first, but later we can have a real house, a permanent place; it will be worth the trouble to keep clean.

Meanwhile I should be doing something contructive instead of sitting around like this. First I should revise the beer questionnaire and make out a report on my findings so I can type it up first thing tomorrow and get it out of the way.

Then perhaps I'll wash my hair. And my room needs a general clean-up. I should go through the dresser-drawers and throw out whatever has accumulated in them, and there are some dresses hanging in the closet I don't wear enough to keep. I'll give them to the Salvation Army. Also a lot of costume jewellery, the kind you get from relatives at Christmas: imitation gold pins in the shapes of poodle dogs and bunches of flowers with pieces of cutglass for petals and eyes. There's a cardboard box full of books, textbooks mostly, and letters from home I know I'll never look at again, and a couple of ancient dolls I've kept for sentimental reasons. The older doll has a cloth body stuffed with sawdust (I know that because I once performed an operation on it with a pair of nail scissors) and hands, feet and head made of a hard woody material. The fingers and toes have been almost chewed off; the hair is black and short, a few frizzy wisps attached to a piece of netting which is coming unglued from the skull. The face is almost eroded but still has its open mouth with the red felt tongue inside and two china teeth, its chief fascination as I remember. It's dressed in a strip of old sheet. I used to leave food in front of it overnight and was always disappointed when it wasn't gone in the morning. The other doll is newer and has long washable hair and a rubbery skin. I asked for her one Christmas because you could give her baths. Neither of them is very attractive any longer; I might as well throw them out with the rest of the junk.

I still can't quite fit in the man at the laundromat or account for my own behaviour. Maybe it was a kind of lapse, a blank in the ego, like amnesia. But there's little chance of ever running into him again—I don't even know his name—and anyway he has nothing at all to do with Peter.

After I finish cleaning my room I should write a letter home. They will all be pleased, this is surely what they've been waiting for. They'll want us to come down for the weekend as soon as possible. I've never met Peter's parents either.

In a minute I'll get off the bed and walk through the pool of sunshine on the floor. I can't let my whole afternoon dribble away, relaxing though it is to sit in this quiet room gazing up at the empty ceiling with my back against the cool wall, dangling my feet over the edge of the bed. It's almost like being on a rubber raft, drifting, looking up into a clear sky.

I must get organized. I have a lot to do.

Part Two

13

☐ Marian was sitting listlessly at her desk. She was doodling on the pad for telephone messages. She drew an arrow with many intricate feathers, then a cross-hatch of intersecting lines. She was supposed to be working on a questionnaire, something about stainless-steel razorblades; she had got as far as the question that directed the interviewer to ask the victim for the used razorblade currently in his razor and offer him a new one in exchange. This had stalled her. She was thinking now that it must be an elaborate plot: the president of the razorblade company had possessed a miraculous razorblade which had been in his family for generations and which not only renewed its shapeness every time it was used but also granted the shaver anything he wished for after every thirteenth shave ... the president, however, had not guarded his treasure carefully enough. One day he had forgotten to replace it in its velvet-lined case and had left it lying around in the bathroom, and one of the maids, trying to be useful, had ... (the story was unclear at this point, but it was very complicated. The razorblade had somehow managed to make its way into a store, a second-hand store where it had been bought by an unsuspecting customer and ...). The president had that very day needed some money in a hurry. He had shaved frantically every three hours to make up the number 13, scraping his face raw; what was his surprise and dismay when. ... So he had found out what had happened, commanded the offending maid to be tossed into a pit full of used razorblades, and had covered the city with a dragnet of middle-aged female private detectives posing as Seymour Surveys interviewers, their eagle-eyes trained to ferret out everyone, male or female, with the least trace of a beard, crying "New Razorblades For Old," in a desperate attempt to recover the priceless lost. ...

Marian sighed, drew a small spider in one corner of the maze of lines, and turned to her typewriter. She typed the section intact from the rough questionnaire— "We would like to examine the condition of your razorblade. Would you give me the razorblade that is *now* in your razor? Here is a new one in return for it,"—adding a "please" before "give". There was no way of rewording the question that would make it sound less eccentric, but at least it could be made more polite.

Around her the office was in a turmoil. It was always either in a turmoil or in a dead flat calm, and on the whole she preferred the turmoils. She could get away with doing less, everyone else was in such a state, skittering about and screeching, that they didn't have time to lounge around and peer over her shoulder and wonder what was taking her so long or what exactly she was doing anyway. She used to feel a sense of participation in the turmoils themselves; once or twice she had even allowed herself to become frenzied in sympathy, and had been surprised at how much fun it was; but ever since she had become engaged and had known she wasn't going to be there forever (they'd talked about it, Peter said of course she could keep working after the wedding if she wanted to, for a while at least, though she didn't need to financially—he considered it unfair to marry, he said, if you couldn't afford to support your wife, but she had decided against it), she had been able to lean back and view them all with detachment. In fact, she found that she couldn't become involved even when she wanted to. They had taken lately to complimenting her on her calmness in emergencies. "Well, thank goodness for Marian," they'd say, as they soothed themselves with cups of tea and patted their overwrought foreheads with pieces of kleenex, breathing hard. "*She* never lets herself get out of control. Do you, dear?"

At the moment they were running around, she thought, like a herd of armadilloes at the zoo. Armadilloes recalled briefly to her mind the man in the laundromat, who had never reappeared, though she had been to the laundromat several times since and had always half-expected to see him there. But that wasn't surprising, he was obviously unstable; he had probably vanished down some drain or other a long time ago. . . .

She watched Emmy as she darted to the filing cabinet and rummaged feverishly among the files. This time it was the coast-to-coast sanitary-napkin survey: something had gone embarassingly wrong in the West. It was supposed to have been what they called a "three-wave" survey: the first wave surging out through the mails, locating and bringing back on its returning crest a shoal of eligible and willing answerers, and the second and third waves following up with interviews of greater depth, done in person. And, Marian hoped, behind closed doors. The whole business, especially some of the questions that were to be asked, had rather shocked her sense of fitness, though Lucy had pointed out over a coffee-break that it was most proper these days, after all it was a respectable product, you could buy it in the supermarket and it had full-page advertisements in some of the best magazines, and wasn't it nice they were getting it out in the open and not being so Victorian and repressed about it. Millie had said of course that was the enlightened view but these surveys were always a pain, not only did you have trouble with people at the doors but you couldn't get the interviewers to do them anyway, lots of them were quite old-fashioned, especially the ones in small towns, some of them even resigned if you asked them to do it (that was the worst of using housewives, they didn't really *need* the money, they were always getting bored with it or fed up or pregnant and resigning and then you had to get new ones and train them up from scratch), the best thing was to send them out a form letter telling them now they must all do their best to better the lot of Womankind—an attempt to appeal, Marian reflected, to the embryonic noble nurse that is supposed to be curled, efficient and self-sacrificing, in the heart of every true woman.

This time something worse had happened. In the West, whoever had been in charge of selecting from the local phone books the names of the women who were to be hit by the first wave (who *had* been in charge out there? Mrs. Lietch in Foam River? Mrs. Hatcher in Watrous? No one could remember, and Emmy said they seemed to

111

have misplaced the file) had not been overly meticulous. Instead of the expected flood of responses, only a mere trickle of filled-in questionnaires had been coming through the mail. Millie and Lucy were scrutinizing these now at the desk opposite Marian's, trying to figure out what had gone wrong.

"Well, some of them obviously went out to men," Millie snorted.

"Here's one with 'Tee Hee' written on it, from a Mr. Leslie Andrewes."

"What I can't understand is the ones that come back from women with NO checked in *all* the boxes. What on earth *do* they use then?" said Lucy peevishly.

"Well this lady's over eighty."

"Here's one who says she's been pregnant for seven years straight."

"Oh *no,* poor thing," gasped Emmy, who was listening. "Why she'll ruin her health."

"I bet that dumb cluck Mrs. Lietch—or Mrs. Hatcher, whoever it was—sent them to Indian reservations again. I specifically *told* her not to. The lord knows what *they* use," sniffed Lucy.

"Moss," Millie said decisively. This wasn't the first time something had gone wrong in the West. She counted once more through the stack of questionnaires. "We're going to have to start it all over again and the client will be furious. All our quotas are thrown off and I hate to think what'll happen to our deadlines."

Marian looked at the clock. It was almost time for lunch. She drew a row of moons across her page; crescent moons, full moons, then crescent moons pointing the other way, then nothing: a black moon. For good measure she drew a star inside one of the crescents. She set her watch, the one Peter had given her for her birthday, though it was only two minutes off by the office clock, and wound it. She typed another question. She was aware of being hungry, and wondered whether her hunger had been produced by her knowledge of the time. She got out of her chair, spun it round a couple of times to raise the height, sat down again and typed another question; she was tired, tired, tired of being a manipulator of words.

At last, unable to remain sitting in her chair at her desk in front of her typewriter a moment longer, she said "Let's go have lunch now."

"Well . . ." Millie hesitated, and looked at the clock. She was still semi-held by the illusion that there was something she could *do* about the mess.

"Yes, let's," said Lucy, "this is driving me bats, I've just got to get out of here." She walked towards the coat-rack, and Emmy followed her. When Millie saw the others putting on their coats she reluctantly abandoned the questionnaires.

On the street the wind was cold. They turned their collars up, holding the fronts of their coats together near the neck with gloved hands, threading two by two among the other lunchtime scurriers, their heels clicking and grating on the bare sidewalk: it had not yet snowed. They had further to walk than usual. Lucy had suggested that they go to a more expensive restaurant than the ones they normally frequented, and in the state of heightened metabolism created by the sanitary-napkin turmoil they had agreed.

"OOoo," Emmy wailed as they leaned into the gritty wind. "In this dry weather I just don't know what I'll do. My skin's just all drying up and flaking away." When it rained she got terrible pains in her feet and when it was sunny she got eye-strain, headaches and freckles and dizzy spells. When the weather was neutral, grey and lukewarm, she got hot flashes and coughs.

"Cold cream's the best," Millie said. "My gran had dry skin too and that's what she used."

"But I've heard it gives you pimples," Emmy said dubiously.

The restaurant was one with old-world English pretensions and stuffed leather chairs and Tudor beams. After a short wait they were led to a table by a black-silk hostess; they settled themselves and slipped off their coats. Marian noticed that Lucy was wearing a new dress, a stately dark-mauve laminated jersey with a chaste silver pin at the neckline. So that's why she wanted to come here today, Marian thought.

Lucy's long-lashed gaze was brushing over the other

lunchers—stolid breadfaced businessmen most of them, gobbling their food and swilling a few drinks to get the interruption of lunch over with as soon and as numbly as possible so they could get back to the office and make some money and get that over with as soon as possible and get back through the rush hour traffic to their homes and wives and dinners and to get those over with as soon as possible too. Lucy had mauve eye-shadow to match her dress, and lipstick with a pale mauve tinge. She was, as always, elegant. She had been lunching out expensively more and more in the last two months, (though Marian wondered how she could afford it), trailing herself like a many-plumed fish-lure with glass beads and three spinners and seventeen hooks through the likely-looking places, good restaurants and cocktail bars with their lush weedbeds of potted philodendrons, where the right kind of men might be expected to be lurking, ravenous as pike, though more maritally inclined. But those men, the right kind, weren't biting, or had left for other depths, or were snapping at a different sort of bait—some inconspicuous brown-plastic minnow or tarnished simple brass spoon, or something with even more feathers and hooks than Lucy could manage. And in this restaurant, and similar ones, it was in vain that Lucy displayed her delicious dresses and confectionery eyes to the tubfulls of pudgy guppies who had no time for mauve.

The waitress came. Millie ordered steak-and-kidney pie, a good substantial lunch. Emmy chose a salad with cottage cheese, to go with her three kinds of pills, the pink, the white, and the orange, which were lined up on the table beside her water glass. Lucy fussed and fretted and changed her mind several times and finally asked for an omelette. Marian was surprised at herself. She had been dying to go for lunch, she had been starving, and now she wasn't even hungry. She had a cheese sandwich.

"How's Peter?" Lucy asked after she had fiddled with her omelette and accused it of being leathery. She took an interest in Peter. He had got into the habit of phoning Marian at the office to tell her what he had done that day and what he was going to do that evening, and when Marian wasn't there he left messages with Lucy, who shared Marian's phone. Lucy thought him most polite, and found his voice intriguing.

Marian was watching Millie as she stowed away her steak-and-kidney pie, methodically, like putting things in a trunk. "There," she'd say, or ought to, when it was finished: "All stored neatly away." And her mouth would close like a lid.

"Just fine," Marian said. She and Peter had decided she shouldn't tell them at the office quite yet. She had been holding out therefore, day after day, but now the question caught her desire to announce off-guard, and she couldn't resist. They might as well know there's hope in the world yet, she rationalized. "I have something to tell you all," she said, "but it isn't to go any further just now." She waited until the three pairs of eyes had transferred their attention from the plates to her, then said, "We're engaged."

She smiled glowingly at them, watching the expression in their eyes change from expectation to dismay. Lucy dropped her fork and gasped, "No!" adding, "how wonderful!" Millie said, "Oh. Jolly good." Emmy hurriedly took another pill.

Then there were flurried questions, which Marian dealt with calmly, doling out the information like candies to small children: one at a time, and not too much: it might make them sick. The triumphant elation she had assumed would follow the announcement, for her at least, was only momentary. As soon as the surprise effect had worn off, the conversation became as remote and impersonal, on both sides, as the razorblade questionnaires: enquiries about the wedding, the future apartment, the possible china and glassware, what would be bought and worn.

Lucy asked finally, "I always thought he was the confirmed bachelor type, that's what you said. How on earth did you ever catch him?"

Marian looked away from the suddenly pathetic too-eager faces poised to snatch at her answer, down at the knives and forks on the plates. "I honestly don't know," she said, trying to convey a becoming bridal modesty. She really didn't know. She was sorry now that she had told

115

them, dangled the effect in front of them that way without being able to offer them a reproducible cause.

Peter phoned almost as soon as they got back to the office. Lucy handed the phone to Marian with a whispered "It's the man!", a little awed by the presence of an actual prospective groom at the other end of the line. Marian felt through the air the tensing of three pairs of ear-muscles, the swivelling of three blonde heads, as she spoke into the phone.

Peter's voice was terse. "Hi honey how are you? Listen, I really can't make it tonight. A case came up suddenly, something big, and I've just got to do some work on it."

He sounded as though he was accusing her of trying to interfere with his work, and she resented this. She hadn't even been expecting to see him in mid-week like that until he'd called the day before and asked her to have dinner; since then she'd been looking forward to it. She said rather sharply, "That's all right, darling. But it would be nice if we could get these things straight before the last minute."

"I told you it came up *suddenly*," he said with irritation.

"Well you needn't bite my head off."

"I wasn't," he said, exasperated. "You know I'd much rather see you, of course, only you've got to understand. . . ." The rest of the conversation was a tangle of retractions and conciliations. Well, we have to learn to compromise, Marian thought, and we might as well begin working at it now. She concluded, "Tomorrow then?"

"Look darling," he said, "I really don't know. It'll really all depend, you know how these things are, I'll let you know, okay?"

When Marian had said good-bye sweetly for the benefit of her audience and had put down the phone she felt exhausted. She must watch how she spoke to Peter, she would have to handle him more carefully, there was evidently a good deal of pressure on him at his office. . . . "I wonder if I'm getting anaemia?" she said to herself as she turned back to the typewriter.

After she had finished the razorblade questionnaire and had begun to work on a different one, the instructions for

116

a product-test of a new dehydrated dog-food, the phone rang again. It was Joe Bates. She had been half-expecting the call. She greeted Joe with false enthusiasm: she knew she had been shirking her responsibilities lately, avoiding the Bates' dinner-invitations even though Clara had been wanting to see her. The pregnancy had gone first one week, then two weeks longer than it was supposed to, and Clara had sounded over the phone as though she herself was being dragged slowly down into the gigantic pumpkin-like growth that was enveloping her body. "I can hardly stand up," she had groaned. But Marian had not been able to face another evening of contemplating Clara's belly and speculating with her on the mysterious behavior of its contents. She had responded the last time only with cheerful but notably uncheering remarks intended to lighten the atmosphere, such as "Maybe it's got three heads," and "Maybe it isn't a baby at all but a kind of parasitic growth, like galls on trees, or elephantiasis of the navel, or a huge bunion. . . ." After that evening she had rationalized that she would do Clara more harm by going to see her than by staying away. In a spurt of solicitude catalysed by guilt, though, she had made Joe promise as she was leaving to let her know as soon as anything happened, even offering heroically to babysit for the others if absolutely necessary; and now his voice was saying, "Well thank god it's all over. It's another girl, ten pounds seven ounces, and she only went into the hospital at two last night. We were afraid she was going to have it in the taxi."

"Well that's marvellous," Marian exclaimed, and added various inquiries and congratulations. She got the visiting hours and the room-number from Joe and wrote them down on her telephone-messages pad. "Tell her I'll come down and see her tomorrow," she said. She was thinking that now Clara was deflating toward her normal size again she would be able to talk with her more freely: she would no longer feel as though she was addressing a swollen mass of flesh with a tiny pinhead, a shape that had made her think of a queen-ant, bulging with the burden of an entire society, a semi-person—or sometimes, she thought, several people, a cluster of hidden personalities that she

117

didn't know at all. She decided on impulse to buy her some roses: a welcoming-back gift for the real Clara, once more in uncontended possession of her own frail body.

She settled the phone in its black cradle and leaned back in her chair. The second-hand on the clock was sweeping around, accompanied by the ticking of typewriters and the click-clack of high-heeled shoes on the hard floor. She could feel time eddying and curling almost visibly around her feet, rising around her, lifting her body in the office-chair and bearing her, slowly and circuitously but with the inevitability of water moving downhill, towards the distant, not-too-distant-anymore day they had agreed on—in late March?—that would end this phase and begin another. Somewhere else, arrangements were being gradually made; the relatives were beginning to organize their forces and energies, it was all being taken care of, there was nothing for her to do. She was floating, letting the current hold her up, trusting to it to take her where she was going. Now there was this day to get through: a landmark to be passed on the shore, a tree not much different from any of the others that could be distinguished from the rest only by being here rather than further back or further on, with no other purpose than to measure the distance travelled. She wanted to get it behind her. To help the propelling second-hand she typed out the rest of the dog-food questionnaire.

Towards the end of the afternoon Mrs. Bogue sauntered out of her cubicle. The upwardly-arranged lines on her brow expressed consternation, but her eyes were level as ever.

Oh dear," she said to the office at large—it was part of her human-relations policy to let them in on minor managerial crises— "What a day. Not only that disturbance in the West, but there's been some trouble with that horrible Underwear Man again."

"Not that filthy man!" Lucy said, wrinkling her opalescently-powdered nose in disgust.

"Yes," said Mrs. Bogue, "it's so upsetting." She wrung her hands together in feminine despair. She was evidently not at all upset. "He seems to have shifted his field of operations to the suburbs, to Etobicoke as a matter of fact.

118

I've had two ladies from Etobicoke on the phone this afternoon complaining. Of course he's probably some nice ordinary man, perfectly harmless, but it's so nasty for the company's image."

"What does he do?" asked Marian. She had never heard about the Underwear Man before.

"Oh," said Lucy, "he's one of those dirty men who phone women and say filthy things to them. He was doing it last year too."

"The trouble is," Mrs. Bogue lamented, still clasping her hands in front of her, "he tells them he's from our company. Apparently he has a very convincing voice. Very official. He says he's doing a survey on underwear, and I guess the first question he asks must sound genuine. Brands and types and sizes and things. Then he gets more and more personal until the ladies get annoyed and hang up. Of course then they phone the company to complain, and sometimes they've accused us of all sorts of indecent things before I can explain that he's not one of our interviewers and our company would never ask questions like that. I wish they'd catch him and ask him to stop, he's such a nuisance, but of course he's almost impossible to trace."

"I wonder why he does it?" Marian speculated.

"Oh, he's probably one of those sex-fiends," Lucy said with a delicate mauve shiver.

Mrs. Bogue puckered her brow again and shook her head. "But they all say he sounds so *nice*. So normal and even intelligent. Not at all like those awful people who call you up and breathe at you."

"Maybe it all proves that some sex-fiends are very nice normal people," Marian said to Lucy when Mrs. Bogue had gone back to her cubicle.

As she put on her coat and drifted out of the office and down the hall and let herself be floated down in the decompression chamber of the elevator, she was still thinking about the Underwear Man. She pictured his intelligent face, his polite, attentive manner, something like that of an insurance salesman; or an undertaker. She wondered what sort of personal questions he asked, and what she would say if he were ever to phone *her* (Oh, you must be the Underwear Man. I've heard *so* much about you. . . . I think we must have some friends in common). She saw him as wearing a business suit and a fairly conservative tie, diagonal stripes in brown and maroon; shoes well-shined. Perhaps his otherwise normal mind had been crazed into frenzy by the girdle advertisements on the buses: he was a victim of society. Society flaunted these slender laughing rubberized women before his eyes, urging, practically forcing upon him their flexible blandishments, and then refused to supply him with any. He had found when he had tried to buy the garment in question at store counters that it came empty of the promised contents. But instead of raging and fuming and getting nowhere he had borne his disappointment quietly and maturely, and had decided, like the sensible man he was, to go systematically in search of the underwear-clad image he so ardently desired, using for his purposes the handy telecommunications network provided by society. A just exchange: they owed it to him.

As she stepped onto the street a new thought came to her. Maybe it was really Peter. Slipping out from his law into the nearest phone booth to dial the numbers of housewives in Etobicoke. His protest against something or other—surveys? housewives in Etobicoke? vulcanization?—or his only way of striking back at a cruel world that saddled him with crushing legal duties and prevented him from taking her to dinner. And he had got the company name and the knowledge of official interviewing procedures, of course, from her! Perhaps this was his true self, the core of his personality, the central Peter who had been occupying her mind more and more lately. Perhaps this was what lay hidden under the surface, under the other surfaces, that secret identity which in spite of her many guesses and attempts and half-successes she was aware she had still not uncovered: he was really the Underwear Man.

14

□The first thing Marian's eyes encountered as her head emerged periscope-like through the stairwell was a pair of naked legs. They were topped by Ainsley, who was standing half-dressed in the small vestibule, gazing down upon her, the usual blankness of her face tinged almost imperceptibly here and there with shades of surprise and annoyance.

"Hi," she said. "I thought you were going out for dinner tonight." She fastened her eyes accusingly upon the small bag of groceries Marian was carrying.

Marian's legs pushed the rest of her body up the remaining stairs before she answered. "I was, but I'm not. Something came up at Peter's office." She went into the kitchen and deposited the paper bag on the table. Ainsley followed her in and sat down on one of the chairs.

"Marian," she said dramatically, "it has to be tonight!"

"What does?" Marian asked vaguely, putting her carton of milk into the refrigerator. She wasn't really listening.

"It. Leonard. You know."

Marian had been so occupied with her own thoughts that it was a moment before she remembered what Ainsley was talking about. "Oh. That," she said. She took off her coat, reflectively.

She hadn't been paying close attention to the progress of Ainsley's campaign (or was it Leonard's?) over the past two months—she'd wanted to keep her hands clean of the whole thing—but she had been force-fed enough with Ainsley's own accounts and analyses and complaints to be able to deduce what had been happening; after all, however clean one's hands, one's ears were of necessity open. Things hadn't gone according to schedule. It appeared that Ainsley had overshot the mark. At the first encounter she had made herself into an image of such pink-gingham purity that Len had decided, after her strategic repulse of him that evening, that she would require an extra-long and careful siege. Anything too abrupt, too muscular, would frighten her away; she would have to be trapped with gentleness and caution. Consequently he had begun by asking her to lunch several times, and had progressed, at intervals of medium length, to dinners out and finally to foreign films, in one of which he had gone so far as to hold her hand. He had even invited her to his apartment once, for afternoon tea. Ainsley said later with several vigorous oaths that he had been on this occasion a model of propriety. Since by her own admission she didn't drink, she could not even pretend to permit him to get her drunk. In conversation he treated her as though she was a little girl, patiently explaining things to her and impressing her with stories about the television studio and assuring her that his interest in her was strictly that of a well-wishing older friend until she wanted to scream. And she couldn't even talk back: it was necessary for her mind to appear as vacant as her face. Her hands were tied. She had constructed her image and now she had to maintain it. To make any advances herself, or to let slip a flicker of anything resembling intelligence, would have been so out of character as to give her dumb-show irrevocably away. So she had been stewing and fussing in private, suffering Len's overly-subtle manoeuvrings with suppressed impatience and watching the all-important calendar days slide uneventfully by.

"If it isn't tonight," Ainsley said, "I don't know what I'll do. I can't stand it much longer—I'll have to get another one. But I've wasted so much *time*." She frowned, as much as she was able to with her embryonic eyebrows.

"And where . . .?" Marian asked, beginning to see why Ainsley had been annoyed at her unexpected return.

"Well he's obviously not going to ask me up to see his camera-lenses," Ainsley said petulantly. "And anyway if I said Yes he'd get suspicious as hell. We're going out to dinner though, and I thought maybe if I invited him up for coffee afterwards. . . ."

"So you'd rather I went out," Marian said, her voice heavy with disapproval.

"Well, it would be an awful help. Ordinarily I wouldn't give a damn if there was a whole camp meeting in the next room, or under the bed for that matter, and I bet he wouldn't either, but you see, he'll think I ought to care. I've got to let myself be backed slowly into the bedroom. Inch by inch."

"Yes, I can see that." Marian sighed. Censure was, at this point, none of her business. "I'm just wondering where I can go."

Ainsley's face brightened. Her main objective had been gained; the rest of the details were secondary. "Well, do you think maybe you could just phone Peter and tell him you're coming over? He shouldn't mind, he's engaged to you."

Marian considered. Previously, in some area of time she could not at the moment remember clearly, she would have been able to; it wouldn't have mattered if he had got peeved. But these days, and especially after their conversation in the afternoon, it would not be a good idea. No matter how unobtrusive she made herself with a book in the living room, he would silently accuse her of being over-possessive, or of being jealous and interfering about his work. Even if she explained the real situation. And she didn't want to do that: though Peter had seen almost nothing of Len since the first evening, having exchanged the free-bachelor image for the mature-fiancé one and adjusted his responses and acquaintances accordingly, there would still be a kind of clan-loyalty that might cause trouble, if not for Ainsley, at least for her. It would give him ammunition. "I don't think I'd better," she said. "He's working awfully hard." There was really no place she could go. Clara's was out. It was getting too cold for sitting in parks or for prolonged walking. She might call one of the office virgins. . . . "I'll see a movie," she said at last.

Ainsley smiled with relief. "Fabulous," she said, and went into her bedroom to finish dressing. She stuck her head out a few minutes later to ask, "Can I use that bottle of scotch if I need it? I'll say it's yours *but* that you won't mind."

"Sure, go ahead," Marian said. The scotch was mutually owned. Ainsley, she knew, would pay her back out of the next bottle. Even if she forgot to, a half-bottle of scotch would be a small enough sacrifice to get the thing decisively over and done with. This vicariously nerve-wracking delay and shilly-shally had gone on for too long. She remained in the kitchen, leaning against the counter and gazing with pensive interest into the sink, which contained four glasses partly filled with opaque water, a fragment of eggshell, and a pot that had recently

123

been used for cooking macaroni and cheese. She decided not to wash the dishes, but as a token gesture of cleanliness she picked out the eggshell and put it in the garbage. She disliked remnants.

When Ainsley reappeared, in a blouse and jumper outfit set off by earrings in the shape of tiny daisies and an extra good eye-job, Marian said to her, "That movie isn't going to last all night, you know. I'll have to come back around twelve-thirty." Even if she expects me to sleep in the gutter, she thought.

"I imagine the situation will be well under control by then," Ainsley said with determination. "If it isn't, neither of us will be there anyway: I'll have thrown him out of the window. And leaped out myself. But just in case, don't go charging through any closed doors without knocking."

Marian's mind selected the most ominous word. *Any* closed doors. "Now look," she said, "I draw the line at my own bedroom."

"Well, it *is* neater," Ainsley said reasonably, "and if I'm being overwhelmed in a moment of passion and swept off my feet I can't very well interrupt and say 'You've got the wrong bedroom,' can I?"

"No, I guess not," said Marian. She was beginning to feel homeless and dispossessed. "I just don't like the thought of stumbling into my bed and finding that there are people in it already."

"Tell you what," said Ainsley, "if we do happen to end up in your room I'll hang a tie on the doorknob, okay?"

"Whose tie?" Marian asked. She knew Ainsley collected things—among the objects covering the floor of her room were several photographs, some letters, and a half-dozen dried out flowers—but didn't know she had collected any ties.

"Why his, of course," said Ainsley.

Marian had a disturbing vision of a trophy room with stuffed and antlered heads nailed to the walls. "Why not just use his scalp?" she asked. Leonard, after all, was supposed to be her friend.

She pondered the situation while she ate her T.V. dinner and drank her tea in solitude, Ainsley having departed, and while she dawdled around the apartment waiting for it to be the right time for the late show. All the way to the nearest movie theatre district she was still pondering it. She had felt for some time, in one of the smaller and more obscure crevices of her mind, that she ought to do something to warn Len, but she didn't know what, or, more importantly, why. She knew he would not readily believe that Ainsley, who seemed as young and inexperienced as a button mushroom, was in reality a scheming superfemale carrying out a foul plot against him, using him in effect as an inexpensive substitute for artificial insemination with a devastating lack of concern for his individuality. And there was no convincing evidence as yet; Ainsley had been most discreet. Marian had thought several times of calling him up in the middle of the night with a nylon stocking over the telephone mouthpiece and whispering "Beware!"; but that would do no good. He would guess what he was supposed to beware of. Anonymous letters . . . he'd think it was some crank; or a jealous former girlfriend trying to foil his own fiendish plans, which would only make his pursuit more eager. Besides, ever since she had become engaged there had been a tacit agreement with Ainsley: neither was to interfere with the other's strategy, though it was apparent that each disapproved of the other's course of action on moral grounds. If she said anything to Len she knew that Ainsley would be perfectly capable of carrying out a successful, or at any rate an unsettling, counter-attack. No, Len must be abandoned to his fate, which he would no doubt embrace with glee. Marian was further confused by the fact that she didn't exactly know whether an early Christian was being thrown to the lions, or an early lion to the Christians. Was she, as Ainsley had asked her during one of their Sunday discussions, on the side of the Creative Life Force, or wasn't she?

There was also the lady down below to be considered. Even if she wasn't peering out a window or standing in ambush behind one of the velvet curtains when Leonard arrived, she would almost certainly be aware that a pair of masculine feet had ascended the stairs; and in her mind, that despotic empire where the proprieties had the rigidity

125

and force of the law of gravity, what went up must come down, preferably before eleven-thirty at night. Though she had never said so: it was merely something one took into account. Marian hoped Ainsley would have the sense either to get him over with and get him out before twelve at the latest, or, if the worst came to the worst, to keep him there, and keep him quiet, all night; what they would do with him the next morning, in that case, she was not sure. He would probably have to be smuggled out in the laundry bag. Even if he was in any condition to walk by himself. Oh, well; they could always find another apartment. But she hated scenes.

Marian got off the subway at the station near the laundromat. There were two movie-theatres close by, across the street from each other. She inspected them. One was offering a foreign film with subtitles, advertised outside by black-and-white fuzzy reproductions of ecstatic newspaper reviews and much use of the words "adult" and "mature". It had won several awards. The other had a low-budget American Western and technicolour posters of horsemen and dying Indians. In her present state she did not feel like writhing through intensities and pauses and long artistic closeups of expressively-twitched skin-pores. She was looking only for warmth, shelter, and something resembling oblivion, so she chose the Western. When she groped her way to a seat in the half-empty theatre the movie had already begun.

She slouched her body down, resting her head on the back of the seat and her knees against the seat in front and half-closing her eyes. Not a lady-like position, but nobody could see in the dark; and the seats on either side of her were empty. She had made sure of that: she didn't want any trouble with furtive old men. She recalled such encounters from early school days, before she had learned about movie theatres. Hands squeezing against knees and similar bits of shuffling pathos, although not frightening (one should just move quietly away), were painfully embarrassing to her simply because they were sincere. The attempt at contact, even slight contact, was crucial for the fumblers in the dark.

The coloured pictures succeeded each other in front of

126

her: gigantic stetsoned men stretched across the screen on their even more gigantic horses, trees and cactus-plants rose in the foreground or faded in the background as the landscape flowed along; smoke and dust and galloping. She didn't attempt to decide what the cryptic speeches meant or to follow the plot. She knew there must be bad people who were trying to do something evil and good people who were trying to stop them, probably by getting to the money first (as well as Indians who were numerous as buffalo and fair game for everyone), but it didn't matter to her which of these moral qualities was incarnate in any given figure presented to her. At least it wasn't one of the new Westerns in which people had psychoses. She amused herself by concentrating on the secondary actors, the bit players, wondering what they did in their no doubt copious spare time and whether any of them still had illusions of future stardom.

It was night, the purplish-blue translucent night that descends only on the technicolour screen. Someone was sneaking through a meadow towards someone else; all was quiet except for the rustling of the grass and the chirping of several mechanical crickets. Close beside her, to the left, she heard a small cracking noise, then the sound of something hard hitting the floor. A gun went off, there was a struggle, and it was day. She heard the cracking noise again.

She turned her head to the left. In the faint reflection from the glare of sunlight on the screen she could barely make out who was sitting beside her, two places away. It was the man from the laundromat. He was slumped in the seat, staring glassily in front of him. Every half-minute or so he would lift his hand to his mouth from a bag he was holding in his other hand, and there would be the small crack and then the sound from the floor. He must be eating something with shells, but they weren't peanuts. That would make a softer noise. She studied his dim profile, the nose and one eye and the shadowed hunch of one shoulder.

She turned her head to the front again and tried to concentrate all her attention on the screen. Although she found herself being glad that he had suddenly materialized in that seat, it was an irrational gladness: she didn't intend to speak to him, in fact she was hoping very much that he had not seen her, would not see her sitting alone there in the movie-theatre. He seemed entranced by the screen, almost totally absorbed in it, and in whatever he was eating—what could possibly make that exasperating thin cracking sound?—and he might not notice her if she kept quite still. But she had the disquieting sense that he knew perfectly well who she was and had been aware of her presence for some time before she had recognized his. She gazed at the vast featureless expanse of prairie before her. At her side the cracking went on, irritatingly regular.

They were fording a river, men and horses together and one blonde woman in a dishevelled dress, when she noticed a peculiar sensation in her left hand. It wanted to reach across and touch him on the shoulder. Its will seemed independent of her own: surely she herself wanted nothing of the kind. She made its fingers grip the arm of her seat. "That would never do," she admonished it silently, "he might scream." But she was also afraid, now that she wasn't looking at him any more, that if she did not reach across, her hand would encounter only darkness and emptiness or the plush surface of movie-theatre upholstery.

The sound-track exploded, spattering the air with yelps and whoops, as a band of Indians swept from their hiding-place for the attack. After they had been demolished and listening was possible again she could no longer hear the small clock-like sound he had been making. She jerked her head round to the side: nobody. Well, he had gone then, or perhaps he had never been there in the first place; or maybe it had been somebody else.

On the screen a gargantuan cowboy was pressing his lips chastely to those of the blonde woman. "Hank, does this mean . . .?" she was whispering. Shortly there would be a sunset.

Then, so close to her ear that she could feel the breath stirring her hair, a voice spoke. "Pumpkin seeds," it said.

Her mind accepted the information calmly. "Pumpkin seeds," it replied in silence, "of course, why not?" But her body was startled, and froze momentarily. When she had

128

overcome its purely muscular surprise enough to turn around, there wasn't anybody behind her.

She sat through the closing scene of the movie, beginning to be convinced that she was the victim of a complicated hallucination. "So I'm finally going mad," she thought, "like everybody else. What a nuisance. Though I suppose it will be a change." But when the lights went on after a brief shot of a waving flag and some tinny music, she took the trouble to examine the floor beneath the seat where he had (possibly) been sitting. She found a little pile of white shells. They were like some primitive signal, a heap of rocks or a sign made with sticks or notches cut in trees, marking a path or indicating something ahead, but though she stared down at them for several minutes while the handful of moviegoers straggled past her up the aisle, she could not interpret them. At any rate, she thought as she left the theatre, this time he left a visible trail.

She took as much time as she could getting home; she did not wish to walk in on the middle of anything. The house, as far as she could tell from the outside, was in darkness, but when she stepped through the door and switched on the hall light, an intercepting form glided out from the dining-room. It was the lady down below, still managing to look dignified even in pincurls and a purple viyella-flannel dressing-down.

"Miss MacAlpin," she said, her eyebrows severe, "I have been so upset. I'm sure I heard a—some man went upstairs earlier this evening with Miss Tewce, and I'm positive I haven't heard him come down yet. Of course, I don't mean to imply that—I know that you are *both* very nice girls, but still, the child. . . ."

Marian looked at her watch. "Well, I don't know," she said doubtfully, "I don't *think* anything like that would happen. Perhaps you were mistaken. After all it's past one, and when she isn't out somewhere Ainsley usually goes to bed before that."

"Well, that's what I thought, I mean I haven't heard any conversation from up there . . . not that I mean to say. . . ."

The mangy old eavesdropper, she's perfectly avid,

129

Marian thought. "Then she *must* have gone to bed," she said cheerfully. "And whoever it was probably came downstairs very quietly so as not to disturb you. But I'll speak to her about it in the morning for you." She smiled with what she intended to be a reassuring efficiency, and escaped up the stairs.

Ainsley is a whited sepulchre, she thought as she climbed, and I've just applied another coat of whitewash. But remember the mote in thy neighbour's eye and the beam in thine own, etcetera. How on earth are we going to convey him, whatever is left of him, down past that old vulture in the morning?

On the kitchen table she found the scotch bottle, three-quarters empty. A tie with green and blue stripes was dangling victoriously on the closed door of her own room.

That meant she'd have to clear some place that could be slept in, more or less, from the tangled crow's-nest of sheets, clothing, blankets and paperback books that was Ainsley's bed.

"Oh rats!" she said to herself as she flung off her coat.

15

☐At four-thirty the next day Marian was walking along a hospital corridor searching for the right room. She had skipped her lunch-hour, substituting a cheese-and-lettuce sandwich—a slice of plastic cheese between two pieces of solidified bubble-bath with several flaps of pallid greenery, brought in a cardboard carton by the restaurant take-out-order boy—for real food, so that she could leave the office an hour early, and had already spent half-an-hour buying the roses and getting to the hospital. Now she had only thirty minutes of visiting time in which to talk with Clara; she wondered whether they would be able to produce, between them, thirty minutes' worth of conversation.

The doors of the rooms were standing open, and she had to pause in front of them and step almost into the rooms to read the numbers. From within each came the high-pitched bibblebobble of women talking together. At last she reached the right number, close to the end of the corridor.

Clara was lying diaphanously on a high white hospital bed, its raised back propping her in a half-sitting position. She was wearing a flannelette hospital gown. Her body under the sheet looked to Marian unnaturally thin; her pale hair was falling loosely over her shoulders.

"Well hi," she said. "Come down to see the old mum at last, eh?"

Marian thrust her flowers foward in place of the guilty apologetic remark she should have made. Clara's fragile fingers unwrapped the cornucopia of green paper from around them. "They're lovely," she said. "I'll have to get that damn nurse to put them in some decent water. She's just as likely to stick them in the bedpan if you don't watch her."

When selecting them, Marian had been uncertain whether to get deep red ones, salmon pink, or white; she was a little sorry now that she had chosen the white. In some ways they went almost too well with Clara; in other ways not at all.

"Draw the curtains a bit," Clara said in a low voice. There were three other women in the room and private conversation was obviously difficult.

When Marian had pulled the heavy canvas curtains that were attached by rings to a curved metal rod suspended like a large oval halo above the bed and had sat down on the visitor's chair she asked, "Well, how do you feel?"

"Oh marvellous; really marvellous. I watched the whole thing, it's messy, all that blood and junk, but I've got to admit it's sort of fascinating. Especially when the little bugger sticks its head out, and you finally know after carrying the damn thing around all that time what it *looks* like; I get so excited waiting to see, it's like when you were little and you waited and waited and finally got to open your Christmas presents. Sometimes when I was pregnant I wished like hell he could just hatch them out of eggs, like the birds and so on; but there's really something to be said for this method." She picked up one of

131

the white roses, and sniffed at it. "You really ought to try it sometime."

Marian wondered how she could be so casual about it, as if she was recommending a handy trick for making fluffier pie-crust or a new detergent. Of course it was something she had always planned to do, eventually; and Peter had begun to make remarks with paternal undertones. But in this room with these white-sheeted out-stretched women the possibility was suddenly much too close. And then there was Ainsley. "Don't rush me," she said, smiling.

"Of course it hurts like hell," Clara said smugly, "and they won't give you anything till quite far along, because of the baby; but that's the funny thing about pain. You can never remember it afterwards. I feel just marvellous now—I keep thinking I'll get post-puerperal depression, like a lot of women do, but I never seem to; I save that till I have to get up and go home. It's so nice to just lie here; I really feel marvellous." She hitched herself up a little against the pillows.

Marian sat and smiled at her. She couldn't think of anything to say in reply. More and more, Clara's life seemed cut off from her, set apart, something she could only gaze at through a window. "What are you going to call her?" she asked, repressing a desire to shout, not quite sure whether Clara would be able to hear her through the glass.

"We don't really know yet. We're sort of considering Vivian Lynn, after my grandmother and Joe's grandmother. Joe wanted to call her after me but I've never liked my own name much. It's really marvellous though to have a man who's just as pleased with a daughter as a son, so many men aren't, you know, though maybe Joe wouldn't be if he didn't have one son already."

Marian stared at the wall above Clara's head, thinking that it was painted the same colour as the office. She almost expected to hear the sound of typewriters from beyond the curtains, but instead there were only the murmuring voices of three other women and their visitors. When she came in she had noticed that one of them, the young one in the pink-lace bedjacket, had been sitting up working at a paint-by-numbers picture. Maybe she should

132

have brought Clara something to do, instead of just flowers: it must be very tiresome lying around like that all day.

"Would you like me to bring you anything to read?" she asked thinking as she did so how much she was sounding like the kind of ladies'-club member who makes a part-time career out of visiting the sick.

"Now that's a kind thought. But really I don't think I could concentrate enough, not for a while. I'll either be sleeping, or," she said in a lower voice, "listening to those other women. Maybe it's the hospital atmosphere, but all they ever talk about are their miscarriages and their diseases. It makes you feel very sickly after a while: you start wondering when it'll be *your* turn to get cancer of the breast or a ruptured tube, or miscarry quadruplets at half-weekly intervals; no kidding, that's what happened to Mrs. Moase, the big one over there in the far corner. And christ they're so *calm* about it, and they seem to think that each of their grisly little episodes is some kind of service medal: they haul them out and compare them and pile on the gory details, they're really *proud* of them. It's a positive gloating about pain. I even find myself producing a few of my own ailments, as though I have to compete. I wonder why women are so morbid?"

"Oh, some men are morbid too, I guess," Marian said. Clara was talking a lot more, and a lot more quickly, then she usually did, and Marian found herself being surprised. During the later, more vegetable stage of Clara's pregnancy she had tended to forget that Clara had a mind at all or any perceptive faculties above the merely sentient and sponge-like, since she had spent most of her time being absorbed in, or absorbed by, her tuberous abdomen. To have her observing, commenting like this, was a slight shock. It might be some kind of reaction, but it certainly wasn't hysteria: she seemed thoroughly in control. Something to do with hormones maybe.

"Well, Joe certainly isn't," Clara said happily. "If he weren't so un-morbid I don't know how I'd ever manage. He's so good about the children and the washing and everything, I don't feel at all uneasy about leaving everything up to him at a time like this. I know he manages

133

just as well as I would if I were there, though we're having a bit of trouble with poor Arthur. He's beautifully toilet-trained now, he uses his plastic potty almost every time, but he's become a hoarder. He rolls the shit into little pellets and hides them places—like cupboards and bottom drawers. You have to watch him like a hawk. Once I found some in the refrigerator, and Joe tells me he just discovered a whole row of them hardening on the bathroom window-sill behind the curtain. He gets very upset when we throw them out. I can't imagine why he does it; maybe he'll grow up to be a banker."

"Do you think it has anything to do with the new baby?" Marian said. "Jealousy perhaps?"

"Oh, probably," Clara said, smiling serenely. She was twirling one of the white roses between her fingers. "But here I am running on about myself," she said, turning herself on the bed so she was facing more directly towards Marian. "I haven't really had a chance to talk to you about your engagement. We both think it's wonderful, of course, although we don't really *know* Peter."

Marian said, "We must all get together sometime, after you're home and have got yourself organized again. I'm sure you'll like him."

"Well he *looks* awfully nice. Of course you never really know someone till you've been married to them for a while and discover some of their scruffier habits. I remember how upset I was when I realized for the first time that after all Joe wasn't Jesus Christ. I don't know what it was, probably some silly thing like finding out he's crazy about Audrey Hepburn. Or that he's a secret philatelist."

"A what?" asked Marian. She didn't know what it was but it sounded perverted.

"Stamp collecting. Not a real one of course, he tears them off the mail. Anyway it takes adjustment. Now," she said, "I just think he's one of the minor saints."

Marian didn't know what to say. She found Clara's attitude towards Joe both complacent and embarrassing: it was sentimental, like the love stories in the back numbers of women's magazines. Also she felt Clara was trying to give her some kind of oblique advice, and this was even

134

more embarrassing. Poor Clara, she was the last person whose advice would be worth anything. Look at the mess she had blundered into: three children at her age. Peter and she were going into it with far fewer illusions. If Clara had slept with Joe before marriage she would have been much better able to cope afterwards.

"I think Joe's a wonderful husband," she said generously.

Clara gave a snort of laughter, then winced. "Oh. Screw. It hurts in the most ungodly places. No you don't; you think we're both shiftless and disorganized and you'd go bats if you lived in all that chaos; you can't understand how we've survived without hating each other." Her voice was perfectly good-natured.

Marian started to protest, thinking it was unfair of Clara to force the conversation out into the open like that; but a nurse popped her head through the doorway long enough to announce that the visiting time was up.

"If you want to see the baby," Clara said as Marian was leaving, "you can probably get someone to tell you where they've stowed it. You can see them through a plate-glass window somewhere; they all look alike, but they'll point out mine if you ask. If I were you I wouldn't bother though, they aren't very interesting at this stage. They look like red shrivelled prunes."

"Maybe I'll wait then," said Marian.

It struck her as she went out the door that there had been something in Clara's manner, especially in the slightly worried twist of her eyebrows once or twice, that had expressed concern; but concern about what, exactly, she didn't know and couldn't stop to puzzle over. She had the sense of having escaped, as if from a culvert or cave. She was glad she wasn't Clara.

Now there was the rest of the day to unravel. She would eat quickly at the nearest restaurant she could find and by the time she was finished the traffic would have cleared somewhat, and she could rush home and grab some laundry. What on earth did she have that was fit to take? Perhaps a couple of blouses. She wondered whether a pleated skirt would do, that would keep him busy and she had one that needed pressing, but on second thought

135

it was the wrong sort of thing, and surely too complicated anyway.

The hours before her were going to be, she felt, as convoluted as that hour in the afternoon during which Peter had called to arrange dinner and they had discussed at length—too great a length, she was afraid—where they were going to eat; and then after all that she had had to call him back and say, "I'm terribly sorry darling, but something really unavoidable has come up; can we put it off? Tomorrow maybe?" He had been peevish, but he couldn't say much about it because he had just finished doing the same thing to her the day before.

There had been a difference, of course, in what had come up. In her case it had been another telephone call.

The voice at the other end had said "This is Duncan."

"Who?"

"The guy at the laundromat."

"Oh. Yes." Now she recognized the voice, though it sounded more nervous than usual.

"I'm sorry I startled you in the movie, but I knew you were dying to know what I was eating."

"Yes, I was actually," she said, glancing at the clock and then at the open door of Mrs. Bogue's cubicle. She had already spent far too much time on the phone that afternoon.

"They were pumpkin seeds. I'm trying to stop smoking, you know, and I find them very helpful. There's a lot of oral satisfaction in cracking them open. I get them at the pet store, they're supposed to be for birds, really."

"Yes," she said, to fill up the pause that followed.

"It was a crummy movie."

Marian wondered whether the switchboard girl downstairs was listening in on the conversation, as she had been known to do, and if so, what she was thinking about it; she must have realized by now that it was not a business call. "Mr. . . . Duncan," she said in her most official voice, "I'm sort of at the office, and we aren't supposed to take much time for outside calls; I mean from friends and so on."

"Oh," he said. He sounded discouraged, but he made no attempt to clarify the situation.

136

She pictured him at the other end of the line, morose, hollow-eyed, waiting for the sound of her voice. She had no idea why he had called. Perhaps he needed her, needed to talk to her. "But I *would* like to talk to you," she said encouragingly. "Some more convenient time?"

"Well," he said, "as a matter of fact I sort of need you; right now. I mean I need—what I need is some ironing. I've just got to iron something and I've already ironed everything in the house, even the dishtowels, and I sort of wondered whether maybe I could come over to your house and maybe iron some of your things."

Mrs. Bogue's eye was now definitely upon her. "Why, of course," she said crisply. Then she suddenly decided that it would be, for some as yet unexamined reason, disastrous if this man were to encounter either Peter or Ainsley. Besides, who could tell what variety of turmoil had broken loose after she had tiptoed out of the house that morning, leaving Len still caught in the toils of vice behind the door ornamented with his own tie? She hadn't heard from Ainsley all day, which might be either a good or an evil omen. And even if Len had managed to escape safely, the wrath of the lady down below, foiled of its proper object, might very well descend on the head of the harmless ironer as a representative of the whole male species. "Maybe I'd better bring some things to your house," she said.

"Actually I'd prefer that. It means I can use my own iron; I'm used to it. It makes me uncomfortable to iron with other people's irons. But please hurry, I really do need it. Desperately."

"Yes, as soon as I can after work," she said, trying both to reassure him and to sound, for the benefit of the office, as though she was making a dentist appointment. "About seven." She realized as soon as she had hung up that this would mean postponing dinner with Peter yet again; but then she could see him any night. The other thing was an emergency.

By the time she had got matters straightened out with Peter she had felt as though she had been trying to unsnarl herself from all the telephone lines in the city. They

137

were prehensile, they were like snakes, they had a way of coiling back on you and getting you all wrapped up.

A nurse was coming towards her, pushing a rubber-wheeled wagon loaded with trays of food. Although her mind was occupied with other things, Marian's eyes registered the white shape and found it out of place. She stopped and looked around. Wherever else she was going it was not towards the main exit. She had been so involved in the threads of her own plans and reflections that she must have got off the elevator on the wrong floor. She was in a corridor exactly similar to the one she had just come from, except that all the room-doors were closed. She looked for a number: 273. Well, that was simple: she had got off a floor too soon.

She turned and walked back, trying to remember where the elevator was supposed to be; she seemed to recall having gone around several corners. The nurse had disappeared. Coming towards her now from the far end of the hallway was a figure, a man wearing a green smock, with a white mask over the lower part of his face. She was aware for the first time of the hospital smell, antiseptic, severe.

It must be one of the doctors. She could see now that he had a thin black thing, a stethoscope, around his neck. As he came nearer she looked at him more closely. In spite of the mask there was something familiar about him; it bothered her that she could not tell what it was. But he passed her, staring straight ahead, his eyes expressionless, and opened one of the doors to the right and went in. When he turned she could see that he had a bald spot on the back of his head.

"Well, nobody I know is going bald, at any rate," she said to herself. She was relieved.

16

□She remembered the way to his apartment perfectly, although she couldn't recall either the number or the street name. She hadn't been in that district for a long time, in fact ever since the day of the beer interviews. She took the right directions and turnings almost automatically, as though she was trailing somebody by an instinct that was connected not with sight or smell but with a vaguer sense that had to do with locations. But it wasn't a complicated route: just across the baseball park, up the asphalt ramp and along a couple of blocks; though the way seemed longer now that she was walking in a darkness illuminated only by the dim street lamps rather than the former searing light of the sun. She walked quickly: already her legs were cold. The grass on the baseball park had been grey with frost.

The few times she had thought about the apartment, in idle moments at the office when she had had nothing but a blank sheet of paper in front of her or at other times when she was bending to pick some piece of clutter off the floor, she had never given it any specific place in the city. She had an image in her mind of the inside, the appearance of the rooms, but not of the building itself. Now it was disconcerting to have the street produce it, square and ordinary and anonymous, more or less exactly where it had been before.

She pushed the buzzer of Number Six and slipped through the inside glass doors as soon as the mechanism started its chain-saw noise. Duncan opened the door part-way. He stared at her suspiciously; in the semi-darkness his eyes gleamed behind his hair. He had a cigarette stub in his mouth, burning dangerously close to his lips.

"Got the stuff?" he asked.

Mutely she held towards him the small cloth bundle she had been carrying under her arm, and he stepped aside to let her come in.

"It's not very much," he said, undoing the clothes. There were only two white cotton blouses, recently washed, a pillowcase, and a few guest towels embroidered with flowers, donated by a great-aunt, that were wrinkled from lying underneath everything else on the linen shelf.

"I'm sorry," she said, "it was really all I had."

"Well, it's better than nothing," he said grudgingly. He turned and walked towards his bedroom.

Marian wasn't certain whether she was supposed to follow him or whether he expected her to go away now that she had made the delivery. "Can I watch?" she asked, hoping he wouldn't consider it an invasion of privacy. She didn't feel like going back to her own apartment right away. There would be nothing to do and she had, after all, sacrificed an evening with Peter.

"Sure, if you want to; though there isn't much to see."

She made her way towards the hall. The living room had not been altered since her former visit, except that there were if possible more stray papers lying about. The three chairs were still in the same positions; a slab of board was leaning against an arm of the red plush one. Only one of the lamps, the one by the blue chair, was turned on. Marian inferred that both of the room-mates were out.

Duncan's room too was much the same as she remembered it. The ironing-board was nearer the centre of the room and the chessmen had been set up in their two opposing rows; the black-and-white chequered board was resting now on top of a stack of books. On the bed were several freshly-ironed white shirts on coathangers. Duncan hung them up in the closet before going over to plug in the iron. Marian took off her coat and sat down on the bed.

He threw his cigarette into one of the crowded ashtrays on the floor, waited for the iron to heat, testing it at intervals on the board, and then began to iron one of the blouses, with slow concentration and systematic attention to collar corners. Marian watched him silently; he obviously didn't want to be interrupted. She found it strange to see someone else ironing her clothes.

Ainsley had given her a peculiar look when she had come out of her bedroom with her coat on and the bundle under her arm. "Where are you going with those?" she had asked. It was too small a lot for the laundromat.

"Oh, just out."

"What'll I say if Peter calls?"

"He won't call. But just say I'm out." She had plunged down the stairs then, not wishing to explain anything at all about Duncan or even to reveal his existence. She felt it might upset the balance of power. But Ainsley had no time at the moment for anything more than a tepid curiosity: she was too elated by the probable success of her own campaign, and also by what she had called "a stroke of luck".

Marian had asked, when she had reached the apartment and had found Ainsley in the living room with a paperback on Baby and Child Care, "Well, how did you get the poor thing out of here this morning?"

Ainsley laughed. "Great stroke of luck," she said. "I was sure the old fossil down there would be lying in wait for us at the bottom of the stairs. I really didn't know what I'd do. I was trying to think of some bluff, like saying he was the telephone man. . . ."

"She tried to pin me down about it last night," Marian interjected. "She knew perfectly well he was up there."

"Well for some reason she actually went *out*. I saw her go from the living room window; just by chance really. Can you imagine? I didn't think she ever went out, not in the mornings. I skipped work today of course and I was just wandering around having a cigarette. But when I saw her go I got Len up and stuck his clothes on him and hustled him down the stairs and out of there before he was quite awake. He had a terrible hangover too, he just about killed that bottle. All by himself. I don't think he's too sure yet exactly what happened." She smiled with her small pink mouth.

"Ainsley, you're immoral."

"Why? He seemed to enjoy it. Though he was terribly apologetic and anxious this morning when we were having breakfast, and then sort of soothing, as though he was trying to console me or something. Really it was embarrassing. And then, you know, as he got wider and wider awake and soberer and soberer, he couldn't wait to get away from me. But now," she said, hugging herself with both arms, "we'll have to wait and see. Whether it was all worth it."

"Yes, well," Marian said, "would you mind fixing the bed?"

Thinking back on it, she found something ominous about the fact that the lady down below had gone out. It wasn't like her at all. She'd be much more likely to lurk

141

behind the piano or the velvet curtains while they were creeping down the stairs and spring out upon them just as they had reached the threshold of safety.

He was starting on the second blouse. He seemed to be unaware of everything but the wrinkled white material spread on the board in front of him, poring over it as though it was an ancient and very fragile manuscript that he couldn't quite translate. Before, she had thought of him as being short, perhaps because of the shrunken child's-face, or because she had mostly seen him sitting down; but now she thought, actually he would be quite tall if he didn't slouch like that.

As she sat watching him she recognized in herself a desire to say something to him, to intrude, to break through the white cloth surface of his absorption: she did not like being so totally closed out. To avoid the emotion she picked up her purse and went into the bathroom, intending to comb her hair, not because it needed combing but as what Ainsley called a substitution-activity; like a squirrel scratching itself when confronted by hazardous or unobtainable breadcrumbs. She wanted to talk to him, but talking to him now, she thought, might cancel out any therapeutic effects the ironing was having.

The bathroom was ordinary enough. Damp towels were mounded on the racks and a clutter of shaving things and men's cosmetics covered the various porcelain ledges and surfaces. But the mirror over the basin had been broken. There were only a few jagged pieces of glass left sticking around the edges of the wooden frame. She tried peering into one of them but it wasn't large enough to be of much use.

When she went back into the room he was doing the pillowcase. He seemed more relaxed: he was ironing with a long easy sweeping motion instead of the exact staccato strokes he had been using on the blouse. He looked up at her as she came in.

"I suppose you're wondering what happened to the mirror," he said.

"Well . . ."

"I smashed it. Last week. With the frying-pan."

"Oh," she said.

"I got tired of being afraid I'd walk in there some morning and wouldn't be able to see my own reflection in it. So I went and grabbed the frying-pan out of the kitchen and gave it a whack. They both got very upset," he said meditatively, "particularly Trevor, he was cooking an omelette at the time and I guess I sort of ruined it. Got it all full of broken glass. But I don't really see why it should disturb them, it was a perfectly understandable symbolic narcissistic gesture, and it wasn't a good mirror anyway. But they've been jittery ever since. Especially Trevor, subconsciously he thinks he's my mother; it's rather hard on him. It doesn't bother me that much, I'm used to it, I've been running away from understudy mothers ever since I can remember, there's a whole herd of them behind me trying to catch up and rescue me, god knows what from, and give me warmth and comfort and nourishment and make me quit smoking, that's what you get for being an orphan. And they're quoting things at me: Trevor quotes T. S. Eliot these days and Fish quotes the Oxford English Dictionary."

"How do you shave then?" Marian asked. She could not quite imagine life without a mirror in the bathroom. She speculated, while she spoke, about whether he even shaved at all. She had never examined him for bristles.

"What?"

"I mean with no mirror."

"Oh," he said, grinning, "I've got my own private mirror. One I can trust, I know what's in it. It's just public ones that I don't like." He seemed to lose interest in the subject, and ironed in silence for a minute. "What grisly things," he said at last; he was doing one of the guest towels. "I can't stand things with flowers embroidered on them."

"I know. We never use them."

He folded the towel, then looked up at her gloomily. "I suppose you believed all that."

"Well . . . all what?" she answered cautiously.

"About why I broke the mirror and my reflection and so on. Really I broke it because I felt like breaking something. That's the trouble with people, they always believe me. It's too much of an encouragement, I can never resist

143

the temptation. And those brilliant insights about Trevor, how do *I* know whether they're true? Maybe the real truth is that I want to think that he wants to think he's my mother. Actually I'm not an orphan anyway, I do have some parents, back there somewhere. Can you believe that?"

"Should I?" She couldn't tell whether or not he was being serious; his expression revealed nothing. Perhaps this was another labyrinth of words, and if she said the wrong thing, took the wrong turning, she would suddenly find herself face to face with something she could not cope with.

"If you like. But the real truth is, of course"—he waved the iron in the air for emphasis, watching the movement of his hand as he did so—"that I'm a changeling. I got switched for a real baby when young and my parents never discovered the fraud, though I must admit they suspected something." He closed his eyes, smiling faintly. "They kept telling me my ears were too big; but really I'm not human at all, I come from the underground. . . ." He opened his eyes and began to iron again, but his attention had wandered away from the ironing-board. He brought the iron too close to his other hand, and gave a yelp of pain. "Damn," he said. He set the iron down and stuck his finger in his mouth.

Marian's first impulse was to go over and see whether it was a bad burn, and suggest remedies, butter or baking-soda; but she decided against it. Instead she sat unmoving and said nothing.

He was looking at her now, expectantly but with a trace of hostility. "Aren't you going to comfort me?" he asked.

"I don't think," she said, "that it's really needed."

"You're right; I enjoy it though," he said sadly. "And it does hurt." He picked up the iron again.

When he had folded the last towel and pulled the plug out of the wall-socket he said, "That was a vigorous session, thanks for the clothes, but it wasn't really enough. I'll have to think of something else to do with the rest of the tension. I'm not a chronic ironer you know, I'm not hooked, it's not one of the habits I ought to kick,

144

but I go on these binges." He came over and sat gingerly down beside her on the bed, and lit a cigarette. "This one started the day before yesterday when I dropped my term-paper in a puddle on the kitchen floor and I had to dry it out and iron it. It was all typed and I couldn't face typing it over again, plowing through all that verbiage, I'd start wanting to change everything. It came out okay, nothing blurred, but you could tell it had been ironed, I scorched one of the pages. But they can't reasonably object, it would sound pretty silly to say, 'We can't accept a term-paper that's been ironed.' So I turned it in and then of course I had to get rid of all that frenzy, so I ironed everything in the house that was clean. Then I had to go to the laundromat and wash some dirty things, that's why I was sitting in that wretched movie, I was waiting for the clothes to get done. I got bored watching them churning around in there, that's a bad sign, if I get bored with the laundromat even, what the hell am I going to do when I get bored with everything else? Then I ironed all the things I'd washed, and then I'd run out."

"And then you phoned me," Marian said. It irritated her slightly that he went on talking to himself about himself, without giving much evidence that he even knew she was there.

"Oh. You. Yes. Then I phoned you. At least, I phoned your company. I remembered the name, I guess it was the switchboard girl I got, and I sort of described you to whoever it was for a while, I said you didn't look like the usual kind of interviewer; and then they figured out who you were. You never told me your name."

It had not occurred to Marian that she hadn't told him her name. She had taken it for granted that he knew it all along.

Her introduction of a new subject seemed to have brought him to a standstill. He stared down at the floor, sucking on the end of his cigarette.

She found the silence disconcerting. "Why do you like ironing so much?" she asked. "I mean, apart from relieving tension and all that; but why ironing? Instead of maybe bowling, for instance?"

He drew his thin legs up and clasped his arms around

145

his knees. "Ironing's nice and simple," he said. "I get all tangled up in words when I'm putting together those interminable papers, I'm on another one by the way, 'Sado-Masochistic Patterns in Trollope,' and ironing—well, you straighten things out and get them flat. God knows it isn't because I'm neat and tidy; but there's something about a flat surface. . . ." He had shifted his position and was contemplating her now. "Why don't you let me touch up that blouse for you a bit while the iron's still hot?" he said. "I'll just do the sleeves and collar. It looks like you missed a few places."

"You mean the one I have on?"

"That's the one," he said. He unwound his arms from around his knees and stood up. "Here, you can wear my dressing-gown. Don't worry, I won't peek." He took a grey object out of the closet, handed it to her, and turned his back.

Marian stood for a moment, clutching the grey bundle, uncertain how to act. Doing as he suggested, she knew, was going to make her feel both uneasy and silly; but to say at this point, "No thank you, I'd rather not," when the request was obviously harmless, would have made her feel even sillier. After a minute she found herself undoing the buttons, then slipping on the dressing-gown. It was much too large for her: the sleeves came down over her hands and the bottom edge trailed along the floor.

"Here you are then," she said.

She watched with a slight anxiety as he wielded the iron. This time the activity seemed more crucial, it was like a dangerous hand moving back and forth slowly an inch away, the cloth had been so recently next to her skin. If he burns it or anything though, she thought, I can always put on one of the others.

"There," he said, "all done." He unplugged the iron again and draped the blouse over the small end of the ironing-board; he seemed to have forgotten that she was supposed to be wearing it. Then, unexpectedly, he came over to the bed, crawled onto it beside her, and stretched himself out on his back with his eyes closed and his arms behind his head.

"God," he said, "all these distractions. How does one

go on? It's like term-papers, you produce all that stuff and nothing is ever done with it, you just get a grade on it and heave it in the trash, you know that some other poor comma-counter is going to come along the year after you and have to do the same thing over again, it's a treadmill, even ironing, you iron the damn things and then you wear them and they get all wrinkled again."

"Well, and then you can iron them again, can't you?" Marian said soothingly. "If they stayed neat you wouldn't have anything to do."

"Maybe I'd do something worthwhile for a change," he said. His eyes were still closed. "Production-consumption. You begin to wonder whether it isn't just a question of making one kind of garbage into another kind. The human mind was the last thing to be commercialized but they're doing a good job of it now; what *is* the difference between the library stacks and one of those used-car graveyards? What bothers me though is that none of it is ever final; you can't ever finish anything. I have this great plan for permanent leaves on trees, it's a waste for them having to produce a new lot each year; and come to think of it there's no reason at all why they have to be green, either; I'd have them white. Black trunks and white leaves. I can hardly wait till it snows, this city in the summer has altogether too much vegetation, it's stifling, and then it all falls off and lies around in the gutters. The thing I like about the place I came from, it's a mining town, there isn't much of anything in it but at least it has no vegetation. A lot of people wouldn't like it. It's the smelting plants that do it, tall smokestacks reaching up into the sky and the smoke glows red at night, and the chemical fumes have burnt the trees for miles around, it's barren, nothing but the barren rock, even grass won't grow on most of it, and there are the slag-heaps too; where the water collects on the rock it's a yellowish-brown from the chemicals. Nothing would grow there even if you planted it, I used to go out of the town and sit on the rocks, about this time of year, waiting for the snow. . . ."

Marian was sitting on the edge of the bed, bending slightly down towards his talking face, only half-listening to the monotonous voice. She was studying the contours of

147

his skull under the papery skin, wondering how anyone could be that thin and still remain alive. She did not want to touch him now, she was even slightly repelled by the hollowness of the eye-sockets, the angular hinge of the jawbone moving up and down in front of the ear.

Suddenly he opened his eyes. He stared at her for a minute as though he couldn't remember who she was and how she happened to be in his bedroom. "Hey," he said finally in a different voice, "you look sort of like me in that." He reached out a hand and tugged at the shoulder of the dressing-gown, pulling her down. She let herself sink.

The transition from the flat hypnotic voice, and then the realization that he had actual flesh, a body like most other people, startled her at first. She felt her own body stiffen in resistance, begin to draw away; but he had both arms around her now. He was stronger than she had thought. She was not sure what was happening: there was an uneasy suspicion in one corner of her mind that what he was really caressing was his own dressing-gown, and that she merely happened to be inside it.

She pulled her face away and gazed down at him. His eyes were closed. She kissed the end of his nose. "I think I ought to tell you something," she said softly; "I'm engaged." At that moment she could not recall exactly what Peter looked like, but the memory of his name was accusing her.

His dark eyes opened and looked up at her vacantly. "That's your problem, then," he said. "It's like me telling you I got an A on my Pre-Raphaelite Pornography paper—interesting, but it doesn't have much of anything to do with anything. Does it?"

"Well, but it does," she said. The situation was rapidly becoming a matter of conscience. "I'm going to get married, you know. I shouldn't be here."

"But you are here." He smiled. "Actually I'm glad you told me. It makes me feel a lot safer. Because really," he said earnestly, "I don't want you to think that all this means anything. It never sort of does, for me. It's all happening really to somebody else." He kissed the end of
148

her nose. "You're just another substitute for the laundromat."

Marian wondered whether her feelings ought to be hurt, but decided that they weren't: instead she was faintly relieved. "I wonder what you're a substitute for, then," she said.

"That's the nice thing about me. I'm very flexible. I'm the universal substitute." He reached up over her head and turned off the light.

Not very much later the front door was opened and closed, admitting a number of heavy footsteps. "Oh, shit," he said from somewhere inside his dressing-gown. "They're back." He pushed her upright, turned the light back on, yanked the dressing-gown closed around her and slithered off the bed, smoothing his hair down over his forehead with both hands, then straightening his sweater. He stood in the middle of the room for an instant, glaring wildly at the bedroom doorway, then dashed across the room, seized the chessboard, dropped it onto the bed, and sat down facing her. He quickly began to set the toppled pieces upright.

"Hi," he said calmly a moment later, to someone who had presumably appeared in the doorway. Marian was feeling too dishevelled to look around. "We were just having a game of chess."

"Oh, good show," said a dubious voice.

"Why get all upset about it?" Marian said, when whoever it was had gone into the bathroom and shut the door. "It's nothing to be disturbed about, it's all perfectly natural, you know. If anything it's their fault for barging in like that." She herself was feeling extraordinarily guilty.

"Well, I told you," he said, staring down at the orderly pattern of chessmen on the board. "They think they're my parents. You know parents never understand about things like that. They'd think you were corrupting me. They have to be protected from reality." He reached across the chessboard and took hold of her hand. His fingers were dry and rather cold.

17

☐ Marian gazed down at the small silvery image reflected in the bowl of the spoon: herself upside down, with a huge torso narrowing to a pinhead at the handle end. She tilted the spoon and her forehead swelled, then receded. She felt serene.

She looked fondly across the white tablecloth and the intervening plates and the basket of rolls at Peter, who smiled back at her. The angles and curves of his face were highlighted by the orange glow from the shaded candle at the side of the table; in the shadow his chin was stronger, his features not so smooth. Really, she thought, anyone seeing him would find him exceptionally handsome. He was wearing one of his suave winter costumes—dark suit, sombrely-opulent tie—not as jaunty as some of his young-man-about-town suits, but more quietly impressive. Ainsley had once called him "nicely packaged", but now Marian decided that she found this quality attractive. He knew how to blend in and stand out at the same time. Some men could never wear dark suits properly, they got flaky on the shoulders and shiny at the back, but Peter never shed and never shone in the wrong places. The sense of proud ownership she felt at being with him there in that more or less public way caused her to reach across the table and take his hand. He put his own hand on top of hers in answer.

The waiter appeared with the wine, and Peter tasted it and nodded. The waiter poured and stepped back into the darkness.

That was another nice thing about Peter. He could make that kind of decision so effortlessly. She had fallen into the habit in the last month or so of letting him choose for her. It got rid of the vacillation she had never found herself displaying when confronted with a menu: she never knew what she wanted to have. But Peter could make up their minds right away. His taste ran towards steak and roast beef: he did not care for peculiar things like sweetbreads, and he didn't like fish at all. Tonight they were having Filet Mignon. Already it was fairly late, they had spent the earlier hours of the evening at Peter's apartment, and they were both, they had told each other, ravenous.

Waiting for their food, they resumed the conversation they had begun earlier, while they were getting dressed again, about the proper education of children. Peter talked theoretically, about children as a category, carefully avoiding any application. But she knew perfectly well that it was their own future children they were really discussing: that was why it was so important. Peter thought that all children ought to be punished for breaches of discipline; even physically. Of course no one should ever strike a child in anger; the main thing was to be consistent. Marian was afraid of warping their emotions.

"Darling, you don't understand these things," Peter said; "you've led a sheltered life." He squeezed her hand. "But I've seen the results, the courts are full of them, juvenile delinquents, and a lot of them from good homes too. It's a complex problem." He compressed his lips.

Marian was secretly convinced she was right and resented being told she had led a sheltered life. "But shouldn't they be given understanding, instead of. . . ?"

He smiled indulgently. "Try giving understanding to some of those little punks: the motorcycle boys and the dope addicts and the draft dodgers up from the States. You've never even seen one up close, I bet; some of them have lice. You think you can solve everything by good will, Marian, but it doesn't work; they have no sense of responsibility at all, they run around smashing things up just because they feel like it. That's how they were brought up, nobody kicked hell out of them when they deserved it. They think the world owes them a living."

"Perhaps," Marian said primly, "somebody kicked hell out of them when they didn't deserve it. Children are very sensitive to injustice, you know."

"Oh, I'm all in favour of justice," Peter said. "What about justice for the people whose property they destroy?"

"You'd teach them not to drive around mowing down other people's hedges, I suppose."

151

Peter chuckled warmly. Her disapproval of that incident and his laughter at her for it had become one of the reference points in their new pattern. But Marian's serenity had vanished with her own remark. She looked intently at Peter, trying to see his eyes, but he was glancing down at his wineglass, admiring perhaps the liquid richness of the red against the white of the tablecloth. He had leaned back a little in his chair and his face was now in shadow.

She wondered why restaurants like this one were kept so dark. Probably to keep people from seeing each other very clearly while they were eating. After all, chewing and swallowing are pleasanter for those doing them than for those watching, she thought, and observing one's partner too closely might dispel the aura of romance that the restaurant was trying to maintain. Or create. She examined the blade of her knife.

The waiter stepped forward from somewhere, soft and deft as a cat on the carpeted floor, and set her order before her: the filet on a wooden platter, oozing juicily within its perimeter of bacon. They both liked it rare: synchronizing the cooking times would never be a problem at any rate. Marian was so hungry she would have liked to devour the steak at one gulp.

She began slicing and chewing, conveying the food to her grateful stomach. She was reconsidering the conversation, trying to get a clearer image of what she had meant by "justice". She thought that it ought to mean being fair, but even her notion of that became hazy around the edges as she looked at it. Did it mean an eye for an eye? And what good did it do anyway to destroy someone else's eye if you had lost your own? What about compensation? It seemed to be a matter of money in things like car accidents; you could even be awarded money for having suffered emotional distress. Once on a streetcar she had seen a mother bite a small child because it had bitten her. She gnawed thoughtfully through a tough piece, and swallowed.

Peter, she decided, wasn't himself today. He had had a difficult case, one that involved a lot of intricate research; he had gone through precedent after precedent only to

152

find that they all favoured the opposition. That was why he was making stern pronouncements: he was frustrated by complications, he wanted simplicity. He should realize though that if the laws weren't complicated he would never make any money.

She searched for her wineglass, and looked up. Peter was watching her. He was three-quarters finished and she wasn't even half.

"Thoughtful?" he said mellowly.

"Not really. Just absent-minded." She smiled at him and returned her attention to the platter.

Lately he had been watching her more and more.

Before, in the summer, she used to think he didn't often look at her, didn't often really see her; in bed afterwards he would stretch out beside her and press his face against her shoulder, and sometimes he would go to sleep. These days however he would focus his eyes on her face, concentrating on her as though if he looked hard enough he would be able to see through her flesh and her skull and into the workings of her brain. She couldn't tell what he was searching for when he looked at her like that. It made her uneasy. Frequently when they were lying side by side exhausted on the bed she would open her eyes and realize that he had been watching her like that, hoping perhaps to surprise a secret expression on that face. Then he would run his hand gently over her skin, without passion, almost clinically, as if he could learn by touch whatever it was that had escaped the probing of his eyes. Or as if he was trying to memorize her. It was when she would begin feeling that she was on a doctor's examination table that she would take hold of his hand to make him stop.

She picked at her salad, turning the various objects in the wooden bowl over with her fork: she wanted a piece of tomato. Maybe he had got hold of one of those marriage-manuals; maybe that was why. It would be just like Peter, she thought with fondness. If you got something new you went out and bought a book that told you how to work it. She thought of the books and magazines on cameras that were part of the collection on the middle shelf in his room, between the law books and the detec-

153

tive novels. And he always kept the car manual in the glove compartment. So it would be according to his brand of logic to go out and buy a book on marriage, now that he was going to get married; one with easy-to-follow diagrams. She was amused.

She spiked and devoured a black olive from her salad. That must be it. He was sizing her up as he would a new camera, trying to find the central complex of wheels and tiny mechanisms, the possible weak points, the kind of future performance to be expected: the springs of the machine. He wanted to know what made her tick. If that was what he was looking for. . . .

She smiled to herself. Now I'm making things up, she thought.

He was almost finished. She watched the capable hands holding the knife and fork, slicing precisely with an exact adjustment of pressures. How skilfully he did it: no tearing, no ragged edges. And yet it was a violent action, cutting; and violence in connection with Peter seemed incongruous to her. Like the Moose Beer commercials, which had begun to appear everywhere, in the subway trains, on hoardings, in magazines. Because she had worked on the pre-marketing survey she felt partially responsible for them; not that they were doing any harm. The fisherman wading in the stream, scooping the trout into his net, was too tidy: he looked as though his hair had just been combed, a few strands glued neatly to his forehead to show he was windblown. And the fish also was unreal; it had no slime, no teeth, no smell; it was a clever toy, metal and enamel. The hunter who had killed a deer stood posed and urbane, no twigs in his hair, his hands bloodless. Of course you didn't want anything in an advertisement to be ugly or upsetting; it wouldn't do, for instance, to have a deer with its tongue sticking out.

She was reminded of the newspaper that morning, the front page story she had skimmed over without paying much attention. The young boy who had gone berserk with a rifle and killed nine people before he was cornered by the police. Shooting out of an upstairs window. She remembered him now, grey and white, gripped by two darker policemen, the eyes remote, guarded. He wasn't
154

the kind who would hit anyone with his fist or even use a knife. When he chose violence it was a removed violence, a manipulation of specialized instruments, the finger guiding but never touching, he himself watching the explosion from a distance; the explosion of flesh and blood. It was a violence of the mind, almost like magic: you thought it and it happened.

Watching him operating on the steak like that, carving a straight slice and then dividing it into neat cubes, made her think of the diagram of the planned cow at the front of one of her cookbooks: the cow with lines on it and labels to show you from which part of the cow all the different cuts were taken. What they were eating now was from some part of the back, she thought: cut on the dotted line. She could see rows of butchers somewhere in a large room, a butcher school, sitting at tables, clothed in spotless white, each with a pair of kindergarten scissors, cutting out steaks and ribs and roasts from the stacks of brown-paper cow-shapes before them. The cow in the book, she recalled, was drawn with eyes and horns and an udder. It stood there quite naturally, not at all disturbed by the peculiar markings painted on its hide. Maybe with lots of careful research they'll eventually be able to breed them, she thought, so that they're born already ruled and measured.

She looked down at her own half-eaten steak and suddenly saw it as a hunk of muscle. Blood red. Part of a real cow that once moved and ate and was killed, knocked on the head as it stood in a queue like someone waiting for a streetcar. Of course everyone knew that. But most of the time you never thought about it. In the supermarket they had it all pre-packaged in cellophane, with name-labels and price-labels stuck on it, and it was just like buying a jar of peanut-butter or a can of beans, and even when you went into a butcher shop they wrapped it up so efficiently and quickly that it was made clean, official. But now it was suddenly there in front of her with no intervening paper, it was flesh and blood, rare, and she had been devouring it. Gorging herself on it.

She set down her knife and fork. She felt that she had turned rather pale, and hoped that Peter wouldn't notice.

"This is ridiculous," she lectured herself. "Everyone eats cows, it's natural; you have to eat to stay alive, meat is good for you, it has lots of proteins and minerals." She picked up her fork, speared a piece, lifted it, and set it down again.

Peter raised his head, smiling. "Christ I was hungry," he said, "I sure was glad to get that steak inside. A good meal always makes you feel a little more human."

She nodded, and smiled back limply. He shifted his glance to her platter. "What's the matter, darling? You aren't finished."

"No," she said, "I don't seem to be hungry any more. I guess I'm full." She meant to indicate by her tone of voice that her stomach was too tiny and helpless to cope with that vast quantity of food. Peter smiled and chewed, pleasantly conscious of his own superior capacity. "God," she thought to herself, "I hope it's not permanent; I'll starve to death!"

She sat twisting her napkin unhappily between her fingers, watching the last of Peter's steak disappear into his mouth.

18

☐Marian was sitting at the kitchen table, disconsolately eating a jar of peanut butter and turning over the pages of her largest cookbook. The day after the filet, she had been unable to eat a pork chop, and since then, for several weeks, she had been making experiments. She had discovered that not only were things too obviously cut from the Planned Cow inedible for her, but that the Planned Pig and the Planned Sheep were similarly forbidden. Whatever it was that had been making these decisions, not her mind certainly, rejected anything that had an indication of bone or tendon or fibre. Things that had been ground up and re-shaped, hot-dogs and hamburgers for instance, or lamb patterns or pork sausages, were all right as long as she didn't look at them too closely, and fish was still permitted. She had been afraid to try chicken: she had been fond of it once, but it came with an unpleasantly complete skeletal structure, and the skin, she predicted, would be too much like an arm with goose bumps. For protein variety she had been eating omelettes and peanuts and quantities of cheese. The quiet fear, that came nearer to the surface now as she scanned the pages—she was in the "Salads" section—was that this thing, this refusal of her mouth to eat, was malignant; that it would spread; that slowly the circle now dividing the non-devourable from the devourable would become smaller and smaller, that the objects available to her would be excluded one by one. "I'm turning into a vege-tarian," she was thinking sadly, "one of those cranks; I'll have to start eating lunch at Health Bars." She read, with distaste, a column headed *Hints for Serving Yoghurt.* "For a taste sensation, sprinkle it with chopped nuts!" the editress suggested with glee.

The telephone rang. She let it ring a couple of times before getting up to answer it. She didn't feel like talking to anyone and it was an effort to pull herself up out of the gentle realm of lettuce and watercress and piquant herb dressings.

"Marian?" It was Leonard Slank's voice. "Is that you?"

"Yes, hi Len," she said. "How are you?" She hadn't see him or even spoken to him for quite a long time.

He sounded urgent. "Are you alone? I mean is Ainsley there?"

"No; she isn't back from work yet. She said she was going to do some shopping." It was the Christmas season; had been, it seemed, for several months; and the stores were staying open till nine. "But I can get her to call you when she comes in."

"No no," he said hastily. "It's you I want to talk to. Can I come over?"

Peter was working on a case that night, so technically she wasn't busy; and her brain did not provide her with any excuse. "Sure, of course Len," she said. So she's told him, she thought as she put down the phone. The idiot. I wonder what she did that for.

Ainsley had been in the highest of spirits for the past few weeks. She had been certain from the beginning that she was pregnant, and her mind had hovered over the activities of her body with the solicitous attention of a scientist towards a crucial test-tube, waiting for the definitive change. She spent more time than usual in the kitchen, trying to decide whether or not she had strange cravings and sampling a multitude of foods to see if they tasted at all different, reporting her findings to Marian: tea, she said, was more bitter, eggs were sulphury. She stood on Marian's bed to examine the profile of her belly in Marian's dresser-mirror, which was bigger than her own. When she wandered around the apartment she hummed to herself, constantly, intolerably; and finally one morning she had retched in the kitchen sink, to her immense satisfaction. At last it had been time to go and see the gynaecologist, and just yesterday she had bounced up the stairs, her face radiant, waving an envelope: the result was Positive.

Marian congratulated her, but not as dourly as she would have done if it had happened several months earlier. At that time she would have had to cope with the resulting problems, such as where Ainsley would live—the lady down below would certainly not tolerate her once she became rotund—and whether she herself should get another room-mate, and if so, whether she would feel guilty about deserting Ainsley, and if not, whether she could face all the intricacies and tensions that would result from living with an unmarried mother and a newborn baby. But now it wasn't her concern, and she could afford to sound genuinely pleased for Ainsley's sake. After all, she herself was getting married; she had contracted out.

It was because she didn't want to be involved that she resented Len's phone call. From the tone of his voice she guessed Ainsley had told him something, but it hadn't been clear from the conversation exactly what he knew. She was already resolved to be as passive as possible. She would listen, of course—she had ears, she couldn't help it—to whatever he had to say (what was there for him to say, anyway? His function, such as it had been, was over); but beyond that there was nothing she could do. She felt incapable of handling the situation, and irritated too: if Len wanted to talk to anyone he should talk to Ainsley. She was the one with the answers.

Marian ate another spoonful of peanut butter, disliking the way it cleaved to the roof of her mouth, and to pass the time turned to the shellfish chapter and read the part about de-veining shrimps (who, she wondered, still bought real shrimps?) and then the instructions for turtles, which she had recently begun to find of interest: precisely what kind of interest, she was not certain. You were supposed to keep your live turtle in a cardboard box or other cage for about a week, loving it and feeding it hamburger to rid it of its impurities. Then just as it was beginning to trust you and perhaps follow you around the kitchen like a sluggish but devoted hard-shelled spaniel, you put it into a cauldron of cold water (where no doubt it would swim and dive happily, at first) and then brought it slowly to the boil. The whole procedure was reminiscent of the deaths of early Christian martyrs. What fiendishness went on in kitchens across the country, in the name of providing food! But the only alternative for that sort of thing seemed to be the cellowrapped and plasticoated and cardboard-cartoned surrogates. Substitutes, or merely disguises? At any rate, whatever killing had gone on had been done efficiently, by somebody else, beforehand.

Down below the doorbell rang. Marian tensed, listening: she didn't want to start down the stairs if it wasn't necessary. She heard a mumble of voices and the reverberation of the closing door. The lady down below had been on the alert. She sighed, closed the cookbook, tossed her spoon into the sink after giving it one last lick, and screwed the top on the peanut butter jar.

"Hi," she said to Len as he rose, white-faced and out of breath, from the stairwell. He looked ill. "Come on in and sit down." Then, because it was only six-thirty, she asked, "Have you had dinner? Can I get you anything?" She wanted to prepare something for him, if only a bacon-and-tomato sandwich. Ever since her own relation to food had become ambiguous she found she took a perverse delight in watching other people eat.

"No thanks," he said, "I'm not hungry. But I could use a drink if you've got one." He walked into the living room and plopped himself onto the chesterfield as though his body was a sack that he was too tired to carry around any longer.

"I've only got beer—that okay?" She went into the kitchen, opened two bottles, and carried them into the living room. With good friends like Len she didn't bother with the formality of glasses.

"Thanks," he said. He upended the squat brown bottle. His mouth, pursed budlike around the bottleneck, was for a moment strangely infantile. "Christ, do I need this," he said, putting the bottle down on the coffee table. "I guess she must've told you."

Marian sipped at her beer before replying. It was Moose Beer; she had bought some out of curiosity. It tasted like all the other brands.

"You mean that she's pregnant," she said in a neutral conversational tone. "Yes, of course."

Len groaned. He took off his hornrimmed glasses and pressed one hand over his eyes. "God, I feel just sick about it," he said. "I was so shocked when she told me, god I'd just called her up to see if she'd have coffee with me, she's been sort of avoiding me ever since that night, I guess all that really shook her up, and then to have *that* hit you over the phone. I haven't been able to work all afternoon. I hung up right in the middle of the conversation, I don't know what she thought about that but I couldn't help it. She's such a little *girl,* Marian, I mean most women you'd feel what the hell, they probably deserved it, rotten bitches anyway, not that anything like that has ever happened to me before. But she's so *young.* The damn thing is, I can't really remember what happened that evening. We came back for coffee, and I was feeing sort of rotten and that bottle of scotch was sitting on the table and I started in on it. Of course I won't deny that I'd been angling for her, but, well, I wasn't expecting it, I mean I wasn't ready, I mean I would have been a lot more careful. What a mess. What'm I going to *do?*"

Marian sat watching him silently. Ainsley, then, hadn't had a chance to explain her motives. She wondered whether she should attempt to unsnarl, for Len's benefit, that rather improbable tangle, or wait and let Ainsley do it herself, as by right she ought to.

"I mean I can't *marry* her," Len said miserably. "Being a husband would be bad enough, I'm too *young* to get married, but can you imagine me as a husband and *father?*" He gave a small gurgle and upended his beer bottle again. "Birth," he said, his voice higher and more distraught, "birth terrifies me. It's revolting. I can't stand the thought of having"—he shuddered—"a baby."

"Well, it isn't you who's going to have it, you know," Marian said reasonably.

Len turned to her, his face contorted, pleading. The contrast between this man, his eyes exposed and weak without their usual fence of glass and tortoise-shell, and the glib, clever, slightly leering Len she had always known was painful. "Marian," he said, "please, can't you try to reason with her? If she'd only decide to have an abortion, of course I'll pay for it." He swallowed; she watched his adam's-apple go up and down. She hadn't known anything could make him this unhappy.

"I'm afraid she won't," she said gently. "You see, the whole point of it was that she *wanted* to get pregnant."

"She what?"

"She did it on purpose. She wanted to get pregnant."

"That's ridiculous!" Len said. "Nobody *wants* to get pregnant. Nobody would deliberately do a thing like that!"

Marian smiled; he was being simple-minded, which she found sweet, in a sticky sort of way. She felt as though she should take him upon her knee and say, "Now Leonard, it's high time I told you about the Facts of Life."

"You'd be surprised," she said, "a lot of people do. It's fashionable these days, you know; and Ainsley reads a lot; she was particularly fond of anthropology at college, and she's convinced that no woman has fulfilled her femininity unless she's had a baby. But don't worry, you won't have to be involved any further. She doesn't want a husband, just a baby. So you've already done your bit."

Len was having trouble believing her. He put on his glasses, stared at her through them, and took them off again. There was a pause while he drank more beer. "So she's been to college, too. I should have known. That's

161

what we get then," he said nastily, "for educating women. They get all kinds of ridiculous ideas."

"Oh, I don't know," Marian said with a touch of sharpness, "there's some men it doesn't do much good for either."

Len winced. "Meaning me, I suppose. But how was I to know? *You* certainly didn't tell me. What a friend."

"Why, I'd never presume to try and tell you how to run your life," Marian said indignantly. "But why should you be upset, now that you know? You don't have to *do* anything. She'll take care of the whole business. Believe me, Ainsley's quite capable of looking after herself."

Leonard's mood seemed to be changing rapidly from despair to anger. "The little slut," he muttered. "Getting me into something like this. . . ."

There were footsteps on the stairs.

"Shhh," Marian said, "here she is. Now keep calm." She went out into the small vestibule to greet Ainsley.

"Hi, just wait till you see what I *got*," Ainsley called, lilting up the stairs. She bustled into the kitchen, setting her parcels on the table and taking off her coat and talking breathlessly. "It was such a jam down there but besides the groceries—have to eat enough for two now, you know—oh, and I got my vitamin pills—and I got the darlingest little patterns, just wait till you see." She produced a knitting book, then some blue baby-wool.

"So it's going to be a boy," Marian said.

Ainsley's eyes widened. "Well of course. I mean, I thought it might be better. . . ."

"Well, maybe you should have discussed it with the prospective father before you took the necessary steps. He's in the living room, and he seems rather annoyed at not being consulted. You see," Marian said maliciously, "he may have wanted a girl."

Ainsley pushed back a strand of auburn hair that had fallen over her forehead. "Oh. Len's here, is he?" she said, with pronounced coolness. "Yes. He sounded a little upset on the phone." She walked into the living room. Marian did not know which of them needed her support more or which she would give it to if forced to choose between them. She followed Ainsley, aware that she should extricate herself before the thing got much messier, but not knowing how.

"Hi Len," Ainsley said lightly. "You hung up on me before I had a chance to explain."

Len wouldn't look at her. "Marian has already explained, thanks."

Ainsley pouted reproachfully. She had evidently wanted to do it herself.

"Well, it was somebody's duty to," Marian said, compressing her lips in a slightly presbyterian manner. "He was suffering."

"Maybe I shouldn't have told you at all," Ainsley said, "but I really couldn't keep it to myself. Just think, I'm going to be a mother! I'm really so happy about it."

Len had been gradually bristling and swelling. "Well I'm not so damn happy about it," he burst out. "All along you've only been *using* me. What a moron I was to think you were sweet and innocent, when it turns out you were actually college-educated the whole time! Oh, they're all the same. You weren't interested in me at all. The only thing you wanted from me was my body!"

"What did you want," Ainsley asked sweetly, "from me? Anyway, that's all I took. You can have the rest. And you can keep your peace of mind, I'm not threatening you with a paternity suit."

Len had stood up and was pacing the floor, at a safe distance from Ainsley. "Peace of mind. Hah. Oh no, you've involved me. You involved me psychologically. I'll have to think of myself as a father now, it's indecent, and all because you"—he gasped: the idea was a novel one for him —"*you* seduced *me!*" He waved his beer-bottle at her. "Now I'm going to be all mentally tangled up in Birth. Fecundity. Gestation. Don't you realize what that will do to me? It's obscene, that horrible oozy. . . ."

"Don't be idiotic," Ainsley said. "It's perfectly natural and beautiful. The relationship between mother and unborn child is the loveliest and closest in the world." She was leaning in the doorway, gazing towards the window. "The most mutually balanced. . . ."

"Nauseating!" interjected Len.

Ainsley turned on him angrily. "You're displaying the

classic symptoms of uterus envy. Where the hell do you think *you* came from, anyway? You're not from Mars, you know, and it may be news but your mother didn't find you under a cabbage-plant in the garden either. You were all curled up inside somebody's *womb* for nine months just like everybody else, and. . . ."

Len's face cringed. "Stop!" he cried. "Don't remind me. I really can't stand it, you'll make me sick. Don't come near me!" he yelped, as Ainsley took a step towards him. "You're unclean!"

Marian decided that he was becoming hysterical. He sat down on the arm of the chesterfield and covered his face with his hands. "She made me do it," he muttered. "My own mother. We were having eggs for breakfast and I opened mine and there was, I swear there was a little chicken inside it, it wasn't born yet, I didn't want to touch it but she didn't *see,* she didn't see what was really there, she said Don't be silly, it looks like an ordinary egg to me, but it wasn't, it wasn't and she made me eat it. And I know, I know there was a little beak and little claws and everything. . . ." He shuddered violently. "Horrible. Horrible, I can't stand it," he moaned, and his shoulders began to heave convulsively.

Marian blushed with embarrassment, but Ainsley gave a maternal coo of concern and hurried to the chesterfield. She sat down beside Len and put her arms around him, pulling him down so that he was resting half across her lap with his head against her shoulder. "There, there," she soothed. Her hair fell down around their two faces like a veil, or, Marian thought, a web. She rocked her body gently. "There, there. It's not going to be a little chicken anyway, it's going to be a lovely nice baby. Nice baby."

Marian walked out to the kitchen. She was coldly revolted: they were acting like a couple of infants. Ainsley was getting a layer of blubber on her soul already, she thought; aren't hormones wonderful. Soon she would be fat all over. And Len had displayed something hidden, something she had never seen in him before. He had behaved like a white grub suddenly unearthed from its burrow and exposed to the light of day. A repulsive blinded writhing. It amazed her though that it had taken so little, really, to reduce him to that state. His shell had not been as thick and calloused as she had imagined. It was like that parlour trick they used to play with eggs: you put the egg endwise between your locked hands and squeezed it with all your might, and the egg wouldn't break; it was so well-balanced that you were exerting your force against yourself. But with only a slight shift, an angle, a re-adjustment of the pressure, the egg would crack, and skoosh, there you were with your shoes full of albumin.

Now Len's delicate adjustment had been upset and he was being crushed. She wondered how he had ever imagined to avoid the issue for so long, to persuade himself that his own much-vaunted sexual activities could have nothing whatever to do with the manufacture of children. What would he have done then if the situation had been as he first imagined it, and he *had* got Ainsley pregnant by accident? Would he have been able to play guilt off against a blamelessness based on no-intent-to-injure, have let them cancel each other out and escaped unscathed? Ainsley couldn't have foreseen his reaction. But it was her decision that was responsible for this crisis. What was she going to do with him now? What *should* she do?

Oh well, she thought, it's their problem, let them solve it; I'm well out of it anyway. She went into her bedroom and closed the door.

The next morning, however, when she opened her soft-boiled egg and saw the yolk looking up at her with its one significant and accusing yellow eye, she found her mouth closing together like a frightened sea-anemone. It's living; it's alive, the muscles in her throat said, and tightened. She pushed the dish away. Her conscious mind was used to the procedure by now. She sighed with resignation and crossed one more item off the list.

19

☐ "There's jelly, salmon, peanut butter and honey, and egg salad," Mrs. Grot said, shoving the platter almost under Marian's nose—not because she was being rude but because Marian was sitting on the chesterfield and Mrs.

Grot was standing up, and the assemblage of vertebrae, inflexible corsetry, and desk-oriented musculature that provided Mrs. Grot with her vertical structure would not allow her to bend very far over.

Marian drew herself back into the soft chintz cushions. "Jelly, thanks," she said, taking one.

It was the office Christmas party, which was being held in the ladies' lunchroom where they could be, as Mrs. Gundridge had put it, "more comfy." So far their comfiness, all-permeating as it was in these close quarters, had been tempered by a certain amount of suppressed resentment. Christmas fell on a Wednesday this year, which meant that they all had to come back to work on Friday, missing by a single day the chance of a gloriously long weekend. It was the knowledge of this fact however that had, Marian was sure, put the twinkle in Mrs. Grot's spectacles and even infused her with gaiety enough to sustain this unprecedentedly-social sandwich-passing. It's because she wants to take a good close look at our sufferings, Marian thought, watching the rigid figure as it progressed around the room.

The office party seemed to consist largely of the consumption of food and the discussion of ailments and bargains. The food had all been brought by the ladies themselves: each of them had agreed to provide a certain item. Even Marian had been pressured into promising some chocolate brownies, which she had actually bought at a bakery and switched to a different bag. She had not felt much like cooking lately. The food was heaped on the table that stood at one end of the lunchroom—much more food than they needed really, salads and sandwiches and fancy breads and desserts and cookies and cakes. But since everyone had brought something, everyone had to eat at least some of everything, or else the contributor would feel slighted. From time to time one or another of the ladies would shriek, "Oh Dorothy, I just *have* to try some of your Orange-Pineapple Delight!" or "Lena, your Luscious Fruit Sponge looks just scrummy!" and heave to her feet and trundle to the table to re-fill her paper plate.

Marian gathered that it had not always been like this. For some of the older girls, there was a memory, fast fading to legend, of a time when the office party had been a company-wide event; that was when the company had been much smaller. In those far-off days, Mrs. Bogue said mistily, the men from upstairs had come down, and they even had drinks. But the office had expanded, finally things reached a stage at which nobody knew everybody any longer, and the parties started to get out of hand. Small ink-stained girls from Mimeo were pursued by wandering executives, there were untimely revelations of smouldering lusts and concealed resentments, and elderly ladies had a papercupful too much and hysterics. Now, in the interests of allover office morale, each department had its own office party; and Mrs. Gundridge had volunteered earlier that afternoon that it was a lot comfier this way anyhow, just all us girls here together, a comment which had produced glutinous murmurs of assent.

Marian was sitting wedged between two of the office virgins; the third was perched on the arm of the chesterfield. In situations like this, the three of them huddled together for self-protection: they had no children whose cutenesses could be compared, no homes whose furnishings were of much importance, and no husbands, details of whose eccentricities and nasty habits could be exchanged. Their concerns were other, though Emmy occasionally contributed an anecdote about one of her illnesses to the general conversation. Marian was aware that her own status among them was doubtful—they knew that she was on the fringe of matrimony and therefore regarded her as no longer genuinely single, no longer able to empathize with their problems—but in spite of their slight coolness towards her she still preferred being with them to joining any of the other groups. There was little movement in the room. Apart from the platter-passers, most of the ladies remained seated, in various clusters and semi-circles, re-clumping themselves every now and then by an exchange of chairs. Mrs. Bogue alone circulated, bestowing a sociable smile here, a mark of attention or a cookie there. It was her duty.

She was working at it the more assiduously because of the cataclysm that had taken place earlier in the day. The giant city-wide instant tomato juice taste-test, in the offing

167

since October but constantly delayed for further refinements, had been due to go out that morning. A record number of interviewers, almost the whole available crew, were to have descended on the unwary front porches of the housewives with cardboard trays on strings around their necks, like cigarette girls (privately, to Lucy, Marian had suggested bleaching them all and dressing them up in feathers and net stockings), carrying small paper cups of real canned tomato juice and small paper cups of Instant tomato juice powder and small pitchers of water. The housewife was to take a sip of the real juice, watch the interviewer mix the Instant right before her astounded eyes, and then try the result, impressed, possibly, by its quickness and ease: "One Stir and you're Sure!" said the tentative advertisement sketches. If they'd done it in October it might have worked.

Unfortunately the snow that had been withholding itself during five uniformly overclouded grey days had chosen that morning at ten o'clock to begin to fall, not in soft drifting flakes or even intermittent flurries, but in a regular driving blizzard. Mrs. Bogue had tried to get the higher-ups to postpone the test, but in vain. "We're working with humans, not with machines," she had said on the phone, her voice loud enough so that they could hear it through the closed door of her cubicle. "It's utterly impossible out there!" But there was a deadline to be met. The thing had already been postponed for so long that it could be kept back no longer, and furthermore a delay of one day at this point would mean an actual delay of three because of the major inconvenience of Christmas. So Mrs. Bogue's flock had been driven, bleating faintly, out into the storm.

For the rest of the morning the office had resembled the base of a mercy-mission in a disaster-area. Phone-calls flooded in from the hapless interviewers. Their cars, antifreeze and snow-tireless, balked and stalled, stranded themselves in blowing drifts, and slammed their doors on hands and their trunk-lids on heads. The paper cups were far too light to withstand the force of the gale, and whirled away over the lanes and hedges, emptying their blood-red contents on the snow, on the interviewers, and,

168

if the interviewers had actually made it as far as a front door, on the housewife herself. One interviewer had her whole tray ripped from her neck and lifted into the air like a kite; another had tried to shelter hers inside her coat, only to have it tipped and spewn against her body by the wind. From eleven o'clock on, the interviewers themselves had come straggling in, wild-haired and smeared with red, to resign or explain or have their faith in themselves as scientific and efficient measurers of public opinion restored, depending on temperament; and Mrs. Bogue had had to cope in addition with the howls of rage from the broadloomed Olympics above who refused to recognize the existence of any storm not of their own making. The traces of the fray were still evident on her face as she moved among the eating women. When she was pretending to be flustered and upset, she was really serene; but now, attempting serenity, she reminded Marian of a club-lady in a flowered hat making a gracious speech of thanks, who has just felt a small many-legged creature scamper up her leg.

Marian gave up half-listening to several conversations at once and let the sound of voices filling the room wash across her ears in a blur of meaningless syllables. She finished her jelly sandwich and went for a piece of cake. The loaded table made her feel gluttonous: all that abundance, all those meringues and icings and glazes, those coagulations of fats and sweets, that proliferation of rich glossy food. When she returned with a piece of spongecake Lucy, who had been talking with Emmy, had turned and was now talking with Millie, so that after she had taken her place again Marian found herself in the middle of their conversation.

"Well naturally they just didn't know what to do about it," Lucy was saying. "You just don't ask someone would they please take a bath. I mean it's not very polite."

"And London's so dirty too," Millie said sympathetically. "You see the men in the evenings, the collars of their white shirts are black, just black. It's all the soot."

"Yes well, and this went on and it got worse and worse, it was getting so bad they were ashamed to even ask their friends in. . . ."

"Who's this?" Marian asked.

"Oh this *girl* who was living with some friends of mine in England and she just stopped *washing*. Nothing else was wrong with her, she just didn't wash, even her *hair* even, or change her clothes or anything, for the longest time, and they didn't want to say anything because she seemed perfectly *normal* in every other way, but obviously underneath it she must have been really *sick*."

Emmy's narrow peaked face swung round at the word "sick", and the story was repeated to her.

"So what happened, then?" Millie asked, licking chocolate icing from her fingers.

"Well," said Lucy, nibbling daintily at a morsel of shortcake, "it got pretty horrible. I mean, she was wearing the same *clothes*, you can imagine. And I guess it must have been three or four months."

There was a murmur of "Oh no's," and she said, "Well, at least two. And they were just about to ask her for god's sake either take a bath or move out. I mean, wouldn't you? But one day she came home and just took off those clothes and burnt them, and had a bath and everything, and she's been perfectly normal ever since. Just like that."

"Well that *is* queer!" Emmy said in a disappointed voice. She had been expecting a severe illness, or perhaps even an operation.

"Of course they're all a lot dirtier Over There, you know," Millie said in a woman-of-the-world tone.

"But *she* was from Over Here!" Lucy exclaimed. "I mean she'd been brought up the right way, she was from a good family and all; it wasn't as if they didn't have a *bathroom, they* were always perfectly clean!"

"Maybe it was one of those things we sort of all go through," said Millie philosophically. "Maybe she was just immature, and being away from the home like that and all. . . ."

"I think she was *sick*," Lucy said. She was picking the raisins out of a piece of Christmas-cake, preparatory to eating it.

Marian's mind grasped at the word "immature", turning it over like a curious pebble found on a beach. It suggested an unripe ear of corn, and other things of a vegetable or fruitlike nature. You were green and then you ripened: became mature. Dresses for the mature figure. In other words, fat.

She looked around the room at all the women there, at the mouths opening and shutting, to talk or to eat. Here, sitting like any other group of women at an afternoon feast, they no longer had the varnish of officialdom that separated them, during regular office hours, from the vast anonymous ocean of housewives whose minds they were employed to explore. They could have been wearing housecoats and curlers. As it was, they all wore dresses for the mature figure. They were ripe, some rapidly becoming overripe, some already beginning to shrivel; she thought of them as attached by stems at the tops of their heads to an invisible vine, hanging there in various stages of growth and decay ... in that case, thin elegant Lucy, sitting beside her, was merely at an earlier stage, a springtime green bump or nodule forming beneath the careful golden calyx of her hair. . . .

She examined the women's bodies with interest, critically, as though she had never seen them before. And in a way she hadn't, they had just been there like everything else, desks, telephones, chairs, in the space of the office: objects viewed as outline and surface only. But now she could see the roll of fat pushed up across Mrs. Gundridge's back by the top of her corset, the ham-like bulge of thigh, the creases around the neck, the large porous cheeks; the blotch of varicose veins glimpsed at the back of one plump crossed leg, the way her jowls jellied when she chewed, her sweater a woolly teacosy over those rounded shoulders; and the others too, similar in structure but with varying proportions and textures of bumpy permanents and dune-like contours of breast and waist and hip; their fluidity sustained somewhere within by bones, without by a carapace of clothing and makeup. What peculiar creatures they were; and the continual flux between the outside and the inside, taking things in, giving them out, chewing, words, potato chips, burps, grease, hair, babies, milk, excrement, cookies, vomit, coffee, tomato-juice, blood, tea, sweat, liquor, tears, and garbage. . . .

For an instant she felt them, their indentities, almost their substance, pass over her head like a wave. At some time she would be—or no, already she was like that too; she was one of them, her body the same, identical, merged with that other flesh that choked the air in the flowered room with its sweet organic scent; she felt suffocated by this thick sargasso-sea of femininity. She drew a deep breath, clenching her body and her mind back into her self like some tactile sea-creature withdrawing its tentacles; she wanted something solid, clear: a man; she wanted Peter in the room so that she could put her hand out and hold on to him to keep from being sucked down. Lucy had a golden bangle on one arm. Marian focussed her eyes on it, concentrating on it as though she was drawing its hard gold circle around herself, a fixed barrier between herself and that liquid amorphous other.

She became aware of a silence in the room. The henyard gabble had ceased. She lifted her head: Mrs. Bogue was standing at the end of the room near the table, holding up her hand.

"Now that we're all gathered together here in this unofficial way," she said, smiling benignly, "I'd like to take this opportunity to make a very pleasant announcement. I've learned recently through the grapevine that one of our girls will soon be getting married. I'm sure we'll all wish Marian MacAlpin the very best in her new life."

There were preliminary squeals and chirps and burbles of excitement; then the whole mass rose up and descended upon her, deluging her with moist congratulations and chocolate-crumbled inquiries and little powdery initiatory kisses. Marian stood up, and was immediately pressed against the more-than-ample bosom of Mrs. Gundridge. She unstuck herself and backed against the wall; she was blushing, but more from anger than from modesty. Someone had let it slip; one of them had told on her; Millie, it must have been.

She said "Thank you" and "September" and "March," the only three words necessary for the questions they were asking. "Wonderful!" and "Marvellous!" cried the chorus. The office virgins remained aloof, smiling wistfully. Mrs. Bogue also stood aside. She had, by the tone of her speech, and by the mere fact of this public announcement coming without warning or prior consultation, made it clear to Marian that she would be expecting her to leave her job whether she wanted to or not. Marian knew, from rumour and from the banishment of a typist just after she had begun to work at the office, that Mrs. Bogue preferred her girls to be either unmarried or seasoned veterans with their liability to unpredictable pregnancies well in the past. Newly-weds, she had been heard to say, were inclined to be unstable. Mrs. Grot from Accounting kept at the rim of the circle too, her smile tight-lipped and acid. I bet her festive mood is quite spoiled now, Marian thought; I'm lost to the Pension Plan forever.

To emerge from the building and walk along the street in the cold air was like throwing open the window of an overheated and stuffy room. The wind had subsided. It was already dark, but the jangling light from the store windows and the Christmas decorations overhead, festoons and stars, made the snow that was falling, softly now, glow like the spray from a gigantic and artificially-lit waterfall. Underfoot, there was less snow than she had anticipated. It was wet, trodden to a brown slush by the pedestrians. The blizzard had not started until after Marian had left for work that morning, and she wasn't wearing boots. Her shoes were soaked through by the time she had reached the subway station.

But in spite of her wet feet she got off the subway a stop before the right one. After that tea-party she could not possibly confront the apartment yet. Ainsley would come in and take up her infernal knitting; and there was the Christmas-tree, a plastic table-model in silver and azure. There were still the presents to be wrapped, lying on her bed; and her suitcase to be packed: early the next morning she had to leave on the bus for a two-day visit with her parents and their town and their relatives. When she thought of them at all, they no longer seemed to belong to her. The town and the people waited for her on some horizon, somewhere, unchanging, monolithic and grey, like the weathered stone ruins of an extinct civilization. She had bought all of the presents last weekend, shoving her way through the crowds that clamoured and shouted at the store-counters, but she no longer felt like giving anybody anything. She felt even less like receiving, having to thank them all for things she didn't need and would never use; and it was no use telling herself, as she had been told all her life, that it was the spirit of the giver and not the value of the gift that counted. That was worse: all the paper tags with Love on them. The kind of love they were given with was also by now something she didn't need and would never use. It was archaic, sadly ornate, kept for some obscure nostalgic reason, like the photograph of a dead person.

She had been walking west but with little sense of direction along a street walled with stores and with elegant mannequins posturing in their bright glass cages. Now she had passed the final store and was walking in a darker space. As she approached the corner, she realized she had been heading toward the Park. She crossed the street and turned south, following the stream of cars. The Museum was on her left, its frieze of stone figures thrown into relief by the garish orange floodlights they seemed to be using more and more for night-lighting.

Peter had been a problem. She hadn't known what she ought to buy him. Clothes were out of the question, she had decided: he would always want to choose his own. What else was there? Something for the apartment, some household object, would be like making a gift to herself. She had finally settled on a handsome expensive technical book about cameras. She knew nothing about the subject but she had taken the word of the salesman, hoping that the book was one he didn't already have. She was glad he had hobbies: he would be less likely to get heart failure after retiring.

She was passing under the arching branches of the trees that grew within these nearby fences and seclusions of the university. The sidewalk was less trampled here, and the snow was deeper, above her ankles in some places. Her feet were aching with the cold. Just as she was beginning to wonder why she kept on walking, she had crossed the street again and was standing in the Park.

It was a huge dimly-white island in the darkness of the night. The cars flowed around it, counter clockwise; on the further side lay the buildings of the university, those places she thought she had known so well only half a year ago but which now radiated a faint hostility towards her through the cold air, a hostility she recognized as coming from herself: in some obscure way she was jealous of them. She would have liked them to have vanished when she left, but they had remained standing, kept going on, as indifferent to her absence as they had actually been, she supposed, to her presence.

She walked further into the Park through the soft ankle-deep snow. Here and there it was criss-crossed by random trails of footprints, already silting over, but mostly it was smooth, untouched, the trunks of the bare trees coming straight up out of the snow as though it was seven feet deep and the trees had been stuck there like candles in the icing of a cake. Black candles.

She was near the round concrete pool that had a fountain in the summers but would be empty of water now, gradually filling instead with snow. She stopped to listen to the distant sounds of the city, which seemed to be moving in a circle around her; she felt quite safe. "You have to watch it," she said to herself, "you don't want to end up not taking baths." In the lunchroom she had felt for a moment dangerously close to some edge; now she found her own reactions rather silly. An office party was merely an office party. There were certain things that had to be got through between now and then, that was all: details, people, necessary events. After that it would be all right. She was almost ready to go back and wrap the presents; she was even hungry enough now to devour half a cow, dotted lines and all. But she wanted to stand for only one more minute with the snow sifting down her in this island, this calm open eye of silence. . . .

"Hello," a voice said.

Marian was hardly startled. She turned: there was a figure seated on the far end of a bench in the darker shadow of some evergreen trees. She walked towards it.

175

It was Duncan, sitting hunched over, a cigarette glowing between his fingers. He must have been there for some time. The snow had settled on his hair and on the shoulders of his coat. His hand, when she took off her glove to touch it, was cold and wet.

She sat down beside him on the snow-covered bench. He flicked away his cigarette and turned towards her, and she undid the buttons of his overcoat and huddled herself inside it, in a space that smelled of damp cloth and stale cigarettes. He closed his arms around her back.

He was wearing a shaggy sweater. She stroked it with one of her hands as though it was a furry skin. Beneath it she could feel his spare body, the gaunt slope of a starved animal in time of famine. He nuzzled his wet face under her scarf and hair and coat collar, against her neck.

They sat without moving. The city, the time outside the white circle of the Park, had almost vanished. Marian felt her flesh gradually numbing; her feet had even ceased to ache. She pressed herself deeper into the furry surface; outside, the snow was falling. She could not begin the effort of getting up. . . .

"You took a long time," he said quietly at last. "I've been expecting you."

Her body was beginning to shiver. "I have to go now," she said.

Against her neck she felt a convulsive movement of the muscles beneath his face.

20

☐Marian was walking slowly down the aisle, keeping pace with the gentle music that swelled and rippled around her. "Beans," she said. She found the kind marked "Vegetarian" and tossed two cans into her wire cart.

The music swung into a tinkly waltz; she proceeded down the aisle, trying to concentrate on her list. She resented the music because she knew why it was there: it was supposed to lull you into a euphoric trance, lower your sales resistance to the point at which all things are desirable. Every time she walked into the supermarket and heard the lilting sounds coming from the concealed loudspeakers she remembered an article she had read about cows who gave more milk when sweet music was played to them. But just because she knew what they were up to didn't mean she was immune. These days, if she wasn't careful, she found herself pushing the cart like a somnambulist, eyes fixed, swaying slightly, her hands twitching with the impulse to reach out and grab anything with a bright label. She had begun to defend herself with lists, which she printed in block letters before setting out, willing herself to buy nothing, however deceptively-priced or subliminally-packaged, except what was written there. When she was feeling unusually susceptible she would tick the things off the list with a pencil as an additional counter-charm.

But in some ways they would always be successful: they couldn't miss. You had to buy something sometime. She knew enough about it from the office to realize that the choice between, for instance, two brands of soap or two cans of tomato juice was not what could be called a rational one. In the products, the things themselves, there was no real difference. How did you choose them? You could only abandon yourself to the soothing music and make a random snatch. You let the thing in you that was supposed to respond to the labels just respond, whatever it was; maybe it had something to do with the pituitary gland. Which detergent had the best power-symbol? Which tomato juice can had the sexiest-looking tomato on it, and did she care? Something in her must care; after all, she did choose eventually, doing precisely what some planner in a broadloomed office had hoped and predicted she would do. She had caught herself lately watching herself with an abstracted curiosity, to see what she would do.

"Noodles," she said. She glanced up from her list just in time to avoid collision with a plump lady in frazzled muskrat. "Oh no, they've put another brand on the market." She knew the noodle business: several of her afternoons had been spent in stores in the Italian section, counting the endless varieties and brands of *pasta*. She

177

glared at the noodles, stacks of them, identical in their cellopaks, then shut her eyes, shot out her hand an' closed her fingers on a package. Any package.

"Lettuce, radishes, carrots, onions, tomatoes, parsley," she read from her list. Those would be easy: at least you could tell by looking at them, though some things came in bags or rubber-banded bunches arranged with some good and some bad in each, and the tomatoes, hothouse-pink and tasteless at this time of year, were prepackaged in cardboard and cellophane boxes of four. She steered her cart towards the vegetable area, where a slickly-finished rustic wooden sign hung on the wall: "The Market "Garden."

She picked listlessly through the vegetables. She used to be fond of a good salad but now she had to eat so many of them she was beginning to find them tiresome. She felt like a rabbit, crunching all the time on mounds of leafy greenery. How she longed to become again a carnivore, to gnaw on a good bone! Christmas dinner had been difficult. "Why Marian, you're not eating!" her mother had fussed when she had left the turkey untouched on her plate. She had said she wasn't hungry, and had eaten huge quantities of cranberry sauce and mashed potatoes and mince pie when no one was looking. Her mother had set her strange loss of appetite down to overexcitement. She had thought of saying she had taken up a new religion that forbade her to eat meat, Yoga or Doukhobor or something, but it wouldn't have been a good idea: they had been pathetically eager to have the wedding in the family church. Their reaction though, as far as she could estimate the reactions of people who were now so remote from her, was less elated glee than a quiet, rather smug satisfaction, as though their fears about the effects of her university education, never stated but always apparent, had been calmed at last. They had probably been worried she would turn into a high-school teacher or a maiden aunt or a dope addict or a female executive, or that she would undergo some shocking physical transformation, like developing muscles and a deep voice or growing moss. She could picture the anxious consultations over cups of tea. But now, their approving eyes said, she was turning

178

out all right after all. They had not met Peter, but for them he seemed to be merely the necessary X-factor. They were curious though: they continued to urge her to bring him home for the weekend soon. As she had moved around the town during those cold days, visiting relatives, answering questions, she could not convince herself she was actually back in it.

"Kleenex," she said. She glanced with distaste at the different brands and colours offered—what difference did it make what you blew your nose on?—and at the fancy printed toilet-paper-flowers and scrolls and polka-dots. Pretty soon they would have it in gold, as though they wanted to pretend it was used for something quite different, like wrapping Christmas presents. There really wasn't a single human unpleasantness left that they had not managed to turn to their uses. What on earth was wrong with plain white? At least it looked clean.

Her mother and her aunts of course had been interested in the wedding dress and the invitations and things like that. At the moment, listening to the electric violins and hesitating between two flavours of canned rice pudding—she had no reservations about eating that, it tasted so synthetic—she couldn't remember what they had all decided.

She looked at her watch; she didn't have much time. Luckily they were playing a tango. She wheeled rapidly towards the canned soup section, trying to shake the glaze out of her eyes. It was dangerous to stay in the supermarket too long. One of these days it would get her. She would be trapped past closing time, and they would find her in the morning propped against one of the shelves in an unbreakable coma, surrounded by all the pushcarts in the place heaped to overflowing with merchandise. . . .

She steered towards the checkout counters. They were having another of their sales-promoting special programmes, some sort of contest that would send the winner on a three-day trip to Hawaii. There was a big poster over the front window, a semi-nude girl in a grass skirt and flowers, and beside it a small sign: PINEAPPLES, Three Cans 65¢. The cashier behind the counter had a paper garland around her neck; her orange mouth was chewing

179

gum. Marian watched the mouth, the hypnotic movements of the jaws, the bumpy flesh of the cheeks with their surface of dark pink makeup, the scaling lips through which glinted several rodent-yellow teeth working as with a life of their own. The cash register totalled her groceries.

The orange mouth opened. "Five twenty-nine," it said. "Just write your name and address on the receipt."

"No thanks," Marian said. "I don't want to go."

The girl shrugged her shoulders and turned away. "Excuse me, you forgot to give me my stamps," Marian said.

That was another thing, she thought as she hoisted the grocery bag and went through the electric-eye door into the slushy grey twilight. For a while she had refused them: it was another hidden way for them to make money. But they still made the money anyway, more of it; so she had begun accepting them and hiding them in kitchen drawers. Now, however, Ainsley was saving for a baby-carrier, so she made a point of getting them. It was the least she could do for Ainsley. The flowery cardboard Hawaiian smiled at her as she trudged off towards the subway station.

Flowers. They had all wanted to know what kind of flowers she was going to carry. Marian herself was in favour of lilies; Lucy had suggested a cascade of pink tearoses and baby's breath. Ainsley had been scornful. "Well, I suppose you have to have a traditional wedding, since it's Peter," she had said. "But people are so hypocritical about flowers at weddings. Nobody wants to admit they're really fertility symbols. What about a giant sunflower or a sheaf of wheat? Or a cascade of mushrooms and cactuses, that would be quite genital, don't you think?" Peter didn't want to be involved in such decisions. "I'll leave all that sort of thing up to you," he would say with fondness when questioned seriously.

Lately she had been seeing more and more of Peter, but less and less of Peter alone. Now that she had been ringed he took pride in displaying her. He said he wanted her to really get to know some of his friends, and he had been taking her around with him to cocktail parties with the more official ones and to dinners and evening get-togethers with the intimates. She had even been to lunch

180

with some lawyers, during which she had sat the whole time silent and smiling. The friends collectively were all well-dressed and on the verge of being successful, and they all had wives who were also well-dressed and on the verge of being successful. They were all anxious; they were all polite to her. Marian found it difficult to connect these sleek men with the happy hunters and champion beer-drinkers that lived in Peter's memories of the past, but some of them were the same people. Ainsley referred to them as "the soap men," because once when Peter had come to pick Marian up he brought with him a friend who worked for a soap company. Marian's greatest apprehension about them was that she would get their names mixed up.

She wanted to be nice to them for Peter's sake; however, she had been feeling somewhat bombarded with them, and she had decided it was time for Peter to start really getting to know some of *her* friends. This was why she had asked Clara and Joe to dinner. She had been guilty of neglecting them anyway; though it was curious, she thought, how married people always assumed they were being neglected when you didn't phone them, even when they themselves had been too dug under to even think of phoning you. Peter had been recalcitrant; he had seen the inside of Clara's living room once.

As soon as she had issued the invitations she realized that the menu would be a major problem. She couldn't feed them milk and peanut butter and vitamin pills, or a salad with cottage cheese, she couldn't have fish because Peter didn't like it, but she couldn't serve meat either—because what would they all think when they saw her not eating any of it? She couldn't possibly explain; if she didn't understand it herself, how could she expect them to? In the past month the few forms that had been available to her had excluded themselves from her diet: hamburger after a funny story of Peter's about a friend of his who had got some analysed just for a joke and had discovered it contained ground-up mouse hairs; pork because Emmy during a coffee break had entertained them with an account of trichinosis and a lady she knew who got it— she mentioned the name with almost religious awe ("She ate it too pink in a restaurant, I'd never dare eat anything like that in a restaurant, just *think*, all those little things curled up in her muscles and they can't ever get them out"); and mutton and lamb because Duncan had told her the etymology of the word "giddy": it came, he said, from "gid", which was a loss of equilibrium in sheep caused by large white worms in their brains. Even hot dogs had been ruled out; after all, her stomach reasoned, they could mash up any old thing and stick it in there. In restaurants she could always hedge by ordering a salad, but that would never do for guests, not for dinner. And she couldn't serve them Vegetarian Baked Beans.

She had fallen back on a casserole, a mushroom-and-meatballs affair of her mother's which would disguise things effectively. "I'll turn off the lights and have candles," she thought, "and get them drunk on sherry first so they won't notice." She could dish herself a very small helping, eat the mushrooms, and roll the meat balls under one of the lettuce leaves from the accompanying salad. It wasn't an elegant solution but it was the best she could do.

Now, hurriedly slicing up the radishes for the salad, she was grateful for several things: that she had made the casserole the night before so all she had to do was stick it in the oven; that Clara and Joe were coming late, after they had put the children to bed; and that she could still eat salad. She was becoming more and more irritated by her body's decision to reject certain foods. She had tried to reason with it, had accused it of having frivolous whims, had coaxed it and tempted it, but it was adamant; and if she used force it rebelled. One incident like that in a restaurant had been enough. Peter had been terribly nice about it, of course; he'd driven her straight home and helped her up the stairs as though she was an invalid and insisted she must have the stomach-flu; but also he had been embarrassed and (understandably) annoyed. From then on she had resolved to humour it. She had done everything it wanted, and had even bought it some vitamin pills to keep its proteins and minerals balanced. There was no sense in getting malnutrition. "The thing to do," she had told herself, "is to keep calm." At times when she had meditated on the question she had concluded that the stand it had taken was an ethical one: it simply refused to eat anything that had once been, or (like oysters on the half-shell) might still be living. But she faced each day with the forlorn hope that her body might change its mind.

She rubbed the wooden bowl with a half-clove of garlic and threw in the onion rings and the sliced radishes and the tomatoes, and tore up the lettuce. At the last minute she thought of adding a grated carrot to give it more colour. She took one from the refrigerator, located the peeler finally in the bread-box, and began to peel off the skin, holding the carrot by its leafy top.

She was watching her own hands and the peeler and the curl of crisp orange skin. She became aware of the carrot. It's a root, she thought, it grows in the ground and sends up leaves. Then they come along and dig it up, maybe it even makes a sound, a scream too low for us to hear, but it doesn't die right away, it keeps on living, right now it's still alive. . . .

She thought she felt it twist in her hands. She dropped it on the table. "Oh no," she said, almost crying. "Not this too!"

When they had finally gone, even Peter, who had kissed her on the cheek and said jokingly, "Darling, we're never going to be like *that*," Marian went out to the kitchen and scraped the plates into the garbage pail and stacked them in the sink. The dinner had not been a good idea. Clara and Joe hadn't been able to get a babysitter so they had brought the children, lugging them up the stairs and putting them to bed, two in Marian's room and one in Ainsley's. The children had wept and excreted, and the fact that the bathroom was down a flight of stairs didn't help. Clara carted them out to the living room to reassure them and change them; she had no qualms. Conversation had ceased. Marian hovered about, handing diaper pins and pretending to be helpful, but secretly wondering whether it would be bad taste to go down and get one of the many odour-killing devices from the lady down below's bathroom. Joe bustled about, whistling and bringing fresh supplies; Clara made apologetic remarks in Peter's direction. "Small children are like this, it's only shit. Perfectly

183

natural, we all do it. Only," she said, joggling the youngest on her knee, "some of us have a sense of timing. Don't we, you little turd?"

Peter had pointedly opened a window; the room became ice-cold. Marian served the sherry, despairingly. Peter was not getting the right impression, but she didn't know what could be done. She found herself wishing that Clara had a few more inhibitions. Clara didn't deny that her children stank, but neither did she take any pains to conceal it. She admitted it, she almost affirmed it; it was as though she wanted it to be appreciated.

When the children had been swathed and pacified and arranged, two on the chesterfield and one in its carrier on the floor, they sat down to dinner. Now, Marian hoped, they will all have a conversation. She was concentrating on how to conceal her meatballs and didn't want the position of referee: she just couldn't think up any bright topical remarks. "Clara tells me you're a philatelist," she had ventured, but for some reason Joe didn't hear her; at least he didn't answer. Peter gave her a quick inquisitive look. She sat fidgeting with a piece of roll, feeling as though she had made an indecent joke and nobody had laughed.

Peter and Joe had started talking about the international situation, but Peter had tactfully changed the subject when it became obvious they would disagree. He said he had once had to take a philosophy course at university and had never been able to understand Plato; perhaps Joe could explain? Joe said he thought not, as he himself specialized in Kant, and asked Peter a technical question about inheritance taxes. He and Clara, he added, belonged to a co-operative burial society.

"I didn't know that," Marian said in an undertone to Clara as she dished herself a second helping of noodles. She felt as though her plate was exposed, all eyes fixed upon it, the hidden meatballs showing up from beneath the lettuce leaves like bones in an X-ray; she wished she had used one candle instead of two.

"Oh yes," said Clara briskly, "Joe doesn't believe in embalming."

Marian was afraid Peter might find this a little too radical. The trouble was, she sighed inwardly, that Joe was

184

idealistic and Peter was pragmatic. You could tell by their ties: Peter's was paisley and dark-green, elegant, functional; while Joe's was—well, it wasn't exactly a tie any more; it was the abstract idea of a tie. They themselves must have realized the difference: she caught them separately eyeing each other's ties, each probably thinking he would never wear a tie like that.

She began putting the glasses into the sink. It bothered her that things hadn't gone well; it made her feel responsible, like being It in a game of tag at recess. "Oh well," she remembered, "he got on with Len." It didn't really matter anyway: Clara and Joe were from her past, and Peter shouldn't be expected to adjust to her past; it was the future that mattered. She shivered slightly; the house was still chilly from when Peter had opened the window. She would smell maroon velvet and furniture polish, behind her there would be rustlings and coughings, then she would turn and there would be a crowd of watching faces, they would move forward and step through a doorway and there would be a flurry of white, the bits of paper blowing against their faces and settling on their hair and shoulders like snow.

She took a vitamin pill and opened the refrigerator door to get herself a glass of milk. Either she or Ainsley should really do something about the refrigerator. In the past couple of weeks their interdependent cleaning cycle had begun to break down. She had tidied up the living room for this evening, but she knew she was going to leave the dishes unwashed in the sink, which meant Ainsley would leave hers, and they would go on like that until they had used up all the dishes. Then they would start washing the top plate when they needed one and the others would sit there undisturbed. And the refrigerator: not only did it need defrosting, but its shelves were getting cluttered up with odds and ends, scraps of food in little jars, things in tinfoil and brown paper bags. . . . Soon it would begin to smell. She hoped that whatever was going on in there wouldn't spread too quickly to the rest of the house, at least not down the stairs. Maybe she would be married before it became epidemic.

Ainsley had not been at dinner; she had gone to the

185

Pre-Natal Clinic, as she did every Friday evening. While Marian was folding the tablecloth, she heard her come upstairs and go into her room, and shortly afterwards her tremulous voice called, "Marian? Could you please come here?"

She went into Ainsley's room, picking her way over the boggy surface of clothes that covered the floor towards the bed where Ainsley had thrown herself. "What's the matter?" she asked. Ainsley looked dismayed.

"Oh Marian," she quavered, "it's too awful. I went to the Clinic tonight. And I was so happy, and I was doing my knitting and everything during the first speaker—he talked about The Advantages of Breast Feeding. They even have an Association for it now. But then they had this psy-psy-psychologist, and he talked about the Father Image." She was on the verge of tears, and Marian got up and rooted around on the dresser until she unearthed a grubby piece of kleenex, just in case. She was concerned: it wasn't like Ainsley to cry.

"He says they ought to grow up with a strong Father Image in the home," she said when she had composed herself. "It's good for them, it makes them *normal*, especially if they're boys."

"Well, but you sort of knew that before, didn't you?" Marian asked.

"Oh no Marian, it's really a lot more drastic. He has all kinds of statistics and everything. They've proved it scientifically." She gulped. "If I have a little boy, he's absolutely *certain* to turn into a ho-ho-ho-homosexual!" At this mention of the one category of man who had never shown the slightest interest in her, Ainsley's large blue eyes filled with tears. Marian extended the kleenex, but Ainsley waved it away. She sat up and pushed back her hair.

"There's got to be a way," she said; her chin lifted, courageously.

21

☐They were holding hands as they went up the wide stone stairway and through the heavy doors, but they had to let go to pass through the turnstile. Once they were inside it didn't seem right to take hands again. The churchlike atmosphere created by the high gold-mosaicked dome under which they were standing discouraged any such fleshly attempts, even if they involved only fingers, and the blue-uniformed and white-haired guard had frowned at them as he took her money. Marian connected the frown with dim recollections of two previous visits during all-day educational bus excursions to the city when she was in elementary school: perhaps it came with the price of admission.

"Come on," Duncan said, almost in a whisper. "I'll show you my favourite things."

They climbed the spiral staircase, round and around the incongrous totem-pole, up towards the geometrical curved ceiling. Marian had not been in this part of the Museum for so long that it seemed like something remembered from a not altogether pleasant dream, the kind you had when recovering from ether after having your tonsils out. When at university she had attended one class on the basement floor (Geology; it had been the only way to avoid Religious Knowledge, and she had felt surly towards rock-specimens ever since), and occasionally she had gone to the Museum Coffee Shop on the main floor. But not up these marble stairs again, into the bowl-shaped space of air that looked almost solid now, shafted with dustmotes whenever the weak winter sunlight became positive enough through the narrow windows high above.

They paused for a minute to look over the balustrade. Down below a batch of schoolchildren was filing through the turnstile and going to pick up folding canvas chairs from the stack at the side of the rotunda, their bodies foreshortened by perspective. The shrill edges of their voices were dulled by the thick encircling space, so that they seemed even further away than they actually were.

"I hope they don't come up here," Duncan said as he pushed himself away from the marble railing. He tugged at her coatsleeve, turning and drawing her with him into one of the branching galleries. They walked slowly along the creaking parquet floor past the rows of glass cases.

She had been seeing Duncan frequently during the past

187

three weeks, by collusion rather than by coincidence, as formerly. He was writing another term-paper, he had told her, called "Monosyllables in Milton," which was to be an intensive stylistic analysis done from a radical angle. He had been stuck on the opening sentence, "It is indeed highly significant that . . ." for two and a half weeks and, having exhausted the possibilities of the laundromat, he had felt a need for frequent escapes.

"Why don't you find a *female* graduate student in English?" she had asked once when their two faces, reflected in a store window, had struck her as particularly ill-matched. She looked like someone who was hired to take him out for walks.

"That wouldn't be an escape," he said, "they're all writing term-papers too; we'd have to discuss them. Besides," he added morosely, "they don't have enough breasts. Or," he qualified after a pause, "some of them have too many."

Marian was being, she supposed, what they called "used", but she didn't at all mind being used, as long as she knew what for: she liked these things to take place on as conscious a level as possible. Of course Duncan was making what they called "demands", if only on her time and attention; but at least he wasn't threatening her with some intangible gift in return. His complete selfcentredness was reassuring in a peculiar way. Thus, when he would murmur, with his lips touching her cheek, "You know, I don't even really *like* you very much," it didn't disturb her at all because she didn't have to answer. But when Peter, with his mouth in approximately the same position, would whisper "I love you" and wait for the echo, she had to exert herself.

She guessed that she was using Duncan too, although her motives eluded her; as all her motives tended to these days. The long time she had been moving through (and it was strange to realize that she had after all been moving: she was due to leave for home in another two weeks, the day after a party Peter was going to give, and two, or was it three, weeks after that she would be married) had been merely a period of waiting, drifting with the current, an endurance of time marked by no real event; waiting for an event in the future that had been determined by an event in the past; whereas when she was with Duncan she was caught in an eddy of present time: they had virtually no past and certainly no future.

Duncan was irritatingly unconcerned about her marriage. He would listen to the few things she had to say about it, grin slightly when she would say she thought it was a good idea, then shrug and tell her neutrally that it sounded evil to him but that she seemed to be managing perfectly well and that anyway it was her problem. Then he would direct the conversation towards the complex and ever-fascinating subject of himself. He didn't seem to care about what would happen to her after she passed out of the range of his perpetual present: the only comment he had ever made about the time after her marriage implied that he supposed he would have to dig up another substitute. She found his lack of interest comforting, though she didn't want to know why.

They were passing through the Oriental section. There were many pale vases and glazed and lacquered dishes. Marian glanced at an immense wall-screen that was covered with small golden images of the gods and goddesses, arranged around a gigantic central figure: an obese Buddha-like creature, smiling like Mrs. Bogue controlling by divine will her vast army of dwarfed housewives, serenely, inscrutably.

Whatever the reasons though she was always glad when he telephoned, urgent and distraught, and asked her to meet him. They had to arrange out-of-the-way places— snowy parks, art galleries, the occasional bar (though never the Park Plaza)—which meant that their few embraces had been unpremeditated, furtive, gelid, and much hampered by muffling layers of winter clothing. That morning he had phoned her at work and suggested, or rather demanded, the Museum: "I crave the Museum," he had said. She had fled the office early, pleading a dental appointment. It didn't matter anyway, she was leaving at last in a week and her successor was already training for the job.

The Museum was a good place: Peter would never go there. She dreaded having Peter and Duncan encounter

189

each other. An irrational dread because for one thing there was no reason, she told herself, why Peter should be upset—it had nothing to do with him, there was obviously no question of competition or anything silly like that—and, for another, even if they did collide she could always explain Duncan as an old friend from college or something of the sort. She would be safe; but what she really seemed to fear was the destruction, not of anything in her relationship with Peter, but of one of the two by the other; though who would be destroyed by whom, or why, she couldn't tell, and most of the time she was surprised at herself for having such vague premonitions.

Nevertheless it was for this reason that she couldn't let him come to her apartment. It would be too great a risk. She had gone to his place several times, but one or both of the room-mates had always been there, suspicious and awkwardly resentful. That would make Duncan more nervous than ever and they would leave quickly.

"Why don't they like me?" she asked. They had paused to look at a suit of intricately embossed Chinese armour.

"Who?"

"Them. They always act as though they think I'm trying to gobble you up."

"Well actually it isn't that they don't like you. As a matter of fact, they've said that you seem like a nice girl and why don't I ask you home to dinner sometime, so they can really get to know you. I haven't told them," he said, suppressing a smile, "that you're getting married. So they want a closer look at you to see if you're acceptable to the family. They're trying to protect me. They're worried about me, it's how they get their emotional vitamins, they don't want me to get corrupted. They think I'm too young."

"But why am I such a threat? What are they protecting you from?"

"Well, you see, you're not in graduate English. And you're a girl."

"Well, haven't they ever seen a girl before?" she asked indignantly.

Duncan considered. "I don't think so. Not exactly. Oh I don't know, what do you ever know about your parents?
190

You always think they live in some kind of primal innocence. But I get the impression that Trevor believes in a version of Mediaeval Chastitie, sort of Spenserian you know. As for Fish, well, I guess he thinks it's all right in theory, he's always talking about it and you ought to hear his thesis-topic, it's all about sex, but he thinks you've got to wait for the right person and then it will be like an electric shock. I think he picked it up from Some Enchanted Evening or D. H. Lawrence or something. God, he's been waiting long enough, he's almost thirty . . ."

Marian felt compassion; she started to make a mental list of ageing single girls she knew who might be suitable for Fish. Millie? Lucy?

They walked on, turned another corner, and found themselves in yet another room full of glass cases. By this time she was thoroughly lost. The labyrinthine corridors and large halls and turnings had confused her sense of direction. There seemed to be no one else in this part of the Museum.

"Do you know where we are?" she asked, a little anxiously.

"Yes," he said. "We're almost there."

They went under another archway. In contrast to the crowded and gilded oriental rooms they had been passing through, this one was comparatively grey and empty. Marian realized, from the murals on the walls, that they were in the Ancient Egyptian section.

"I come up here occasionally," Duncan said, almost to himself, "to meditate on immortality. This is my favourite mummy-case."

Marian looked down through the glass at the painted golden face. The stylized eyes, edged with dark-blue lines, were wide open. They gazed up at her with an expression of serene vacancy. Across the front of the figure, at chest-level, was a painted bird with outstretched wings, each feather separately defined; a similar bird was painted across the thighs, and another one at the feet. The rest of the decorations were smaller: several orange suns, gilded figures with crowns on their heads, seated on thrones or being ferried in boats; and a repeated design of odd symbols that were like eyes.

"She's beautiful," Marian said. She wondered whether she really thought so. Under the surface of the glass the form had a peculiar floating drowned look; the golden skin was rippling. . . .

"I think it's supposed to be a man," Duncan said. He had wandered over to the next case. "Sometimes I think I'd like to live forever. Then you wouldn't have to worry about Time anymore. Ah, Mutabilitie; I wonder why trying to transcend time never even succeeds in stopping it. . . ."

She went to see what he was looking at. It was another mummy-case, opened so that the shrivelled figure inside could be seen. The yellowed linen wrappings had been removed from the head, and the skull with its dried grey skin and wisps of black hair and curiously perfect teeth was exposed. "Very well preserved," Duncan commented, in a tone that implied he knew something about the subject. "They could never do a job like that now, though a lot of those commercial body-snatchers pretend they can."

Marian shuddered and turned away. She was intrigued, not by the mummy itself—she didn't enjoy looking at things like that—but by Duncan's evident fascination with it. From somewhere the thought drifted into her mind that if she were to reach out and touch him at that moment he would begin to crumble. "You're being morbid," she said.

"What's wrong with death?" Duncan said, his voice suddenly loud in the empty room. "There's nothing morbid about it; we all do it, you know, it's perfectly natural."

"It's not natural to like it," she protested, turning toward him. He was grinning at her.

"Don't take me seriously," he said. "I've warned you about that. Now come on and I'll show you my womb-symbol. I'm going to show it to Fish pretty soon. He's threatening to write a short monograph for *Victorian Studies* called 'Womb-Symbols in Beatrix Potter.' He has to be stopped."

He led her to the far corner of the room. At first in the rapidly fading light she couldn't make out what was inside the case. It looked like a heap of rubble. Then she saw that it was a skeleton, still covered in places with skin, lying on its side with its knees drawn up. There were some clay pots and a necklace lying beside it. The body was so small it looked like that of a child.

"It's sort of a pre-pyramid," Duncan said. "Preserved by the sands of the desert. When I get really fed up with this place I'm going to go and dig myself in. Maybe the library would serve the purpose just as well; except this city is kind of a dump. Things would rot."

Marian leaned further over the glass case. She found the stunted figure pathetic: with its jutting ribs and frail legs and starved shoulder-blades it looked like the photographs of people from underprivileged countries or concentration camps. She didn't exactly want to gather it up in her arms, but she felt helplessly sorry for it.

When she moved away and glanced up at Duncan, she realized with an infinitesimal shiver of horror that he was reaching out for her. Under the circumstances, his thinness was not reassuring, and she drew back slightly.

"Don't worry," he said. "I'm not going to return from the tomb." He passed his hand over the curve of her cheek, smiling down at her sadly. "The trouble is, especially with people and when I'm touching them and so on, I can't concentrate on the surface. As long as you only think about the surface I suppose it's all right, and real enough; but once you start thinking about what's inside. . . ."

He bent to kiss her. She swerved, rested her head against his winter-coated shoulder, and closed her eyes. He felt more fragile than usual against her: she was afraid of holding him too tightly.

She heard a creaking of the parquet floor, opened her eyes, and found herself confronted by a pair of austere grey scrutinizing eyes. They belonged to a blue-uniformed guard, who had come up behind them. He tapped Duncan on the shoulder.

"Pardon me, sir," he said, politely though firmly, "but—ah—kissing in the Mummy Room is not permitted."

"Oh," said Duncan. "Sorry."

They wound their way back through the maze of rooms and reached the main staircase. A stream of schoolchildren carrying folding stools was coming out of the gallery opposite, and they were caught up by the current of small moving feet and swept down the marble stairs in a waterfall of strident laughter.

Duncan had suggested that they go for coffee, so they were sitting at a square grubby-surfaced table in the Museum Coffee Shop, surrounded by groups of selfconsciously disconsolate students. Marian had for so long associated having coffee in a restaurant with the office and morning coffee breaks that she kept expecting the three office virgins to materialize across the table from her, beside Duncan.

Duncan stirred his coffee. "Cream?" he asked.

"No thanks," she said, but changed her mind and took some after she had reflected that it was nourishing.

"You know, I think it might be a good idea if we went to bed," Duncan said conversationally, putting his spoon down on the table.

Marian blenched inwardly. She had been justifying whatever had been happening with Duncan (whatever *had* been happening?) on the grounds that it was, according to her standards, perfectly innocent. It had seemed to her lately that innocence had some imperfectly-defined connection with clothing: the lines were drawn by collars and long sleeves. Her justifications always took the form of an imagined conversation with Peter. Peter would say, jealously, "What's this I hear about you seeing a lot of some scrawny academic type?" And she would reply, "Don't be silly Peter, it's perfectly innocent. After all, we're getting married in two months." Or a month and a half. Or a month.

"Don't be silly Duncan," she said, "that's impossible. After all, I'm getting married in a month."

"That's your problem," he said, "it has nothing to do with me. And it's me I thought it would be a good idea for."

"Why?" she asked, smiling in spite of herself. The extent to which he could ignore her point of view was amazing.

"Well of course it's not you. It's just it. I mean you personally don't arouse exactly a raging lust in me or any-
194

thing. But I thought you would know how, and you'd be competent and sensible about it, sort of calm. Unlike some. I think it would be a good thing if I could get over this thing I have about sex." He poured some of the sugar out onto the table and started tracing designs in it with his index-finger.

"What thing?"

"Well, maybe I'm a latent homosexual." He considered that for a moment. "Or maybe I'm a latent heterosexual. Anyway I'm pretty latent. I don't know why, really. Of course I've taken a number of stabs at it, but then I start thinking about the futility of it all and I give up. Maybe it's because you're expected to do something and after a certain point all I want to do is lie there and stare at the ceiling. When I'm supposed to be writing term-papers I think about sex, but when I've finally got some willing lovely backed into a corner or we're thrashing about under hedges and so on and everybody is supposed to be all set for the *coup de grâce*, I start thinking about term-papers. I know it's an alternation of distractions, both of those things are basically distractions you know, but what am I really being distracted from? Anyway they're all too literary, it's because they haven't read enough books. If they'd read more they'd realize that all those scenes have been done already. I mean *ad nauseum*. How can they be so trite? They sort of get limp and sinuous and passionate, they try so hard, and I start thinking oh god it's yet another bad imitation of whoever it happens to be a bad imination of, and I lose interest. Or worse, I start to laugh. Then they get hysterical." He licked the sugar from his fingers, thoughtfully.

"What makes you think it would be any different with me?" She was beginning to feel very experienced and professional: almost matronly. The situation, she thought, called for stout shoes and starched cuffs and a leather bag full of hypodermic needles.

"Well," he said, "it probably wouldn't be. But now that I've told you at least you wouldn't get hysterical."

They sat in silence. Marian was thinking about what he had said. She supposed that the impersonality of his request was quite insulting. Why didn't she feel insulted

195

then? Instead she felt she ought to do something helpful and clinical, like taking his pulse.

"Well ..." she said, deliberating. Then she wondered whether anyone had been listening. She glanced around the coffee shop, and her eyes met those of a large man with a beard who was sitting at a table near the door, looking in her direction. She thought he might be an anthropology professor. It was a moment before she recognized him as one of Duncan's room-mates. The blond man with him, sitting with his back to her, must be the other one.

"That's one of your parents over there," she said.

Duncan swivelled round. "Oh," he said. "I'd better go say hello." He got up, walked over to their table, and sat down. There was a huddled conversation and he got up and came back. "Trevor wants to know if you'd like to come to dinner," he said in the tone of a small child delivering a memorized message.

"Do you want me to?" she asked.

"Me? Oh, sure. I guess so. Why not?"

"Tell him then," she said, "that I'd be delighted." Peter was working on a case and it was Ainsley's night at the clinic.

He went to convey her acceptance. After a minute the two room-mates got up and went out, and Duncan slouched back and sat down. "Trevor said that's thrilling," he reported, "and he'll just rush off and pop a few things in the oven. Nothing fancy, he says. We're expected in an hour."

Marian started to smile, then put her hand over her mouth: she had suddenly remembered all the things she couldn't eat. "What do you think he'll have?" she asked faintly.

Duncan shrugged. "Oh, I don't know. He likes skewering things and setting fire to them. Why?"

"Well," she said, "there are a lot of things I can't eat; I mean, I haven't been eating them lately. Meat, for instance, and eggs and certain vegetables."

Duncan did not seem in the least surprised. "Well, okay," he said, "but Trevor's very proud of his cooking. I mean I don't care, I'd just as soon eat hamburger any day, but he'll be insulted if you don't eat at least some of what's on your plate."

"He'll be even more insulted if I throw it all up," she said grimly. "Maybe I'd better not come."

"Oh, come along, we'll work something out." His voice had a hint of malicious curiosity.

"I'm sorry, I don't know why I do it, but I can't seem to help it." She was thinking, maybe I can say I'm on a diet.

"Oh," said Duncan, "you're probably representative of modern youth, rebelling against the system; though it isn't considered orthodox to begin with the digestive system. But why not?" he mused. "I've always thought eating was a ridiculous activity anyway. I'd get out of it myself if I could, though you've got to do it to stay alive, they tell me."

They stood up and put on their coats.

"Personally," he said as they went out the door, "I'd prefer to be fed through the main artery. If I only knew the right people I'm sure it could be arranged. . . ."

22

☐As they entered the vestibule of the apartment building Marian, who had taken off her gloves, slipped her hand into her coat pocket and turned her engagement ring half-way around on her finger. She did not think it would be courteous to the room-mates, who had misunderstood with such touching concern, to flaunt the enlightening diamond too ostentatiously. Then she took the ring off altogether. Then she thought, "What am I doing? I'm getting married in a month. Why shouldn't they find out?" and put it back on. Then she thought, "But I'll never see them again. Why complicate things at this point?" and took it off for the second time and deposited it for safe-keeping in her change-purse.

By now they had gone up the stairs and were at the door of the apartment, which was opened before Duncan had touched the handle by Trevor. He was wearing an apron and was surrounded by a delicate aroma of spices.

"I thought I heard you two out there," he said. "Do come in. Dinner'll be a few more minutes, I'm afraid. I'm so glad you could come, ah. . . ." He fixed his pale blue eyes enquiringly on Marian.

"Marian," Duncan said.

"Oh yes," said Trevor, "I don't think we've really met—formally." He smiled, and a dimple appeared in each cheek. "You're just getting pot-luck tonight—nothing fancy." He frowned, sniffed the air, gave a shriek of alarm, and scuttled sideways into the kitchenette.

Marian left her boots on the newspapers outside the door and Duncan took her coat into the bedroom. She walked into the living room, searching for a place to sit down. She didn't want to sit in Trevor's purple chair, nor in Duncan's green one—that would create a problem for Duncan when he came out of the bedroom—nor on the floor among the papers: she might be disarranging someone's thesis; and Fish was barricaded into the red chair with the slab of board across its arms in front of him, writing with great concentration on yet another piece of paper. There was an almost-empty glass by his elbow. Finally she balanced herself on one of the arms of Duncan's chair, folding her hands in her lap.

Trevor warbled out of the kitchenette, bearing a tray with crystal sherry glasses. "Thank you, this is very nice," Marian said politely as he dispensed hers. "What a beautiful glass!"

"Yes, isn't it elegant? It's been in the family for years. There's so little elegance left," he said, gazing at her right ear as though he could see inside it a vista of an immemorially-ancient but fast-vanishing history. "Especially in this country. I think we all ought to do our bit to preserve some of it, don't you?"

With the arrival of the sherry Fish had put down his pen. He was now staring fixedly at Marian, not at her face but at her abdomen, somewhere in the vicinity of the navel. She found it disconcerting, and said, to distract him, "Duncan tells me you've been doing some work on Beatrix Potter. That sounds exciting."

198

"Huh? Oh yeah. I was contemplating it, but I've got into Lewis Carroll, that's really more profound. The nineteenth century is very hot property these days, you know." He threw his head back against the chair and closed his eyes; his words rose in a monotonously-intoned chant through the black thicket of his beard. "Of course everybody knows *Alice* is a sexual-identity-crisis book that's old stuff, it's been around for a long time, I'd like to go into it a little deeper though. What we have here, if you only look at it closely, this is the little girl descending into the very suggestive rabbit-burrow, becoming as it were pre-natal, trying to find her role," he licked his lips, "her role as a Woman. Yes, well that's clear enough. These patterns emerge. Patterns emerge. One sexual role after another is presented to her but she seems unable to accept any of them, I mean she's really blocked. She rejects Maternity when the baby she's been nursing turns into a pig, nor does she respond positively to the dominating-female role of the Queen and her castration cries of 'Off with his head!' And when the Dutchess makes a cleverly concealed lesbian pass at her, sometimes you wonder how *conscious* old Lewis was, anyway she's neither aware nor interested; and right after that you'll recall she goes to talk with the Mock-Turtle, enclosed in his shell and his self-pity, a definitely pre-adolescent character; then there are those most suggestive scenes, most suggestive, the one where her neck becomes elongated and she is accused of being a serpent, hostile to eggs, you'll remember, a rather destructively-phallic identity she indignantly rejects; and her negative reaction to the distatorial Caterpillar, just six inches high, importantly perched on the all-too-female mushroom which is perfectly round but which has the power to make you either smaller or larger than normal, I find that particularly interesting. And of course there's the obsession with time, clearly a cyclical rather than a linear obsession. So anyway she makes a lot of attempts but she refuses to commit herself, you can't say that by the end of the book she has reached anything that can be definitely called maturity. She does much better though in *Through the Looking Glass*, where, as you'll remember. . . ."

There was a smothered but audible snicker. Marian

jumped. Duncan must have been standing in the doorway: she hadn't noticed him come in.

Fish opened his eyes, blinked, and frowned at Duncan, but before he could make any comment Trevor bustled into the room.

"Has he been going on about those horrid symbols and things again? I don't approve of that kind of criticism myself, I think *style's* so much more important, and Fischer gets much too Viennese, especially when he drinks. He's very wicked. Besides, he's so out of *date*," he said cattily. "The very latest approach to *Alice* is just to dismiss it as a rather charming children's book. I'm almost ready, Duncan could you just help me set the table?"

Fischer sat watching them, sunk in the depths of his chair. They were putting up two card tables, placing the legs carefully in the gaps between the piles of paper, shifting the papers when necessary. Then Trevor spread a white cloth over the two tables and Duncan started to arrange the silverware and dishes. Fish picked up his sherry glass from his board and swallowed the contents at one gulp. He noticed the other glass that was standing there, and emptied that one also.

"There now!" Trevor cried. "Dinner will be served!"

Marian stood up. Trevor's eyes were glittering and a round red spot of excitement had appeared in the centre of each of his flour-white cheeks. A strand of blond hair had come detached and was hanging limply across his high forehead. He lit the candles on the table, and went around the living room turning off the floorlamps. Finally he removed the board from in front of Fish.

"You sit here, ah, Marian," he said, and disappeared into the kitchen. She sat down in the card table chair indicated. She could not get as close to the table as she would have liked, because of the legs. She ran her eyes over the dishes, checking: they were to begin with shrimp cocktail. That was all right. She wondered apprehensively what else would be produced for her body's consumption. Evidently there would be many more objects: the table bristled with silverware. She noted with curiosity the ornately-garlanded silver Victorian salt-cellar and the tasteful flower-decoration which stood between the two candles. They were real flowers too, chrysanthemums in an oblong silver dish.

Trevor returned and sat down in the chair nearest the kitchen and they began to eat. Duncan was seated opposite, and Fish to her left, at what she supposed was the foot of the table, or possibly the head. She was glad they were dining by candlelight: it would be easier to dispose of things if necessary. She hadn't as yet the least idea of how she was going to cope, if coping was going to be required, and it did not look as though Duncan would be much help. He seemed to have retreated into himself; he ate mechanically, and while chewing fixed his gaze on the candle flames, which made his eyes appear to be slightly crossed.

"Your silverware is beautiful," she said to Trevor.

"Yes, isn't it," he smiled. "It's been in the family for ages. The china too, I think it's rather heavenly, so much nicer than those stark Danish things everybody is using nowadays."

Marian inspected the pattern. It was a burgeoning floral design with many scallops, flutings and scrolls. "Lovely," she said. "I'm afraid you've taken far too much trouble."

Trevor beamed. She was obviously saying the right things. "Oh, no trouble at all. I think eating *well* is awfully important, why eat just to stay alive as most people do? The sauce is my own, do you like it?" He went on without waiting for an answer. "I can't stand these bottled things, they're so standardized; I can get real horse-radish at the Market down near the waterfront but of course it's so difficult to get fresh shrimp in this city...." He cocked his head to one side as though listening, then sprang out of his chair and pivoted round the corner into the kitchenette.

Fischer, who had not said anything since they had sat down, now opened his mouth and began to speak. Since he continued to eat at the same time, the intake of food and the output of words made a rhythm, Marian commented to herself, much like breathing, and he seemed to be able to handle the alternation quite as automatically; which was a good thing because she was sure that if he paused to think about it something would go down the wrong way. It would be more than painful to have a shrimp caught in one's windpipe; especially with horse-radish sauce. She watched him, fascinated. She was able to stare openly because he had his eyes shut most of the time. His fork found its way to his mouth by some mech-anism or sense peculiar to himself, she couldn't imagine how: perhaps batlike supersonic, radar-waves bounced back from the fork; or perhaps his individual whiskers functioned like antennae. He didn't break his pace even when Trevor, who had been busily removing the shrimp-cocktail dishes, set his soup plate in front of him, though he opened his eyes long enough to pick up his soup-spoon after a preliminary trial with his fork.

"Now my proposed thesis-topic," he had begun. "They may not approve of it, they're very conservative around here, but even if they turn it down I can always write it up for one of the journals, no human thought is ever wasted; anyway it's publish or perish these days, if I can't do it here I can always do it in the States. What I have in mind is something quite revolutionary, 'Malthus and the Creative Metaphor,' Malthus being of course merely a symbol for what I want to get at, that's the inescapable connection between the rise of the birth-rate in modern times, say the past two or three centuries, especially the eighteenth to the middle of the nineteenth, and the change in the way the critics have been thinking about poetry, with the consequent change in the way poets have been writing it, and oh I could safely extend the thing to cover all of the creative arts. It'll be an interdisciplinary study, a crossing over the presently much too rigid field-lines, a blend of say economics, biology, and literary criticism. People get much too narrow, too narrow, they're special-izing too much, that makes you lose sight of a lot of things. Of course I'll have to get some statistics and draw some graphs; thus far I've merely been doing the ground-work thinking, the primary research, the necessary exam-ination of the works of ancient and modern authors. . . ."

They were having sherry with the soup. Fish groped for his sherry glass, almost upsetting it.

Marian was now under cross-fire, since as soon as Trev-or had sat down again he had begun to talk at her from the other side, telling her about the soup, which was clear and subtly flavoured: how he had extracted its essences, painstakingly, moment by moment, at a very low heat; and since he was the only person at the table who was looking more or less at her she felt obliged to look at him in return. Duncan wasn't paying any attention to anyone and neither Fish nor Trevor seemed at all disconcerted by the fact that both of them were talking at once. They were evidently used to it. She found however that she could manage by nodding and smiling from time to time and keeping her eyes riveted on Trevor and her ears on Fish, who was continuing, "You see as long as the population, per square mile especially, was low and the infant mortality rate and the death-rate in general was high, there was a premium on Birth. Man was in harmony with the purposes, the cyclical rhythms of Nature, and the earth said, Produce, Produce. Be fruitful and multiply, if you'll recall. . . ."

Trevor sprang up and dashed around the table, removing the soup plates. His voice and his gestures were becoming more and more accelerated; he was popping in and out of the kitchen like the cuckoo in a cuckoo-clock. Marian glanced at Fish. Apparently he had missed several times with the soup: his beard was becoming glutinous with spilled food. He looked like a highchaired and bewhiskered baby; Marian wished someone would tie a bib around his neck.

Trevor made an entrance with clean plates, and another exit. She could hear him fidgeting about the kitchen, in the background of Fish's voice: "And so then consequently the poet also thought of himself as the same kind of natural producer; his poem was something begotten so to speak on him by the Muses, or let's say maybe Apollo, hence the term 'inspiration,' the instilling of breath as it were into, the poet was pregnant with his work, the poem went through a period of gestation, often a long one, and when it was finally ready to see the light of day the poet was delivered of it often with much painful labour. In this way the very process of artistic creation was itself an imitation of Nature, of the thing in nature that was most important to the survival of Mankind. I mean birth; birth. But what do we have nowadays?"

There was a fizzling sound, and Trevor appeared dramatically in the doorway, holding a flaming blue sword in either hand. Marian was the only person who even looked at him.

"Oh my goodness," she said appreciatively. "That's quite an effect!"

"Yes, isn't it? I just love things flambé. It's not really shishkebab of course, its a little more French, not so blatant as the Greek kind. . . ."

When he dexterously slid whatever was impaled on the skewers onto her plate, she could see that most of it was meat. Well, now her back was to the wall. She would have to think of something. Trevor poured the wine, explaining how hard it was to find really fresh tarragon in this city.

"What we have now, I say, is a society in which all the values are anti-birth. Birth control, they all say, and, It's the population explosion not the atomic explosion that we must all worry about. Malthus, you see, except that war no longer exists as a means of seriously diminishing the population. It's easy to see in this context that the rise of Romanticism . . ."

The other dishes contained rice with something in it, an aromatic sauce which went on the meat, and an unidentifiable vegetable. Trevor passed them round. Marian put some of the dark green vegetable substance into her mouth, tentatively, as one would make an offering to a possibly angry god. It was accepted.

". . . coincides most informatively with the population increase which had started of course some time earlier but which was reaching almost epidemic proportions. The poet could no longer see himself with any self-congratulation as a surrogate mother-figure, giving birth to his works, delivering as it were another child to society. He had to become a something else, and what really is this emphasis on individual expression, notice it's *expression*, a pressing out, this emphasis on spontaneity, the instantaneous creation? Not only does the twentieth century have . . ."

204

Trevor was in the kitchen again. Marian surveyed the chunks of meat on her plate with growing desperation. She thought of sliding them under the tablecloth—but they would be discovered. She would have been able to put them into her purse if only she hadn't left it over by the chair. Perhaps she could slip them down the front of her blouse or up her sleeves. . . .

". . . painters who splatter the paint all over the canvas in practically an orgasm of energy but we have writers thinking the same way about themselves . . ."

She reached under the table with her foot and prodded Duncan gently on the shin. He started, and looked across at her. For a moment his eyes held no recognition whatsoever; but then he watched, curious.

She scraped most of the sauce from one of the hunks of meat, picked it up between thumb and finger, and tossed it to him over the candles. He caught it, put it on his plate, and began to cut it up. She started to scrape another piece.

". . . no longer as giving birth however; no, long meditation and bringing forth are things of the past. The act of Nature that Art now chooses to imitate, yes is *forced* to imitate, is the very act of copulation. . . ."

Marian flung the second chunk, which was also neatly caught. Maybe they should quickly exchange plates, she thought; but no, that would be noticed, he had finished his before Trevor left the room.

"What we need is a cataclysm," Fish was saying. His voice had become almost a chant, and was swelling in volume; he seemed to be building up to some kind of crescendo. "A cataclysm. Another Black Death, a vast explosion, millions wiped from the face of the earth, civilization as we know it all but obliterated, then Birth would be essential again, then we could return to the tribe, the old gods, the dark earthgods, the earth goddess, the goddess of waters, the goddess of birth and growth and death. We need a new Venus, a lush Venus of warmth and vegetation and generation, a new Venus, big-bellied, teeming with life, potential, about to give birth to a new world in all its plenitude, a new Venus rising from the sea. . . ."

Fischer decided to stand up, perhaps to give rhetorical

205

emphasis to his last words. To lift himself he placed his hands on the card table, two of whose legs jackknifed, sending Fish's plate slithering into his lap. At that moment the chunk of meat which Marian had just hurled was in mid-air; it caught Duncan squarely in the side of the head, then deflected, bounced across the floor, and landed on a pile of term-papers.

Trevor, a small salad dish in either hand, had stepped through the doorway just in time to witness both events. His jaw dropped.

"At last I know what I really want to be," Duncan said into the suddenly quiet room. He was gazing serenely at the ceiling, a whitish-grey trace of sauce in his hair. "An amoeba."

Duncan had said he would walk her part way home: he needed a breath of fresh air.

Luckily none of Trevor's dishes had been broken, although several things had been spilled; and when the table had been straightened and Fischer had subsided, muttering to himself, Trevor had gracefully dismissed the whole incident, though for the remainder of the meal, through the salad and the *pêches flambées* and the coconut cookies and the coffee and liqueurs, his manner to Marian had been cooler.

Now, crunching along the snowy street, they were discussing the fact that Fischer had eaten the slice of lemon out of his fingerbowl. "Trevor doesn't like it, of course," Duncan said, "and I told him once that if he doesn't like Fish eating it he shouldn't put one in. But he insists on doing these things properly, though as he says, nobody appreciates his efforts much. I generally eat mine, too, but I didn't today: we had company."

"It was all very . . . interesting," Marian said. She was considering the total absence all evening of any reference to or question about herself, though she had assumed she was invited because the two room-mates wanted to know more about her. Now, however, she thought it more than likely that they were merely desperate for new audiences.

Duncan looked at her with a sardonic smile. "Well, now you know what it's like for me at home."

"You might move out," she suggested.

"Oh no, Actually I sort of like it. Besides, who else would take such good care of me? And worry about me so much? They do, you know, when they aren't engrossed in their hobbies or off on some other tangent. They spend so much time fussing about my identity that I really shouldn't have to bother with it myself at all. In the long run they ought to make it a lot easier for me to turn into an ameoba."

"Why are you so interested in amoebas?"

"Oh, they're immortal," he said, "and sort of shapeless and flexible. Being a person is getting too complicated."

They had reached the top of the asphalt ramp that led down to the baseball park. Duncan sat down on the snow bank at one side and lit a cigarette; he never seemed to mind the cold. After a moment she sat down beside him. Since he made no attempt to put his arm around her, she put hers around him.

"The thing is," he said after a while, "I'd like something to be real. Not everything, that's impossible, but maybe one or two things. I mean Dr. Johnson refuted the theory of the unreality of matter by kicking a stone, but I can't go around kicking my room-mates. Or my professors. Besides, maybe my foot's unreal anyway." He threw the stub of his cigarette into the snow and lit another. "I thought maybe you would be. I mean if we went to bed, god knows you're unreal enough now, all I can think of is those layers and layers of woolly clothes you wear, coats and sweaters and so on. Sometimes I wonder whether it goes on and on, maybe you're woollen all the way through. It would be sort of nice if you weren't. . . ."

Marian couldn't resist this appeal. She knew she wasn't woollen. "All right, suppose we did," she said, speculating. "We can't go to my place though."

"And we can't go to mine," Duncan said, showing neither surprise nor glee at her implied acceptance.

"I guess we'd have to go to a hotel," she said, "as married people."

"They'd never believe it," he said sadly. "I don't look married. They're still asking me in bars whether I'm sixteen yet."

"Don't you have a birth certificate?"

"I did once, but I lost it." He turned his head and kissed her on the nose. "I suppose we could go to the kind of hotel where you don't have to be married."

"You mean ... you'd want me to pose as a—some kind of prostitute?"

"Well? Why not?"

"No," she said, a little indignantly. "I couldn't do that."

"I probably couldn't either," he said in a gloomy voice. "And motels are out, I can't drive. Well I guess that's that." He lit another cigarette. "Oh well, it's true anyway: doubtless you would be corrupting me. But then again," he said with mild bitterness, "maybe I'm incorruptible."

Marian was looking out over the baseball park. The night was clear and crisp, and the stars in the black sky burnt coldly. It had snowed earlier, fine powdery snow, and the park was a white blank space, untracked. Suddenly she wanted to go down and run and jump in it, making footmarks and mazes and irregular paths. But she knew that in a minute she would be walking sedately as ever across it towards the station.

She stood up, brushing the snow from her coat. "Coming any further?" she asked.

Duncan stood up too and put his hands into his pockets. His face was shadowed in places and yellowed by the light from the feeble street lamp. "Nope," he said. "See you, maybe." He turned away, his retreating figure blurring almost noiselessly into the blue darkness.

When she had reached the bright pastel oblong of the subway station, Marian took out her change purse and retrieved her engagement ring from among the pennies, nickels and dimes.

23

□ Marian was resting on her stomach, eyes closed, an ashtray balanced in the hollow of her bare back where Peter had set it. He was lying beside her, having a cigarette and finishing his double scotch. In the living room the hi-fi set was playing cocktail music.

Although she was keeping her forehead purposefully unwrinkled, she was worrying. That morning her body had finally put its foot down on canned rice pudding, after accepting it with scarcely a tremor for weeks. It had been such a comfort knowing she could rely on it: it provided bulk, and as Mrs. Withers the dietician had said, it was fortified. But all at once as she had poured the cream over it her eyes had seen it as a collection of small cocoons. Cocoons with miniature living creatures inside.

Ever since this thing had started she had been trying to pretend there was nothing really wrong with her, it was a superficial ailment, like a rash: it would go away. But now she had to face up to it; she had wondered whether she ought to talk to someone about it. She had already told Duncan, but that was no good; he seemed to find it normal, and what was essentially bothering her was the thought that she might not be normal. This was why she was afraid to tell Peter: he might think she was some kind of freak, or neurotic. Naturally he would have second thoughts about getting married; he might say that they should postpone the wedding until she got over it. She would say that, too, if it was him. What she would do after they were married and she couldn't conceal it from him any longer, she couldn't imagine. Perhaps they could have separate meals.

She was drinking her coffee and staring at her uneaten rice pudding when Ainsley came in, wearing her dingy green robe. These days she no longer hummed and knitted; instead she had been reading a lot of books, trying, she said, to nip the problem in the bud.

She assembled her ironized yeast, her wheat-germ, her orange juice, her special laxative and her enriched cereal on the table before sitting down.

"Ainsley," Marian said, "do you think I'm normal?"

"Normal isn't the same as average," Ainsley said cryptically. "Nobody is normal." She opened a paperback book and began to read, underlining with a red pencil.

Ainsley wouldn't have been much help anyway. A couple of months ago she would have said it was something wrong with Marian's sex life, which would have been ridiculous. Or some traumatic experience in her childhood, like finding a centipede in the salad or like Len and the baby chicken; but as far as Marian knew there wasn't anything like that in her past. She had never been a picky eater, she had been brought up to eat whatever was on the plate; she hadn't even balked at such things as olives and asparagus and clams, that people say you have to *learn* to like. Lately though Ainsley had been talking a lot about Behaviourism. Behaviourists, she said, could cure diseases like alcholism and homosexuality, if the patients really wanted to be cured, by showing them images associated with their sickness and then giving them a drug that stopped their breathing.

"They say whatever causes the behaviour, it's the behaviour itself that becomes the problem," Ainsley had told her. "Of course there are still a few hitches. If the cause is deep-rooted enough, they simply switch their addiction, like from alcohol to dope; or they commit suicide. And what I need is not a cure but a prevention. Even if they can cure him—if he *wants* to be cured," she said darkly, "he'll still blame me for causing it in the first place."

But Behaviourism, Marian thought, wouldn't be much use in her case. How could it work on any condition so negative? If she were a glutton it would be different; but they couldn't very well show her images of *non*-eating and then stop her breathing.

She had gone over in her mind the other people she might talk to. The office virgins would be intrigued and would want to hear all about it, but she didn't think they would be able to give her any constructive advice. Besides, if she told one they'd all know and soon everyone they knew would know: you could never tell how it might get back to Peter. Her other friends were elsewhere, in other towns, other cities, other countries, and writing it in a letter would make it too final. The lady down below ... that was the bottom of the barrel; she would be like the relatives, she would be dismayed without understanding. They would all think it in bad taste for

Marian to have anything wrong with what they would call her natural functions.

She decided to go and see Clara. It was a faint hope—surely Clara wouldn't be able to offer any concrete suggestions—but at least she would listen. Marian telephoned her to make certain she would be in, and left work early.

She found Clara in the play-pen with her second youngest child. The youngest was asleep in its carrier on the dining room table, and Arthur was nowhere to be seen.

"I'm so glad you came," she said, "Joe's down at the university. I'll get out in a minute and make the tea. Elaine doesn't like the play-pen," she explained, "and I'm helping her get used to it."

"I'll make the tea," Marian said; she thought of Clara as a perpetual invalid and connected her with meals carried on trays. "You stay where you are."

It took her some time to find everything but at last she had the tray arranged, with tea and lemon and some digestive biscuits she had discovered in the laundry basket, and she carried it in and set it on the floor. She handed Clara her cup over the bars.

"Well," said Clara when Marian had settled herself on the rug, so as to be on the same level, "how's everything? I bet you're busy these days, getting ready and all."

Looking at her sitting in there with the baby chewing on the buttons of her blouse, Marian found herself being envious of Clara for the first time in three years. Whatever was going to happen to Clara had already happened: she had turned into what she was going to be. It wasn't that she wanted to change places with Clara; she only wanted to know what she was becoming, what direction she was taking, so she could be prepared. It was waking up in the morning one day and finding she had already changed without being aware of it that she dreaded.

"Clara" she said, "do you think I'm normal?" Clara had known her a long time; her opinion would be worth something.

Clara considered. "Yes, I would say you're normal," she said, removing a button from Elaine's mouth. "I'd say you're almost abnormally normal, if you know what I mean. Why?"

Marian was reassured. That was what she herself would have said. But if she was so normal, why had this thing chosen to attack *her?*

"Something's been happening to me lately," she said. "I don't know what to do about it."

"Oh, what's that? No, you little pig, that's mummy's."

"I can't eat certain things; I get this awful feeling." She wondered whether Clara was paying as much attention as she ought to.

"I know what you mean," said Clara, "I've always felt that way about liver."

"But these are things I used to be able to eat. It isn't that I don't like the taste; it's the whole. . . ." It was difficult to explain.

"I expect it's bridal nerves," Clara said; "I threw up every morning for a week before my wedding. So did Joe," she added. "You'll get over it. Did you want to know anything about . . . sex?" she asked, with a delicacy Marian found ludicrous, coming from Clara.

"No, not really thanks," she had said. Though she was sure Clara's explanation wasn't the right one she had felt better.

The record had begun to play from the middle again. She opened her eyes; from where she was lying she could see a green plastic aircraft carrier floating in the circle of light from Peter's desk lamp. Peter had a new hobby, putting together model ships from model ship kits. He said he found it relaxing. She herself had helped with that one, reading the directions out loud and handing him the pieces.

She turned her head on the pillow and smiled at Peter. He smiled back at her, his eyes shining in the semi-darkness.

"Peter," she said, "am I normal?"

He laughed and patted her on the rump. "I'd say from my limited experience that you're marvellously normal, darling." She sighed; she didn't mean it that way.

"I could use another drink," Peter said; it was his way of asking her to get him one. The ashtray was removed from her back. She turned over and sat up, pulling the top sheet off the bed and wrapping it around her. "And while you're up, flip over the record, that's a good girl."

Marian turned the record, feeling naked in the open expanse of the living room in spite of the sheet and the venetian blinds; then she went into the kitchen and measured out Peter's drink. She was hungry—she hadn't had much for dinner—so she unboxed the cake she had bought that afternoon on the way back from Clara's. The day before had been Valentine's Day and Peter had sent her a dozen roses. She had felt guilty, thinking she ought to have given him something but not knowing what. The cake wasn't a real gift, only a token. It was a heart with pink icing and probably stale, but it was the shape that mattered.

She got out two of Peter's plates and two forks and two paper napkins; then she cut into the cake. She was surprised to find that it was pink in the inside too. She put a forkful into her mouth and chewed it slowly; it felt spongy and cellular against her tongue, like the bursting of thousands of tiny lungs. She shuddered and spat the cake out into her napkin and scraped her plate into the garbage; after that she wiped her mouth off with the edge of the sheet.

She walked in to the bedroom, carrying Peter's drink and the plate. "I've brought you some cake," she said. It would be a test, not of Peter but of herself. If he couldn't eat his either then she was normal.

"Aren't you nice." He took the plate and the glass from her and set them on the floor.

"Aren't you going to eat it?" For a moment she was hopeful.

"Later," he said, "later." He was unwinding her from the sheet. "You're a bit chilly, darling; come here and be warmed up." His mouth tasted of scotch and cigarettes. He pulled her down on top of him, the sheet rustling whitely around them, his clean familiar soap-smell enfolding her; in her ears the light cocktail music went on and on.

Later, Marian was resting on her stomach with an ashtray balanced in the hollow of her back; this time her eyes were open. She was watching Peter eat. "I really

213

worked up an appetite," he said, grinning at her. He didn't seem to notice anything odd about the cake: he hadn't even winced.

<h2 style="text-align:center">24</h2>

□ All at once it was the day of Peter's final party. Marian had spent the afternoon at the hairdresser's: Peter had suggested that she might have something done with her hair. He had also hinted that perhaps she should buy a dress that was, as he put it, "not quite so mousy" as any she already owned, and she had duly bought one. It was short, red, and sequined. She didn't think it was really her, but the saleslady did. "It's you, dear," she had said, her voice positive.

It had needed an alteration so she had picked it up when she came from the hairdresser's and was carrying it now in its pink and silver cardboard box as she walked towards the house across the slippery road, balancing her head on her neck as though she was a juggler with a fragile golden bubble. Even outside in the cold late-afternoon air she could smell the sweetly-artificial perfume of the hairspray he had used to glue each strand in place. Though she'd asked him not to put on too much; but they never did what you wanted them to. They treated your head like a cake: something to be carefully iced and ornamented.

She usually did her hair herself, so she had got the name of the establishment from Lucy, thinking she would know about such places; but perhaps that had been a mistake. Lucy had a face and shape that almost demanded the artificial: nailpolish and makeup and elaborate arrangements of hair blended into her, became part of her. Surely she would look peeled or amputated without them; whereas Marian had always thought that on her own body these things looked extra, stuck to her surface like patches or posters.

As soon as she had walked into the large pink room—

everything had been pink and mauve, it was amazing how such frivolously feminine decorations could look at the same time so functional—she had felt as passive as though she was being admitted to a hospital to have an operation. She had checked her appointment with a mauve-haired young woman who despite her false eye-lashes and iridescent talons was disturbingly nurse-like and efficient; then she had been delivered over to the waiting staff.

The shampoo girl wore a pink smock and had sweaty armpits and strong professional hands. Marian had closed her eyes, leaning back against the operating-table, while her scalp was soaped and scraped and rinsed. She thought it would be a good idea if they would give anaesthetics to the patients, just put them to sleep while all these necessary physical details were taken care of; she didn't enjoy feeling like a slab of flesh, an object.

Then they had strapped her into the chair—not really strapped in, but she couldn't get up and go running out into the winter street with wet hair and a surgical cloth around her neck—and the doctor had set to work. A young man in a white smock who smelled of cologne and had deft spindly fingers and shoes with pointed toes. She had sat motionless, handing him the clamps, fascinated by the draped figure prisoned in the filigreed gold oval of the mirror and by the rack of gleaming instruments and bottled medicines on the counter in front of her. She couldn't see what he was doing behind her back. Her whole body felt curiously paralysed.

When at last all the clamps and rollers and clips and pins were in place, and her head resembled a mutant hedgehog with a covering of rounded hairy appendages instead of spikes, she was led away and installed under a dryer and switched on. She looked sideways down the assembly-line of women seated in identical mauve chairs under identical whirring mushroom-shaped machines. All that were metal domes. Inert; totally inert. Was this what various shapes and hands that held magazines and heads that were metal domes. Inert; totally inert. Was this what she was being pushed towards, this compound of the sim-

215

ply vegetable and the simply mechanical? An electric mushroom.

She resigned herself to the necessity of endurance, and picked up a movie star magazine from the stack at her elbow. A blonde woman with enormous breasts spoke to her from the back cover: "Girls! Be Successful! If You Wan to Really Go Places, Develop Your Bust. . . ."

After one of the nurses had pronounced her dry she was returned to the doctor's chair to have the stitches taken out; she found it rather incongruous that they weren't wheeling her back on a table. She passed along the gently-frying line of those who were not yet done, and soon her head was being unwound and brushed and combed; then the doctor was smiling and holding a hand mirror at an angle so that she could see the back of her head. She looked. He had built her usually straight hair up into a peculiar shape embellished with many intricate stiff curved wisps, and had manufactured two tusk-like spitcurls which projected forward, one on each cheekbone.

"Well," she said dubiously, frowning at the mirror, "it's a little—um—extreme for me." She thought it made her look like a callgirl.

"Ah, but you should wear it this way more often," he said with Italianate enthusiasm, his rapturous expression nevertheless fading a shade. "You should try new things. You should be *daring,* eh?" He laughed roguishly at her, displaying an unnatural number of white even teeth and two gold ones; his breath was flavoured with peppermint mouthwash.

She considered asking him to comb out some of his special effects, but decided not to, partly because she was intimidated by his official surroundings and specialist implements and dentist-like certainty—he must know what was right, it was his business—but partly because she found herself shrugging mentally. After all, she had taken the leap, she had walked through that gilded chocolate-box door of her own free will and this was the consequence and she had better accept it. "Peter will probably like it. Anyway," she reflected, "it will go with the dress."

Still half etherized, she had plunged into one of the large department stores nearby, intending to take a short-

216

cut through the basement to the subway station. She had gone quickly through the Household Wares section, past the counters that held frying pans and casserole dishes, and the display models of vacuum-cleaners and automatic washers. They reminded her, uneasily, both of the surprise shower the girls at the office had given her the day before, her last day of work, which had involved the bestowing of tea-towels and ladles and beribboned aprons and advice, and of the several anxious letters she had got recently from her mother, urging her to choose her patterns—china and crystal and silverware—because people were wanting to know what to get for wedding presents. She had taken trips to various stores for the purpose of making the selection, but had been so far quite unable to make up her mind. And she was leaving on the bus for home the next day. Well, she would do it later.

She rounded a counter lush with artificial plastic flowers and walked along what seemed to be a main aisle that led somewhere. In front of her a small frantic man was standing on a pedestal, demonstrating a new kind of grater with an apple-coring attachment. He was pattering and grating simultaneously, non-stop, holding up a handful of shredded carrot, then an apple with a near round hole in its centre. A cluster of women with shopping-bags watched silently, their heavy coats and overshoes drab in the basement light, their eyes shrewd and sceptical.

Marian stopped for a minute on the outer fringe of the group. The little man made a radish-rose with yet another attachment. Several of the women turned and glanced at her in an appraising way, summing her up. Anyone with a hair-style like that, they must have been thinking, would be far too trivial to be seriously interested in graters. How long did it take to acquire that patina of lower-middle income domesticity, that weathered surface of slightly mangy fur, cloth worn thin at cuff-edges and around buttons, scuffed leather of handbags; the tight slant of the mouth, the gauging eyes; and above all that invisible colour that was like a smell, the underpainting of musty upholstery and worn linoleum that made them in this bargain basement authentic in a way that she was not? Some-

217

how Peter's future income cancelled the possibility of graters. They made her feel like a dilettante.

The little man started briskly to reduce a potato to a pulp. Marian lost her interest and continued her search for the yellow subway sign.

When she opened the front door she was met by a gabble of female voices. She took off her boots in the vestibule and put them on the newspapers that were there for that purpose. A number of other pairs had been deposited, many with thick soles and some with black fur tops. As she went past the parlour doorway she caught a glimpse of dresses and hats and necklaces. The lady down below was having a tea party; they must be the Imperial Daughters, or perhaps they were the Women Christian Temperates. The child, in maroon velvet with a lace collar, was passing cakes.

Marian climbed the stairs as noiselessly as she could. For some reason she had not yet spoken to the lady down below about giving up the apartment. She should have done it weeks ago. The delay might mean having to pay another month's rent for insufficient notice. Maybe Ainsley would want to keep it on with another room-mate; but she doubted it. In another few months that would be impossible.

When she had climbed the second flight of stairs she could hear Ainsley talking in the living room. The voice was harder, more insistent, angrier than she had ever heard it before: Ainsley did not usually lose her temper. Another voice was interrupting, answering. It was Leonard Slank's.

"Oh no," Marian thought. They seemed to be having an argument. She definitely did not want to get involved. She intended to slip quietly into her room and close the door, but Ainsley must have heard her coming up the stairs: her head appeared abruptly from the living room, followed by quantities of loose red hair and then by the rest of her body. She was dishevelled and had been crying.

"Marian!" she half-wailed, half-commanded. "You've got to come in here and talk to Len. You've got to make
218

him listen to *reason*! I like your hair," she added perfunctorily.

Marian trailed after her into the living room, feeling like a child's wheeled wooden toy being pulled along by a string, but she didn't know on what grounds, moral or otherwise, she could base a refusal. Len was standing in the middle of the room, looking even more disturbed than Ainsley.

Marian sat down on a chair, keeping her coat on as a shock-absorber. The other two both stared angrily and beseechingly at her in silence.

Then, "My God!" Len almost shouted. "After all that, now she wants me to *marry* her!"

"Well, what's the matter with you anyway! You don't want a homosexual son, do you?" Ainsley demanded.

"Goddam it, I don't want any son at all! I didn't want it, you did it yourself, you should have it removed, there must be some kind of pill. . . ."

"That's not the *point,* don't be ridiculous, the point is of course I'm going to have the baby; but it should have the best circumstances, and it's your responsibility to provide it with a father. A father-image." Ainsley was now trying a slightly more patient and cool-headed approach.

Len paced across the floor. "How much do they cost? I'll buy you one. Anything. But I'm *not* going to marry you, dammit. Dont' give me that responsibility stuff either, I'm not responsible anyway. It was all your doing, you deliberately allowed me to get myself drunk, you seduced me, you practically *dragged* me into. . . ."

"That isn't quite how I remember it," Ainsley said, "and I was in a condition to remember it a lot more clearly than you can. Anyway," she continued with relentless logic, "you thought you were seducing me. And after all, that's important too, isn't it: your motives. Suppose you really *had* been seducing me and I'd got pregnant accidentally. What would you do then? You'd certainly be responsible then, wouldn't you? So it *is* your responsibility."

Len contorted his face, his smile an anaemic parody of cynical sarcasm. "You're like all the rest of them, you're a sophist," he said in a quaveringly-savage voice. "You're twisting the truth. Let's stick to the facts, shall we dear? I *didn't* seduce you really, it was. . . ."

"That doesn't *matter*," Ainsley said, her voice rising. "You *thought* you. . . ."

"For God's sake can't you be *realistic*!" Leonard shrieked.

Marian had been sitting quietly, looking from one to the other, thinking how peculiarly they were acting; so out-of-control. Now she said, "Could we please be a little less noisy? The lady down below might hear."

"Oh, SCREW the lady down below!" Len roared.

This novel idea was so blasphemous and at the same time so ludicrous that both Ainsley and Marian broke into horrified and delighted giggles. Len glared at them. This was the final outrage, the final feminine insolence—after putting him through all that, she was laughing at him! He snatched up his coat from the back of the chesterfield and strode towards the stairs.

"You and your goddamn fertility-worship can go straight to hell!" he shouted, plunging downwards.

Ainsley, seeing the father-image escaping, remoulded her features into an imploring expression and ran after him. "Oh Len, come back and let's talk it over seriously," she pleaded. Marian followed them down the stairs, impelled less by a sense of being able to do anything concrete or helpful than by some obscure herd- or lemming-instinct. Everyone else was leaping over the cliff, she might as well go too.

Len's descent was halted by the spinning-wheel on the landing. He was temporarily snarled in it, and tugged and swore loudly. By the time he was able to start down the next flight of stairs Ainsley had caught up to him and was pulling at his sleeve, and all the ladies, as alert to the symptoms of wickedness as a spider to the vibrations of its web, had come fluttering out of the parlour and were gathered at the foot of the stairs, gazing up with a certain gloating alarm. The child was among them, still holding a plate of cakes, her mouth slackly open, her eyes wide. The lady down below in black silk and pearls was being dignified in the background.

Len looked over his shoulder, then down the stairs. Retreat was impossible. He was surrounded by the enemy; there was no choice but to go bravely forward.

Not only that, he had an audience. His eyes rolled in his head like those of a frenzied spaniel. "All you clawed scaly bloody predatory whoring fucking bitches can go straight to hell! All of you! Underneath you're all the same!" he shouted, with, Marian thought, rather good enunciation.

He wrenched his sleeve out of Ainsley's clutch. "You'll never get me!" he screamed, charging down the stairs, his coat streaming behind him like a cape, scattering the assembled ladies before him in a blither of afternoon prints and velvet flowers, and gained the front door, which closed behind him with a thunderous crash. On the wall the yellowed ancestors rattled in their frames.

Ainsley and Marian retreated up the stairs, to the sound of excited bleating and twittering from the ladies in the parlour. The voice of the lady down below was rising above the others, calm and soothing: "The young man was obviously inebriated."

"Well," Ainsley said in a clipped practical voice when they were in the living room once more, "I guess that's that."

Marian didn't know whether she was referring to Leonard or to the lady down below. "What's what?" she asked.

Ainsley pushed her hair back over her shoulders and straightened her blouse. "I don't think he's going to come round. It's just as well: I doubt if he'd make a very good one anyway. I'll simply have to get another one, that's all."

"Yes; I guess so," Marian said vaguely. Ainsley went into the bedroom, her firm stride expressing determination, and shut the door. The matter sounded ominously settled. She seemed to have decided on another plan already, but Marian didn't even want to think about what it might be. Thinking would be of no use anyway. Whatever course it took, there would be nothing she herself could do to prevent it.

25

☐ She went into the kitchen and took off her coat. Then she ate a vitamin-pill, remembering as she did so that she had not had any lunch that day. She ought to put something in her stomach.

She opened the refrigerator to see what was in there that might be edible. The freezing-compartment was so thickly encrusted with ice that its door wouldn't stay shut. It contained two icecube trays and three suspicious-looking cardboard packages. The other shelves were crowded with various objects, in jars, on plates with bowls inverted over them, in waxed-paper packets and brown-paper bags. The ones toward the back had been there longer than she cared to remember. Some of them were definitely beginning to smell. The only thing she could see that interested her at all was a hunk of yellow cheese. She took it off the rack: it had a thin layer of green mould on the underside. She put it back and closed the door. She decided she wasn't hungry anyway.

"Maybe I'll have a cup of tea," she said to herself. She looked into the cupboard where they kept the dishes: it was empty. That meant she would have to wash a cup, they had all been used. She went to the sink and peered in.

It was full of unwashed dishes: stacks of plates, glasses half-filled with organic-looking water, bowls with vestiges of things that had ceased to be recognizable. There was a saucepan that had once held macaroni-and-cheese; its inner surface was spotted with bluish mould. A glass dessert dish sitting in the puddle of water at the bottom of the pot was filmed over with a grey slippery-looking growth reminiscent of algae in ponds. The cups were in there too, all of them, standing one inside another, ringed with dregs of tea and coffee and scums of cream. Even the white porcelain surface of the sink had developed a skin of brown. She did not want to disturb anything for fear of discovering what was going on out of sight: heaven only knew what further botulisms might be festering underneath. "Disgraceful," she said. She had a sudden urge to make a clean sweep, to turn the taps full on and squirt everything with liquid detergent; her hand even moved forward; but then she paused. Perhaps the mould had as much right to life as she had. The thought was not reassuring.

She wandered into the bedroom. It was too early to start dressing for the party, but she couldn't think of anything else she could do to fill up the time. She took her dress out of its cardboard box and hung it up; then she put on her dressing-gown and gathered together her bath equipment. She would be descending into the lady down below's territory and might have to brave an encounter; but, she thought, I'll just deny any connection with the whole mess and let her battle it out with Ainsley.

When the bathtub was filling she brushed her teeth, examining them in the mirror over the basin to make sure she hadn't missed anything, an established habit, she did it even when she hadn't been eating; it was remarkable, she thought, how much time you spend with a scouring brush in your hand and your mouth full of foam, peering down your own throat. She noticed that a tiny pimple had appeared to the right of one of her eyebrows. That's because I'm not eating properly, she decided: my metabolism or chemical balance or something has got upset. As she gazed at the small red spot it seemed to shift position a fraction of an inch. She ought to have her eyes examined, things were beginning to blur; it must be an astigmatism, she thought as she spat into the sink.

She took off her engagement ring and deposited it in the soap dish. It was a little too large for her—Peter had said they should get it cut down to size, though Clara said No, it would be best to leave it, since your fingers swelled up as you got older, especially when you were pregnant—and she had developed a fear of seeing it disappear down the drain. Peter would be furious: he was very fond of it. Then she clambered into the bathtub over the high old-fashioned side and lowered herself into the warm water.

She occupied herself with the soap. The water was lulling, relaxing. She had lots of time; she could indulge her

223

desire to lie back with her enamelled hair placed for security against the slope of the tub, to float with the water washing gently over her nearly-submerged body. From their elevated position her eyes had a long vista of white concave enclosing walls and semi-transparent water, her body islanded, extending in a series of curves and hollows down towards the terminal peninsula of legs and the reefs of toes; and beyond that a wire rack with the soap dish, and then the taps.

There were two taps, one for the hot and one for the cold. Each had a round bulb-shaped silver base and there was a third bulb in the middle with the spout where the water came out. She looked more closely: in each of the three silver globes she could see now that there was a curiously-sprawling pink thing. She sat up, stirring the water into minor tidal waves, to see what they were. It was a moment before she recognized, in the bulging and distorted forms, her own waterlogged body.

She moved, and all three of the images moved also. They were not quite identical: the two on the outside were slanted inwards towards the third. How peculiar it was to see three reflections of yourself at the same time, she thought; she swayed herself back and forth, watching the way in which the different bright silver parts of her body suddenly bloated or diminished. She had almost forgotten that she was supposed to be taking a bath. She stretched one hand towards the taps, wanting to see it grow.

There were footsteps outside the door. She had better get out: it must be the lady down below trying to get in. She began to splash off the remaining traces of soap. Looking down, she became aware of the water, which was covered with a film of calcinous hard-water particles of dirt and soap, and of the body that was sitting in it, somehow no longer quite her own. All at once she was afraid that she was dissolving, coming apart layer by layer like a piece of cardboard in a gutter puddle.

She pulled the plug hastily and scrambled out of the tub. It was safer on the dry beach of the cold tiled floor. She slid her engagement ring back onto her finger, seeing the hard circle for a moment as a protective talisman that would help keep her together.

But the panic was still with her as she climbed the stairs. She could not face the party, all those people, Peter's friends were nice enough but they didn't really know her, fixing their uncomprehending eyes on her, she was afraid of losing her shape, spreading out, not being able to contain herself any longer, beginning (that would be worst of all) to talk a lot, to tell everybody, to cry. She contemplated bleakly the festive red dress hanging in her closet. What can I do? her mind kept thinking. She sat down on her bed.

She remained sitting on the bed, gnawing idly on the end of one of her fringed dressing-gown ties, closed in a sodden formless unhappiness that seemed now to have been clogging her mind for a long time, how long she could not remember. With its weight pressing around her it was most improbable that she would ever manage to get up off the bed. I wonder what time it is? she said to herself. I've got to get ready.

The two dolls which she had never thrown out after all were staring blankly back at her from the top of the dresser. As she looked at them their faces blurred, then re-formed, faintly malevolent. She was irritated with them for sitting there inertly on either side of the mirror, just watching her, not offering any practical suggestions. But now that she examined their faces more closely she could see that it was only the dark one, the one with the peeling paint, that was definitely watching her. Perhaps the blonde one didn't even see her, the round blue eyes in its rubbery face were gazing straight through her.

She substituted one of her fingers for the dressing-gown tie, biting at the side of her nail. Or perhaps it was a game, an agreement they had made. She saw herself in the mirror between them for an instant as though she was inside them, inside both of them at once, looking out: herself, a vague damp form in a rumpled dressing-gown, not quite focussed, the blonde eyes noting the arrangement of her hair, her bitten fingernails, the dark one looking deeper, at something she could not quite see, the two overlapping images drawing further and further away

225

from each other; the centre, whatever it was in the glass, the thing that held them together, would soon be quite empty. By the strength of their separate visions they were trying to pull her apart.

She couldn't stay there any longer. She pushed herself off the bed and into the hallway, where she found herself crouching over the telephone and dialing a number. There was ringing, then a click. She held her breath.

"Hullo?" said a sullen voice.

"Duncan?" she said tentatively. "It's me."

"Oh." There was a pause.

"Duncan, could you come to a party tonight? At Peter's place? I know it's late to ask you, but. . . ."

"Well, we're supposed to be going to a brain-picking graduate English party," he said. "The whole family."

"Well, maybe you could come on later. And you could even bring them with you."

"Well, I don't know. . . ."

"*Please,* Duncan, I don't really know anybody there, I *need* you to come," she said with an intensity which was unfamiliar to her.

"No you don't," he said. "But maybe we'll come though. This other thing sounds pretty dull, all they ever do is talk about their Orals, and it would be sort of a kick to see what you're getting married to."

"Oh thank you," she said gratefully, and gave him directions.

When she had put down the phone she felt a lot better. So that was the answer, then: to make sure there were people at the party who really knew her. That would keep everything in the right perspective, she would be able to cope. . . . She dialled another number.

She spent half an hour on the phone; by that time she had rounded up a sufficient number of people. Clara and Joe were coming if they could get a baby-sitter, that made five counting the other three; and the three office virgins. After their initial hesitations, caused she supposed by the lateness of the invitation, she had hooked the three firmly by saying that she hadn't asked them before because she thought it was going to be mostly married people, but that several unescorted bachelors were coming, and could they

226

do her the favour of coming along too? Things got so dull for single men at couple-parties, she had added. That made eight altogether. As an afterthought she had asked Ainsley—it would be good for her to get out—and she accepted, surprisingly: it wasn't her kind of party.

Although she considered it in passing, Marian did not think it would be a wise move to ask Leonard Slank.

Now she was all right she could begin to dress. She oozed herself into the new girdle she had got to go with the dress, noting that she hadn't really lost much weight: she had been eating a lot of noodles. She hadn't intended to buy one at all, but the saleslady who was selling her the dress and who was thoroughly corseted herself said that she ought to, and produced an appropriate model with satin panelling and a bow of ribbon at the front. "Of course you're very *thin* dear, you don't really need one, but still that *is* a close-fitting dress and you wouldn't want it to be obvious that you haven't got one on, would you?" She had lifted her pencilled brows. At that time it had seemed like a moral issue. "No, of course not," Marian had said hastily, "I'll take it."

When she had slithered into her red dress, she found she couldn't reach behind far enough to do up the zipper. She knocked on Ainsley's door. "Do up my zipper, please?" she asked.

Ainsley was in her slip. She had begun to put on her makeup, but thus far only one of her eyes had acquired its outline of black and her eyebrows hadn't appeared at all, which made her face look unbalanced. After she had done up Marian's zipper and the little hook at the top, she stood back and examined her critically. "That's a good dress," she said, "but what are you going to wear with it?"

"With it?"

"Yes, it's very dramatic; you need some good heavy earrings or something to set it off. Have you got any?"

"I don't know," said Marian. She went into her own room and brought back the drawer that held the trinkets accumulated from her relatives. They were all variations of clustered imitation pearls and pastel arrangements of seashells and metal-and-glass flowers and cute animals.

Ainsley pawed through them. "No," she said, with the decisiveness of someone who really knew. "These won't do. I've got a pair that'll work, though." After a search which involved much rustling in drawers and overturning of things on the bureau, she produced a couple of chunky dangly gold objects, which she screwed to Marian's ears. "That's better," she said. "Now smile."

Marian smiled, weakly.

Ainsley shook her head. "Your hair's okay," she said, "but really you'd better let me do your face for you. You'll never manage it by yourself. You'd just do it in your usual skimpy way and come out looking like a kid playing dress-up in her mother's clothes."

She wadded Marian into her chair, which was lumpy with garments in progressive stages of dirtiness, and tucked a towel around her neck. "I'll do your nails first so they can be drying," she said, adding while she began to file them, "looks like you've been biting them." When the nails had been painted a shimmering off-white and Marian was holding her hands carefully in the air, she went to work on Marian's face, using mixtures and instruments from the jumble of beauty-aids that covered her dressing-table.

During the rest of the procedure, while strange things were being done to her skin, then to each eye and each eyebrow, Marian sat passively, marvelling at the professional efficiency with which Ainsley was manipulating her features. It reminded her of the mothers backstage at public-school plays, making up their precocious daughters. She had only a fleeting thought about germs.

Finally Ainsley took a lipstick-brush and painted the mouth with several coats of glossy finish. "There," she said, holding a hand-mirror so that Marian could see herself. "That's better. But be careful till the eyelash-glue is dry."

Marian stared into the egyptian-lidded and outlined and thickly-fringed eyes of a person she had never seen before. She was afraid even to blink, for fear that this applied face would crack and flake with the strain. "Thank you," she said doubtfully.

"Now smile," said Ainsley.

Marian smiled.

Ainsley frowned. "Not like *that*," she said. "You've got to throw yourself *into* it more. Sort of droop your eyelids."

Marian was embarrassed: she didn't know how. She was experimenting, looking in the mirror, trying to find out which particular set of muscles would produce the desired effect, and had just succeeded in getting an approximate droop that still however had a suggestion of squint in it, when they heard footsteps ascending the stairs; and a moment later the lady down below stood in the doorway, breathing heavily.

Marian removed the towel from her neck and stood up. Now that she had got her eyelids drooped she could not immediately get them undrooped again, back to their usual capable and level width. It was going to be impossible in this red dress and this face to behave with the ordinary matter-of-fact politeness that the situation was going to require.

The lady down below gasped a little when she saw Marian's new ensemble—bare arms and barish dress and well-covered face—but her real target was Ainsley, who stood bare-footed in her slip with one eye black-ringed and her auburn hair tendrilling over her shoulders.

"Miss Tewce," the lady down below began. She was still wearing her tea-dress and her pearls: she was going to attempt dignity. "I have waited until I am perfectly calm to speak to you. I don't want any unpleasantness, I've always tried to avoid scenes and unpleasantness, but now I'm afraid you'll have to go." She was not at all calm: her voice was trembling. Marian noticed that she was clenching a lace handkerchief in one hand. "The drinking was bad enough, I know all those bottles were yours, I'm sure Miss MacAlpin never drank, not more than one should"—her eyes flicked again over Marian's dress; her faith was somewhat shaken, but she let the comment pass—"though at least you were fairly discreet about all the liquor you were carrying into the house; and I couldn't say anything about the untidyness and disorder, I'm a tolerant person and what a person does in their own living-quarters has always been entirely their own

229

business as far as I'm concerned. And I turned the other way when that young man as I'm prefectly aware, don't try to *lie* to me, was here overnight, I even went out the next morning to avoid unpleasantness. At least the child didn't know. But to make it so public"—she was shrilling now, in a vibrant accusing voice—"dragging your disreputable, drunken friends out into the open, where people can *see* them . . . and it's such a bad example for the child. . . ."

Ainsley glared at her; the black-rimmed eye flashed. "So," she said in an equally accusing voice, tossing back her hair and planting her bare feet further apart on the floor, "I've always suspected you of being a hypocrite and now I know. You're a bourgeois fraud, you have no real convictions at all, you're just worried about what the neighbours will say. Your precious reputation. Well, I consider that kind of thing immoral. I'd like you to know that *I'm* going to have a child too, and I certainly wouldn't choose to bring him up in *this* house—you'd teach him dishonesty. You'd be a bad example, and let me tell you that you're by far the most anti-Creative-Life-Force person I've ever met. I will be most pleased to move and the sooner the better; I don't want you exerting any negative pre-natal influences."

The lady down below had turned quite pale. "Oh," she said faintly, clutching at her pearls. "A baby! Oh, oh, oh!" She turned, emitting small cries of outrage and dismay, and tottered away down the stairs.

"I guess you'll have to move," said Marian. She felt safely remote from this fresh complication. She was leaving for home the next day anyway; and now that the lady down below had finally forced a confrontation she couldn't imagine why she had ever been even slightly afraid of her. She had been so easily deflated.

"Yes, of course," Ainsley said calmly, and sat down and began to outline her other eye.

Downstairs the doorbell rang.

"That must be Peter," Marian said, "already." She had no idea it was so late. "I'm supposed to go over with him and help get things ready—I wish we could give you a ride, but I don't think we'll be able to wait."

"That's okay," said Ainsley, drawing a long gracefully-curved artistic eyebrow on her forehead in the place where hers ought to have been. "I'll come on later. I've got some things to do anyway. If it's too cold for the baby I can always take a taxi, it isn't that far."

Marian went into the kitchen, where she had left her coat. I really should have eaten something, she said to herself, it's bad to drink on an empty stomach. She could hear Peter coming up the stairs. She took another vitamin pill. They were brown, oval-shaped, with pointed ends: like hard-cased brown seeds. I wonder what they grind up to put into these things, she thought as she swallowed.

26

☐ Peter unlocked the glass door with his key and fixed the latch so that the door would remain open for the guests. Then they stepped into the lobby and walked together across the wide tiled floor towards the staircase. The elevator was not yet in working order, though Peter said it would be the end of next week. The service elevator was running but the workmen kept it locked.

The apartment building was almost finished. Each time Marian had come there she had been able to notice a minor alteration. Gradually the clutter of raw materials, pipes and rough boards and cement blocks, had disappeared, transmuted by an invisible process of digestion and assimilation into the shining skins that enclosed the space through which they were moving. The walls and the line of square supporting pillars had been painted a deep orange-pink; the lighting had been installed, and was blazing now at its full cold strength, since Peter had turned the lobby switches on for his party. The floor-length mirrors on the pillars were new since the last time she had been there; they made the lobby seem larger, much longer than it really was. But the carpets, the furniture (imitation-leather sofas, she predicted) and the inevitable broad-leaved philodendrons twining around pieces of driftwood had not yet arrived. They would be the final rich layer, and would add a touch of softness, however synthetic, to this corridor of hard light and brittle surfaces.

They ascended the staircase together, Marian leaning on Peter's arm. In the hallways of each floor they passed as they went up Marian could see gigantic wooden crates and oblong canvas-covered shapes standing outside the apartment doors: they must be installing the kitchen equipment, the stoves and refrigerators. Soon Peter would no longer be the only person living in the building. Then they would turn the heat up to its full capacity; as it was, the building, all except Peter's place, was kept almost as cold as the outside air.

"Darling," she said in a casual tone when they had reached the fifth floor and were pausing for a moment on the landing to catch their breath, "something came up and I've invited a few more people. I hope you don't mind."

All the way there in the car she had been pondering how she would tell him. It would not be a good thing for those people to arrive with Peter now knowing anything about it, though it had been a great temptation to say nothing, to rely on her ability to cope with the situation when the moment came. In the confusion she would not have to explain how she had come to invite them, she didn't want to explain, she couldn't explain, and she dreaded questions from Peter about it. Suddenly she felt totally without her usual skill at calculating his reactions in advance. He had become an unknown quantity; just after she had spoken, blind rage and blind ecstasy on his part seemed equally possible. She took a step away from him and gripped the railing with her free hand: there was no telling what he might do.

But he only smiled down at her, a slight crease of concealed irritation appearing between his eyebrows. "Did you, darling? Well the more the merrier. But I hope you didn't ask too many: we won't have enough liquor to go around, and if there's anything I hate it's a party that goes dry."

Marian was relieved. Now he had spoken she saw that it was exactly what he would have said. She was so pleased with him for answering predictably that she pressed his arm. He slid it around her waist, and they be-

232

gan to climb again. "No," she said, "only about six." Actually there were nine, but since he had been so polite about it she made the courteous gesture of minimizing.

"Anyone I know?" he asked pleasantly.

"Well . . . Clara and Joe," she said, her momentary elation beginning to vanish. "And Ainsley. But not the others: not really. . . ."

"My, my," he said, teasing, "I wasn't aware you had that many friends I've never met. Been keeping little secrets, eh? I'll have to make a special point of getting to know them so I can find out all about your private life." He kissed her ear genially.

"Yes," Marian said, with feeble cheerfulness. "I'm sure you'll like them." Idiot, she raged at herself. Idiot, idiot. How could she have been so stupid? She foresaw how it was going to be. The office virgins would be all right— Peter would just look somewhat askance at them, particularly Emmy; and Clara and Joe would be tolerated. But the others. Duncan would not give her away—or would he? He might think it was funny to drop an insinuating remark; or he might do it out of curiosity. She could take him aside when he arrived though and ask him not to. But the room-mates were an insoluble problem. She did not think either of them knew yet that she was engaged, and she could picture Trevor's shriek of surprise when he found out, the way he would glance at Duncan and say, "But my dear, *we* thought . . ." and trail off into a silence weighted with innuendoes that would be even more dangerous than the truth. Peter would be furious, he would think someone had been infringing on his private property rights, he wouldn't understand at all, and what would happen then? Why in heaven's name had she invited them? What a colossal mistake; how could she stop them from coming?

They reached the seventh floor and walked along the corridor towards the door of Peter's apartment. He had spread several newspapers outside his door for people to put their overshoes and boots on. Marian took off her own boots and stood them neatly beside Peter's overshoes. "I hope they'll follow our example," Peter said. "I just had the floors done, I don't want them getting all

233

tracked up." With no others beside them yet, the two pairs looked like black leathery bait in a large empty newspaper trap.

Inside, Peter took off her coat for her. He put his hands on her bare shoulders and kissed her lightly on the back of the neck. "Yum yum," he said, "new perfume." Actually it was Ainsley's, an exotic mixture she had selected to go with the ear-rings.

He took off his own coat and hung it up in the closet just inside the door. "Take your coat into the bedroom, darling," he said, "and then come on out to the kitchen and help me get things ready. Women are so much better at arranging things on plates."

She walked across the living room floor. The only addition Peter had made to its furniture recently was another matching Danish-modern chair; most of the space was still unoccupied. At least it meant that the guests would have to circulate: there wasn't room for all of them to sit down. Peter's friends did not, as a rule, sit on floors until rather late in the evening. Duncan might though. She imagined him crosslegged in the centre of the bare room, a cigarette stuck in his mouth, staring with gloomy incredulity perhaps at one of the soap-men or at one of the Danish-modern sofa legs while the other guests circled around him, not noticing him much but being careful not to step on him, as though he were a coffee table or a conversation-piece of some kind: a driftwood-and-parchment mobile. Maybe it wasn't too late to phone them and ask them not to come. But the phone was in the kitchen and so was Peter.

The bedroom was meticulously neat as always. The books and the guns were in their usual places; four of Peter's model ships now served as book-ends. Two of the cameras had been taken out of their cases and were standing on the desk. One of them had a flash-attachment on it with a blue flashbulb already clipped inside the silver saucer-shaped reflector. More of the blue bulbs were lying near an opened magazine. Marian placed her coat on the bed; Peter had told her that the coat closet by the door wouldn't be large enough for all the coats and that the women were to put their coats in his bedroom. Her coat

234

then, lying with its arms at its sides, was really more functional than it looked: it was acting as a sort of decoy for the other coats. By it they would see where they were supposed to go.

She turned, and saw herself reflected in the full-length mirror on the back of the cupboard door. Peter had been so surprised and pleased. "Darling, you look absolutely marvellous," he had said as soon as he had come up through the stairwell. The implication had been that it would be most pleasant if she could arrange to look like that all the time. He had made her turn around so he could see the back, and he had liked that too. Now she wondered whether or not she did look absolutely marvellous. She turned the phrase over in her mind: it had no specific shape or flavour. What should it feel like? She smiled at herself. No, that wouldn't do. She smiled a different smile, drooping her eyelids; that didn't quite work either. She turned her head and examined her profile out of the corner of her eye. The difficulty was that she couldn't grasp the total effect: her attention caught on the various details, the things she wasn't used to—the fingernails, the heavy ear-rings, the hair, the various parts of her face that Ainsley had added or altered. She was only able to see one thing at a time. What was it that lay beneath the surface these pieces were floating on, holding them all together? She held both of her naked arms out towards the mirror. They were the only portion of her flesh that was without a cloth or nylon or leather or varnish covering, but in the glass even they looked fake, like soft pinkish-white rubber or plastic, boneless, flexible. . . .

Annoyed with herself for slipping back towards her earlier panic, she opened the cupboard door to turn the mirror to the wall and found herself staring at Peter's clothes. She had seen them often enough before, so there was no particular reason why she should stand, one hand on the edge of the door, gazing into the dark cupboard. . . . The clothes were hanging neatly in a row. She recognized all the costumes she had ever seen Peter wearing, except of course the dark winter suit he had on at the moment: there was his midsummer aspect, beside it his tweedy casual jacket that went with his grey flannels, and then the series of his other phases from late summer through fall. The matching shoes were lined up on the floor, each with its own personal shoe-tree inside. She realized that she was regarding the clothes with an emotion close to something like resentment. How could they hang there smugly asserting so much invisible silent authority? But on second thought it was more like fear. She reached out a hand to touch them, and drew it back: she was almost afraid they would be warm.

"Darling, where are you?" Peter called from the kitchen.

"Coming, darling," she called back. She shut the cupboard door hastily, glanced into the mirror and patted one of her fronds back into place, and went to join him, walking carefully inside her finely-adjusted veneers.

The kitchen table was covered with glassware. Some of it was new: he must have bought it especially for the party. Well, they would always be able to use it after they were married. The counters held rows of bottles in different colours and sizes: scotch, rye, gin. Peter seemed to have everything well under control. He was giving some of the glasses a final polish with a clean teatowel.

"Anything I can do to help?" she asked.

"Yes darling, why don't you fix up some of these things on some dishes? Here, I've poured you a drink, scotch and water, we might as well get a head start." He himself had wasted no time; his own glass was standing half-empty on the counter.

She sipped at her drink, smiling at him over the rim. It was far too strong for her; it burnt as it went down her throat. "I think you're trying to get me drunk," she said. "Could I have another icecube?" She noticed with distaste that her mouth had left a greasy print on the rim of the glass.

"There's lots of ice in the fridge," he said, sounding pleased that she felt in need of dilution.

The ice was in a large bowl. There was more in reserve, two polyethylene bags. The rest of the space was taken up by bottles, bottles of beer stacked on the bottom shelf, tall green bottles of gingerale and short colourless bottles of tonic water and soda on the shelves beside the freezing

236

compartment. His refrigerator was so white and spotless and arranged; she thought with guilt of her own.

She busied herself with the potato chips and peanuts and olives and cocktail mushrooms, filling the bowls and platters that Peter had indicated, handling the foods with the very ends of her fingers so as not to get her nail-polish dirty. When she had almost finished Peter came up behind her. He put one arm around her waist. With the other hand he half-undid the zipper of her dress; then he did it back up again. She could feel him breathing down the back of her neck.

"Too bad we don't have time to hop into bed," he said, "but I wouldn't want to get you all mussed up. Oh well, plenty of time for that later." He put his other arm around her waist.

"Peter," she said, "do you love me?" She had asked him that before as a kind of joke, not doubting the answer. But this time she waited, not moving, to hear what he would say.

He kissed her lightly on the ear-ring. "Of course I love you, don't be silly," he said in a fond tone that indicated he thought he was humouring her. "I'm going to marry you, aren't I? And I love you especially in that red dress. You should wear red more often." He let go of her, and she transferred the last of the pickled mushrooms from the bottle to the plate.

"Come in here a minute, darling," his voice called. He was in the bedroom. She rinsed off her hands, dried them, and went to join him. He had switched on his desk lamp and was sitting at the desk adjusting one of his cameras. He looked up at her, smiling. "Thought I'd get some pictures of the party, just for the record," he said. "They'll be fun to have later, to look back on. This is our first real party together, you know; quite an occasion. By the way, have you got a photographer for the wedding yet?"

"I don't know," she said, "I think they have."

"I'd like to do it myself, but of course that's impossible," he said with a laugh. He began doing things to his light meter.

She leaned affectionately against his shoulder, glancing over it at the objects on the desk, the blue flashbulbs, the concave silver circle of the flashgun. He was consulting the open magazine; he had marked the article entitled, "Indoors Flash Lighting". Beside the column of print there was an advertisement: a little girl with pigtails on a beach, clutching a spaniel. "Treasure It Forever," the caption read.

She walked over to the window and looked down. Below was the white city, its narrow streets and its cold winter lights. She was holding her drink in one of her hands; she sipped at it. The ice tinkled against the glass.

"Darling," Peter said, "it's almost zero-hour, but before they come I'd like to get a couple of shots of you alone, if you don't mind. There are only a few exposures left on this roll and I want to put a new one in for the party. That red ought to show up well on a slide, and I'll get some black-and-whites too while I'm at it."

"Peter," she said hesitantly, "I don't think. . . ." The suggestion had made her unreasonably anxious.

"Now don't be modest," he said. "Could you just stand over there by the guns and lean back a little against the wall?" He turned the desk-lamp around so that the light was on her face and held the small black light-meter out towards her. She backed against the wall.

He raised the camera and squinted through the tiny glass window at the top; he was adjusting the lens, getting her in focus. "Now," he said. "could you stand a little less stiffly? Relax. And don't hunch your shoulders together like that, come on, stick out your chest, and don't look so worried darling, look natural, come on, smile. . . ."

Her body had frozen, gone rigid. She couldn't move, she couldn't even move the muscles of her face as she stood and stared into the round glass lens pointing towards her, she wanted to tell him not to touch the shutter-release but she couldn't move. . . .

There was a knock at the door.

"Oh damn," Peter said. He set the camera on the desk. "Here they come. Well, later then, darling." He went out of the room.

Marian came slowly from the corner. She was breathing quickly. She reached out one hand, forcing herself to touch it.

"What's the matter with me?" she said to herself. "It's only a camera."

27

☐ The first to arrive were the three office virgins, Lucy alone, Emmy and Millie almost simultaneously five minutes later. They were evidently not expecting to see each other there: each seemed annoyed that the others had been invited. Marian performed the introductions and led them to the bedroom, where their coats joined hers on the bed. Each of them said in a peculiar tone of voice that Marian should wear red more often. Each glanced at herself in the mirror, preening and straightening, before going out to the living room. Lucy refrosted her mouth and Emmy scratched hurriedly at her scalp.

They lowered themselves carefully onto the Danish-modern furniture and Peter got them drinks. Lucy was in purple velvet, with silver eyelids and false lashes; Emmy was in pink chiffon, faintly suggestive of high-school formals. Her hair had been sprayed into stiff wisps and her slip was showing. Millie was encased in pale blue satin which bulged in odd places; she had a tiny sequin-covered evening-bag, and sounded the most nervous of the three.

"I'm so glad you could all come," Marian said. At that moment she was not at all glad. They were so excited. They were each expecting a version of Peter to walk miraculously through the door, drop to one knee and propose. What would they do when confronted with Fish and Trevor, not to mention Duncan? Moreover, what would Fish and Trevor, not to mention Duncan, do when confronted with *them*? She pictured two trios of screams and a mass exodus, one set through the door and one through the window. What have I done now? she thought. But she had almost ceased to believe in the existence of the three graduate students; they were becoming more and more

239

improbable as the evening and the scotch wore on. Maybe they would just never show up.

The soap-men and their wives were filtering in. Peter had put a record on the hi-fi and the room was noisier and more crowded. Every time there was a knock on the door the three office virgins swivelled their heads towards the entrance; and every time they saw another successful and glittering wife step into the room with her sleek husband, they turned back, a little more frantic, to their drinks and their interchange of strained comments. Emmy was fiddling with one of her rhinestone ear-rings. Millie picked at a loose sequin on her evening-bag.

Marian, smiling and efficient, led each wife to the bedroom. The pile of coats grew higher. Peter got everybody drinks and had a number of them himself. The peanuts and potato chips and other things were circulating from hand to hand, from hand to mouth. Already the group in the living room was beginning to divide itself into the standard territories, wives on the sofa-side of the room, men on the hi-fi side, an invisible no-man's-land between. The office virgins had got stuck on the wrong side: they listened unhappily to the wives. Marian felt another pang of remorse. But she couldn't attend to them right now, she thought: she was passing the pickled mushrooms. She wondered what was keeping Ainsley.

The door opened again, and Clara and Joe walked into the room. Behind them was Leonard Slank. Marian's nerves twitched, and one of the cocktail mushrooms fell from the plate she was carrying, bounced along the floor, and disappeared under the hi-fi set. She set down the plate. Peter was already greeting them, shaking Len's hand effusively. His voice was getting louder with every drink. "How the hell are you, good to see you here, god I've been meaning to call you up," he was saying. Len responded with a lurch and a glazed stare.

Marian clamped her hand firmly on Clara's coatsleeve and hustled her into the bedroom. "What's *he* doing here?" she asked, rather ungraciously.

Clara took off her coat. "I hope you don't mind us bringing him, I didn't think you would because after all you're old friends, but really I thought we'd better, we didn't want him going off somewhere alone. As you can see, he's in piss-poor shape. He turned up just after the baby-sitter got there and he looked really awful, he'd obviously had a lot. He told us an incoherent story about some woman he's been having trouble with, it sounded quite serious, and he said he was afraid to go back to the apartment, I don't know why, what could anybody do to him? So, poor thing, we're going to keep him up in that back room on the second floor. It's Arthur's room really, but I'm sure Len won't mind sharing. We both feel so sorry for him, what he needs is some nice home-loving type who'll take care of him, he doesn't seem to be able to cope at all. . . ."

"Did he say who she was?" Marian asked quickly.

"Why no," Clara said, raising her eyebrows, "he doesn't usually tell the names."

"Let me get you a drink," Marian said. She was feeling like another one herself. Of course Clara and Joe couldn't have known who the woman was or they never would have brought Len with them. She was surprised he had even come; he must have known there was a good chance Ainsley would be at the party, but probably by this time he was too far gone to care. What worried her most was the effect his presence might have on Ainsley. It might upset her enough to make her do something unstable.

When they reached the living room, Marian saw that Leonard had been spotted at once by the office virgins as single and available. They had him backed against the wall in the neuter area now, two of them on the sides cutting off flank escape and the third, in front. He had one of his hands pressed against the wall for balance; the other held a glass stein full of beer. While they talked he shifted his gaze continually from face to face as though he didn't want to remain looking for too long at any one of them. His own face, which was the flat whitish-grey colour of uncooked piecrust and oddly bloated, expressed a combination of sodden incredulity, boredom, and alarm. But they seemed to have pried a few words out of him, because Marian heard Lucy exclaim, "Television! How exciting!" while the others giggled tensely. Leonard swallowed a desperate mouthful of beer.

Marian was passing the ripe olives when she saw Joe coming towards her from the men's territory. "Hi," he said to her. "I'm very glad you asked us here tonight. Clara has so few chances to get out of the house."

Both of them turned their eyes towards Clara, who was over at the sofa-side of the room, talking with one of the soap-wives.

"I worry about her a lot, you know," Joe continued. "I think it's a lot harder for her than for most other women; I think it's harder for any woman who's been to university. She gets the idea she has a mind, her professors pay attention to what she has to say, they treat her like a thinking human being; when she gets married, her core gets invaded. . . ."

"Her what?" Marian asked.

"Her core. The centre of her personality, the thing she's built up; her image of herself, if you like."

"Oh. Yes," said Marian.

"Her feminine role and her core are really in opposition; her feminine role demands passivity from her. . . ."

Marian had a fleeting vision of a large globular pastry, decorated with whipped cream and maraschino cherries, floating suspended in the air above Joe's head.

"So she allows her core to get taken over by the husband. And when the kids come, she wakes up one morning and discovers she doesn't have anything left inside, she's hollow, she doesn't know who she is any more; her core has been destroyed." He shook his head gently and sipped at his drink. "I can see it happening with my own female students. But it would be futile to warn them."

Marian turned to look at Clara where she stood talking, dressed in simple beige, her long hair a delicate pear-pale yellow. She wondered whether Joe had ever told Clara her core had been destroyed; she thought of apples and worms. As she watched, Clara made an emphatic gesture with one of her hands and a soap-wife stepped back looking shocked.

"Of course it doesn't help to realize all that," Joe was saying. "It happens, whether you realize it or not. Maybe women shouldn't be allowed to go to university at all;

then they wouldn't always be feeling later on that they've missed out on the life of the mind. For instance when I suggest to Clara that she should go out and do something about it, like taking a night course, she just gives me a funny look."

Marian looked up at Joe with an affection the precise flavour of which was blurred by the drinks she had had. She thought of him shuffling about the house in his undershirt, meditating on the life of the mind and doing the dishes and tearing the stamps raggedly off the envelopes; she wondered what he did with the stamps after that. She wanted to reach out and touch him, reassure him, tell him Clara's core hadn't really been destroyed and everything would be all right; she wanted to give him something. She thrust forward the plate she was holding. "Have an olive," she said.

Behind Joe's back the door was opened and Ainsley came through it. "Excuse me," Marian said to Joe. She set the olives on the hi-fi set and went over to intercept Ainsley; she had to warn her.

"Hi," Ainsley said breathlessly. "Sorry I'm later than I thought but I got this urge to start packing. . . ."

Marian hurried her into the bedroom, hoping that Len hadn't seen her. She noted in passing that he was still fully enclosed.

"Ainsley," she said when they were alone with the coats, "Len's here and I'm afraid he's drunk."

Ainsley unswathed herself. She looked magnificent. She was dressed in a shade of green that bordered on turquoise, with eyelids and shoes to match; her hair coiled and shone, swirled around her head. Her skin glowed, irradiated with many hormones; her stomach was not yet noticeably bulbous.

She studied herself in the mirror before answering. "Well?" she said calmly, widening her eyes. "Really Marian, it doesn't matter to me in the least. After that talk this afternoon I'm sure we know where we stand and we can both behave like mature adults. There's nothing he could say now that could disturb me."

"But," said Marian, "he seems quite upset; that's what Clara says. Apparently he's gone to stay at their place. I

243

saw him when he came in, he looks terrible; so I hope you won't say anything that could disturb *him*."

"There's no reason at all," Ainsley said lightly, "why I should even talk to him."

In the living room the soapmen on their side of the invisible fence were becoming quite boisterous. They gave forth bursts of laughter: one of them was telling dirty jokes. The women's voices too were rising in pitch and volume, soaring in strident competitive descants over the baritone and bass. When Ainsley appeared, there was a general surge towards her: some of the soapmen predictably deserted their side and came to be introduced, and the corresponding wives, ever alert, rose from the sofa and took rapid steps to head them off at the pass. Ainsley smiled vacantly.

Marian went into the kitchen to get a drink for Ainsley and another one for herself. The previous order of the kitchen, the neat rows of glasses and bottles, had disintegrated in the process of the evening. The sink was full of melting icecubes and shreds of food, people never seemed to know what to do with their olive-pits, and the pieces of a broken glass; bottles were standing, empty and partially-empty, on the counters and the table and the top of the refrigerator; and something unidentifiable had been spilled on the floor. But there were still some clean glasses. Marian filled one for Ainsley.

As she was going out of the kitchen she heard voices in the bedroom.

"You're even handsomer than you sound on the phone." It was Lucy's voice.

Marian glanced into the bedroom. Lucy was in there, gazing up at Peter from under her silver lids. He was standing with a camera in his hand grinning boyishly, though somewhat foolishly, down at her. So Lucy had abandoned the siege of Leonard. She must have realized it was futile, she had always been more astute about those things than the other two. But how touching of her to try instead for Peter; pathetic, actually. After all Peter was off the market almost as definitely as if he was already married.

Marian smiled to herself and retreated, but not before
244

Peter had spotted her and called, waving the camera, his face guiltily over-cheerful. "Hi honey, the party's really going! Almost picture-time!" Lucy turned her head towards the doorway, smiling, her eyelids raising themselves like window shades.

"Here's your drink, Ainsley," Marian said, breaking through the circle of soapmen to hand it.

"Thanks," said Ainsley. She took it with a certain abstraction that Marian sensed as a danger-signal. She followed the direction of Ainsley's gaze. Len was staring across the room towards them, his mouth slightly open. Millie and Emmy were still tenaciously holding him at bay. Millie had moved round to the front, blocking as much space with her wide skirt as possible and Emmy was side-stepping back and forth like a basketball guard; but one of the flanks was unprotected. Marian looked back in time to see Ainsley smile: an inviting smile.

There was a knock on the door. I'd better get it, Marian thought, Peter's busy in the bedroom.

She opened the door and found herself confronting Trevor's puzzled face. The other two were behind him, and an unfamiliar figure, probably female, in a baggy Harris-tweed coat, sunglasses and long black stockings. "Is this the right number?" Trevor asked. "A Mr. Peter Wollander?" He evidently did not recognize her.

Marian blenched inwardly; she had forgotten all about them. Oh well, there was so much noise and chaos in there anyway that Peter might not even notice them.

"Oh, I'm so glad you could come," she said. "Do come in. By the way, I'm Marian."

"Oh, hahaha, of *course,*" shrilled Trevor. "How stupid of me! I didn't recognize you, my dear you look elegant, you should really wear red more often."

Trevor and Fish and the other one passed by her into the room, but Duncan remained outside. He took hold of her arm, tugged her into the hall, and closed the door behind her.

He stood for a moment peering silently at her from under his hair, examining every new detail. "You didn't tell me it was a masquerade," he said at last. "Who the hell are you supposed to be?"

Marian let her shoulders sag with despair. So she didn't look absolutely marvellous after all. "You've just never seen me dressed up before," she said weakly.

Duncan began to snicker. "I like the ear-rings best," he said, "where did you dredge them up?"

"Oh stop that," she said with a trace of petulance, "and come inside and have a drink." He was very irritating. What did he expect her to wear, sackcloth and ashes? She opened the door.

The sound of talking and music and laughter swelled into the corridor. Then there was a bright flash of light, and a loud voice cried triumphantly, "Aha! Caught you in the act!"

"That's Peter," Marian said, "he must be taking pictures."

Duncan stepped back. "I don't think I want to go in there," he said.

"But you *have* to. You have to meet Peter, I'd like you to really." It was suddenly very important that he come with her.

"No no," he said, "I can't. It would be a bad thing, I can tell. One of us would be sure to evaporate, it would probably be me; anyway it's too loud in there, I couldn't take it."

"*Please*," she said. She was reaching for his arm, but already he was turning, almost running back down the corridor.

"Where are you going?" she called after him plaintively.

"To the laundromat!" he called back. "Good-bye, have a nice marriage," he added. She caught a last glimpse of his twisted smile as he rounded the corner. She could hear his footsteps retreating down the stairs.

For an instant she wanted to run after him, to go with him: surely she could not face the crowded room again. But, "I have to," she said to herself. She walked back through the doorway.

The first thing she encountered was Fischer Smythe's broad woolly back. He was wearing an aggressively-casual striped turtleneck sweater. Trevor, standing beside him, was immaculately suited, shirted and tied. They were both talking to the creature in the black stockings: something about death-symbols. She sidestepped the group deftly, not wanting to be forced to account for Duncan's disappearance.

She discovered that she was standing behind Ainsley, and realized after a minute that Leonard Slank was on the other side of that rounded bluegreen form. She couldn't see his face, Ainsley's hair was in the way, but she recognized his arm and the hand holding the beer stein: freshly filled, she noted. Ainsley was saying something to him in a low urgent voice.

She heard his slurred answer: "NO, dammit! You'll never get me. . . ."

"Alright then." Before Marian realized what Ainsley was doing she had raised her hand and brought it down, hard, smashing her glass against the floor. Marian jumped back.

At the sound of shattering glass the conversation stopped as though its plug had been pulled out, and Ainsley said into the silence that was filled, incongruously, only by the soft sighing of violins, "Len and I have a marvellous announcement to make." She hesitated for effect, her eyes glittering. "We're going to have a baby." Her voice was bland. Oh dear, Marian thought, she's trying to force the issue.

There were a few audible gasps from the sofa-side of the room. Somebody sniggered, and one of the soapmen said, "Atta boy Len, whoever you are." Marian could see Len's face now. The white surface had developed a random scattering of red blotches; the underlip was quivering.

"You rotten bitch!" he said thickly.

There was a pause. One of the soap-wives began a rapid conversation about something else, but trailed off quickly. Marian watched Len: she thought he was going to hit Ainsley, but instead he smiled, showing his teeth. He turned to the listening multitudes.

"That's right folks," he said, "and we're going to have the christening right now, in the midst of this friendly little gathering. Baptism in utero. I hereby name it after me." He shot out one hand and grasped Ainsley's shoul-

247

der, lifted his beer stein, and poured its contents slowly and thoroughly over her head.

The soap-wives all gave delighted screams; the soap-men bellowed "Hey!" As the last of the suds were descending, Peter came charging in from the bedroom, jamming a flashbulb into his camera. "Hold it!" he shouted, and shot. "Great! That'll be a great one! Hey, this party's really getting off the ground!"

Several people gave him annoyed glances, but most paid no attention. Everyone was moving and talking at once; in the background the violins still played, saccharine-sweet. Ainsley was standing there, drenched, a puddle of foam and beer forming at her feet on the hardwood floor. Her face contorted: in a minute she would have decided whether it would be worth the effort to cry. Len had let go of her. His head dropped; he mumbled something inaudible. He looked as though he had only an imperfect idea of what he had just done and no idea at all of what he was going to do next.

Ainsley turned and started to walk towards the bathroom. Several of the soap-wives trotted forward, uttering throaty cooing noises, eager to share the spotlight by helping; but someone was there before them. It was Fischer Smythe. He was pulling his woolly turtleneck sweater over his head, exposing a muscular torso covered with quantities of tufted black fur.

"Allow me," he said to her, "we wouldn't want you to catch a chill, would we? Not in your condition." He began to dry her off with his sweater. His eyes were damp with solicitude.

Ainsley's hair had come down and was lying in dripping strands over her shoulders. She smiled up at him through the beer or tears beading her eyelashes. "I don't believe we've met," she said.

"I think I already know who you are," he said, patting her belly tenderly with one of his striped sleeves, his voice heavy with symbolic meaning.

It was later. The party, miraculously, was still going on, having somehow closed itself smoothly together over the rent made in it earlier by Ainsley and Len. Someone had cleaned the broken glass and beer off the floor, and in the

248

living room now the currents of talk and music and drink were flowing again as though nothing had happened.

The kitchen however was a scene of devastation. It looked as though it had been hit by a flash-flood. Marian was scrabbling through the debris, trying to locate a clean glass; she had set her own down there somewhere, she couldn't remember where, and she wanted another drink.

There weren't any more clean glasses. She picked up a used one, swished it under the tap, slowly and carefully poured herself another shot of scotch. She felt serene, a floating sensation, like lying on one's back in a pond. She went to the doorway and leaned in it, gazing out over the room.

"I'm coping! I'm coping!" she said to herself. The fact amazed her somewhat, but it pleased her immensely. They were all there, all of them (except, she noted as she scanned, Ainsley and Fischer, and oh yes Len—she wondered where they had gone), doing whatever people did at parties; and she was doing it, too. They were sustaining her, she could float quite watertight, buoyed up by the feeling that she was one of them. She had a warm affection for them all, for their distinct shapes and faces that she could see now so much more clearly than usual, as though they were being illuminated by a hidden floodlight. She even liked the soap-wives and Trevor gesturing with one of his hands; and those people from the office, Millie, laughing over there in her shining light-blue dress, even Emmy, moving unconscious of her frazzled slip-edge. . . . Peter was among them too; he was still carrying his camera and every now and then he would raise it to take a picture. He reminded her of the home-movie ads, the father of the family using up rolls and rolls of film on just such everyday ordinary things, what subjects could be better: people laughing, lifting glasses, children at birthday-parties. . . .

So that's what was in there all the time, she thought happily: this is what he's turning into. The real Peter, the one underneath, was nothing surprising or frightening, only this bungalow-and-double-bed man, this charcoal-cooking-in-the-backyard man. This home-movie man.

And I called him out, she thought, I evoked him. She swallowed some of her scotch.

It had been a long search. She retraced through time the corridors and rooms, long corridors, large rooms. Everything seemed to be slowing down.

If that's who Peter really is, she thought, walking along one of the corridors, will he have a pot-belly at forty-five? Will he dress sloppily on Saturdays, in wrinkled blue jeans for his workshop in the cellar? The image was reassuring: he would have hobbies, he would be comfortable, he would be normal.

She opened the door to the right and went in. There was Peter, forty-five and balding but still recognizable as Peter, standing in bright sunlight beside a barbecue with a long fork in his hand. He was wearing a white chef's apron. She looked carefully for herself in the garden, but she wasn't there and the discovery chilled her.

No, she thought, this has to be the wrong room. It can't be the last one. And now she could see there was another door, in the hedge at the other side of the garden. She walked across the lawn, passing behind the unmoving figure, which she could see now held a large cleaver in the other hand, pushed open the door and went through.

She was back in Peter's living room with the people and the noise, leaning against the doorframe holding her drink. Except that the people seemed even clearer now, more sharply focussed, further away, and they were moving faster and faster, they were all going home, a file of soapwomen emerged from the bedroom, coats on, they teetered jerkily out the door trailing husbands, chirping goodnights, and who was that tiny two-dimensional small figure in a red dress, posed like a paper woman in a mail-order catalogue, turning and smiling, fluttering in the white empty space. . . . This couldn't be it; there had to be something more. She ran for the next door, yanked it open.

Peter was there, dressed in his dark opulent winter suit. He had a camera in his hand; but now she saw what it really was. There were no more doors and when she felt behind for the doorknob, afraid to take her eyes off him, he raised the camera and aimed it at her; his mouth opened in a snarl of teeth. There was a blinding flash of light.

"No!" she screamed. She covered her face with her arm.

"What's the matter, darling?" She looked up. Peter was standing beside her. He was real. She put up her hand and touched his face.

"It startled me," she said.

"You really can't hold your liquor, can you darling," he said, fondness and irritation blending in his voice. "You should be used to it, I've been taking pictures all evening."

"Was that one of me?" she asked. She smiled at him in conciliation. She sensed her face as vastly spreading and papery and slightly dilapidated: a huge billboard smile, peeling away in flaps and patches, the metal surface beneath showing through. . . .

"No, actually it was of Trigger over at the other side of the room. Never mind, I'll get you later. But you'd better not have another drink darling, you're swaying." He patted her on the shoulder and walked away.

She was still safe then. She had to get out before it was too late. She turned and set her drink down on the kitchen table, her mind suddenly rendered cunning by desperation. It all depended on getting as far as Duncan: he would know what to do.

She glanced around the kitchen, then picked up her glass and poured its contents down the sink. She would be careful, she would leave no clues. Then she picked up the telephone and dialled Duncan's number. The phone rang and rang: no answer. She put it down. From the living room there was another flash of light, and the sound of Peter laughing. She should never have worn red. It made her a perfect target.

She edged into the bedroom. I must be sure not to forget anything, she told herself; I can't come back. Before, she had wondered what their bedroom would look like after they were married, trying out various arrangements and colour-schemes. Now she knew. It would always look exactly like this. She dug among the coats, looking for her own, and could not for a moment remember what it

251

looked like, but at last she recognized it and slipped it on; she avoided the mirror. She had no idea what time it was. She glanced at her wrist: it was blank. Of course; she had taken her watch off and left it at home because Ainsley said it didn't go with the total effect.

In the living room Peter was calling above the noise "Come on now, let's get a group portrait. Everybody all together."

She had to hurry. Now there was the living room to negotiate. She would have to become less visible. She took her coat back off and bundled it under her left arm, counting on her dress to act as a protective camouflage that would blend her with the scenery. Staying close to the wall, she made her way towards the door through the thicket of people, keeping behind the concealing trunks and bushes of backs and skirts. Peter was over at the other side of the room, trying to get them organized.

She opened the door and slid out; then, pausing only long enough to get her coat on again and to pick her overboots out from the tangle of trapped feet on the newspaper, she ran as fast as she could down the hallway towards the stairs. She could not let him catch her this time. Once he pulled the trigger she would be stopped, fixed indissolubly in that gesture, that single stance, unable to move or change.

She stopped on the sixth-floor landing to put on her boots, then continued down, holding on to the bannister for balance. Under the cloth and the metal bones and elastic her flesh felt numbed and compressed; it was difficult to walk, it took concentration.... I'm probably drunk, she thought. Funny I don't feel drunk; idiot, you know perfectly well what happens to drunk people's capillaries when they go out into the cold. But it was even more important to get away.

She reached the empty lobby. Although there was no one following her, she thought she could hear a sound; it was the thin sound glass would make, icy as the tinkle of a chandelier, it was the high electric vibration of this glittering space....

She was outside in the snow. Running along the street, the snow squeaking under her feet, as quickly as her hampered legs would move, balancing with her eyes on the sidewalk, in winter even level surfaces were precarious, she couldn't afford to fall down. Behind her even now Peter might be tracing, following, stalking her through the crisp empty streets as he had stalked his guests in the living room, waiting for the exact moment. That dark intent marksman with his aiming eye had been there all the time, hidden by the other layers, waiting for her at the dead centre: a homicidal maniac with a lethal weapon in his hands.

She slipped on a patch of ice and almost fell. When she had recovered her balance she looked behind. Nothing.

"Take it easy," she said, "keep calm." Her breath was coming in sharp gasps, crystallizing in the freezing air almost before it had left her throat. She continued on, more slowly. At first she had been running blindly; now however she knew exactly where she was going. "You'll be all right," she said to herself "if only you can make it as far as the laundromat."

28

☐ It had not occurred to her that Duncan might not be in the laundromat. When she finally reached it and pulled open the glass door, breathless but relieved at having got that far at all, it was a shock to find it empty. She couldn't believe it. She stood, confronted only by the long white row of machines, not knowing where to move. She hadn't considered the time beyond that imagined encounter.

Then she saw a wisp of smoke ascending from one of the chairs at the far end. It would have to be him. She walked forward.

He was sitting slouched so far down that only the top of his head was showing over the back of the chair, his eyes fixed on the round window of the machine directly in front of him. There was nothing inside it. He didn't look up as she sat down in the chair beside his.

"Duncan," she said. He didn't answer.

She took off her gloves and stretched out one of her hands, touching his wrist. He jumped.

"I'm here," she said.

He looked at her. His eyes were even more shadowed than usual, more deeply-sunk in the sockets, the skin of his face bloodless in the fluorescent light. "Oh. So you are. The Scarlet Woman herself. What time is it?"

"I don't know," she said, "I haven't got my watch on."

"What're you doing here? You're supposed to be at the party."

"I couldn't stay there any longer," she said. "I had to come and find you."

"Why?"

She couldn't think of a reason that wouldn't sound absurd. "Because I just wanted to be with you."

He looked at her suspiciously and took another drag on his cigarette. "Now listen, you should be back there. It's your duty, what's-his-name needs you."

"No, you need me more than he does."

As soon as she had said it, it sounded true. Immediately she felt noble.

He grinned. "No I don't. You think I need to be rescued but I don't. Anyway I don't like being a test-case for amateur social-workers." He shifted his eyes back to the washing-machine.

Marian fidgeted with the leather fingers of one of her gloves. "But I'm not trying to rescue you," she said. She realized he had tricked her into contradicting herself.

"Then maybe you want me to rescue you? What from? I thought you had it all worked out. And you know I'm totally inept anyway." He sounded faintly smug about his own helplessness.

"Oh, let's not talk about rescuing," Marian said desperately. "Can't we just go some place?" She wanted to get out. Even talking was impossible in this white room with its rows of glass windows and its all-pervading smell of soap and bleach.

"What's wrong with here?" he said. "I sort of like it here."

Marian wanted to shake him. "That isn't what I mean," she said.

254

"Oh," he said. "Oh, that. You mean tonight's the night, it's now or never." He dug out another cigarette and lit it. "Well, we can't go to my place, you know."

"We can't go to mine either." For a moment she wondered why not, she was moving out anyway. But Ainsley might turn up, or Peter. . . .

"We could stay here, it suggests interesting possibilities. Maybe inside one of the machines, we could hang your red dress over the window to keep out the dirty old men. . . ."

"Oh come on," she said, standing up.

He stood up too. "Okay, I'm flexible. I guess it's about time I found out the real truth. Where are we going?"

"I suppose," she said, "we will have to find some sort of hotel." She was vague about how they were going to get the thing accomplished, but tenaciously certain that it had to be done. It was the only way.

Duncan smiled wickedly. "You mean I'll have to pretend you're my wife?" he said. "In those ear-rings? They'll never believe it. They'll accuse you of corrupting a minor."

"I don't care," she said. She reached up and began to unscrew one of the ear-rings.

"Oh, leave them on for now," Duncan said. "You don't want to spoil the effect."

When they were outside on the street she had a sudden horrible thought. "Oh no," she said, standing still.

"What's the matter?"

"I don't have any money!" Of course she hadn't thought she would need any for the party. She had only her evening-bag with her, stuffed in a coat pocket. She felt the energy that had been propelling her through the streets, through this conversation, draining away. She was powerless, paralysed. She wanted to cry.

"I think I may have some," Duncan said. "I usually carry some. For emergencies." He began to search through his pockets. "Hold this." Into her cupped hands he piled a chocolate-bar, then several neatly folded silver chocolate-bar wrappers, a few white pumpkin-seed shells, an empty cigarette package, a piece of grubby string tied in knots, a key-chain with two keys, a wad of chewing-gum wrapped in paper, and a shoelace. "Wrong pocket," he said. From his other pocket he pulled, in a cascade of small change that scattered over the sidewalk, a few crumpled bills. He picked up the change and counted all the money. "Well, it won't be the King Eddie," he said, "but it'll get us something. Not around here though, this is expense-account territory; it'll have to be further downtown. Looks like this is going to be an underground movie rather than a technicolour extravaganza spectacular." He put the money and the handsful of junk back into his pocket.

The subway was closed down, its iron latticed gate pulled across the entrance.

"I guess we could take a bus," Marian said.

"No; it's too cold to stand and wait."

They turned at the next corner and walked south down the wide empty street, past the lighted storefronts. There were few cars and fewer people. It must be really late, she thought. She tried to imagine what was going on at the party—was it over? Had Peter realized yet that she was no longer there?—but all she could picture was a confusion of noises and voices and fragments of faces and flashes of bright light.

She took Duncan's hand. He wasn't wearing gloves, so she put both his hand and her own into her pocket. He looked down at her then with an almost hostile expression, but he did not remove his hand. Neither of them spoke. It was getting colder and colder: her toes were beginning to ache.

They walked for what seemed hours, gently downwards toward the frozen lake although they were nowhere near it, past blocks and blocks that contained nothing but tall brick office buildings and the vacant horizontal spaces of car-dealers, with their strings of coloured lights and little flags; not what they were looking for at all. "I think we're on the wrong street," Duncan said after a time. "We should be further over."

They went along a dark narrow cross-street whose sidewalks were treacherous with packed snow and emerged finally on a larger street gaudy with neon signs. "This looks more like it," said Duncan.

"What are we going to do now?" she asked, conscious of the plaintive tone in her own voice. She felt helpless to decide. He was more or less in charge. After all, he was the one with the money.

"Hell, *I* don't know how one goes about these things," he said. "I've never done this before."

"Neither have I," she said defensively. "I mean, not like this."

"There must be an accepted formula," he said, "but I guess we'll just have to make it up as we go along. We'll take them in order, from north to south." He scanned the street. "It looks as though they get crummier as you go down."

"Oh, I hope it's not a real dump," she wailed, "with bugs!"

"Oh, I don't know, bugs might make it sort of more interesting. Anyway we'll have to take what we can get."

He stopped in front of a narrow red brick building sandwiched between a formal-rental store with a gritty bride in the window and a dusty-looking florist's. "Royal Massey Hotel," its dangling neon sign said; underneath the writing there was a coat-of-arms. "You wait here," Duncan said. He went up the steps.

He came back down the steps. "Door's locked," he said.

They walked on. The next one had a more promising aspect. It was dingier, and the stone grecian-scrolled cornices over the windows were dark-grey with soot. "The Ontario Towers," it said, in a red sign whose preliminary "O" had gone out. "Cheap Rates." It was open.

"I'll come in and stand in the lobby," she said. Her feet were freezing. Besides, she felt a need to be courageous: Duncan was coping so well, she ought to provide at least moral support.

She stood on the dilapidated matting, trying to look respectable, and conscious of her ear-rings and of the improbability of the attempt. Duncan walked over to the night clerk, a wizened shred of a man who was staring at her suspiciously through his puckers. He and Duncan had a low-voiced conversation; then Duncan came back and took her arm and they walked out.

"What did he say?" she asked when they were outside.

"He said it wasn't that sort of place."

"That's rather presumptuous," she said. She was offended, and felt quite self-righteous.

Duncan snickered. "Come now," he said, "no outraged virtue. All it means is that we've got to find one that *is* that sort of place."

They turned a corner and went east along a likely-looking street. They passed a few more shabby-genteel establishments before they came to one that was even shabbier, but definitely not genteel. In place of the crumbled brick facade characteristic of the others, it had pink stucco with large signs painted on it: "BEDS 4$ A NITE." "T.V. IN EVERY ROOM." "VICTORIA AND ALBERT HOTEL." "BEST BARGAIN IN TOWN." It was a long building. Further down they could see the "MEN" and "LADIES AND ESCORTS" sign that signalled a beer-parlour, and it seemed to have a tavern too: though both would be closed at this hour.

"I think this is it," said Duncan.

They went in. The night clerk yawned as he took down the key. "Sort of late buddy, isn't it?" he said. "That'll be four."

"Better late," Duncan said, "than never." He took a handful of bills out of his pocket, scattering assorted change over the carpet. As he stooped to pick it up, the night clerk looked over at Marian with an undisguised though slightly jaded leer. She drooped her eyelids at him. After all, she thought grimly, if I'm dressed like one and acting like one, why on earth shouldn't he think I really am one?

They ascended the sparsely-carpeted stairs in silence.

The room when they finally located it was the size of a large cupboard, furnished with an iron bedstead, a straight-backed chair, and a dresser whose varnish was peeling off. There was a miniature quarter-in-the-slot T.V. set bolted to the wall in one corner. On the dresser were a couple of folded thread-bare towels in baby-blue and pink. The narrow window opposite the bed had a blue neon sign hanging outside it; the sign flashed on and off, making an ominous buzzing noise. Behind the room-door was another door that led to a cubbyhole of a bathroom.

Duncan bolted the door behind them. "Well, what do we do now?" he said. "You must know."

Marian removed her boots, then her shoes. Her toes tingled with the pain of thawing. She looked at the gaunt face peering at her from between an upturned coat collar and a mass of windy hair; the face was dead white, all but the nose, which was red from the cold. As she watched he produced a tattered grey piece of kleenex from some recess in his clothing and wiped it.

God, she thought, what am I doing here? How did I get here anyway? What would Peter say? She walked across the room and stood in front of the window, looking out at nothing in particular.

"Oh boy," said Duncan behind her, enthusiastically. She turned. He had discovered something new, a large ashtray that had been sitting on the dresser behind the towels. "It's genuine." The ashtray was in the form of a seashell, pink china with scalloped edges. "It says A Gift From Burk's Falls on it," he told her with glee. He turned it over to look on the bottom and some ashes fell out of it onto the floor. "Made In Japan," he announced.

Marian felt a surge of desperation. Something had to be done. "Look," she said, "for heaven's sake put down that damned ashtray and take off your clothes and get into that bed!"

Duncan hung his head like a rebuked child. "Oh, all right," he said.

He shed his clothes with such velocity that it looked as though he had concealed zippers somewhere, or one long zipper so his clothes came off together like a single skin. He tossed them in a heap onto the chair and scuttled with alacrity into the bed and lay with the sheets pulled up around his chin, watching her with barely disguised and only slightly friendly curiosity.

With tight-lipped determination she began to undress. It was somewhat difficult to wisp off her stockings in reckless abandon or even a reasonable facsimile of it with those two eyes goggling at her in such a frog-like manner from over the top of the sheet. She scrabbled with her fingers for the zipper at the back of her dress. She could not quite reach it.

"Unzip me," she said tersely. He complied.

She threw the dress over the back of the chair and struggled out of her girdle.

"Hey!" he said. "A real one! I've seen them in the ads but I never got that far in real life, I've always wondered how they worked. Can I look at it?"

She handed it over to him. He sat up in bed to examine it, stretching it all of its three ways and flexing the bones. "God, how medieval," he said. "How can you stand it? Do you have to wear one all the time?" He spoke of it as though it was some kind of unpleasant but necessary surgical appliance: a brace or a truss.

"No," she said. She was standing in her slip, wondering what to do next. She refused, somewhat prudishly she supposed, to undress the rest of the way with the lights on; but he seemed to be having such a good time at the moment that she didn't want to interrupt. On the other hand the room was cold and she was beginning to shiver.

She walked doggedly towards the bed, gritting her teeth. It was an assignment that was going to take a lot of perseverance. If she had had any sleeves on she would have rolled them up. "Move over," she said.

Duncan flung away the girdle and pulled himself back into the bedclothes like a turtle into its shell. "Oh no," he said, "I'm not letting you into this bed until you go in there and peel that junk off your face. Fornication may be all very well in its way, but if I'm going to come out looking like a piece of flowered wallpaper I reject it."

She saw his point.

When she returned, scraped more or less clean, she snapped off the light and slithered into bed beside him. There was a pause.

"I guess now I'm supposed to crush you in my manly arms," Duncan said out of the darkness.

She slid her hand beneath his cool back.

He groped for her head, snuffing against her neck. "You smell funny," he said.

Half an hour later Duncan said, "It's no use. I must be incorruptible. I'm going to have a cigarette." He got up, stumbled the few steps across the room in the dark, located his clothes and rummaged around in them till he found the pack, and returned. She could see parts of his face now and the china seashell gleaming in the light of the burning cigarette. He was sitting propped against the iron scrollwork at the head of the bed.

"I don't exactly know what's wrong," he said. "Partly I don't like not being able to see your face; but it would probably be worse if I could. But it's not just that, I feel like some kind of little stunted creature crawling over the surface of a huge mass of flesh. Not that you're fat," he added, "you aren't. There's just altogether too much flesh around here. It's suffocating." He threw back the covers on his side of the bed. "That's better," he said. He rested the arm with the cigarette across his face.

Marian knelt beside him in the bed, holding the sheet around her like a shawl. She could barely trace the outlines of his long white body, flesh-white against bed-white, faintly luminous in the blue light from the street. Somebody in the next room flushed a toilet; the gurgling of the water in the pipes swirled through the air of the room and died away with a sound between a sigh and a hiss.

She clenched her hands on the sheet. She was tense with impatience and with another emotion that she recognized as the cold energy of terror. At this moment to evoke something, some response, even though she could not predict the thing that might emerge from beneath that seemingly-passive surface, the blank white formless thing lying insubstantial in the darkness before her, shifting as her eyes shifted trying to see, that appeared to have no temperature, no odour, no thickness and no sound, was the most important thing she could ever have done, could ever do, and she couldn't do it. The knowledge was an icy desolation worse than fear. No effort of will could be worth anything here. She could not will herself to reach out and touch him again. She could not will herself to move away.

The glow of the cigarette vanished; there was the hard china click of the ashtray being set down on the floor. She could sense that he was smiling in the darkness, but with what expression, sarcasm, malevolence, or even kindness, she could not guess.

"Lie down," he said.

She sank back, still with the sheet clutched around her and her knees drawn up.

He put his arm around her. "No," he said, "you have to unbend. Assuming the foetal position won't be any help at all, god knows I've tried it long enough." He stroked her with his hand, gently, straightening her out, almost as though he was ironing her.

"It isn't something you can dispense, you know," he said. "You have to let me take my own time."

He edged over, closer to her now. She could feel his breath against the side of her neck, sharp and cool, and then his face pressing against her, nudging into her flesh, cool; like the muzzle of an animal, curious, and only slightly friendly.

29

□ They were sitting in a grimy coffee-shop around the corner from the hotel. Duncan was counting the rest of his money to see what they could afford to have for breakfast. Marian had undone the buttons of her coat, but was holding it together at the neck. She didn't want any of the other people to see her red dress: it belonged too obviously to the evening before. She had put Ainsley's ear-rings in her pocket.

Between them on the green arborite-surfaced table was an assortment of dirty plates and cups and crumbs and splashes and smears of grease, remnants of the courageous breakfasters who had pioneered earlier into the morning when the arborite surface was innocent as a wilderness, untouched by the knife and fork of man, and had left behind them the random clutter of rejected or abandoned articles typical of such light travellers. They knew they would never pass that way again. Marian looked at their waste-strewn trail with distaste, but she was trying to be casual about breakfast. She didn't want her stomach to make a scene. I'll just have coffee and toast, maybe with jelly; surely there will be no objections to that, she thought.

A waitress with harassed hair appeared and began to clear the table. She flapped a dog-eared menu down in front of each of them. Marian opened hers and looked at the column headed "Breakfast Suggestions".

Last night everything had seemed resolved, even the imagined face of Peter with its hunting eyes absorbed into some white revelation. It had been simple clarity rather than joy, but it had been submerged in sleep; and waking to the sound of water sighing in the pipes and loud corridor voices, she could not remember what it was. She had lain quietly, trying to concentrate on it, on what it might possibly have been, gazing at the ceiling, which was blotched with distracting watermarks; but it was no use. Then Duncan's head had emerged from beneath the pillow where he had placed it during the night for safe-keeping. He stared at her for a moment as though he didn't have the least idea who she was or what he was doing in that room. Then "Let's get out of here," he said. She had leaned over and kissed him on the mouth, but after she had drawn back he had merely licked his lips, and as though reminded by the action said, "I'm hungry. Let's go for breakfast. You look awful," he had added.

"You're not exactly the picture of health yourself," she replied. His eyes were heavily circled and his hair looked like a raven's nest. They got out of bed and she examined her own face briefly in the yellowed wavery glass of the bathroom mirror. Her skin was drawn and white and strangely dry. It was the truth: she did look awful.

She had not wanted to put those particular clothes back on but she had no choice. They dressed in silence, awkward in the narrow space of the room whose shabbiness was even more evident in the grey daylight, and furtively descended the stairs.

She looked at him now as he sat hunched over across the table from her, muffled again in his clothes. He had lit a cigarette and his eyes were watching the smoke. The eyes were closed to her, remote. The imprint left on her mind by the long famished body that had seemed in the darkness to consist of nothing but sharp crags and angles, the memory of its painfully-defined almost skeletal rib-cage, a pattern of ridges like a washboard, was fading as

263

rapidly as any other transcient impression on a soft surface. Whatever decision she had made had been forgotten, if indeed she had ever decided anything. It could have been an illusion, like the blue light on their skins. Something had been accomplished in his life though, she thought with a sense of weary competence; that was a small comfort; but for her nothing was permanent or finished. Peter was there, he hadn't vanished; he was as real as the crumbs on the table, and she would have to act accordingly. She would have to go back. She had missed the morning bus but she could get the afternoon one, after talking to Peter, explaining. Or rather avoiding explanation. There was no real reason to explain because explanations involved causes and effects and this event had been neither. It had come from nowhere and it led nowhere, it was outside the chain. Suddenly it occurred to her that she hadn't begun to pack.

She looked down at the menu. "Bacon and Eggs, Any Style," she read. "Our Plump Tender Sausages." She thought of pigs and chickens. She shifted hastily to "Toast." Something moved in her throat. She closed the menu.

"What do you want?" Duncan asked.

"Nothing, I can't eat anything," she said, "I can't eat anything at all. Not even a glass of orange juice." It had finally happened at last then. Her body had cut itself off. The food circle had dwindled to a point, a black dot, closing everything outside. . . . She looked at the grease-spot on the cover of the menu, almost whimpering with self-pity.

"You sure? Oh well then," said Duncan with a trace of alacrity, "that means I can spend it all on me."

When the waitress came back he ordered ham and eggs, which he proceeded to consume voraciously, and without apology or comment, before her very eyes. She watched him in misery. When he broke the eggs with his fork and their yellow centres ran viscously over the plate she turned her head away. She thought she was going to be sick.

"Well," he said when he had paid the cheque and they were standing outside on the street, "thanks for everything. I've got to go home and get to work on my term paper."

Marian thought of the cold fuel-oil and stale cigar smell there would be inside the bus. Then she thought of the dishes in the kitchen sink. The bus would get warm and stuffy as she travelled inside it along the highway, the tires making their high grinding whine. What was living, hidden and repulsive, down there among the plates and dirty glasses? She couldn't go back.

"Duncan," she said, "please don't go."

"Why? Is there more?"

"I can't go back."

He frowned down at her. "What do you expect me to do?" he asked. "You shouldn't expect me to do anything. I want to go back to my shell. I've had enough so-called reality for now."

"You don't have to do anything, couldn't you just. . . ."

"No," he said, "I don't want to. You aren't an escape any more, you're too real. Something's bothering you and you'd want to talk about it; I'd have to start worrying about you and all that, I haven't time for it."

She looked down at their four feet, standing in the trodden slush of the sidewalk. "I really can't go back."

He peered at her more closely. "Are you going to be sick?" he asked. "Don't do that."

She stood mutely before him. She could offer him no good reason for staying with her. There was no reason: what would it accomplish?

"Well," he said, hesitating, "all right. But not for very long, okay?"

She nodded gratefully.

They walked north. "We can't go to my place, you know," he said. "They'd make a fuss."

"I know."

"Where do you want to go then?" he asked.

She hadn't thought about that. Everything was impossible. She put her hands over her ears. "I don't know," she said, her voice rising towards hysteria, "I don't know, I might as well go back. . . ."

"Oh come now," he said genially, "no histrionics. We'll

265

go for a walk." He pulled her hands away from her ears. "All right," she said, letting herself be humoured.

As they walked Duncan swung their linked hands back and forth. His mood seemed to have changed from its breakfast sullenness to a certain vacant contentment. They were going uphill, away from the lake; the sidewalks were crowded with furred Saturday ladies trudging inexorably as icebreakers through the slush, brows furrowed with purpose, eyes glinting, shopping bags hung at either side to give them ballast. Marian and Duncan dodged past and around them, breaking hands when an especially threatening one bore down upon them. In the streets the cars fumed and splattered by. Pieces of soot fell from the grey air, heavy and moist as snowflakes.

"I need some clean air," Duncan said when they had walked wordlessly for twenty minutes or so. "This is like being in a fishbowl full of dying pollywogs. Can you face a short subway ride?"

Marian nodded. The further away, she thought, the better.

They went down the nearest pastel-tiled chute, and after an interval smelling of damp wool and mothballs let themselves be carried up by the escalator and out again into daylight.

"Now we take the streetcar," Duncan said. He seemed to know where he was going, for which Marian could only be thankful. He was leading her. He was in control.

On the streetcar they had to stand. Marian held on to one of the metal poles and stooped so she could see out the window. Over the top of the tea-cosy-shaped green and orange wool hat with large gold sequins sewed to it an unfamiliar landscape jolted past: stores first, then houses, then a bridge, then more houses. She had no idea what part of the city they were in.

Duncan reached over her head and pulled the cord. The streetcar ground to a halt and they squeezed their way towards the back and jumped down.

"Now we walk," said Duncan. He turned down a side street. The houses were smaller and a little newer than the ones in Marian's district, but they were still dark and tall, many with square pillared wooden porches, the paint grey or dingy white. The snow on the lawns was fresher here. They passed an old man shovelling a walk, the scrape of the shovel sounding strangely loud in the silent air. There was an abnormal number of cats. Marian thought of how the street would smell in the spring when the snow melted: earth, bulbs coming up, damp wood, last year's leaves rotting, the winter's accumulations of the cats who had thought they were being so clean and furtive as they scratched holes for themselves in the snow. Old people coming out of the grey doors with shovels, creaking over the lawns, burying things. Spring cleaning: a sense of purpose.

They crossed a street and began to go down a steep hill. All at once Duncan started to run, dragging Marian behind him as if she was a toboggan.

"Stop!" she called, alarmed at the loudness of her own voice. "I can't run!" She felt the curtains in all the windows swaying perilously as they went past, as though each house contained a dour watcher.

"No!" Duncan shouted back at her. "We're escaping! Come on!"

Under her arm a seam split. She had a vision of the red dress disintegrating in mid-air, falling in little scraps behind her in the snow, like feathers. They were off the sidewalk now, slithering down the road towards a fence; there was a yellow and black chequered sign that said "Danger." She was afraid they would to splintering through the wooden fence and hurtle over an unseen edge, in slow motion almost, like movies of automobiles falling off cliffs, but at the last minute Duncan swerved around the end of the fence and they were on a narrow cider path between high banks. The footbridge at the bottom of the hill came rapidly towards them; he stopped suddenly and she skidded, colliding.

Her lungs hurt: she was dizzy from too much air. They were leaning against a cement wall, one of the sides of the bridge. Marian put her arms on the top and rested. Level with her eyes there were tree-tops, a maze of branches, the ends already pale yellow, pale red, knotted with buds.

"We aren't there yet," Duncan said. He tugged at her arm. "We go down." He led her to the end of the bridge.

At one side was an unofficial path: the imprints of feet, a muddy track. They climbed down gingerly, their feet sideways like children learning to go down stairs, step by step. Water was dripping on them from the icicles on the underside of the bridge.

When they had reached the bottom and were standing on level ground Marian asked, "Are we here yet?"

"Not yet," said Duncan. He began to walk away from the bridge. Marian hoped they were going to a place where they could sit down.

They were in one of the ravines that fissured the city, but which one she didn't know. She had gone for walks close to the one that was visible from their living room window, but nothing she saw around her was familiar. The ravine was narrow here and deep, closed in by trees which looked as though they were pinning the covering of snow to the steep sides. Far above, towards the rim, some children were playing. Marian could see their bright jackets, red and blue, and hear their faint laughter.

They were going single file along a track in the crusted snow. Some other people had walked there, but not many. At intervals she noticed what she thought were the marks of horses' hooves. All she could see of Duncan was his slouched back and his feet lifting and setting down.

She wished he would turn around so she could see his face; his expressionless coat made her uneasy.

"We'll sit down in a minute," he said as if in answer.

She didn't see any place they might possibly sit. They were walking now through a field of tall weedstalks whose stiff dried branches scraped against them as they passed: goldenrod, teasles, burdocks, the skeletons of anonymous grey plants. The burdocks had clusters of brown burrs and the teazles their weathered-silver spiked heads but otherwise nothing interrupted the thin branching and re-branching monotony of the field. Beyond it on either side rose the walls of the ravine. Along the top now were houses, a line of them perched on the edge, careless of the erosion-gullies that scarred the ravine-face at irregular intervals. The creek had disappeared into an underground culvert.

Marian looked behind her. The ravine had made a

curve; she had walked around it without noticing; ahead of them was another bridge, a larger one. They kept walking.

"I like it down here in winter," Duncan's voice said after a while. "Before I've only been down here in summer. Everything grows, it's so thick with green leaves and stuff you can't see three feet in front of you, some of it's poison-ivy. And it's populated. The old drunks come down here and sleep under the bridges and the kids play here too. There's a riding-stable down here somewhere, I think what we're on is one of the bridal-paths. I used to come down because it was cooler. But it's better covered with snow. It hides the junk. They're beginning to fill this place up with junk too, you know, beginning with the creek, I wonder why they like throwing things around all over the landscape . . . old tires, tin cans. . . ." The voice came from a mouth she couldn't see, as though from nowhere; it was foreshortened, blunted, as if it was being blotted up, absorbed by the snow.

The ravine had widened out around them and in this place there were fewer weeds. Duncan turned off the path, breaking the crusted snow; she followed him. They plodded up the side of a small hill.

"Here we are," Duncan said. He stopped and turned, and reached a hand to draw her up beside him.

Marian gasped and took an involuntary step back: they were standing on the very edge of a cliff. The ground ended abruptly beyond their feet. Below them was a huge roughly circular pit, with a spiral path or roadway cut round and round the sides, leading to the level snow-covered space at the bottom. Directly across from where they were standing, separated from them by perhaps a quarter of a mile of empty space, was a long shed-like black building Everything seemed closed, deserted.

"What is it?" she asked.

"It's only the brickworks," Duncan said. "That's pure clay down there. They go down that road with steam-shovels and dig it out."

"I didn't know there was anything like that in the ravines," she said. It seemed wrong to have this cavity in the city: the ravine itself was supposed to be as far down as you could go. It made her suspect the white pit-bottom also; it didn't look solid, it looked possibly hollow, dangerous, a thin layer of ice, as though if you walked on it you might fall through.

"Oh, they have lots of good things. There's a prison down here somewhere, too."

Duncan sat down on the edge, dangling his legs nonchalantly, and took out a cigarette. After a moment she sat down beside him, although she didn't trust the earth. It was the kind of thing that caved in. They both gazed down into the gigantic hole scooped into the ground.

"I wonder what time it is," Marian said. She listened as she spoke: the open space had swallowed up her voice.

Duncan didn't answer. He finished his cigarette in silence; then he stood up, walked a short way along the brink till he came to a flat area where there were no weeds, and lay down in the snow. He was so peaceful, stretched out there looking up at the sky, that Marian walked over to join him where he was lying.

"You'll get cold," he said, "but go ahead if you want to."

She lay down at arm's length from him. It did not seem right, here, to be too close. Above, the sky was a uniform light grey, made diffusely bright by a sun concealed somewhere behind it.

Duncan spoke into the silence. "So why can't you go back? I mean, you are getting married and so on. I thought you were the capable type."

"I am," she said unhappily. "I was. I don't know." She didn't want to discuss it.

"Some would say of course that it's all in your mind."

"I know that," she said, impatient: she wasn't a total idiot yet. "But how do I get it out?"

"It ought to be obvious," Duncan's voice said, "that I'm the last person to ask. They tell me I live in a world of fantasies. But at least mine are more or less my own, I choose them and I sort of like them, some of the time. But you don't seem too happy with yours."

"Maybe I should see a psychiatrist," she said gloomily.

"Oh no, don't do that. They'd only want to adjust you."

"But I want to be adjusted, that's just it. I don't see any point in being unstable." It occurred to her also that she didn't see any point in starving to death. What she really wanted, she realized, had been reduced to simple safety. She thought she had been heading towards it all these months but actually she hadn't been getting anywhere. And she hadn't accomplished anything. At the moment her only solid achievement seemed to be Duncan. That was something she could hang on to.

Suddenly she needed to make sure he was still there, hadn't vanished or sunk down beneath the white surface. She wanted verification.

"How was it for you last night?" she asked. He had not yet said anything about it.

"How was what? Oh. That." He was silent for several minutes. She listened intently, waiting for his voice as though for an oracle. But when he spoke at last he said, "I like this place. Especially now in winter, it's so close to absolute zero. It makes me feel human. By comparison. I wouldn't like tropical islands at all, they would be too fleshy, I'd always be wondering whether I was a walking vegetable or a giant amphibian. But in the snow you're as near as possible to nothing."

Marian was puzzled. What did this have to do with it?

"You want me to say it was stupendous, don't you?" he asked. "That it got me out of my shell. Hatched me into manhood. Solved all my problems."

"Well. . . ."

"Sure you do, and I could always tell you would. I like people participating in my fantasy life and I'm usually willing to participate in theirs, up to a point. It was fine; just as good as usual."

The implication sank in smoothly as a knife through butter. She wasn't the first then. The starched nurse-like image of herself she had tried to preserve as a last resort crumpled like wet newsprint; the rest of her couldn't even work up the energy to be angry. She had been so thoroughly taken in. She should have known. But after she had thought about it for a few minutes, gazing up at the blank sky, it didn't make that much difference. There was the possibility also that this revelation was just as fraudulent as so much else had been.

She sat up, brushing the snow from her sleeves. It was time for action. "All right, that was your joke," she said. She would let him wonder whether or not she believed him. "Now I've got to decide what I'm going to do."

He grinned at her. "Don't ask me, that's your problem. It does look as though you ought to do something: self-laceration in a vacuum eventually gets rather boring. But it's your own personal cul-de-sac, you invented it, you'll have to think of your own way out." He stood up.

Marian stood up too. She had been calm but now she could feel desperation returning in her, seeping through her flesh like the effects of a drug. "Duncan," she said, "could you maybe come back with me and talk to Peter? I don't think I can do it, I don't know what to say, he's not going to understand. . . ."

"Oh no," he said, "you can't do that. I'm not part of that. It would be disastrous, don't you see? I mean for me." He wrapped his arms around his torso and held on to his own elbows.

"Please " she said. She knew he would refuse,

"No," he said, "it wouldn't be right." He turned and looked down at the two imprints their bodies had made in the snow. Then he stepped on them, first on his own and then on hers, smearing the snow with his foot. "Come here," he said, "I'll show you how to get back." He led her further along. They came to a road which rose and then dipped. Below was a giant expressway, sloping up, and in the distance another bridge, a familiar bridge with subway cars moving on it. Now she knew where she was.

"Aren't you coming with me even that far?" she asked.

"No. I'm going to stay here for a while. But you have to go now." The tone of his voice closed her out. He turned and started to walk away

The cars rocketed past. She looked back once when she had trudged halfway up the hillside towards the bridge. She almost expected him to have evaporated into the white expanse of the ravine, but he was still there, a dark shape against the snow, crouched on the edge and gazing into the empty pit.

272

30

☐ Marian had just got home and was struggling with her wrinkled dress, trying to get the zipper undone, when the phone rang. She knew who it would be.

"Hello?" she said.

Peter's voice was icy with anger. "Marian, where the hell have you been? I've been phoning everywhere." He sounded hung-over.

"Oh," she said with airy casualness, "I've been somewhere else. Sort of out."

He lost control. "Why the hell did you leave the party? You really disrupted the evening for me. I was looking for you to get you in the group picture and you were gone, of course I couldn't make a big production of it with all those people there but after they'd gone home I looked all over for you, your friend Lucy and I got in the car and drove up and down the streets and we called your place half a dozen times, we were .both so worried Damn nice of her to take the trouble, it's nice to know there are *some* considerate women left around. . . ."

I'll bet it is, Marian thought with a momentary twinge of jealousy, remembering Lucy's silver eyelids; but out loud she said, "Peter, please don't get upset. I just stepped outside for a breath of fresh air and something else came up, that's all. There is absolutely nothing to get upset about. There have been no catastrophes."

"What do you mean, upset!" he said. "You shouldn't go wandering around the streets at night, you might get *raped,* if you're going to do these things and god knows it isn't the first time why the hell can't you think of other people once in a while? You could at least have told me where you were, your parents called me long-distance, they're frantic because you weren't on the bus and what was I supposed to tell them?"

Oh yes, she thought; she had forgotten about that. "Well, I'm perfectly all right," she said.

"But where were you? When we'd discovered you'd left and I started quietly asking people if they'd seen you I must say I got a pretty funny story from that prince-charming friend of yours, Trevor or whatever the hell his name is. Who's the guy he was telling me about anyway?"

"Please, Peter," she said, "I just hate talking about things like this over the phone." She had a sudden desire to tell him the whole story, but what good would that do since nothing had been proved or accomplished? Instead she said, "What time is it?"

"Two-thirty," he said, his voice surprised into neutrality by this appeal to simple fact

"Well, why don't you come over a bit later? Maybe about five-thirty. For tea. And then we can talk it all over." She made her voice sweet, conciliatory. She was conscious of her own craftiness. Though she hadn't made any decisions she could feel she was about to make one and she needed time.

"Well, all right," he said peevishly, "but it better be good." They hung up together.

Marian went into the bedroom and took off her clothes; then she went downstairs and took a quick bath. The lower regions were silent; the lady down below was probably brooding in her dark den or praying for the swift destruction of Ainsley by heavenly thunder-bolts. In a spirit approaching gay rebellion Marian neglected to erase her bath-tub ring.

What she needed was something that avoided words, she didn't want to get tangled up in a discussion. Some way she could know what was real: a test, simple and direct as litmus-paper. She finished dressing—a plain grey wool would be appropriate—and put on her coat, then located her everyday purse and counted the money. She went out to the kitchen and sat down at the table to make herself a list, but threw down the pencil after she had written several words. She knew what she needed to get.

In the supermarket she went methodically up and down the aisles, relentlessly out-manoeuvring the muskrat-furred ladies, edging the Saturday children to the curb, picking the things off the shelves. Her image was taking shape. Eggs. Flour. Lemons for the flavour. Suger, icing-sugar, vanilla, salt, food-colouring. She wanted everything new, she didn't want to use anything that was already in the house. Chocolate—no, cocoa, that would be better. A glass tube full of round silver decorations. Three nesting plastic bowls, teaspoons, aluminium cake-decorator and a cake tin. Lucky, she thought, they sell almost everything in supermarkets these days. She started back towards the apartment, carrying her paper bag

Sponge or angel-food? she wondered. She decided on sponge. It was more fitting.

She turned on the oven. That was one part of the kitchen that had not been over-run by the creeping skin-disease-covering of dirt, mostly because they hadn't been using it much recently. She tied on an apron and rinsed the new bowls and the other new utensils under the tap, but did not disturb any of the dirty dishes. Later for them. Right now she didn't have time. She dried the things and began to crack and separate the eggs, hardly thinking, concentrating all her attention on the movements of her hands, and then when she was beating and sifting and folding, on the relative times and the textures. Spongecake needed a light hand. She poured the batter into the tin and drew a fork sideways through it to break the large air-bubbles As she slid the tin into the oven she almost hummed with pleasure. It was a long time since she had made a cake

While the cake was in the oven baking she re-washed the bowls and mixed the icing. An ordinary butter icing, that would be the best. Then she divided the icing into three parts in the three bowls. The largest portion she left white, the next one she tinted a bright pink, almost red, with the red food-colouring she had bought, and the last one she made dark brown by stirring cocoa into it.

What am I going to put her on? she thought when she had finished. I'll have to wash a dish. She unearthed a long platter from the very bottom of the stack of plates in the sink and scoured it thoroughly under the tap. It took quite a lot of detergent to get the scum off.

She tested the cake; it was done. She took it out of the oven and turned it upside-down to cool.

She was glad Ainsley wasn't home: she didn't want any interference with what she was going to do. In fact it didn't look as though Ainsley had been home at all. There was no sign of her green dress. In her room a suitcase was lying open on the bed where she must have left it the night before. Some of the surface flotsam was eddying into it, as though drawn by a vortex. Marian wondered in passing how Ainsley was ever going to cram the random contents of the room into anything as limited and rectilineal as a set of suitcases.

While the cake was cooling she went into the bedroom and tidied her hair, pulling it back and pinning it to get rid of the remains of the hairdresser's convolutions. She felt lightheaded, almost dizzy: it must be the lack of sleep and the lack of food. She grinned into the mirror, showing her teeth.

The cake wasn't cooling quickly enough. She refused to put it into the refrigerator though. It would pick up the smells. She took it out of the tin and set it on the clean platter, opened the kitchen window, and stuck it out on the snowy sill. She knew what happened to cakes that were iced warm—everything melted.

She wondered what time it was. Her watch was still on the top of the dresser where she had left it the day before but it had run down. She didn't want to turn on Ainsley's transistor, that would be too distracting She was getting jittery already. There used to be a number you could plone . . . but anyway she would have to hurry.

She took the cake off the sill, felt it to see if it was cool enough, and put it on the kitchen table. Then she began to operate. With the two forks she pulled it in half though the middle. One half she placed flat side down on the platter. She scooped out part of it and made a head with the section she had taken out. Then she nipped in a waist at the sides. The other half she pulled into strips for the arms and legs. The spongy cake was pliable, easy to mould. She stuck all the separate members together with white icing, and used the rest of the icing to cover the shape she had constructed. It was bumpy in places and had too many crumbs in the skin, but it would do. She reinforced the feet and ankles with tooth-picks.

276

Now she had a blank white body. It looked slightly obscene, lying there soft and sugary and featureless on the platter. She set about clothing it, filling the cake-decorator with bright pink icing. First she gave it a bikini, but that was too sparse. She filled in the midriff. Now it had an ordinary bathing-suit, but that still wasn't exactly what she wanted. She kept extending, adding to top and bottom, until she had a dress of sorts. In a burst of exuberance she added a row of ruffles around the neckline, and more ruffles at the hem of the dress. She made a smiling lush-lipped pink mouth and pink shoes to match. Finally she put five pink fingernails on each of the amorphous hands.

The cake looked peculiar with only a mouth and no hair or eyes. She rinsed out the cake-decorator and filled it with chocolate icing. She drew a nose, and two large eyes, to which she appended many eyelashes and two eyebrows, one above each eye. For emphasis she made a line demarcating one leg from the other, and similar lines to separate the arms from the body. The hair took longer. It involved masses of intricate baroque scrolls and swirls, piled high on the head and spilling down over the shoulders.

The eyes were still blank. She decided on green—the only other possibilities were red and yellow, since they were the only other colours she had—and with a toothpick applied two irises of green food-colouring.

Now there were only the globular silver decorations to add. One went in each eye, for a pupil. With the others she made a floral design on the pink dress, and stuck a few in the hair. Now the woman looked like an elegant antique china figurine. For an instant she wished she had bought some birthday candles; but where could they be put? There was really no room for them. The image was complete.

Her creation gazed up at her, its face doll-like and vacant except for the small silver glitter of intelligence in each green eye. While making it she had been almost gleeful, but now, contemplating it, she was pensive. All that work had gone into the lady and now what would happen to her?

"You look delicious," she told her. "Very appetizing.

And that's what will happen to you; that's what you get for being food." At the thought of food her stomach contracted. She felt a certain pity for her creature but she was powerless now to do anything about it. Her fate had been decided. Already Peter's footsteps were coming up the stairs.

Marian had a swift vision of her own monumental silliness, of how infantile and undignified she would seem in the eyes of any rational observer. What kind of game did she think she was playing? But that wasn't the point, she told herself nervously, pushing back a strand of hair. Though if Peter found her silly she would believe it, she would accept his version of herself, he would laugh and they would sit down and have a quiet cup of tea.

She smiled gravely at Peter as he came up out of the stairwell. The expression on his face, a scowl combined with a jutting chin, meant he was still angry. He was wearing a costume suitable for being angry in: the suit stern, tailored, remote, but the tie a paisley with touches of sullen maroon.

"Now what's all this . . ." he began.

"Peter, why don't you go into the living room and sit down? I have a surprise for you. Then we can have a talk if you like." She smiled at him again.

He was puzzled, and forgot to sustain his frown; he must have been expecting an awkward apology. But he did as she suggested. She remained in the doorway for a moment, looking almost tenderly at the back of his head resting against the chesterfield. Now that she had seen him again, the actual Peter, solid as ever, the fears of the evening before had dwindled to foolish hysteria and the flight to Duncan had become a stupidity, an evasion; she could hardly remember what he looked like. Peter was not the enemy after all, he was just a normal human being like most other people. She wanted to touch his neck, tell him that he shouldn't get upset, that everything was going to be all right. It was Duncan that was the mutation.

But there was something about his shoulders. He must have been sitting with his arms folded. The face on the other side of that head could have belonged to anyone.

And they all wore clothes of real cloth and had real bodies: those in the newspapers, those still unknown, waiting for their chance to aim from the upstairs window; you passed them on the streets every day. It was easy to see him as normal and safe in the afternoon, but that didn't alter things. The price of this version of reality was testing the other one.

She went into the kitchen and returned, bearing the platter in front of her, carefully and with reverence, as though she was carrying something sacred in a procession, an icon or the crown on a cushion in a play. She knelt, setting the platter on the coffee-table in front of Peter.

"You've been trying to destroy me, haven't you," she said. "You've been trying to assimilate me. But I've made you a substitute, something you'll like much better. This is what you really wanted all along, isn't it? I'll get you a fork," she added somewhat prosaically.

Peter stared from the cake to her face and back again. She wasn't smiling.

His eyes widened in alarm. Apparently he didn't find her silly.

When he had gone—and he went quite rapidly, they didn't have much of a conversation after all, he seemed embarrassed and eager to leave and even refused a cup of tea—she stood looking down at the figure. So Peter hadn't devoured it after all. As a symbol it had definitely failed. It looked up at her with its silvery eyes, enigmatic, mocking, succulent.

Suddenly she was hungry. Extremely hungry. The cake after all was only a cake. She picked up the platter, carried it to the kitchen table and located a fork. "I'll start with the feet," she decided.

She considered the first mouthful. It seemed odd but most pleasant to be actually tasting and chewing and swallowing again. Not bad, she thought critically; needs a touch more lemon though.

Already the part of her not occupied with eating was having a wave of nostalgia for Peter, as though for a style that had gone out of fashion and was beginning to turn up on the sad Salvation Army clothes racks. She could see him in her mind, posed jauntily in the foreground of an elegant salon with chandeliers and draperies, impeccably dressed, a glass of scotch in one hand; his foot was on the head of a stuffed lion and he had an eyepatch over one eye. Beneath one arm was strapped a revolver. Around the margin was an edging of gold scrollwork and slightly above Peter's left ear was a thumbtack. She licked her fork meditatively. He would definitely succeed.

She was halfway up the legs when she heard footsteps, two sets of them, coming up the stairs. Then Ainsley appeared in the kitchen doorway with Fischer Smythe's furry head behind her. She still had on her bluegreen dress, much the worse for wear. So was she: her face was haggard and in only the past twenty-four hours her belly seemed to have grown noticeably rounder.

"Hi," said Marian, waving her fork at them. She speared a chunk of pink thigh and carried it to her mouth.

Fischer had leaned against the wall and closed his eyes as soon as he reached the top of the stairs, but Ainsley focussed on her. "Marian, what have you got there?" She walked over to see. "It's a woman—a woman made of cake!" She gave Marian a strange look.

Marian chewed and swallowed. "Have some," she said, "it's really good. I made it this afternoon "

Ainsley's mouth opened and closed, fishlike, as though she was trying to gulp down the full implication of what she saw. "Marian!" she exclaimed at last, with horror. "You're rejecting your femininity!"

Marian stopped chewing and stared at Ainsley, who was regarding her through the hair that festooned itself over her eyes with wounded concern, almost with sternness. How did she manage it, that stricken attitude, that high seriousness? She was almost as morally earnest as the lady down below.

Marian looked back at her platter. The women lay there, still smiling glassily, her legs gone. "Nonsense," she said. "It's only a cake." She plunged her fork into the carcass, neatly severing the body from the head.

Part Three

31

☐ I was cleaning up the apartment. It had taken me two days to gather the strength to face it, but I had finally started. I had to go about it layer by layer. First there was the surface debris. I began with Ainsley's room, stuffing everything she had left behind into cardboard cartons: the half-empty cosmetic jars and used lipsticks, the strata of old newspapers and magazines on the floor, the desiccated banana-peel I found under the bed, the clothes she had rejected. All the things of mine I wanted to throw out went into the same boxes.

When the floors and furniture had been cleared I dusted everything in sight, including the mouldings and the tops of the doors and the window sills. Then I did the floors, sweeping and then scrubbing and waxing. The amount of dirt that came off was astounding: it was like uncovering an extra floor. Then I washed the dishes and after that the kitchen window-curtains. Then I stopped for lunch. After lunch I tackled the refrigerator. I did not examine closely the horrors that had accumulated inside it. I could see well enough from holding the little jars up to the light that they had better not be opened. The various objects within had been industriously sprouting hair, fur or feathers, each as its nature dictated, and I could guess what they would smell like. I lowered them carefully into the garbage bag. The freezing compartment I attacked with an icepick, but I discovered that the thick covering of ice, though mossy and spongelike on the outside, was hard as a rock underneath, and I left it to melt a little before attempting to chip or pry it loose.

I had just begun on the windows when the phone rang. It was Duncan. I was surprised; I had more or less forgotten about him.

"Well?" he asked. "What happened?"

"It's all off," I said. "I realized Peter was trying to destroy me. So now I'm looking for another job."

"Oh," said Duncan. "Actually I didn't mean that. I was wondering more about Fischer."

"Oh," I said. I might have known.

"I mean, I think I know what happened but I'm not sure why. He's abandoned his responsibilities, you know."

"His responsibilities? You mean graduate school?"

"No," said Duncan. "I mean me. What am I going to do?"

"I haven't the faintest idea," I said. I was irritated with him for not wanting to discuss what I was going to do myself. Now that I was thinking of myself in the first person singular again I found my own situation much more interesting than his.

"Now, now," Duncan said, "we can't both be like that. One of us has to be the sympathetic listener and the other one gets to be tortured and confused. You were tortured and confused last time."

Face it, I thought, you can't win. "Oh all right. Why don't you come over for some tea a bit later then? The apartment's a mess," I added apologetically.

When he arrived I was finishing the windows, standing on a chair and wiping off the white glass-cleaner I had spread on them. We hadn't cleaned them for a long time and they had got quite silted over with dust, and I was thinking it was going to be curious to be able to see out of them again. It bothered me that there was still some dirt on the outside I couldn't reach: soot and rainstreaks. I didn't hear Duncan come in. He had probably been standing in the room for several minutes watching me before he announced his presence by saying "Here I am."

I jumped. "Oh hi," I said, "I'll be right with you as soon as I finish this window." He wandered off in the direction of the kitchen.

After giving the window one last polish with a sleeve torn from one of Ainsley's abandoned blouses I got down from the chair, somewhat reluctantly—I like to finish things once I've begun them and there were still several windows left uncleaned; besides, the prospect of discussing the love life of Fischer Smythe wasn't all that compelling—and went out to the kitchen. I found Duncan sitting in one of the chairs, regarding the open refrigerator door with a mixture of distaste and anxiety.

"What smells in here?" he asked, sniffing the air.

"Oh, various things," I answered lightly. "Floor polish and window cleaner and some other things." I went over and opened the kitchen window. "Tea or coffee?"

"Doesn't matter," he said. "Well, what's the real truth?"

"You must know they're married." Tea would be easier, but a quick root through the cupboards didn't uncover any. I measured the coffee into the percolator.

"Well, yes, sort of. Fish left us a rather ambiguous note. But how did it happen?"

"How do these things ever happen? They met at the party," I said. I turned on the coffee and sat down. I had thoughts of holding out on him but he was beginning to look hurt. "Of course there are a few complications, but I think it will work out." Ainsley had come in the day before after another prolonged absence and had packed her suitcases while Fischer waited in the living room, head thrown back against the cushions of the chesterfield, beard bristling with the consciousness of its own vitality, eyes closed. She had given me to understand in the few sentences she had time for that they were going to Niagara Falls for their honeymoon and that she thought Fischer would make, as she put it, "a very good one".

I explained all this to Duncan as well as I could. He did not seem either dismayed or delighted, or even surprised, by any of it.

"Well," he said, "I guess it's a good thing for Fischer, mankind cannot bear too much unreality. Trevor was quite disturbed though. He's gone to bed with a nervous headache and refuses to get up even to cook. What it all means is that I'm going to have to move out. You've heard how destructive a broken home can be and I wouldn't want my personality to get warped."

"I hope it will be all right for Ainsley." I really did hope so. I was pleased with her for justifying my superstitious belief in her ability to take care of herself: for a while there I had begun to lose faith. "At least," I said,

285

"she's got what she thinks she wants, and I suppose that's something."

"Cast out into the world again," Duncan said reflectively. He was gnawing on his thumb. "I wonder what will become of me." He did not seem overly interested in the question.

Talking about Ainsley made me think of Leonard. I had called Clara shortly after I had heard the news about Ainsley's marriage, so she could tell Len it was safe to come out of hiding. Later she had called back. "I'm quite worried," she said, "he didn't seem nearly as relieved as he ought to have been. I thought he would go back to his apartment right away but he said he didn't want to. He's afraid to go outside the house, though he seems perfectly happy as long as he stays in Arthur's room. The children adore him most of the time and I must say it's rather nice having someone who takes them off my hands a bit, but the trouble is he plays with all of Arthur's toys and sometimes they get into fights. And he hasn't been going to work at all, he hasn't even phoned them to tell them where he is. If he just lets himself go like this much longer I'm not sure how I'm going to cope." Nevertheless she had sounded more competent than usual.

There was a loud metallic clunk from inside the refrigerator. Duncan jerked, and took his thumb out of his mouth. "What was that?"

"Oh, just falling ice, I expect," I said. "I'm defrosting the refrigerator." The coffee smelled done. I set two cups on the table and poured.

"Well, are you eating again?" Duncan asked after a moment of silence.

"As a matter of fact I am," I said. "I had steak for lunch." This last remark had been motivated by pride. It still was miraculous to me that I had attempted anything so daring and had succeeded.

"Well, it's healthier that way," Duncan said. He looked at me directly for the first time since he had come in. "You look better too. You look jaunty and full of good things. How did you do it?"

"I told you," I said. "Over the phone."

"You mean that stuff about Peter trying to destroy you?" I nodded.

"That's ridiculous," he said gravely. "Peter wasn't trying to destroy you. Thas't just something you made up. Actually you were trying to destroy him."

I had a sinking feeling. "Is that true?" I asked.

"Search your soul," he said, gazing hypnotically at me from behind his hair. He drank some coffee and paused to give me time, then added, "But the real truth is that it wasn't Peter at all. It was me. I was trying to destroy you."

I gave a nervous laugh. "Don't say that."

"Okay," he said, "ever eager to please. Maybe Peter was trying to destroy me, or maybe I was trying to destroy him, or we were both trying to destroy each other, how's that? What does it matter, you're back to so-called reality, you're a consumer."

"Incidentally," I said, remembering, "would you like some cake?" I had half the torso and the head left over.

He nodded. I got him a fork and took the remains of the cadaver down from the shelf where I had put it. I unwrapped its cellophane shroud. "It's mostly the head," I said.

"I didn't know you could bake cakes," he said after the first forkful. "It's almost as good as Trevor's."

"Thank you," I said modestly. "I like to cook when I have the time." I sat watching the cake disappear, the smiling pink mouth first, then the nose and then one eye. For a moment there was nothing left of the face but the last green eye; then it too vanished, like a wink. He started devouring the hair.

It gave me a peculiar sense of satisfaction to see him eat as if the work hadn't been wasted after all—although the cake was absorbed without exclamations of pleasure, even without noticeable expression. I smiled comfortably at him.

He did not smile back; he was concentrating on the busines at hand.

He scraped the last chocolate curl up with his fork and pushed away the plate. "Thank you," he said, licking his lips. "It was delicious."